THE CONTEST

AND
OTHER
STORIES

JOE DIBUDUO

KATE ROBINSON

THE CONTEST

AND OTHER STORIES

A TOOTIE-DO PRESS ORIGINAL

Cover design by Clarissa Yeo, Yocla Designs
Editorial and interior design by Starstone Lit

ISBN-10: 0692973680
ISBN-13: 978-0692973684

*For artists and writers discovering inspiration in everything,
and in turn, inspiring viewers and readers everywhere.*

— JD & KR

Art is a lie that makes us realize truth...

— Pablo Picasso, "Statement to Marius de Zayas," 1923

Acknowledgments

In Chapter Order:

"Night Café" won the quarterly New Short Fiction Award and first appeared at Jerry Jazz Musician (2012).

"A Twisted Garden" first appeared in *Say Goodnight to the Bad Guy* as "The Yellow House" (May December Press, 2011).

"Lost Memories" first appeared in *The Memory Eater* (CP Anthologies, 2012).

"The Snow Globe" first appeared in *Best Served Cold: An Eye for an Eye* (Runewright, 2011).

"Cheater" first appeared in *Manifest West #4, Weird West* (Western State Colorado University–Western State Press, 2015).

Many thanks to the Stasis critique group in Prescott, Arizona, to sci-fi author Tom A. Wright for creative feedback, and to our Indiegogo donors who assisted with publication expenses.

We are grateful to Clarissa Yeo – Yocla Designs for the snazziest cover art in the universe!

2017 Book Cover of the Year – Cassie Loves Covers

2018 Eric Hoffer – The Da Vinci Eye Finalist (Excellence in Cover Art)

2018 New Generation Indie Book Award Finalist

2018 Recommended – The US Review of Books

2019 Literary Titan Book Award

2019 Global Ebook Awards Silver Medalist

Contents

Chapters

1 A Lonely Death   15

2 A New Routine   33

3 Exposé Expansion   40

4 The Editors Grimm   55

5 Progress   66

6 Saving the Day   75

7 Doomed to Disaster   88

8 Black Magazine Monday   98

9 Two Steps Back   108

10 Trouble in Spades   122

11 Treasure Map   134

12 Clout vs. Integrity   147

13 On a Roll   159

14 Stumbling Blocks or Stepping Stones?   169

15 Slow Afternoon   186

16 Competition   194

17 Who, What, When, Where, Why & How?   204

18 Breaking Even   210

19 New & Improved   222

20 Story of a Lifetime   233

Stories

NIGHT CAFÉ   24

VASILY   37

HERO   43

PRAISE NEPTUNE!   60

THE CONQUISTADORS' SURPRISE   68

LOST MEMORIES   77

THE SNOW GLOBE   90

A LIFE IN FLOWERS   102

A TWISTED GARDEN   112

THE ISLAND   124

NICOR   136

MASTERPIECE   152

LOOKING OUT FOR HARRY   162

THE IMPOSTER   172

ALONE   189

CHEATER   196

SUCCESS   207

THE JONAH   212

HEAVEN OR HELL?   227

SUGGESTED READING   239

ABOUT THE AUTHORS   243

Inspiration: Artists and Artwork

Le Café de Nuit
Vincent van Gogh, 1888

The Bachelor Guitarist
Vasily Gregorevich Perov, 1865

The Accolade
Sir Edmund Blair Leighton, 1901

The Abduction of the Sabine Women
Nicolas Poussin, 1635

Emperor Charles V at Muhlberg
Titian, 1548

The Gallery of H.M.S. Calcutta-Portsmouth
James Jacques Joseph Tissot, 1877

The Horse-Race
Jean-Louis Forain, 1890

Le Chevalier aux Fleurs
Georges-Antoine Rochegrosse, 1894

Jardin des Peupliers
Vincent van Gogh, 1889

New York Harbor
Alfred Thompson Bricher, 1877

Morning by the Stream
T.C. Steele, 1893

The Knife Grinder (Principle of Scintillation)
Kasimir Malevich, 1912

Avenue de Clichy: Five O'Clock in the Evening
Louis Anquetin, 1887

Napoleon on Board the Bellerophon
Sir William Quiller Orchardson, 1880

Snow at Louveciennes
Alfred Sisley, 1874

The Cowboy
Frederick Remington, 1902

Dance at Bougival
Pierre-Auguste Renoir, 1882

Y Une Place Animee a Paris
Joaquin Pallares y Allustante, 1898

Dante & Virgil in Hell
William-Adolphe Bouguereau, 1850

1

A Lonely Death

AS MY CAB ARRIVED AT Fairhaven Cemetery, I spied a lone Catholic priest standing by my Uncle John`s coffin, a study in black and white. Heavy snowflakes fell in swirling eddies like confetti from heaven over the monuments scored with epitaphs for mothers and daughters, fathers and sons, husbands and wives, all long dead and in some cases, long forgotten. Soon the snow would blanket one and all for the long winter`s slumber.

I exited the cab reluctantly and pulled my collar up to stop the snow determined to swirl down my neck. As surprised by my presence as I was by his, the priest locked eyes with me for nearly a minute as though fishing for my soul, then bowed his head to read a blessing for my recently departed uncle from a battered prayer book. When he finished praying, he nodded at me and turned to walk toward the street into the blowing snow, a raven-like figure bobbing through the storm. Two workmen, gravediggers, emerged from the flurries on a pathway beyond the open grave and when they arrived, they lowered the casket into the ground. I threw a clod of dirt onto Uncle`s coffin, startled by the finality of the hollow thump as it met the polished wood. But the clod soon whitened and disappeared under the falling snow as the workmen began to shovel in syncopated rhythms from a low pile of icy, moist earth beside the grave.

I walked away and waved the cab on so I could stroll alone through the storm toward my office at First Fiduciary Savings. When I arrived, I lay my damp overcoat across a meeting table near my desk and grabbed a cup of steaming coffee from the employee`s lounge. I tried to concentrate on the never-ending stack of paperwork filling my inbox, still shivering twenty minutes later. The phone jangled suddenly, startling me even though my secretary picked it up at her desk outside my door. "Line two, Mr. Rizzo," Ruth said over the intercom.

"Peter John Rizzo," a clipped voice demanded when I answered.

"Speaking."

"Are you nephew to John Rizzo of Brooklyn, New York?"

"Who wants to know?"

"Harold O`Neill, attorney at law, calling the nephew of John Rizzo, called Peter John Rizzo. Am I speaking to the aforementioned nephew or not?"

What kind of person would actually talk like this? "Yes, John Rizzo is my uncle, and my name is Peter John Rizzo."

"I`m very sorry for your loss," O`Neill said tersely. "The reading of John Rizzo`s last will and testament is at half-past three at my office tomorrow. 211 Broad St."

Without warning, Mr. O`Neill hung up and left me to sift through my thoughts.

I had trouble attending to my work because I still couldn`t believe Uncle John was gone. Granted, I`d not seen him for years, but I never thought about losing him permanently. My eyes brimmed with tears, but I held back the storm by taking deep breaths. Shuffling blindly through the papers on my desk, I could only think about him. Because he and Aunt Millie had no children of their own to grieve for them, I`d made the trip to the cemetery. I had little knowledge of Uncle`s social life and concluded he must have been a loner after Aunt Millie`s death. I`d expected to see my father present, supposing that in the face of death he would drop his bitterness about his only brother. That I carried his brother`s middle name probably didn`t help the situation any—I had no clue why Mother insisted upon naming me after both Father and Uncle John. I remember well how he snorted every time he heard my middle name when I was a kid. Father hadn`t cared to remember his estranged brother at all.

❦

I was the only person present again the next afternoon in the tastefully appointed conference room at the law office of Harrison, Shearer and O`Neill.

"To my nephew, Peter John Rizzo, I leave my entire estate," Harold O`Neill solemnly read from the legal-sized sheaf of papers he pulled from a dark leather binder embossed with gold lettering.

Uncle John`s entire estate consisted of "Classic Art Exposé," a bi-weekly magazine with art, and sometimes literature, as the main content, located in an old warehouse in New York City, plus seven hundred dollars in cash. I felt touched he`d thought of me, but I didn`t have any interest in running his magazine because of my position at the bank and my need to placate my father.

O`Neill looked over his narrow reading glasses at me. "Peter John Rizzo, it`s my duty to make certain you`re aware that this bequest is conditional."

"Oh? What kind of conditions could Uncle John possibly place on a barely functioning publishing business and seven hundred dollars? I earn enough working for my father to buy and sell magazines like his anytime I want." After I spoke, I bit my lip, not liking the smarmy rich-boy declaration.

"I know you probably expected more, but your uncle went into debt to pay your university expenses."

"Wait a minute—I had a scholarship that paid for everything."

"Surely you did. But who do you think the donor was?"

My jaw nearly hit the floor. "Why did he do that if he couldn`t afford it?"

"I`m not certain. Perhaps he wanted to annoy your father. . ." Mr. O`Neill said, speculating with feigned interest. "Here`s the note for the loan he took out to pay for your scholarship." He handed me an itemized statement of loan payments and corresponding interest typewritten on a bank`s letterhead.

Why would Uncle John go into debt just to annoy my father? I remember how proud he was that I had similar artistic inclinations. I believed he wanted me to follow my heart. He knew how my father always manipulated people to do exactly what he wanted. My uncle wanted me to be free of that trait, and I suspect he may have been a bit envious of my father`s wealth as well. To Father, my university tuition and living expenses were small change.

"Uncle John owned the magazine for years. Maybe he really could afford it," I stubbornly insisted.

"He chose to publish exactly what he wanted, not always what was best for the magazine. The business is breaking even right now, but Mr. Rizzo`s notes are due in eighteen months. Unfortunately, he took out a second mortgage to pay for the scholarship as well as a loan to keep the magazine afloat. One of his conditions is that you increase the circulation from ten thousand to forty thousand. By accomplishing that, you`ll have enough cash flow to meet his expenses."

Who, What, When, Where, Why and *How* streamed through my mind and I barely heard the financial details. Uncle John had paid for my education—my feelings were in turmoil. Why didn`t he tell me? Did my mother know? I knew I`d never figure out the answers. Now that Uncle was dead, I couldn`t even thank him.

"Your uncle felt you could easily meet this stipulation. He always said how clever you are, and he was proud of that."

I still couldn`t say anything. It had been almost thirteen years since my uncle and I had communicated. Though we both loved the arts, I wondered where he got the idea I am clever.

"The condition attached to this stipulation is that if you can`t increase the circulation prior to the due date of his notes, then you're to forfeit all assets to his creditors, and you must donate seven hundred dollars to the Artists' Benevolent Society. But if you do meet his stipulations, you can do whatever you desire with the business. Likely he wanted you to gain experience in his field and still be able to sell the magazine if you choose."

Uncle John couldn't increase circulation in the last thirteen years and he wanted me to quadruple it in a year and a half? Why bother? He had no children and no other relative need assume his debts. Why not donate the seven hundred dollars to the Artists' Benevolent Society and let the magazine go? But something nagged at me, maybe my sense of decency. After all, I loved Uncle John and he'd miraculously paid for my education. I had made it through and now had an opportunity to try my hand at using my education to pay for my education. . .

"Can I have time to think about this?"

Mr. O'Neill nodded as he scooped my uncle's will into the binder. "You have thirty days to make a decision."

❦

I went home and asked my father pointblank if Uncle John had paid for my schooling.

He scowled at the thought. "You're not deaf, are you? I've told you many times that your stupid uncle never did anything right in his life. He lived on dreams. He thought that when you received your journalism degree, you'd work with him at the magazine and save his ass with your abilities. How could he possibly afford to pay for a scholarship?"

My mother, quietly threading a needle across the room, lowered her embroidery hoop and cast him a disapproving look, as if to say *how cruel to speak of your recently departed brother that way.*

I admitted I'd attended Uncle John's lonely burial and that I was considering taking the helm of the magazine.

"You know I'm counting on you to stay aboard at the bank. I envision a distinguished line of Rizzo men heading it in perpetuity. . . I'm getting on in years and you're the only son I have." His anger gave way to a rare heartbroken look.

Father's reply didn't surprise me. Seeing him distraught, I almost succumbed to his passive-aggressive behavior. But my mother's quiet disdain made me reconsider. After all, I had thirty days to make a final decision.

I announced at breakfast the next morning that I would quit my job at the bank and take over the magazine. Father reacted with his usual vigor and jumped up from his chair. "John has been borrowing for years to keep the magazine afloat. I approved the second mortgage on his run-down dump of a building. I'm

⚜

going to buy every note he has and close the rag down. You`ll be back begging for work," he shouted, waving his fork with a bit of egg still attached.

I turned my back and raced from the dining room, flinging the front door open to the sputtering of new threats from my father.

My mother watched me from the dining room. She nodded once as I looked back, then bit her lip and lowered her eyes as I pushed the screen door open and let it slam behind me.

When I stepped from the cab in Brooklyn with one small suitcase to stand before the magazine`s office the next morning, I wasn`t surprised to find it in a rundown part of town. A large sign on top of the dilapidated one-story brick building had the magazine`s name spelled out in faded and peeling red letters: CLASSIC ART EXPOSÉ. My Aunt Millie had created the magazine logo and she also wrote features for it. She`d worked with Uncle John on the magazine layout as well, along with his assistant, Jason. Aunt Millie concentrated upon analyzing literature and writing about the concerns of the local literary community. The word "classic" in the title was a misnomer, as they actually criticized nearly any genre of art. They critiqued or interviewed any deceased or living artist they thought worthy of praise or criticism.

After Aunt Millie died two years ago, Uncle John worked overtime and delegated some of her work to Jason, hoping I`d step in to help him out after I graduated, according to my father. To everyone`s surprise the magazine managed to do fairly well, the readership holding while other magazines rose and fell, dwarfed by the giants Life, Saturday Evening Post, and other household names, and surpassed as well by more highbrow art magazines.

As I entered the building, I heard my father`s angry words echo in my head again, but I shook them off, determined to follow my heart. No one appeared at the receptionist`s desk, so I made myself comfortable in a well-worn chair in the front lobby. I found out why the magazine`s numbers held steady as I thumbed through the collection of old issues held in a sagging bookcase. The modest success of the magazine was due to the fact that Uncle John's and Aunt Millie's readers, mostly artists themselves, relished their critiques. Classic Art Exposé was a combination of the New York Times and the National Enquirer of the art and literary world, and my uncle's "exposés"–his features of little-known facts about artists—were of particular interest. His final issue cover story, "Did Picasso`s foot fetish influence his painting?" discussed Picasso`s obsession with feet and how easily this fetish could have influenced all his work, to the outrage of some Picasso devotees. These controversial or investigative features helped to keep the magazine`s circulation steady.

I knew it would be difficult but not entirely impossible to quadruple the circulation inside eighteen months and to pay off the debt Uncle John had acquired. My savings were substantial for someone my age because of working with my father, but just a fraction of the notes due. I was familiar with analyzing art and in particular, literature because of my schooling in English and journalism, and I obviously understood financial undertakings because of my banking experience, but I had no clue how to run a publishing business. I was no longer a figurehead executive vice-president of a respected banking institution but the editor-in-chief of a quirky art magazine. Standing at the helm of a magazine wasn`t exactly like steering a bank.

I peeked into a doorway leading from the lobby and into the pressroom, where two workers sat at a table drinking beer and playing rummy. The scene raised my hackles a bit, but I rationalized that the workers probably didn`t know what to do with Uncle John gone. Later I found out how delusional I was. These guys hardly ever worked. They belonged to a union with the power to shut down production if the members were overworked. Their agreement included a provision to produce the number of magazines sold every two weeks and not one more. In two days, they could print the entire circulation, and the rest of the week, they played cards and drank beer. In other words, these guys were paid for a full workweek but they only worked a fraction of it.

I found my only employee, Jason, in the editorial office. He sat with his sneaker-shod feet on Millie`s desk, lazily smoking a reefer cigarette and gazing out the window, studying birds on the telephone wires. He looked to be about twenty-five, a bit older than me, and he had the rebellious air of James Dean or Marlon Brando, with a rumpled beatnik look as if he`d never learned about personal grooming. But he knew how to run the magazine and I knew I`d best make friends with him at any cost.

I held my hand out. "Hi, Jason. I`m Pete Rizzo, John`s nephew. . . the new owner."

Jason brushed a stray lock from his forehead, gave my hand one firm shake and held out the reefer, looking at my tidy banking clothes with some dismay. "How`s it going?"

I`d seen Negroes in bars smoke reefer cigarettes when I was out joyriding at Yale, but had never witnessed anyone do so in a workplace. I sucked on it without inhaling much, exhaled quickly and passed it back. "Not so well, I`m afraid."

"Why, man? What`s not s`well?"

I coughed and hesitated for a second and then decided, what the hell, I`m the boss. "I have to quadruple the circulation of this magazine in a year and a half, and it looks like all I have for employees are beer-swilling, reefer-smoking do-nothings."

"Hold on, man, what do you mean, `do-nothings?` I`ve finished my work for the week." Jason showed me a stack of papers. I looked through his work and found his critiques and features well written and explicit. Then he pointed at the table where the layout boards lay pasted with copy and photos for the next issue.

I took a step back and then stepped forward again. "Um, maybe I misjudged you guys. It`s just that I have some business experience and a degree in journalism, but really have no idea how to run this thing, never mind quadruple its size."

Jason smiled as if he wanted to roll his eyes. "No problem. I`d been telling your Uncle John the last few months about my contest idea."

"Contest? What`s a contest got to do with increasing readership?"

"Come on man, you know to attract readers you need something to interest them. Promotions. Freebies."

"Of course."

"Then we have a writing contest."

"How will a writing contest significantly increase readership of an art magazine?"

"People are interested in two things. One is money and the other is sex. Everything else just leads to those, you know?"

"Okay, I agree to some degree, but how are those going to help the magazine?"

"Simple, man," Jason said. "We offer a cash prize and publication for the best short story inspired by a painting. Preferably some well-known artwork—artwork by well-known artists." He pointed to the wall where a reproduction of one of van Gogh`s paintings hung. "Like that one. Everybody knows van Gogh."

"Yeah. So, how would this contest work?"

"Simple again. We vote, you and me, on the best story, and the writer wins a cash prize."

"Good idea, but where am I going to get cash for the prize?"

"Simple once again. Charge a five-dollar entry fee and the winner takes some of the pot. You hold back some each time, to cover your expenses. The word gets around, more people buy the magazine to enter the next contest, and you make a little profit too."

"Five dollars! Isn`t that a bit high?"

Jason shrugged. "Makes it seem more valuable or prestigious. Plus, you have to pay your debt *and* the short story awards. We could offer a critique for the winner and a critique for an unpublished runner-up to justify the fee and give the contest more credibility. Besides, entering any contest is a gamble, even with a creative entry, so no one is forcing anyone to spend their five dollars."

"Okey dokey. . . So, what about professional writers? Won`t they make the contest meaningless for the majority of emerging writers?"

Jason grinned. "Simple. Man, I`m getting tired of saying simple. Make the contest for unpublished or emerging writers who don`t make a living writing. You won`t lose many entries, because professional writers are busy pitching stories to literary magazines and don`t usually waste time entering a new contest that won`t advance their careers."

"So how does this guarantee a larger circulation? A small contest with a small prize doesn`t guarantee magazine sales either, as far as I can see. What if people enter who don`t subscribe?"

"Man, no offense intended, but you`ve got to start thinking for yourself." Jason explained his idea to print an entry form and the painting prompt inside the magazine so anyone who wanted to enter had to buy a copy.

The next deadline was just two days away, so I worked late compiling the guidelines for the contest. I decided to run *Le Café de Nuit*, the print hanging on the office wall, as the first artwork prompt for the contest. Van Gogh thought it the ugliest piece he`d ever painted, but Jason said it was a favorite of our printing crew.

At midnight, I lay down to sleep with a burlap bag pillow on a row of oak office chairs. I would literally work, eat, and sleep in the office for the next few months.

❧

After the next printing and mailing, we received eleven entries inspired by the van Gogh painting. After a quick read and deliberation, Jason and I declared an oddball story, "The Night Café"—an English translation of the van Gogh painting`s French title—the unanimous winner. We voted for it because the strong writing made us fall in love with the Green Goddess. And we liked the offbeat, magical realist theme. The subject of addiction gained Jason`s vote as well, because he hadn`t known about absinthe`s fascinating characteristics until we read the story.

Our readers had no idea how many judges voted on the contest entries. Night Café would appear along with my editorial debut in the first official contest issue. We didn`t disclose the amount of the prize awarded because the first winner had to settle for publication and a few measly bucks, a shame for such an interesting story.

"Well, the story isn`t exactly a literary classic, but it`s great in a Ray Bradbury sort of way." I didn`t know how else to describe the winning story, but I loved Bradbury`s novels—*The Martian Chronicles* and *Fahrenheit 451*—and his short stories in *The Illustrated Man,* and I hoped that students would study Bradbury in lit classes along with classic literary fiction someday.

"Agreed. . ." Distracted, Jason turned to a page in the oversized *Great International Painters* Volume I—a full plate of van Gogh`s *Red Vineyard.* "Can you believe van Gogh only sold one painting in his entire life?"

I looked at the page. "You`ve got to be kidding," I said. "Hard to believe that van Gogh didn`t strike it rich with his unique, colorful style. Like Bradbury, his work always affects me, somehow, some way. So how much did he get for the painting he sold?"

"Four hundred francs—about a thousand dollars in today`s money."

Now I knew why my father had such a disdain for artistic pursuits. That wasn`t much money for years of work. "I sure hope I won`t have to die to sell enough copies of this magazine to keep it afloat."

Jason grinned. "You and I can fix the situation. Trust me."

I dream my painting and I paint my dream.

NIGHT CAFÉ

WHEN MY DOCTOR RELEASED ME from the asylum in Saint Rémy, he warned me to stay away from absinthe or my hallucinations would worsen. I didn`t tell him I had no need for absinthe to hallucinate. I often had company, even when there wasn`t anyone with me.

I`d spent some of my time in the asylum playing billiards. Everyone assured me that I was a natural, the best player they`d ever seen. Maybe, instead of painting, I`d play billiards for a living. As soon as I walked past the gates of the asylum, I headed to windswept Arles and the Café de la Gare at 30 Place Lamartine. I`d heard many stories about the fine billiards table in this tavern and the ample crowd of gamblers willing to bet large sums of money on every game.

Night descended as I entered the café, lit by four hanging lamps made of lemon-lime glass that emanated a greenish light. The blood red walls seemed to ooze into a lower section painted in a dark yellow, and the green billiard table in the middle of the room added to the eerie sensation of color revolving around me in kaleidoscopic circles.

The odor of stale beer and cigarette smoke penetrated my senses and my clothes. I ordered a beer from a heavy-set man behind the bar. "Is there much action at your table?"

"You bet there is. The best players come here from all over to play pocket billiards." His deep, raspy words came out as a growl. "Do you play?"

I wanted to tell him yes, but my companion, Guy de Maupassant, who accompanied me from the asylum, disagreed. "Be quiet, Vincent, and don`t tell him."

I shrugged my shoulders. "A little," I said. I remembered then that Guy had died while confined in the asylum. But he sometimes still hung around and gave me advice about billiards.

The players began to shoot. Judging by the plays, I could easily beat any of them.

"Monsieur, you can play next if you`ve money to bet," said a small raggedy man who stood waiting his turn.

I stared at this undignified man who didn`t measure up to my level. He turned and took his shots, and to my surprise, his technique was so smooth and perfect that I drank to the game he was about to win.

The drink caused me to see flashing colors. Suddenly, this nondescript billiards player changed into a princely figure. His attire changed from lackluster working-class garb to well-tailored clothing bedecked with shiny buttons and gold chains, a man worthy of my challenge. I lay all my money on the billiards table.

"I`ll play you—straight pocket billiards."

He gazed at the sum I`d placed on the table, went around to his compatriots, and borrowed money until he matched my bet.

"I want to be certain I understand the rules, so when I beat you there will be no question," I said.

Together we went over the rules. We agreed the object would be to reach one hundred points, meaning a hundred balls pocketed to win. One point scored for each ball pocketed with no foul made. He agreed to let me shoot first, a distinct advantage for me.

I royally beat him by running one hundred balls without a miss. While waiting for them to decide who would play next, I went for another pint.

"Bière de Chartres," I said, and threw some coins on the countertop.

"All I have is du Croissant, de Monaco, or de Vezelise," the barman replied.

I gazed at the posters advertising the different beers behind the bar. A beautiful woman dressed as a goddess caught my eye. She sipped from a mug of beer while swinging on a pale greenish-yellow moon. I ordered the same beer, "du Croissant." The lovely lady seemed to be staring at the end of the bar. I followed her gaze to a gallon glass jug that had coins and a few franc notes filling but a small portion of it. A large sign pasted to it read *Help The Widows & Orphans, Please*. But I couldn`t help them. The rest of my money sat on the billiards table.

I closed my eyes to fantasize about the moon woman, and before I knew it, I found myself sitting beside her on the quarter moon.

"Hello, I`m Vincent," I said.

I was close enough to feel her breath on my face when she turned to me.

"We`ll play, you and I," she said. "Is that all?" a gruff voice asked. I opened my eyes to the barman`s ugly face and stinking breath. I tilted the glass and the aroma of barley and hops washed the foul smell away.

I hoped I could meet the moon lady again. I returned to my winnings along with my original bet on the billiards table. Men gathered in groups and more money changed hands as they debated who would play me next. I won another game and decided to try another beer.

A new barkeep was on duty and he introduced himself as Joseph, the owner of the cafe. Gazing at the posters again, I fancied the one that said *La Célèbre Bières de Monaco,* with a picture of two women and a huge mug of the "famous Monaco beer." The greenish color from the hanging lights mixed with the colors of the poster. Everything spun, mixed, and swirled faster and faster until the mug of beer disappeared and the entire room filled with spiraling colors.

I found myself standing between the two beautiful women draped in shimmering red and yellow dresses. Sweet perfume mixed with the unmistakable aroma of fine beer mingled amidst the vibrant colors. Hot, sweet female breath flowed over both sides of my face as they leaned in close to whisper, "Bières de Monaco, Bières de Monaco, Bières de Monaco."

They recited this over and over until finally, I too shouted, "Bières de Monaco." Joseph put a full glass in front of me, bringing my imagination to a sudden halt.

"Are you going to play?" A well-dressed gentleman in black approached me, chosen by the anxious gamblers to challenge me in an attempt to win their money back.

I played the gentleman and although a better player than my previous opponents, I easily beat him. I pocketed my money, nearly four times greater than my original sum.

I returned to sit at the bar. My emotions demanded I paint this barroom scene. My ear itched as it always did before one of my "visions." If I didn`t scratch, I knew the itch would turn into a burn I couldn`t stand. One of these days, I`d fix that damn ear, visions or no.

A sound from heaven soothed my itching ear, and the mellow tones caused my whole being to drink in the beauty. Not only did I feel it, but I could also see the sound vibrating and dancing in vivid yellows and blues that lifted me to the heavens, and browns and blacks that sank me to the depths of despair.

This emotion-filled sound seemed to issue from the goddess poster. The lovely moon-green goddess extended her arms, urging me to come and sit beside her. Her voice compelled me to fly to her side and partake of the beauty filling the night sky that only we could see from the vantage point of the quarter moon.

The goddess sang on and on until I too began to sing. I tried to match her note for note, but my voice sounded off-key in comparison to hers.

My bellowing voice and swinging motion attracted the attention of Joseph.

"Hey, hey, take it easy," he said, mopping the counter with a rag. "Calm down. Let me buy you another drink, and then you can go home."

"Home, I have no home. I search for beauty and I find it here. This will be my home."

"This can be your home, for a price. I have rooms for rent in the rear," Joseph said.

"I can afford lodging. Look, I've won this playing on your table." I showed him a large roll of franc notes. "Not only am I the best billiards player in the land, I'm an artist of great renown—someday." I bowed my head to accept his recognition of my greatness to be.

"Quite a bit of that money in your hand used to be mine," Joseph said. "I bet for your challengers."

I saw the dismay at losing in his eyes. I knew he'd be happy if I returned some francs to him as payment for room and board.

I stored my belongings in one of the rooms and returned to the bar to spend more of my winnings. "No more beer for me," I told Joseph as he set a glass in front of me. "I want a Green Fairy."

The billiards players smiled. They knew those who drank absinthe usually lost their skills for shooting billiards. I watched as the barkeep poured the absinthe in a glass with a bubble in the lower portion denoting the measurement. He placed a slotted spoon inside the glass and dropped a sugar cube into the spoon's bowl, taking great care in adding ice-cold water, drop by single drop, onto the cube. Each individual drip cut a milky swathe through the peridot-green absinthe. As the pungent smell of aniseed refreshed me, a swirling mist in the glass became a solid cloud. Joseph let the milky louche sit for a moment to let the herbs blossom and bring out flavors overpowered by the anise.

"There you go, *le Feé Verte*." He left the bottle so I could make myself another.

I put the glass to my lips and slowly let the bitter liquid, now sweetened with sugar, flow over my teeth and swirl around them. I held the liquid in my mouth, trying to absorb it rather than drink it. I swallowed the drink in small dribbles, sipping another bit, and then another.

I paid for the absinthe and my room. Then I handed Joseph some coins. "Here, put these in the widows and orphans jar." The Goddess smiled and our eyes met in mutual sympathy.

Those who watched me drink challenged me to play again. Joseph must have had the next challenger specially sent for because of his reputation as the best billiards player in Arles.

I knew I could play even better when imbibing absinthe. I laid the remainder of my franc notes on the billiards table and watched as my opponent matched the pile, note for note. We ran over the rules of the game and lagged to see who shot first. He ran eighty-eight balls before missing. I, on the other hand, shot one-hundred balls and won the game. I now had more money than I ever dreamed of in my entire life.

Then I sat at the bar and drank much too much absinthe.

❧

Where was I, how was it I still sat there? I don`t know. I must have passed out. But the empty absinthe bottle on the bar was evidence of my debauchery. Joseph had used the entire bottle for my drinks. Sadly, I sat all alone in the eerie, glowing light.

Then she approached me and I couldn`t believe my eyes. The beauty of the Green Goddess overwhelmed my senses. She floated above the floor wearing an almost transparent gown. Her full lips moved in a song so beautiful that I began to weep. I glanced up at the poster but the quarter moon shone like a lonely beacon. The goddess no longer sat on it, but of course, how could she? She was standing before me at the bar.

The warmth became heat and my blood felt as though it would boil. Desire spread with the heat and compelled me to touch her. As if she could read my thoughts, she leaned forward and touched my hand with a fingertip. Celestial sparks flew, blood boiled. Weak from so much wanting, I collapsed and dreamt the night away on the floor of the Green Goddess`s heavenly abode.

❧

Joseph poked me with a dirty mop. "Wake up!"

The Green Goddess had vanished with my sleep. Bright, brain-piercing, yellow sunlight streamed through the windows, revealing the debris on the floor where I lay amongst spittoons, cigar and cigarette butts, and tobacco chewers` spittle. Disgusted with myself, I crawled to the window to lower the shade to shut off the penetrating light that felt like hot needles pricking my eyes. Inconceivable relief came when Joseph stomped past me and dropped the shade.

Joseph`s face contorted in anger. "I can`t have a drunken sot sleeping on my floor. Sleep in your room from now on."

In the now cool gloom, I looked for my Green Goddess even though I knew I drank too much absinthe

❧

and let my imagination run wild. Still, unbelievable despair rolled through me at the thought I had only imagined her, a woman like no mortal woman. She enthralled me with a touch of her finger. Any touching with more than a finger would be pure ecstasy for me.

I couldn't accept my goddess's absence. I hungered for her touch and knew the absinthe could bring her back. I ordered another Green Fairy, and as I put it to my lips, my eyes roved over the posters behind the bar. I gagged and spat the drink all over the polished wood. My unbelieving eyes stopped on the Bière du Croissant poster. The Green Goddess had disappeared. The quarter moon hung in a star-spangled sky without her.

"Where is she? What have you done with her?" I demanded.

"That stuff is going to your head. Why do you drink it in the morning? What are you talking about?"

I pointed to the poster.

Joseph looked at it and shrugged his shoulders. "What?"

I pointed at the spot where she sat only yesterday. "The goddess, you fool, she's gone."

He grabbed the bottle of absinthe. "No more of this for you," he growled.

Astonished that he had taken my absinthe away, my hands shook. Knowing I couldn't have another drink made me need one desperately.

A debonair man strode through the door and approached me. He ignored my disheveled state. "Joseph has told me, Monsieur, that you're a good billiards player. I want you to know that I'm a fair player myself. I have adequate funds to cover any bet you wish to make."

I knew he had to be one of the best billiards players in France or he wouldn't be here challenging me. He pulled a stack of franc notes from his overcoat to show he indeed had more than enough funds to cover any bet. I counted my remaining notes and coins. To me it was a small fortune. I could paint for a long time without any financial worries with what I already had. Should I risk it all? My hands trembled. *No more absinthe*, Joseph had said. But I couldn't play billiards with shaking hands.

"I'll play for all I have," I told the debonair man. I was sure he was a ringer that Joseph had brought here to beat me. "But it's a bit early. I need time to freshen up before I play."

"Take all the time you want as long as it isn't more than an hour. I have business elsewhere," he said.

I returned to my room, splashed water on my face, combed my hair, and changed my shirt. Then I did what I always do when I need to focus. I opened my box of paints, filled my mixing cup half-full of linseed oil, squeezed a few drops from a tube of ultramarine blue into it, and added a few drops of cadmium red. Red was expensive, so I used just a tad out of habit. Then I added a quarter tube of titanium white and stirred it with a mixing stick.

I watched the blue and red swirl around in the oil, slowly becoming a vortex of purple swirls. Tendrils of white flowed into the mixed color, making swirls of lilac. When the liquid mixed thoroughly it became a striking lavender color. I wished my blood could become this color. A royal hue, I thought, light enough not to be a blue blood. I swirled the liquid around, making sure all the colorant dissolved, and then put it to my lips. The taste needed a dash of raw umber to give it a proper flavor.

I mixed in a few capfuls, put the drink to my lips, and closed my eyes. I envisioned a Green Goddess drink in my hand and let the liquid flow over my teeth. If not for the smell of linseed oil, I would have sworn I was drinking absinthe.

Soon my hands stopped shaking and Guy appeared at my side. He told me not to worry. "You can beat any player in the entire country," he said.

I returned to the billiards table, and lagged the debonair man for the break.

The balls rolled so close to the rail he called a tie. "Wait," I said. I picked up a playing card and handed it to him. "See if that fits between your ball and the rail."

He snatched the card from my hand and slid it between his ball and the rail.

"Now see if it`ll fit behind mine."

He tried, but my ball was dead against the rail. That meant I won the lag and would shoot first. Whoever won the lag would run one hundred balls without missing. He knew it as well as I did, and his face fell into a frown.

He tried to distract me, and Joseph watched intently as I again ran one hundred balls without missing. "I`m the best! I can beat anyone on this table, man, beast or immortal," I foolishly shouted.

I picked up my cash and returned to the bar as the debonair man walked out the door with slumping shoulders.

Joseph`s face twisted in grief or anger, I didn`t know which. He must have lost more money on the game I just won. I ordered a bottle of absinthe. Joseph was so upset about losing that he forgot he had said no more for me. Before long, an empty bottle lay before me as I stared at the poster with the empty quarter moon. Broken-hearted, I wondered if my Green Goddess had floated off to the sky, never to return.

The bar filled for the evening and then emptied. How long ago, I didn`t know. I sat alone in the dim light. Although I had plenty of cash, my life would be nothing without my Green Goddess.

Relief spread through me when I suddenly heard her singing. I wept again from the resonance of her mysterious language and her soulful voice. I turned as she floated toward the billiards table, her long golden hair enveloping her face. Her skin shone with an ethereal radiance, her transparent gown revealing more than it obscured. The greenish light transformed her into a glowing apparition.

Feelings flashed through me: joy, desire, gratitude, and of course, love. For I now knew I truly loved this immortal woman. If I couldn`t have her in this world, I must have her in the next.

She began to speak to me in the mysterious language she sang in, but I understood every word. "A mere mortal can never claim a goddess unless he can best her in at least one trial."

How could I ever best a goddess? I almost gave up hope when I saw her gaze at the billiards table. I wondered if she had heard my boast.

She reached a long, translucent arm toward the rack of billiards cues hanging on the wall. "Bet your winnings against me, win, and I`m yours. Lose, and the widows and orphans get your money."

I thanked the gods for the opportunity presented to me. Thoughts of possessing this goddess paralyzed my mind. I lay all my winnings on the billiards table and reached for a billiards cue.

She lifted the wooden rack from the balls and looked into my eyes. How could I have missed the whirling colors in her irises? Hues spun, changed, purple, gray, blue, and green, whirling in a vortex so swift I felt I`d become sucked into the whirlpool if I didn`t look away. But I couldn`t look away. My body floated toward her, my eyes locked to her spinning irises. I floated into her and became part of her until her eyes closed and shut me out.

My Green Goddess never stopped singing while she racked fifteen balls. With open eyes and new resolve, I strode to the billiards table. I took careful aim and shot hard and straight as I called, "Five in the corner." The cue ball hit the rack dead on, and the colorful balls rolled in all directions. The rainbow of shades filled me with wonder—I wanted to paint these orbs of moving color. I saw in my mind the beauty of the canvas blended with the bright yellows and reds of the room on a wavery, deep green background. I knew this would be my masterpiece. The best painting I`d ever create was already painted in my mind, thanks to my Green Goddess.

The five ball sank in the corner pocket. I ran five complete tables. Then I looked at my love, and when I did, her sea-green eyes disoriented me. I missed the intended target.

She floated to the end of the table, picked the cue ball from the pocket, and placed it on the table. Leaning over to aim her shot, her long lustrous golden hair framed her face as it reached to the table, flowed around her arms, and covered the green felt tabletop. She lifted one leg and bent it at the knee, an erotically beautiful pose, possibly never before seen by a mortal man. Inspired, I knew she was my muse, sent by fate. Once she was mine, I`d be able to paint beauty as never seen before, and she`d star in every painting.

Her shots were flawless. She sank every ball she aimed at, sometimes without looking. All the while, she trilled that hauntingly beautiful song in the mysterious language I was beginning to understand. Soon she sank her ninety-ninth ball. Despair washed over me. My goddess would beat me and I`d lose her if she sank the next ball. I had to do something to stop her from winning. As she gauged her next shot, I put my hand on her arm to cause her to miss. I hoped she would think it an accident.

As soon as my hand touched her arm, her warmth spread through me like wildfire. My blood boiled. I spun her around to face me and put both arms around her. When I brought her body into contact with mine, a fire consumed me, so hot it sizzled and cooled me all at the same time. I strove to put my lips on hers, still moving with song. My mistake became clear when she sang, "a goddess would never belong to a man who would cheat."

My Green Goddess vanished, instantly gone. I frantically looked around for her, but she was nowhere to be found. I searched for the money I had bet, and it was gone too, all gone. Distraught, I shuffled to the bar and fixed another glass of absinthe. The milky white liquid rolled over my teeth, bringing the bittersweet flavor to my tongue. I closed my eyes for a minute, and saw the Green Goddess, but only on the insides of my eyelids. I finished the absinthe and cried myself to sleep atop the table where her memory lay.

❦

"Wake up! I can`t have you sleeping on my billiards table and drinking all my liquor," Joseph said as the bright yellow light pierced my brain again.

I pointed. "The shade."

For whatever reason, maybe because he was a decent man, Joseph dropped the sunshade. My brain stopped burning and I opened my teary eyes. Memories of the Green Goddess flooded through me, and I wept for my loss. My muse was gone, dragging the colors and music from my imagination. The tavern was now a drab, dark place where I didn`t want to be. Even Guy had deserted me.

"Don`t cry, come have a drink," Joseph said, cutting lemons for drinks he would mix later. My eyes landed on the knife blade that so easily sliced through the rinds.

Joseph glanced at the widows and orphans jug filled with what must be my winnings from the night before. His face spread in a friendly smile.

I sat and sipped the beer he handed to me. Remorse filled me. Not for the cash the Green Goddess had donated—I never had much money before, so it didn`t bother me to be without any now. But why had I tried to cheat my muse? Shouldn`t I have known I couldn`t, that she would be lost to me?

I knew mine would be a one-sided love unless I could somehow demonstrate my commitment. I glanced up and saw the Green Goddess was again upon her poster, sitting on the quarter moon with a mug of beer in one hand.

I looked at the widows and orphans jug full of money, smiled, and raised my glass to my lovely moon lady, the Green Goddess. She looked at the jug, smiled, and raised her glass, returning my salutation. Our eyes met in mutual understanding as I picked up the sharp blade from the bar, slashed at my ear, and held my sacrifice out, hoping for her forgiveness.

✺

2

A New Routine

WHILE WE ADDED THE FIRST contest submission guidelines and entry form to the magazine layout, Jason and I decided our bi-weekly publication schedule was too hectic and too expensive. We could lower the subscription price but add features for a more exciting monthly publication, and still generate enough money to cover expenses. The addition of the contest plus a few more pages would fill up our slack time and our illustrious union printers would still meet the terms of their contract. Hopefully the contest would increase our circulation overall. Nothing ventured, nothing gained, so to speak.

I started to wear casual clothing on the job and looked much less the uptown banker-sophisticate and more the rumpled, cerebral type. Jason, on the other hand, seemed to relish his newfound responsibility as my advisor, and he stopped wearing sweatshirts with cropped sleeves with dirty jeans and sneakers, and now sported polo shirts and pullover sweaters with chinos and saddle oxfords instead. The only thing that didn`t change was his reefer habit, but it only seemed to enhance his creativity, so why interfere?

I`d decided to continue living in the building to avoid using my savings for personal expenses. I had cordoned off a sleeping area in one corner of the editorial office with clothesline and some old drapes, just a few steps away from our small public restroom. Not exactly a place to bring a date home to, but I`d be too busy for romance until I paid off Uncle John`s notes.

I furnished my lair with an old twin bed, a small wardrobe, and a hotplate that I kept on a little metal shop table along with a three-legged shop stool, all from a secondhand store down the street. The old oak icebox, like the ones still used by poorer families around Brooklyn, was more than sufficient for my modest needs. It would keep the rats and mice out of any food not in a can or jar. I filled an old Blue Goose apple crate under the table with a cast-iron pan, a speckled aluminum saucepan, an army mess kit, a can opener and the requisite bachelor cans of pork and beans and beef stew.

Jason continued to teach me all the tricks of the magazine publishing trade. Under his watchful eye, I started playing with layout, managing this without slicing my fingers too many times with the X-acto knives and one-edged razor blades.

I gained his respect when I started re-designing the cover and page layouts.

"You`ve got a good touch, man," he said from his post behind my left shoulder as I sketched out a new logo and master page plan for the upcoming monthly in colored pencil.

"Honest? You really think this looks good?"

"Yeah. I tried to get John and Millie to switch some stuff up," Jason said, "but they always said you`d come around when you graduated from Yale."

I thought of how Aunt Millie doted on me the few times she`d seen me and how Uncle John had quietly hoped to spend more time with me. Their kindness and their love of Classic Art Exposé made me even more determined to fulfill the terms of the will.

Jason became judge and jury for the new color scheme on the mag cover and the new typography. In a couple of days, I`d created a fresh, new design inside and out, careful to preserve some old conservative elements while jazzing the layout up to attract younger subscribers. I wondered if I really had the touch or if Jason just wanted to brownnose me. So far, he seemed nice enough, but honestly, I was the boss, so what could he say?

Once we had the design elements put to bed, we composed our critiques and features on our respective typewriters, me clacking away on Uncle John`s big gray Remington with the green keys and Jason on Aunt Millie`s small black Royal Aristocrat.

When it came time to choose a painting for the next contest story, we both agreed another painting by a universally known painter would fill the bill. Our readers seemed to like both our choice of painting and the winning story in the first contest, so we hoped for a similar result the second time around.

"Since Uncle John`s last feature was about Picasso, I`d like to use one of Picasso`s paintings in his honor. I had a postcard art print of Picasso`s *The Old Guitarist* propped up against the pencil holder on John`s old desk, with a Picasso quote inked at the bottom: *Art is the lie that enables us to see the truth.*

That might be a problem," Jason said.

"Why?"

"Well, for one thing, we need to get permission to publish images of Picasso paintings. When John ran the Picasso article, he borrowed a close-up photo of Picasso in his studio taken by a photographer friend. The article was not so much about Picasso`s work, but about Picasso himself. Using an image of his painting is another thing entirely. Van Gogh has been dead a long time, so his work is in the public domain. Picasso is still alive. He might give us permission if we ask because it`s good publicity for him, that is, if he`s not upset about John`s controversial article. But we might not have enough time to get permission since we`re making this decision so close to press."

"Of course." I pretended to smack my forehead with the palm of my hand. "It would be a nice touch to choose a painting in the public domain with a musician or musicians in it, something atmospheric like *The Old Guitarist.*"

Jason riffled through the big art book that usually lay on a side table in the waiting area. When he found what he was looking for, he turned the book around and pushed it toward me.

I gazed at the plate of a careworn nineteenth-century guitarist. "Wow. It`s not stark and iconic like *The Old Guitarist,* but it certainly has a magnetic quality. . . *The Bachelor Guitarist* by Vasily Perov it will be."

Vasily Gregorevich Perov lived in Russia at a time when an
artist`s indifference to social problems was considered immoral.

VASILY

ON THE DAY I WAS born, our Mayor made a public proclamation in the village square: "He`s the prettiest baby ever born here. This calls for a celebration!"

My mother glowed with newfound devotion. My father rejoiced. "Roll out the barrels of our best wine! Our son will make the village famous with his beauty and fine demeanor."

Truly, my birth brought joy to everyone in the entire village who celebrated my family`s good fortune for three days and three nights of feasting.

On my first day of school, I basked in the light of joy glowing from the teacher`s eyes as she gazed upon me. The students too were awestruck by my beauty. Beauty seemed a strong and perhaps an inappropriate word for a boy, but as I grew older, even I could see why people often gazed at and admired me. Whenever I passed a mirror, a face that would make an angel proud stared back at me. Tall and lithe, I wore a halo of light blond hair that shone like spun gold.

When I walked the streets, wagons and pedestrians alike slowed and stopped to stare at me. I in turn flexed my muscles, and tightened my gluteus maximi to create an even better spectacle. Women swooned and men wished upon their lucky stars that they could look just like me.

At sixteen, one of my many admirers gave me a guitar. "Legato," she teased, "would you sing a song for me?"

I surprised myself, as my singing voice perfectly matched my appearance, something I hadn`t explored before this moment. My friends and family thought so too, as I began to produce melodious sounds never heard before. My voice could soar to any heights, and could also descend to the lowest, richest notes. I could sing anything, opera or ballads. Soon I found myself in demand all over the land as a balladeer and performer, and I drew many wealthy admirers who filled my every need.

I traveled village-to-village, town-to-town, and whenever I performed I composed songs aplenty about how everyone in the land admired me. The years passed quickly and though I had the pick of many fine women, I was loathe to choose one and take her to wife, because I had so many choices and so many lovely evenings spent a-courting.

Finally, I reached the magic age of thirty-three in 1865. Thirty-three years of bringing joy wherever I went was not such a bad destiny, I thought. On that very evening, I stopped at a fair inn where I intended to sing for my supper and look for the company of some sweet maiden to warm me. I entered a roomful of men and women who were watching an artist as he finished painting a winsome young woman. I could see they had come as much to see her nude as to see the artist paint because her beauty took my breath away too. The throng turned at the opening of the door as I entered, and a hush overcame the room.

The innkeeper`s wife hurried to my side. "Would you like to sit there?" She guided me to a comfortable seat close to both the bar and the young subject of the painting. I knew also that she chose the spot so she could remain close to me.

The artist completed his final stroke for the day. The nude model began to wrap herself in a dressing gown, avoiding eye contact with all the people who remained frozen in place to stare at her. Nearly overcome with her long raven hair and her lithe olive limbs, I had to speak to her. "We`d make a fine couple," I whispered as she passed my table. "Your ebony to my ivory."

The maiden looked at me askance, and continued walking through an inner door to the lodging rooms. The artist finished packing his paints and looked my way. I knew he wouldn`t be able to resist painting an image of me any more than he could resist the charms of the lovely young brunette. My image of course, would sell just as well. He walked toward me carrying the newly painted canvas gingerly between his fingertips, a bag with his paints stashed over one shoulder.

"My name is Vasily and I`d like to paint your portrait," he said.

I nodded, a little drunk from hubris and the tankard of ale. "May I see the painting you`ve just finished?"

He turned the painting to face me and the maiden`s image nearly took my breath away. The clarity, the colors, the lifelike visage. . . this nude nymph was more alive, more luminous in the painting than when I admired her beauty as she walked past me.

I raised my nose a bit as I always did in my certainty that everything always went my way. "If you can capture my likeness as well as you did hers, then yes, oh yes, you can paint my image."

While Vasily set up his easel and paints, I removed my guitar from its case. "Is there a song you`d like to hear?" After his initial request, I sang many ballads. The women who had begun to scatter when the maiden disappeared returned to gather round and gaze into my eyes. As always, their men pondered my voice and my face, wishing to be me. The ballads, of course, were all about me, how I was met with love and respect wherever I traveled.

After I drank many tankards of ale provided by my admirers, I began to sing some of my private ballads jesting about what fools they are for supporting me. Downing too much drink, I began to sing also of my many conquests, the lustful things no decent man should do outside the bonds of holy matrimony.

Vasily narrowed his eyes, observing me closely and painting quickly. When I took a break from my performance, I attempted to look at his work. He spoke to me in a vicious way I wasn`t accustomed to. "Sit down. You`ll see the painting when it`s finished."

I began another song that told the story of how I bested many a man in games of chance. Who believed an angel like me would ever cheat with a smile? Of course I knew, true or not, that these simple folk would view my truth as merely a song. Then I fashioned an impromptu ditty about how Vasily would find fame because he`d painted me in all my glory.

Finally, as I finished this song, Vasily finished the painting. "You can see yourself now," he said, eyeing me coolly.

I eagerly stepped behind him to see my image, but stopped dead in my tracks. Before me was a picture of an older man, a ragged itinerant who looked as though the grim reaper would soon visit. When I found my voice, I shouted, "You blind fool! How can you paint a horrendous image such as that and say it`s me? Maybe this works in Moscow, but we love to see things the way they really are here!"

"I paint what I see within," said Vasily, handing me the painting. He packed his paints and brushes and left the inn without another word.

I held the painting up to the patrons. "Does anyone here see me in this grotesque piece of artwork?"

Not one eye met mine; not one voice rang out to disagree.

I threw the canvas to the plain-looking barmaid and told her it was hers to keep. She stood on tiptoe to hang it on an empty nail on the wall behind the bar.

She turned sadly toward me and looked me in the eye. "I do see what Vasily saw," she whispered. "I do see."

3

❧

Exposé Expansion

JASON AND I WORKED LATE two or three evenings in a row to read our second batch of contest stories and discuss our reactions. We finally settled on the winning story for its appealing simplicity, and we liked how *The Bachelor Guitarist* captured the subject`s soul in the composition and color, and how the author had engaged the artist and artwork in the story.

The winner of the guitarist story received sixty-five dollars and the magazine banked a bonus of one hundred dollars. We wanted to give the writers a larger percentage of the entry kitty than we kept, but at this early stage, we`d never satisfy the terms of the bequest with too much generosity, I reluctantly decided. The threefold increase in stories seemed encouraging, though, and if our good fortune continued long-term—especially if we gained a corresponding increase in circulation—we would meet our financial goals in eighteen months. Heartened by the numbers, I decided to revise the contest submission guidelines.

"The best stories of the lot so far have the artist featured in them. Although I like that, I don`t want writers to feel the stories *must* have the artist as a character or *must* feature the artwork in any way," I told Jason. "It was never my intention to limit the free flow of ideas or entries."

The new clarification emphasized that the stories could be any flight of fancy inspired by the artwork, as oblique and diverse as the writers` imaginations.

Two days after printing my second edition of Classic Art Exposé, we began to receive phone calls and later, some letters from writers and artists who requested new subscriptions or requests to reserve a copy of the magazine so they could clip an entry form for the next contest. We added another hundred copies to the next print run to accommodate these requests. The pressroom employees would now work a day and a quarter to print the next issue.

I felt Jason's contest idea and my new submission guidelines would be a Midas touch, relatively speaking. But an unexpected downside emerged too—we received a few phone calls and letters from armchair literary and art critics saying whoever picked the second winning story must have been insane themselves. The judges and the author of the story were clearly not writers, they complained, and the story belonged in some freshman college anthology and not in the pages of a serious art magazine. One or two people pronounced the story "too prescriptive."

Like us, some subscribers loved the simplicity of the story, but others took offense at the story's implication that Perov had painted the portrait of the guitar player to depict the musician's egocentric inner self. How could anyone write a story unfair to a distinguished artist? Blasphemy, blasphemy. I laughed when I read the letter airing this complaint. After all, Uncle John had enjoyed pushing the envelope.

"Controversy is good. It sells magazines," Jason also said often during the past few weeks, and I agreed. I reached over and slapped Jason on the back. "We picked two fine stories," I told him. "It finally dawned on me that any complaints are just as good for the contest as any praise. Thank you for sharing that revelation."

Jason grinned. "Told ya. Simple." He went back to poring over a rumpled copy of Sunday's New York Times to look at some paintings on the walls of homes belonging to the well-heeled to see what artwork we might choose for story inspiration in future contests.

"Did you know this, Pete?" Jason folded his newspaper section in half, tapped a finger on Picasso's photo, and read from the text. "Pablo Ruiz Picasso founded a magazine named Arte Joven (Young Art), and only published five issues."

"Makes me feel a little insecure," I said. "If a great artist like him can't make a go of an art magazine, why the hell am I trying to make this one a success?"

Jason grinned at me. "Simple, man; we've got skills and technology he didn't have to help propel us to the top."

❦

If the contest continued to produce ever-increasing numbers of entries, I didn't want to spend so much time reading them and debating their merits with Jason. Though our schedule was less hectic than Uncle John's, we still had a lot on our plates.

Jason and I decided to interview some students from Brooklyn College to serve as our intern. We both liked Shirley, an English major, and figured she`d bring a nice feminine balance to the office. She`d screen story entries as they arrived, giving Jason and me only the best from which to choose a winner. To keep expenses in check, I offered her a modest stipend each month. So far, we`d had to plow our profits back into upcoming issues and now had to add Shirley to our payroll. We weren`t much closer to paying off the notes than when I`d taken the helm.

Pretty and approachable, Shirley was easy to talk to and Jason and I hung around her every chance we got. One rainy day when we were all in a slump, she blurted out her real feelings. "Go away, I don`t even want to be close to you," she huffed at Jason. "You always smell like reefer and I think I`m allergic to it."

Jason had to make a choice, either quit his reefer cigarettes, or leave Shirley alone. Much to my surprise, he continued to smoke and let her be.

But the three of us put our heads together anyway to choose a new painting for the next contest—*The Accolade* by Edward Blair Leighton. As I`d discovered with the first two stories, it seems there is nothing more compelling to writers and artists than a theme with romantic possibilities. Leighton`s work highlighted adventure as well as romance, and we`d surely get some dashing stories about chivalrous knights and the beautiful ladies who loved them.

Drawing is the backbone of the whole thing.

HERO

LONG AGO IN THE NORTHERN climes, unbeknownst to but a few, the North Star`s orbit moved slightly on two days at Midsummer, allowing Earth`s creatures to fully understand one another. At this time, the Earl of Shrewsbury`s animals, domestic and wild, met in the woods surrounding his castle to share their tales of triumph and woe.

On this night, bright moonlight streaked through tree branches and a warm breeze carried the scent of a gathering storm. Owl convened the annual gathering. "Anyone with a complaint must voice it now, or wait a year," he said. The usual complaints arose between predator and prey, domestic and wild creatures, who continuously quibbled until midnight, when the tales commenced.

Hero the horse edged to the front of the crowd and all eyes turned to him.

"You`re not going to believe what happened to me."

Murmurs of encouragement arose from the animals.

"Yesterday I galloped around the pasture, hoping to rendezvous with a filly or two when a human sentry yelled, `Sound the alarm.`

"`*Damut*, the *Damut* are coming,` a villager shouted. `See the dragons on the ship`s prow. . .`

"`Dragons mean trouble in the form of Vikings, the *Damut*,` I`d always heard the Earl say. Hero tried to describe these symbolic images and the fierce tribes who sailed from the rugged lands to the north. "The Vikings worship Odin, king of all their gods, and they believe he rides through the air mounted on an eight-footed horse fleeter than an eagle."

An eagle spread his mighty wings. "A horse fleeter than I?" he cried. "Impossible!"

Hero nodded at the eagle. "I didn`t believe the story either. I wanted to destroy their myth by showing them how brave a real four-legged horse could be."

When the eagle settled on his perch in the great chestnut tree, Hero continued his story. "All the humans and all the dogs and horses gazed at the menacing dragon prows carved on the ships. Soon calls of `There be dragons` and the frenzied cries of the animals sounded across the moors."

Hero gazed at the assembly, pausing to create suspense. "The Earl`s men set up a command post atop a hill overlooking the coastline. If the invaders ascended the trails where the Earl`s soldiers gathered in wait, it would be an easy matter to defeat them.

"Robin, a young squire who chose me for his mount," Hero said, lifting his head in pride, "helped plan the defense and held my reins while the Earl conferred with his officers in the commanders` wedge tent. A soldier astride that cute filly from the East Meadow raced past shouting, `Flee, the battle is lost.`"

Hero bobbed his head and whinnied. "The Earl of Shrewsbury stepped from the tent. `What`s happening?` he shouted at Robin, who pointed to the troops.

"`All your troops are retreating,` Robin cried. Terrified of the advancing enemy, he jumped onto my back. `I`ll lead the retreat,` he shouted, and I cantered off, leaving the Earl stranded. But I disobeyed Robin`s commands and turned to charge straight at the advancing enemy troops. `Whoa, turn, Hero, turn!`"

Hero chuckled again. "I ignored Robin. He tried to rein me in again and again. I ran headlong towards the invaders while he screamed at the top of his lungs.

"`There goes Hero.` Sir Orville, one of the Earl`s commanders and Robin`s rival for Lady Mary`s hand, shouted in disbelief. His face crumpled as he watched Robin advance toward the invading army rather than retreat. After all, Robin had earned the name `Coward of the County` for his fear of physical combat.

"Sir Orville shook off his surprise and yelled again at the top of his lungs. `Stop! If Robin`s advancing, we can`t retreat. Follow him.`

"The men turned and followed Sir Orville, who followed Robin, who kept advancing towards the enemy against his will because I wouldn`t turn `round. I wanted to live up to my name!"

Hero stopped his narrative to whinny in laughter and the creatures laughed with him, some audibly, some telepathically.

"The rain stopped, the sun came out, and a rainbow appeared. One of the advancing invaders shouted, `Look, a rainbow bridge like *Bifröst*.` I heard later from the soldiers that in Viking tales, *Bifröst* is a bridge that stretches from the realm of mortals to the realm of the gods. The invaders at the bottom of the cliff thought I rode the rainbow with Robin screaming on my back. They thought a god was arrayed against them! `He must be leading a cavalry attack,` one invader shouted.

"`Yes, and a god with the fiercest knights in the land behind him means we`ll be slaughtered,` another cried.

"The warriors stopped advancing. One screamed, `The gods and the knights are coming!` and turned to flee. A second later, another followed him, and another, and another. Soon the entire horde ran, clattering and swearing, back towards the sea.

"Now Robin, alone amidst the enemy, swung his sword with what appeared to be bravery, but he was truly swinging wildly to chase away a swarm of bees disturbed by the conflict. The Earl observed this seemingly brave action from the hilltop.

"`Lucky for the boy that not one of the heathens stopped to fight. If they had, he surely would have been slain,` Sir Orville jested as they caught up to Robin.

"But when the Earl arrived to speak to his troops, he beamed with joy. He hadn`t seen the event from Sir Orville`s vantage point. `I don`t know where or how Robin summoned his newfound courage,` the Earl said, `but I want my army to emulate him.`"

Hero paused to whinny thrice in horse laughter. "What appeared to be *his* courage was actually *mine*. Only I knew the truth, that I`d won the battle, not cowardly Robin. I got nothing but an extra portion of oats and a five-minute rubdown from Robin for my effort."

Hero gazed around at the assembly of animals and finished his story. "The next day, Lady Mary brought me an apple. I said, `You all know I`m the one who caused those seafaring Vikings to retreat yesterday, and Robin`s lauded for my courage,` but she didn`t understand horse language. Frustrated, I tried harder and harder to make her understand, but the more I whinnied and neighed, the more amused she became."

A weasel stepped out of the shadows and interrupted the story. "Face it, Hero, you ain`t nothing but a horse. Naturally, Robin will receive all the accolades. Men always do."

Hero hung his head. "There must be something I can do."

A little voice piped up from a throng of rabbits. "You must become human; then you will gain recognition for your heroic deeds."

Hero`s ears sagged. "Impossible. How could I ever achieve that?"

An old, grizzled rabbit stepped forward. "A witch lives in these woods. Go and fertilize her garden. If Griselda listens closely she can understand any animal, but she must truly desire this. If you can convince her to listen, she will cast a spell to transform you."

❦

The following day, before the North Star returned to its normal orbit, Hero trotted deep into the woods to find the witch Griselda`s cottage. When he came upon her vegetable garden, he walked slowly amidst the rows spreading his dung, careful not to step on pea vines and carrot tops.

Griselda stepped outside her cottage to pat Hero. "Good boy," she said.

Hero whinnied, trying to relay his story, but she wasn`t listening or couldn`t understand. Dejected, he returned to the stable. If he couldn`t communicate with Griselda under the influence of the North Star, how could he possibly communicate with her in the future?

Still, he didn`t give up. Whenever Hero went out to pasture over the following week, he snuck away and returned to Griselda`s cottage in the woods. Each time he dropped his dung in the garden, he whinnied to her in horse language. To show her appreciation for the fertilizer, Griselda always pulled a carrot from her garden and fed him.

"Thank you," Hero neighed on his fifth visit.

"You`re welcome," Griselda said.

Hero stopped in his tracks. "You understand me?"

"Of course I understand horse."

"Why didn`t you reply before?"

"I thought you were just another dumb animal, but now I see you can think on your feet and are smart enough to give me something before requesting a boon."

Hero began to explain his difficulty with the squire.

"Master Robin is using my heroic deed to further his career. Once the Earl of Shrewsbury knights him, he will ask for Lady Mary`s hand in marriage. I risked everything by attacking those bloodthirsty invaders, and now the coward is taking credit for my bravery. Not that I mind the marriage part—more apples for me," Hero said, thinking about Lady Mary`s visits to the stable. "But I should be rewarded since I was the one who turned defeat into victory."

Griselda looked thoughtful and Hero held his breath, waiting for an answer. When she finally spoke, he flicked his tail with anticipation.

"I can transform you into a man or even a handsome prince. You may be knighted and you may even ask for Lady Mary`s hand, but what reward do I receive?"

Hero pawed the ground. "If you turn me into a prince, I`ll bring the Lady here and you can change places with her. At the least you`ll always understand me, whether I`m a man or a horse. It seems everything I tell Mary goes in one ear and out the other."

The witch shook her head. "What about Robin? The Lady is in love with him, not you. After all, in her eyes he is a hero, even if you dispute his story."

"Robin claims he loves the Lady more for her inner beauty than her outer beauty," Hero said. "After you exchange bodies with her, we`ll see how much the coward loves her then."

Griselda cackled and Hero snorted, both amused at the thought of Robin`s awkward position.

Early the next morning, Lady Mary brought Hero an apple as he rested in the stable. After she fed him and patted his neck, his form began to change before her eyes. His snout shrank, gradually changing into lips, and then his head morphed into a human skull. His forelegs became muscular arms and his hind legs assumed the form of stout, hairy man legs. The Lady stopped patting Hero and closed her eyes, as if she were hallucinating. When she opened her eyes, the handsomest man she had ever gazed upon stood naked before her.

Hero noted her admiration as her eyes flickered below his waist. Wonderful me, he thought. He looked down too, wondering if the hair atop his head was also the color of his lower mane, but other than hair color, he could see he didn`t resemble the old Hero at all.

While Lady Mary stared at him, seemingly mesmerized, Hero seized her and forcibly took her into the woods to the cottage. She swooned in his arms, expecting to be ravished. But Griselda had all the ingredients ready for her transference spell. As he shoved Mary through the cottage door, Griselda filled an urn with a foul-smelling concoction she`d boiled over the fire. Then she sprinkled the Lady with the concoction and recited an ancient spell for body transference. Mary`s body melted like hot candle wax into a puddle of liquid. Griselda soaked it up with a sponge. Then she squeezed the liquid into the kettle, adding a pinch of a special potion to the hot concoction. She stirred the potion over the fire until it bubbled, and filled a spoon with the mixture, careful not to burn her fingers. She then sprinkled it over herself. Almost immediately, her wrinkles began to smooth out and her rough, grizzled hair changed into Lady Mary`s silky, golden hair.

Hero watched with delight as Griselda`s gnarled, arthritic body straightened and filled out, her bodice splitting at the seams as her breasts bloomed into ripe globes.

When the transformation was complete, Griselda said, "Hero, tell me how beautiful I am." She took off her dark rags, picked up Lady Mary`s gown from the floor where it had fallen, and put it on.

Hero looked at her blankly. What was wrong? Then it dawned on him. He might have a man`s body, but he still had the mind of a horse. He didn`t find women beautiful. To him, beauty meant the filly in the East Meadow. To make Griselda happy, he said, "You`re as beautiful as a song. . . as beautiful as a spring sunrise."

"I hear some hesitation in your words," Griselda grumbled. "And?"

"And I have a question—how will we lure Robin here if you don`t give Lady Mary your old body?"

"Simple," Griselda said. "I have a twin cooking in the kettle." She poked her wooden spoon into the boiling potion and pulled out a deflated body that resembled her. She laid the thing on the floor and sprinkled a potion onto it. The wrinkles began to fill out and before long, it plumped up into an exact duplicate.

Lady Mary saw the transformed witch through eyes that now peered at the world from inside Griselda`s duplicate body. "What an improvement—you look just like me. Can I leave now?" She put her hand to her mouth in amazement as a cackle came from her lips.

Griselda laughed with sweet, melodious notes. "You can never leave, dearie, because my spell will keep you confined to these woods for the rest of your days. No one shall be able to see you other than Robin. If he`ll even want to see you again." She laughed once more, just to hear that sweet youthful soprano emanating from her soft red lips.

"Why wouldn`t he want to see me?"

Griselda handed her a looking glass. Mary dropped it. Her scream of horror and the breaking glass startled Hero. Mary rushed to a mirror on the wall and watched in revulsion as her wrinkled lips curled up into her withered old face. Her eyes were buried in her skull like shiny marbles sunk into a prune. A wart with thick, black bristles sprouted from her crooked nose and her once thick, glossy, and golden hair had turned stringy and gray. Lady Mary`s sobs sounded like a frog`s croaking. She clawed at her face with arthritic hands and the long, crooked nails drew blood. "Why? Why did you do this to me?"

"So you can see what it`s like living here in the middle of the woods, as I was forced to do by your father. Once I deal with him, I`ll marry Hero and we`ll rule the land together."

"And you, Hero? I brought you apples and rubbed you down after riding you." Mary stared at him with narrowed eyes. "My God, man, put some clothes on. If you`re going to walk on two legs, you`d do well to become civilized."

Hero shook his hips at her. "Yes, you brought me sweet apples. But you also rode me, whipped me, and spurred me. Put the god-awful bit in my mouth to force me to ride wherever you wanted. And your father—he was twice as cruel with his iron-tipped whip."

Hero took a cloth Griselda handed to him, ran it between his legs and tied a knot around his waist. He began to wonder if being a man was all it was cracked up to be. If he had to wear this rag all the time, he'd rather be a horse.

"Don't worry, Lady, I'll bring Robin here to keep you company." Griselda laughed again, enjoying the melodious voice that previously belonged to Mary.

❦

When the time came for Robin's knighting, he kneeled before Griselda turned Mary. In a loud voice she proclaimed, "Your Lordship, I take exception to this ceremony. The man you're about to knight is not deserving of the honor. He was dragged into battle by Hero the horse."

Aghast, the Earl's face turned red and his eyes bulged. Was she insane? Lady Mary had begged him since the battle to knight the young squire.

Hero stepped forward from the knot of onlookers, still wearing only a loincloth. "I—Hero the horse—forced Robin to attack. All the while, Robin screamed in fear, trying to turn me around."

The Earl motioned Hero forward, looking at him with disdain. "What's this foolishness? I witnessed Robin leading the attack myself. Who are you to parade in here dressed like a barbarian and make accusations?"

Hero bowed on one knee in deference to the Earl. "I am Hero, formerly your horse and now an applicant for knighthood, at your service, my Lord."

Mutterings of disbelief echoed behind Hero until Sir Orville stepped forward. "My Lord, I can vouch for everything he said as true." He described Hero's bravery in carrying Robin into battle. "I saw it all with my own eyes."

An uproar ensued. The courtiers laughed and pointed. Many pawed the ground and uttered whinnies and neighs at the stranger.

"And what is this nonsense about you being Hero the horse transformed? I hereby delay this ceremony until I determine the truth of this matter," the Earl declared.

When the crowd dispersed and the Earl consulted his advisors behind closed doors, Hero sought out Robin. "You know what I said about you is true, Robin. The best course you can take now is to go live in the woods with the Lady."

"What nonsense are you spouting? The Lady is standing right over there."

Hero laughed. "That's her double. Lady Mary has been banished to the woods and it is best if you join her."

Upon hearing this, Robin wondered how his good fortune had diminished in such a drastic reversal. Or had it? He knew a coward`s heart beat in his chest, but the stranger`s claim he was Hero the horse and that Lady Mary had a double was much too bizarre to be true. Robin rushed to the stable to find the groom, who sadly confirmed that Hero was nowhere to be found. Hero`s stall stood empty and he was not among the herd in the East Meadow. But the stranger could have hidden Hero. Robin rushed into the woods towards Griselda`s cottage.

When he knocked on the cottage door, he heard shuffling sounds within. He lifted the latch and opened the door. He started with fright. The old woman apparently had been taking a bath. She made her way to answer the door, but had forgotten, or not cared, to dress. Robin shrank back with revulsion at the sight of her sagging flesh, the stringy hair plastered around her wrinkled, shrunken face. If a shriveled prune could walk, he thought, this is exactly how it would look.

The hag`s frog-like voice croaked in what sounded like joy. "Robin, I`m so happy to see you." Lady Mary turned Griselda threw her arms around him.

Robin pulled back. His first impulse had been to flee, but curiosity compelled him to go back inside.

The hag sat on the floor and began to weep. "Don`t you recognize me, Robin? I`m Lady Mary, your betrothed." She wiped her eyes with an arthritic hand.

Robin wondered if anyone had ever seen a more pitiful sight—this scrawny, withered old woman crouched in the dust, croaking like a frog. He grappled with his feelings. If this truly was Lady Mary, it was not the girl he fell in love with. Though he appreciated any person`s inner beauty, his skin puckered and crawled at the thought of touching this ancient crone. Revulsion filled him and he couldn`t control this feeling. What horrible witchcraft had Griselda wrought?

Mary slashed at the air with one claw-like hand. "You men are all the same. You`ll love us when we`re young and beautiful, but add a few years and you want someone else."

"You`ve added about a hundred years. . . Oh, Mary, please forgive me. Give me some time. I`ll try to get used to your condition. In the meantime, will you dress yourself?"

"Please help me up."

Reluctantly, Robin extended a hand and looked away as Mary rose from the floor. As she dressed, he looked around the hearth and found that Griselda had been so excited about her newfound beauty that she had left a potion standing by the fire and her book of magic open on the table nearby. Robin studied the incantation, pondering how he might reverse the spell by sprinkling Griselda and Hero with the still-warm potion.

Encouraged by this good fortune, Robin paged through the book, searching for the transference spell that would return Mary to her old body.

Mary stepped into the room. Robin still found her revolting, but at least there was hope. He showed her the book of spells and described how they could restore her real body.

Mary rushed to the book and began to read. Although physically ancient, her mind remained sharp and she spotted the small print right away. "Robin, the task will not be simple. There`s an obstacle right here." She put her crooked old finger on the page and read. "'To reverse a transference spell, each party of the transference must joust in a tournament, and the winner will decide if the spell shall be broken.` This means you must challenge Hero to a joust."

"You jest—Hero is, as they say, as strong as a horse."

"It`s the only way."

Robin`s knees trembled at the thought. "I`ve never been a fighter. I get so weak I can barely lift my sword, let alone a jousting lance. Do you think this book contains a spell to give me the courage I need?"

Mary paged through the spells, searching for a courage incantation. Finally, upon reading the final page, she breathed a sigh of relief. "This says it makes one 'unafraid of any man or beast`." She then read from the list of ingredients.

"I hope we can find these plants and creatures from the garden and the river bottom," Robin said.

Mary reached for another kettle and stoked the fire in the hearth. Robin went into the woods and returned with the ingredients she requested. After she measured and chopped the twigs and leaves, she gingerly sprinkled them along with a shiny May beetle, a tadpole halfway grown to a toad, and a newly hatched newt into the kettle and filled it with river water.

Robin bent over the kettle and inhaled the stew-like potion. The pollywogs and river snails made the leafy concoction smell almost delicious.

Mary put a steaming bowl in front of him. "All finished. Eat this."

Robin spooned the broth into his mouth. "It`s good. What do you call it?"

"Liquid courage. One bowl and you`ll never fear anyone as long as you live."

"Give me another measure so I won`t be afraid of anyone after I die!"

Warriors dreamed of great battles in the sky, but Robin had had nightmares his entire life about an eternity of battles in which the entire population of warrior heaven called him the "Holy Coward."

"But wait," Mary said, paging again through the book. "Yes, that`s it." She found the incantation that bound her to the cottage in the woods and recited it backwards three times. It must have worked because nothing happened when she took Griselda`s walking stick and shuffled behind Robin out of the cottage and through the woods. When they neared the castle, Robin had to gather breathless, elderly Mary into his arms and carry her up the hill.

A young page running towards the stable breathlessly told Robin that the Earl of Shrewsbury had made a decision. Hero the horse had indeed become a man and would be knighted the following day.

"We`ve got to stop this," Mary said, holding his chin and forcing him to gaze into her eyes. "You must challenge him now. Once he is knighted he need not respond to a challenge from a squire."

Robin walked past the guards, who lowered and then raised their spears in confusion. They grumbled among themselves and then allowed Robin inside. He stepped into the royal hall and found Hero and the lovely Griselda turned Mary in the great room, where a meeting had just adjourned.

"Sir Horseface, I challenge you to a joust."

"Oh-ho," Hero countered. "The coward desires to joust! He wants to win the hand of this lovely lady!"

The courtiers exploded with mocking laughter at poor Mary turned Griselda and the thought of timid Robin facing off against a perfect specimen of knightly manhood.

Hero waved his hand to quiet them. "I`m more than happy to oblige. I`m sure the Coward of the County will be easily separated from his horse. . . Oh dear, but he does not have a horse!"

The courtiers exploded into jeers and laughter again.

"Neither of you are knights," the Earl declared, "but I will provide armor, lances, and steeds of equal measure to you both. The stakes? I say the victor of the tournament wins knighthood and my daughter`s hand."

The Earl obviously knew nothing about Lady Mary`s plight, and neither the real Mary nor Griselda wanted him to find out. Robin looked at the crone with dismay. Maybe if she`d confess, her father would put a stop to this nonsense. Both men bowed to the Earl and made their way from the hall, the women walking behind them.

"You must win," Griselda turned Mary whispered to Hero as they exited the great door before Robin with Mary turned Griselda. "If you lose, the spell will be broken."

This news aroused profound fear in Hero. Though he didn`t fancy wearing clothing, no way did he wish to return to his former fate. Manhood had advantages over his life as a beast of burden. Hero excused himself from the witch and strode to the stable to borrow a mount. He would channel his worries into practice for the joust. He spurred and whipped the horse without hesitation or mercy, because who knew better than he how to handle a horse?

❦

After two bowls of liquid courage, Robin felt ready to whip not only Hero, but any knight who dared challenge him. He walked with a strut to show he feared no one. He practiced with his armor and lance until he no longer fell sideways off a horse and could face an adversary`s lance without his knees shaking.

⚶

On the day of the joust, Robin borrowed a cart and a donkey to carry Mary turned Griselda to the tournament. He stood before the crowd with more courage than he'd ever felt in his life. Even though he was small in comparison to Hero, weighing perhaps half as many stone as the transformed horse, he felt his chances of victory were good. At the very least, he looked magnificent fully arrayed on the fine white stallion that the Earl had provided for the tournament.

When Hero appeared leading a brightly caparisoned chestnut stallion, a fine brute nearly seventeen hands high and much like the horse he had once been, the crowd went wild. "Hero, Hero, Hero," they chanted, "Hero Horse is our hero!"

A page led the white stallion to Robin and he took his bows before the crowd. As he mounted his steed, the crowds jeered. "Coward, better run while you're able."

Hero and Robin rode to their stations and faced off across the tournament field. At the signal, the men shut their visors, lowered their lances, and spurred the horses.

At the slamming point of contact, Hero's horse suddenly stopped. Robin's lance struck him square in the chest and splayed him from his mount. Hero lay struggling on the ground, encased in his massive armor like an upturned turtle.

The crowd roared. Even Hero's supporters were yelling, "Coward, here's your chance!"

Robin dismounted and sat on the fallen man. He pulled the vial of transference potion from his gauntlet and sprinkled it over Hero while reciting the magic chant Mary made him memorize.

"Look," a spectator shouted, "Hero's armor is splitting!"

All gasped as Hero's arms and legs stretched into horse legs. His armor shattered as his bulk increased. In a matter of seconds, the crowd was crowing at the sight of Robin sitting astride Hero, the horse he had ridden to lead the counterattack against the Viking invaders.

Robin dug his heels into Hero's sides and urged him to the box where Griselda turned Lady Mary rose to leave her seat as the crowd went wild, shouting, "Victor, victor, victor!"

Robin pulled another vial from his gauntlet. "Now you're going to get what you deserve, witch."

He sprinkled her with the potion.

"Nooo," she wailed, but to no avail as she puddled onto the ground.

As the Earl rushed towards him, shouting about the "demise" of his daughter, Robin hurried to soak up the liquid with a sponge he carried under his breastplate. He searched for Lady Mary turned Griselda and gave her the sponge that contained Griselda's juices, helping her astride Hero's back. "We'll ride posthaste to the cottage."

Robin urged Hero to a gallop through the woods, the Earl and a phalanx of his knights not far behind. At the cottage, Mary squeezed the sponge into a kettle, stoked the fire, and heated the liquid before mixing it into the potion that Robin sprinkled over her.

"My beauty," he shouted as her wrinkles and warts faded away and her body filled out into youthful curves. Lady Mary`s cornflower blue eyes popped from the depths of the prune-like face, her lips plumped into cherries, her big hook nose shrank and turned up, and the stringy gray hair shone golden again.

After much kissing and embracing, Mary went outside. "No more apples for you, Hero. This is what you get from now on. She picked up Griselda`s walking stick from the ground and gave the horse a good whacking on the hindquarters. She returned to the steaming kettle on the hearth and pulled out the deflated image of Griselda from it with a spoon, then sprinkled the potion on it that inflated the witch back to her ugly, stinky self. Griselda crawled to cower in a corner, blinking in fear at the young couple.

"Just think, Mary, after I`m knighted tomorrow, we can finally be married," Robin said brightly.

Mary gave him a long look.

"Mary. . . did you hear me?" Robin reached out to embrace her again.

Mary pushed his arms away. "Surely you jest! With the spells I`ve learned from Griselda`s book, I can create any sort of man I want any time I desire!"

Lady Mary put the book of spells under her arm, strode outside, and mounted Hero.

The Earl of Shrewsbury and his knights arrived in a cloud of dust. As they reined in their mounts, they exchanged perplexed stares with Robin as Lady Mary nodded politely and dug her heels into Hero`s flanks to send him trotting away.

❦

At midnight on the following midsummer`s eve, Hero nodded his head and whinnied. "That`s the end of my tale of manhood, believe it or not."

At that, Hero turned from the assembly of animals in the Earl of Shrewsbury`s woods and cantered away towards the East Meadow, where the filly turned mare waited for him in the midsummer moonlight.

4

The Editors Grimm

THOUGH SHIRLEY MADE SHORT WORK of reading and crafting a shortlist for the month`s top stories, we debated a long time over their merits. I found *Hero* amusing but too childish for our readership, yet Shirley and Jason outvoted me when we discussed the stories. On the other hand, with no one the winner in the story, it shone as an interesting piece of fabulist fiction, if you enjoy that sort of thing.

I felt vindicated when negative comments poured in by mail and phone. Horse lovers appreciated the story but hated the ending. Literature buffs thought the story unworthy of the space and ridiculed us not only for promoting fantasy but for fracturing fairy tales as well. One critic called Jason and I the "Editors Grimm."

"You may not like the story, man, and some subscribers may not like it, but again, more controversy, bigger circulation. Besides, it wouldn`t hurt to attract some younger subscribers. We could do a regular feature slanted for students. . ." Jason drifted off to tally up our new requests and figured we reeled in nearly a hundred more subscriptions and requests to reserve the next issue.

"I`m not sure it`s fair to the writers to keep choosing whimsical fantasy stories. On the other hand, our circulation may only be inching up, but up is up," I conceded, relieved to view our glass half-full rather than half-empty. By now, our story contest winners were receiving an impressive monetary award for a new writing competition in a regional art magazine. Our bank account wasn`t looking too shabby either. I had to admit that I kinda liked the odd stories despite their shortcomings; plus, it was brilliant to lighten up and widen the audience by appealing to the younger set.

Shirley suggested we bring in her kid sister Evelyn as an intern to help her review the next batch of contest entries. Jason started hanging around Evelyn`s desk whenever he had free time. Even cuter than Shirley, Evie didn`t have her sister`s "reefer allergy."

All was right in our world until press day. Evie was humming a new rock and roll tune, *Save the Last Dance for Me*, to the chattering rhythm of the printing press as she opened the morning mail with her fingernail file. When I walked past her desk, she glanced up and handed me a typewritten business-sized envelope.

The letterhead inside made my hair stand on end—a foreclosure notice from my father`s bank. He`d never wanted me to study journalism and hadn`t wanted me to leave my job at the bank, but why the hell would he do this?

"Goddamn it," I said, grabbing the phone. "Sorry, Evie, it`s not you, just business."

She motioned to Shirley and Jason, and the three stepped out of the office.

I called my Uncle John`s attorney, Mr. O`Neill, who now represented the magazine.

"Don`t worry about a thing, Pete. Let`s consider filing a bankruptcy petition for the magazine. You`ll have plenty of time to reorganize the debt, and no one will be able to foreclose. At any rate, Mr. Rizzo can accept your conditions—you`re able to give him a substantial payment, after all; or if you`d rather, you can let him foreclose and put you out of your misery."

O`Neill chuckled as though the project was failing and didn`t mean a thing to me. I jerked on the curly cord of the telephone receiver, nearly pulling it out. "Like hell! There will be no foreclosures. I`m going to meet all the requirements put forth if it`s the last thing I do. So you better think of some way to support my side."

O`Neill got my drift and promised to do his best.

I fumed in a blue funk the rest of the day over the torment my father had put me through regarding my education. A few days after my high school graduation, he took me to Yale, where he and Uncle John had graduated years before. He showed me around and introduced me to some professors he`d studied with, old men who still had a bit of smarts under their hats even though their bodies had slowed to a shuffle.

"I can hardly believe he`s still teaching," he said about one particularly piebald gentleman. Evidently these professors were all in their sixties and seventies. Father thought anyone over fifty-five was much too old to retain their edge. That`s why he wanted me at the bank, so I could carry on his legacy when he retired. He always said, "The day I turn fifty-five is the last day I`ll work in this world." His father, my grandfather, had died of a heart attack at sixty and I guessed Father was afraid he`d die young, before enjoying his retirement.

"You know I want to study journalism at Princeton," I said when he pushed me to fill out application papers for Yale`s business program at the admissions office. His face tightened and became so red I thought he might have a heart attack. "I`m not spending my money to make a newspaperman out of you. Either you study business at Yale or I`m not paying a cent toward your education." He huffed back to the car and I followed in silence. I thought his anger only temporary, so I continued with my plans to apply at Princeton with Mother`s blessing.

After I applied to and was accepted by Yale`s journalism program, hoping to please Father with my choice of schools while pleasing myself with my chosen studies, Mother did some creative juggling with her household expense money and made the necessary payment to hold my place open for the fall semester. I unexpectedly received a notice from the university bursar of a substantial scholarship from an unknown sponsor. It covered every educational expense I foresaw during the next three-and-a-half years. The scholarship contract covered not only my class tuition and fees, but also covered university accommodation and meals as well. In the fine print, there were stipulations about access to another fund if I had unforeseen expenses. I couldn`t wait to tell Father about my good fortune, thinking he would be pleased he wouldn`t have to pay a cent toward my "wasteful dabbling in useless artistic pursuits."

Father wasn`t yet aware of Mother`s meddling in my registration when I handed him the letter. "I received a wonderful scholarship from Yale. You don`t have to worry about my tuition," I said, my chest swelling with pride.

He read the letter and thrust it back at me. "You can`t accept this. You don`t even know who the donor is."

"But if I don`t accept it, are you going to pay for my journalism program?"

He stared at me for a moment, putting on his stubborn face. "I`ll gladly pay if you major in business. For journalism, never."

"Then I`m going to accept the scholarship. I love to write and I know I can make a living as a journalist." I always emphasized journalism when I talked to Father about writing, rarely mentioning my love of literature. I filled the blank account books he had given me with poems and short stories and kept these in a box under my bed. Though keeping secrets from him made me feel like a liar, I pled with my eyes for him to understand. More than anything, I wanted his love and support.

Father expressed nothing but his bitter disappointment. "Take the damn scholarship then. I`m not wasting my money so you can write trash."

I took his statement as a positive one. And I made a concession. During the remainder of summer vacation that year, I worked at the bank. Father went out of his way to give me interesting work, trying to entice me to stay with the firm. He staunchly avoided discussing my classes and never mentioned the scholarship again. After four summers, banking routines became familiar, almost comforting, and of course, I could rely on the income. Though Father seemed proud enough at Yale`s large outdoor graduation ceremony—he heartily threw his arm around my shoulder when Mother snapped the obligatory photograph of us displaying my diploma, though I knew he considered my degree worthless. "At least you graduated with honors, even if you only earned a degree in journalism," he said in an incongruous happy tone after the flash bulb popped.

When he offered me a generous starting position at the bank as vice president the day after commencement, with what to me (or any young reporter) was an astronomical salary, I couldn`t refuse. I knew I could save money and still work on my fiction for a few hours before or after work every day. I wondered if it would spoil me because I wouldn`t have to go hungry for my art or have to endure the pressures of a reporter`s life right off the bat. But no matter. There would be plenty of time later on to suffer and pursue a real writing career.

❧

When Shirley, Evie, and Jason wanted to go to lunch and take the afternoon off to celebrate another issue put to bed, as we had last month, I almost snapped at them, but caught myself. "Go ahead, knock yourselves out," I said. "Here, take this." I pulled a twenty out of my pocket. Treating them to a good time was the least I could do for all their hard work. Twenty dollars one way or the other wouldn`t break Classic Art Exposé.

I spent the afternoon poring over my account books, trying to figure out a way to rob Peter to pay Paul. In this case, the situation was more like robbing Pete to pay Peter, I thought sourly, cursing my father for being such an ass. I picked up the phone and called my mother.

"I warned you that something would happen," she reminded me. "He`s still bitter about you leaving the bank."

"It`s been three months. Surely he`s used to it by now."

"Petey, you know your father. He doesn`t let much go."

"But taking his disappointment to this extent? What kind of father does that?"

She remained silent. I thought back to the tense undercurrent in our household that had simmered during much of my childhood. Mother had told me Uncle John had wanted to be a painter. He`d loved both literature and art, and Father often called him "a jack of all trades and master of none." The cliché fit my uncle like the favorite old slippers he sometimes wore as street shoes because of the gout attacks that made his big toes sore.

As I grew older, I learned about Father`s and Uncle John`s fractured relationship. Before I was born, my uncle convinced my father to loan him money for a down payment to purchase a floundering local newspaper. He gushed that the business had potential to be a moneymaker, that the Rizzo family would emerge as publishing barons. He thought his artistic talent combined with the cutting edge of his witty editorials would help the newspaper's circulation grow. After he purchased the press with my father's money, Uncle John's editorials were indeed widely read and frequently commented upon by many county residents. But the newspaper seemed to operate under a cloud and Uncle John lost money just as steadily as he made it. Even with a crackerjack advertising man, the paper barely attracted enough ads to pay the bills and the endeavor never gained that magic balance of subscriptions, advertising, and reporting to pull a dependable profit. Within a few short years, Uncle John's vision failed and my father lost his thousands. After that, Uncle John never visited or called, because one thing my father couldn't tolerate was losing money.

So not only was my choice to work in a field related to my education bothering Father, so was the fact that the magazine I inherited had been owned by Uncle John.

Mother wasn't mentioning the D word, but I felt responsible for her marital woes, never mind all the water under the bridge between my uncle and my father. I made a mental note to call a florist and send her a bouquet of roses. Spending another few bucks on flowers wouldn't make or break Classic Art Exposé either.

As I ended the call with my mother, I looked over at the art print book propped up in Jason's chair. Evie and Shirley had urged us to try something different and more challenging this time. I picked it up and paged through it briefly until I found an unfamiliar but classic scene. Entrants of the next story contest, I decided then and there, would interpret *The Abduction of the Sabine Women* by Nicolas Poussin.

*Colors in painting are as allurements for persuading
the eyes, as the sweetness of meter is in poetry.*

PRAISE NEPTUNE!

WHENEVER I FILL OUR AMPHORAE at the village cistern, I share stories with the other maidens. There is always discontent circulating among us. No one wants to disobey their fathers, but neither do we want to marry the men our fathers choose for our arranged marriages. We are influenced by the rumors that in Rome, the new city, many handsome young men are looking for wives. We chatter about romance, what it is like to fall in love and marry, and our embarrassed giggles twitter like birdsong across the village square.

When I return home after one of these water chats, as we call them, my father sits me down. "Caecina, I finalized an agreement for your marriage to Julius six months from today."

Behind him, my mother holds a finger to her lips, but I cannot remain silent. "My *old, fat, ugly* cousin? You cannot be serious."

My father looks at me with shock that I have the audacity to question his decision. "Yes, you will wed the day after your fourteenth birthday. You should have been married this year."

My mother waves at me frantically to stop talking. "As if I am an old crone," I grumble.

My father lifts one eyebrow as he always does when close to losing his temper. "You will do as I command."

My mother looks relieved when a knock sounds on the door and my father rises to answer it.

"Caecina," she scolds in a whisper, "you must not talk back to your father. What you did not give him a chance to say is that he will take you to Rome to buy you more things for your trousseau. Is that not wonderful?"

I pout, but I am secretly excited to visit the city. We village girls say we would much rather live in Rome than stay in remote, dusty, run-down Collemia. For the young and adventurous, life in the new city has appeal. Now I will actually see all the wonderful things that my friends and I talk about. My older brother Cassius often accompanies my father to Rome to buy and trade goods. Only slaves carry water in Rome, he says, because the city has aqueducts and the water runs into the homes of merchants like my father. Cassius mentions that the young men there come from all over to live as freemen, to have some say about how they conduct their lives. Roman women are viewed as equals under the law. I am quick to notice this, and when Cassius mentions that the lack of women in Rome means the great city might wane in a generation or two due to lack of male offspring, I am even more intrigued.

At the middle of the following week, I rise before dawn and ride with Cassius and our father to Rome in his four-wheeled cart. As we enter the market in the middle of the city, I am awestruck at all the hustle and bustle. There are buildings under construction on every corner and hundreds of young men walk the streets. Father warns me to speak to no one unless he gives me permission. Rome scandalized the villages nearest it when it granted citizenship to criminals and lawless persons so it would grow quickly and therefore win the wars against its neighbors.

My father reins the horses in and stops in front of a building of three stories. "Go through that door and you will find the best weaver in all of Rome. Vibia is waiting for you and knows how much I will spend to purchase the lengths of silk and wool for your wedding garments. She also trades in goods for women, mirrors, and jewelry. I have business on a street nearby. Cassius will fetch you when you are finished."

As I dismount from the cart and walk toward the weaver's shop, I cannot help but notice the building next door. It is not the house that impresses me so much as the muscular young men working on it. If only my cousin looked like any of these handsome brutes!

A vibrant woman with wavy hair and sparkling gold earrings greets me at the door. "Hello, I am Vibia. Your father said you were pretty, Caecina, but you are far more beautiful than his description." She motions me to a seat of low cushions near a window. "Please sit here while I finish with Miss Tiberius."

I gaze at the stacks of linens and other fabric lining the walls while Vibia disappears into another room and brings back a cool drink. When she returns to her other customer, I cannot help but eavesdrop on their conversation.

Miss Tiberius` face screws up in disgust. "I am appalled at all the rough men roaming the streets."

"They say the law was passed so Rome can grow sufficiently and recruit enough men for the army," Vibia says softly.

"If I look on the bright side, I suppose there are benefits when the men outnumber us three to one." Miss Tiberius replies. "My father had five offers for my hand last week. He told me I could choose, and of course, I picked Tullius the potter, by far the handsomest suitor. My father said if Rome doesn`t remedy the city`s shortage of women soon, the city will never grow."

I listen for a long time and learn many amazing facts about Rome. Before today, I only knew what my brother shares. I also knew from the water chats that the Sabine elders look down upon the Romans, and refuse to consider Roman requests to marry our women.

When it is my turn to shop, Vibia helps me choose the softest woolens and linens and the prettiest silks. I try on a pair of golden earrings with ruby ovals that glow on my ears like the setting sun. Even if my wedding day won`t be a happy one, I want to look stunning. When Cassius comes to take me back to our father`s cart, I feel a little more spring in my step. The wedding is still months away. Maybe some unforeseen opportunity will arise to give me a choice, like Miss Tiberius.

The following month, the village is abuzz with news. The Sabine elders have received an invitation to attend a festival in honor of the Roman god Neptune. Not wanting to offend our neighboring state, they graciously accepted.

I am overjoyed to hear of the feast. This is another chance to see the wonders of Rome—if my father will allow our family to attend. I hurry around the village to learn everything I can about Neptune. Not that I am interested in the Roman god, but it might be nice to know more about the ceremonies performed throughout the festival. I ask my friends at the cistern if they know anything about Neptune or the festival. Most shake their heads, but Flavia, a girl of almost fifteen, says I should ask the seers and priests, or the older women of the village. "I think many may know about Neptune."

Over the coming days, whenever I finish my household chores, I do just this. I share what I learn about customs with the other girls when we fill amphorae at the cistern. We grow giddy with anticipation and hope we may all attend the feast. Roman "Wear white tunics on the feast day, as you may march in the festival parade. Oh, and carry a flower. The parade ends at the seashore where a great statue of Neptune stands," I proudly say, showing off my knowledge.

When the feast day finally arrives, scores of young Sabine women all dressed in white line up to march in the parade. I am proud to stand among them. The young Roman men have heard about the arrival of maidens and their families from the Sabine villages. Though we are not to talk to them, they line the streets three and four deep, straining to look over one another to catch a glimpse of us.

At my signal, we girls from Collemia each toss a flower to a young man we find attractive. The other women from Sabine villages notice, and they too offer up their flowers. Ironically, though our elders have refused to allow us to marry Roman men, there are more families from Sabine villages than all the others outside Rome. Because we Sabines march at the end of the procession, it is easy for the young men to follow us. Our parents and guardians grow wary and chide us, but the crowds are large and the parade continues to flow through the streets like a river toward the sea.

When the throng finally arrives at the foot of the statue, each young man keeps an eye on their Sabine admirer. Some girls` families are trying to shoo these young men away, and some are surrounding their daughters to protect them.

I rush to the speaker`s platform erected in the shadow of Neptune and raise my arms. A murmur runs through the crowd, people wondering aloud why a Sabine woman addresses them, and then people hush one another so they can hear what I say.

I raise my voice to a shout. "I have studied the laws of Rome concerning Neptune. They state "any man and woman who sincerely admire one another in the festival parade may be joined as man and wife if they so desire."

Yells of disbelief arise from the Sabine families. Shrieks of joy erupt from the youngest Sabine women, followed by an even louder shout of joy from the young Roman bucks, who begin running toward the Sabine girls who have tossed flowers to them. All chaos breaks out as they pick up their admirers, heft them to their shoulders and carry them away. For some it was not so easy, what with angry fathers, brothers, uncles, and grandfathers attempting to prevent these abductions. Some fists, and even stones, go flying. A scrap breaks out near me, but I watch as Flavia escapes her family. When my young man takes me by the hand, my father surges forward to stop him, but my mother and Cassius hold him back, trying to reason with him. I don`t think they really want me to marry my ugly old cousin.

Soon, even some married women let Roman men capture them. This shocks me at first, but I note that one of my neighbors, a young woman unhappy with the spouse her father has chosen, is smiling as a strapping young

Roman I noticed weeks before at the construction project dumps her over his shoulder like a bag of wheat. May she be blessed with happiness, I think, as our young men carry us away.

❦

Soon a flood of wedding processions ebb and flow in the Roman streets and many young men carry their Sabine brides over the thresholds of Roman homes. Imagine my surprise when I see that Vibia is my new sister-in-law! My husband Julius swiftly unknots my silken marriage belt in his home after our torch and water ceremony, and our hearts and bodies flame with joy at our newfound love.

Horrified by this open breach of the rules of hospitality, the Sabine men return home to prepare for war. By the time the Sabine army arrives at the gates of Rome, most Sabine brides are with child. I am terrified by the thought of Julius killing my father, or my father killing Julius. In the midst of the gathering storm, I summon up my courage. Though my belly is heavy, I rush through the streets to the main gate. The Roman and Sabine commanders and their front lines stand ready with spears and shields, snarling insults at one another, working up their courage. I only hope I can somehow appeal to them not to bring a curse upon themselves by staining their hands with the blood of a father-in-law or a son-in-law.

What words will move them? I place myself as near to the commanders as I dare. "If," I cry, "you are weary of these ties of kindred marriage-bonds, then turn your anger upon me. It is I who have caused the war; it is I who have risked the deaths of many fathers and husbands. Better for me to perish rather than live as a widow or as an orphan."

The commanders take a long look at me. The Roman commander lays down his spear and within moments, the Sabine commander lets his fall to the ground. Then the entire field of soldiers on both sides do the same. Couriers begin to rush to and fro from the gate into the city as the commanders petition the ambassadors to begin negotiations.

After a day of negotiations, the Sabines retreat. We daughters made our choices willingly and there is no point in creating unhappiness where there is none. But to salve their wounded pride, my Sabine countrymen will continue to tell the tale, generation after generation, of the Sabine women`s abduction by uncouth Romans.

❦

On one of his monthly visits to Rome, my father dandles my newest baby on his knee while entertaining my eldest son and middle daughter with toys made of clay. What a wonderful grandfather, I think, watching them play together. How things change. I remember that horrible look Father gave me as Julius carted me away at the feast of Neptune. Mother later told me how Father had vowed to kill Julius. But now my husband, along with my brother Cassius, are key merchants in my father`s trade cooperative.

⚶

Father smiles at me. "Caecina, where on Earth did you learn about the Neptune proclamation that said couples who admire one another could be married if they so choose? Isn`t it true that Romans must receive special permission to marry outsiders?"

I turn from my cooking and wait a moment before I confess. "I did not learn it, Father. I made it up," I say, smiling at him.

Julius wraps his arms around me from behind and laughs. "Praise Neptune!"

5

⚜

Progress

BY THE END OF NINETY DAYS, I`d settled into my role as Publisher and Managing Editor of Classic Art Exposé. While I didn`t exactly have the world by the tail, I felt content with my editorial routines even though I could never seem to work quickly and efficiently or to get ahead. At least my father had quieted down since his last attack and I could only hope he would soon forget his rancor.

This month we`d negotiated over the contest winner for much longer than ever before, three entire mornings, because Shirley and Evie held out in favor of *Praise Neptune!* until I finally cast the tiebreaking vote. Though one male reader enjoyed the "amusing alternate history," most men reacted like the one who dropped a gruff postcard describing the story as a "frivolous historical romance." Or the one who seethed in scrawled capital letters on a full typewritten page about the "disrespectful and degrading alternate history."

Thanks to the girls, our female readers showed overwhelming support for the issue nonetheless, and we gained more new subscriptions and requests for single copies of the next issue. Not so many as after the first three contests, but I couldn`t complain because again, progress is progress. Jason pouted a bit because he felt the other top story, a dashing adventure, would placate the male readers disgruntled by the previous two stories, but it didn`t hurt to soften up and please the ladies, I figured.

This time I kept four hundred dollars of the six-hundred-dollar contest pot, glad we hadn`t promised the entire take to contest winners. Two hundred dollars was a generous payment for a two thousand-word short story, and I kept reminding myself that I didn`t have to feel guilty about it. I worried about diverting contest money into Classic Art Exposé`s outstanding debt kitty because I didn`t have the cold heart of a business "bankster" and wanted to see the writers prosper.

Shirley and Evie were dying to run another feminine painting for the next contest, but Jason and I leaned toward doing something more adventurous again. We gathered around the big art book, and Evie paged to the work of Tiziano Vecellio, better known as Titian.

"I don`t know, ladies," Jason said. "Those are beautiful women but romance always seems to sillify the story, if you know what I mean."

I understood Jason`s concern but I also respected the girl`s desires to make the female experience accessible in art and literature.

"Oh," Shirley said, her face reddening with irritation. "You two are just misogynists."

"Who cares that he has so many female subjects—just look at Titian`s subtle use of deep colors. That`s enough to use his work in this contest."

I looked closer. I could see why Titian is lauded as one of the most influential artists of the Italian Renaissance because even his lesser-known painting, *Emperor Charles V at Muhlberg,* fired my imagination with its grand, equestrian flourish. I couldn`t help but override the girls this time around.

EMPEROR CHARLES V AT MUHLBERG
Titian, 1548

He who improvises can never make a perfect line of poetry.

THE CONQUISTADORS' SURPRISE

PROFESSOR MENDES SMOOTHED THE TWO sheets of parchment on his desktop with gloved hands. "Senhor Cabrilho, you`ve come a long way to see this. . . Some students visiting Santa Catalina Island found the entrance to an unknown cave, and then my university colleagues found these in a cache nearby. This report explains what happened during Juan Cabrillo`s last day on the island."

João Cabrilho wiggled his broad fingers into the cotton gloves provided by the professor and leaned over the desk to survey his illustrious ancestor`s still-visible signature. *Juan Rodríguez Cabrillo* scrawled across the page in vigorous, looped letters right under Father Cabeza de Vaca`s name. The Spanish priest`s hand had likely inscribed the entire report.

Mendes opened a book and read aloud, sharing with Cabrilho some family history he already knew. "When Cabrillo was commissioned by the Viceroy of New Spain to command a search along the Pacific coast of Alta California for trade opportunities and the mythical Strait of Anián, Cabrillo had promised his lover he would return within a year. But five months into his journey, he died, and the notary`s official report was lost. Two centuries passed before Spain sent soldiers, missionaries, and settlers to Alta California to make good on Cabrillo`s claims. . ."

Juan Rodriguez Cabrillo (known also as the Português) was legendary in the Cabrilho family. Every child in the clan knew how he had shipped for Havana as a boy and joined forces with Hernán Cortés in New Spain, how he profited from every trade he had attempted and had died one of the richest of *Conquistadores.*

Though the bedraggled remnant of Cabrillo`s expedition returned to New Spain with some fragments of the ship`s log and his crewmembers` conflicting stories, the true details of his demise remained sketchy.

Until now. Senhor Cabrilho gazed at the top of the page.

"We united on this expedition to serve God, his Royal Highness Carlos I de España y V de Alemania, and to seek riches by the authority of Antonio de Mendoza, Viceroy of New Spain. . ."

Just after dawn on 7 October, in the Year of Our Lord 1542, the armada approached an island some leagues distant from the Baja coast. I duly noted the location of this island and the two islands sighted nearby as possible trading or settlement points on our journey north to locate the Strait of Anián, the passage that surely connects the Pacific and Atlantic Oceans.

As soon as I lifted my quill from the log, a score of canoes cut through the sun-swept blue waters to greet us. We invited the savages aboard to exchange trinkets—their stone pipes and quaint carvings—for our metal fishhooks. Through many attempts at speaking with them, we determined that these people call their island *Pimu* or *Pimugna,* and themselves, *Pimuvit* or *Pimugnans.*

We are two hundred and twenty-two men: fortune hunters, merchants, slaves, and two priests. The priests, of course, will confirm that we explore in the name of God. I believe that the priests are sincere, but we conquistadores explore for profit. Some of my younger men wanted to invade the Pimuvit village, but we experienced conquistadores scoffed. We have learned after many wild goose chases that the rumors of golden cities and mountains are just that, mere tales told to distract us. Outside the early ransacking of rich cities in the South, we must engage in trade and mining in the New World with the same old-fashioned methods employed in the Old World, by the sweat of our brow. I sternly reminded these youngsters of our mission to trade on friendly terms with the natives and to take careful note of their languages and religion.

"That doesn`t mean we cannot look for silver and gold," these young men grumbled.

I conceded that point. Once these simple people understood what we were looking for, they pointed west toward a low mountain where they said we could find shiny gray metal. But they warned us of some monster who lives there. The young men made many jokes, disappointed that the metal wasn`t gold.

When we reached a suitable cove and the men reassembled, I claimed the island in the name of His Majesty, the King of Spain, and christened it San Salvador.

"We continue our journey to find the Strait of Anián at high noon," I told them. "On the return journey we will determine if this tale that the mountain contains silver is true or not."

The expedition made many landfalls and established good relations with Indian settlements along the Alta California coast. But as the gloom gathered into winter`s implacable fogs and gales, I was forced to command the armada to turn south without having located the elusive Strait.

On the chill, foggy morning of 23 November 1542, we made landfall again at San Salvador. This time only two canoes of unenthusiastic warriors, two in each vessel, came to greet us. Immediately, I organized a party of twenty volunteers, including one priest, two slaves and a horse to board our landing pirogue and accompany our taciturn hosts toward the village. We thought it a simple task to hire a guide or guides to show us the entrance to the cave the Pimuvit had referred to months before, but this time the people were much less friendly. Again, when questioned about the mountain, even the most seasoned of the Pimuvit spoke in fearful and animated tones of the god or creature that protected the silver there. Perhaps it was simply the lair that this creature defended? At any rate, Father Portillo gained some fluency in a similar tongue during an expedition he had accompanied further inland, but even he could not be certain exactly what these frightened and superstitious men said.

Even so, one grizzled Pimuvit elder scratched a primitive map in the sand to show us where we could find the entrance to a cavern, and displayed a primitive bead made from silver ore and strung on a strand of twisted fiber that dangled from his neck. I noted that he seemed to do so with a disingenuous glimmer in his eyes, as though to trick us, but his subtle visage was lost upon my men. They still grumbled that the silver wasn`t gold, but even this small windfall was enough for them to ignore the Indians` fright. Naturally, we were equipped with superior weapons and had no use for the savages` superstitions.

The elder who drew the map seemed unnaturally pleased when our company proceeded toward the mountain. The walk took a little more than an hour and the faint trail was clear enough, but locating the entrance to the cave took another hour, as it was simply a small hole in the ground covered by a boulder and some overgrowth rather than the expected doorway leading into a large chamber.

I directed the slaves to hobble the horse near this hole and left them to keep watch. There were some tense moments as we squirmed feet first into the dark hole, and one sweaty, plump young man, Junipero Garcia Valdes, almost shot back outside when he disturbed a serpent that rattled, lashed out at him, and then retreated. We had fashioned some short, crude torches from driftwood taken from a port further north, and we lit these from an ember box supplied from our galley when we began to grope along in the gloom.

The suspense grew strong as we walked along a tunnel two men wide, barren of anything save the same type of stone outside the entrance. Rather than lead into a main cavern, the tunnel narrowed again, and we were forced to crawl through it, this time on our bellies. We had to pass our torches through and two were extinguished, but fortunately, we were able to relight these from the others. Soon we were able stand again, thank the Lord Our Savior, but this small chamber was also unremarkable. We raised our torches and saw a narrow crack in the back of the chamber. We had to ease ourselves through this at considerable discomfort, but at least we were able to remain on our feet this time.

Those who carried the torches held them aloft.

"Holy Mother of God," Valdes said, crossing himself with his sausage-like fingers.

We stood with mouths agape, looking at a wall of enormous white quartz crystals laced with streaks of slightly shimmering gray silver that extended as far as we could see into the murky darkness. Thin at the entrance, the veins of silver became thicker and thicker as they extended into the cavern. Even Father Portillo gazed with his mouth open, impressed by these worldly riches.

I broke the silence. "Move forward, men. Let`s see how thick these veins become."

We walked further into the cavern. Fool that I am, I should have followed military protocol and posted a sentry or two at this spot, but I did not.

This cavern was deeper and longer than it first looked. I feared that the floor might disappear and that we would find ourselves on a precipice and so I edged forward, tapping my rapier in front of me. Many men behind me did the same, and our tap-tapping filled the cavern with ghostly echoes.

About seventy paces into the cave I stopped, struck by the sight of a solid gray wall that shimmered strongly in the torch light, surrounded by enormous translucent crystals. The glimmer of the vein took everyone in its grip. Irrationally, we started chipping chunks of silver from the wall. There was talk of how even the lowliest among us would lead a life of luxury from now on.

I heard an odd sound, or maybe I felt a vibration running through my body before it manifested.

"Silence," I shouted. Suddenly a deafening rumbling noise that sounded like thunder roared through the cavern. Everyone stood transfixed as the thunder became louder and louder.

"*Mira, mira,*" someone shouted, and the men with torches held them higher as a shadow began to descend upon the wall of crystal and silver. Our party all turned to see a stone barricade fall from the ceiling behind us, turning the cavern even blacker than before. Instantly I knew I had led my expedition into a trap. The men`s voices rose and fell in consternation until I shouted again for silence.

By now, our torches had dimmed and would not burn much longer without fresh air.

"Form a line," I yelled. I counted off as each man stood side by side with weapons drawn.

"Now I see why the Pimuvit were so helpful," I said. "They knew what would happen. Use your belts to tie yourselves together, side to side, so if our torches die and attack comes, we can slash our adversaries without killing one another."

While the men complied, I considered extinguishing the torches but wanted the advantage of seeing our attackers. If worse came to worse, and we had to fight in total darkness, at least it would be an even fight.

We stood there for a few moments, silent, listening to one another breathe. Nothing.

Finally, I spoke. "We will search for a way out while we still have light." At my proclamation, one of the torches sputtered and died. The others would soon follow. We turned first to investigate the massive barrier. We pounded, kicked, and stabbed at it, but there was nothing but rock to rage against.

Then another torch failed. To be honest, I didn`t know what to do next save move forward. "Fall back into line and move forward," I ordered, my voice sounding hollow. I motioned to the priest. "Father, stay behind me."

As we began to creep forward, the last three torches sputtered out, leaving us in darkness so deep there was no hope of ever seeing anything. We began to tap forward again, breathing hard. Tension oozed through the cavern like a dull poison.

Just behind us, so close we could almost touch the sufferer, a piercing scream cut through the thickening air. A moment later, a pleading voice wailed, "Please, please stop."

Another piercing scream bounced from the walls. "No! No! Please. . ." The pain in the voice penetrated into my gut. I could almost feel the combined shock of the entire party running down my spine. Because of this shock, we seemed to lose our way even though we edged forward only a few paces. I tried to turn the party back toward the barrier, where we could at least reorient ourselves.

"Silence," I shouted, as the men began to utter epithets and the horrific wailing began again. But we were hopelessly lost, turning in circles. I had never experienced darkness like this before.

Another wailing scream started behind us.

"Mother of God," young Valdes whimpered, as the wailing transformed into weeping and moaning.

Then a long, agonized scream came from yet another direction. We were surrounded by screams of pain and terror. I stumbled down the line to count bodies. There were four missing. I did not report this, wondering if the men already knew. How could this have happened unless they untied themselves?

"Untie yourselves and retie yourselves back to back," I ordered. "Be ready to fight."

Suddenly the air went so quiet I could hear myself breathe again as the men repositioned themselves.

"Stand down and sing."

"Sing, at a time like this?" a rough voice sputtered.

I began to chant a seafaring ballad, and one by one, all sixteen men joined in, reluctantly at first, until all sounded as if enjoying a night on the town. But another sudden scream, louder than all our combined voices, soon engulfed the cavern. We stopped singing, but the screaming continued. My legs grew weak while imagining what could cause this much misery and pain. When I counted pairs of men, there were only six trembling, sobbing men left.

"¡*Dios mío*!" I shouted. "Did no one feel these men disappear? What is happening?"

No one answered, but under the subdued weeping, I could hear the uneasy shuffling of feet, and a low voice that began to pray.

"Sir, what will we do?" Valdes whined, fear dripping from his voice.

Panic stuck in my gullet like a fishbone. How could I answer? If I felt awry, then I am sure this pathetic remnant of my party was disintegrating as well. How could we fight an unseen enemy?

Self-preservation took over. "Untie yourselves. Dig for your life," I shouted. "Each man for himself!"

The men began to hack with their scabbards and rapiers. I knelt on the cool, damp earth and stabbed at it with my dagger, digging as fast and as hard as I could. The screams could still be heard, but they were receding as though the men were being dragged deeper into the bowels of the cavern. When the hole was barely deep enough for me to curl up in, I lay down and pulled as much earth over me as best I could, leaving a small space around my mouth to breathe. From what I could hear, the other men seemed to have done the same.

We crouched like this for what seemed like hours. But I startled awake, I don`t know when, to the sound of rock grinding against rock. I rose from my hole in disbelief, felt around on the ground, but all I found was an empty hollow. I felt around again but felt only bare ground, damp and pungent against my fingertips. Even the holes of the other men seemed not to be there. The grinding sound stopped. Had I been dreaming? Had the barrier been lifted?

I staggered left and right, tearing my shin on what I presumed was one of the projecting crystals. I tried to walk in a straight line, but bumped into another wall. I turned in another direction and tapped forward with my rapier. I kept going this time. Forward and forward.

Finally, I reached the crack where we had entered this godforsaken cavern. I called behind me. Nothing. I shouted again, and a third time, but still no one returned my call. I could only assume that all my men were dead, killed in some unspeakable way.

I only hoped to find the entrance. The dark disrupted my senses, making my head spin. My eyes could see only swirling colors and shapes that did not exist in the blackness. I entered the crack and moved forward until released from the close walls. Then I careened around the smaller cavern on my hands and knees, looking for the tight passage we had crawled through.

When hope finally dimmed that I could locate it and I almost gave up in despair, my hand found the spot. I wormed through it frantically until I could stand again. With my extreme hunger and thirst, I could barely recall what to do next. My bladder was bursting and I stopped to relieve myself, close to tears. Then I put one foot in front of the other until the crack released me into the small chamber. Above me, like an eye from heaven, sunlight burst from the world above.

I looked down and found myself covered in gore. My own blood dribbled from the deep gash in my shin, and a small fragment of bone protruded from it. The dirt all over my tunic was sticky with clotted blood. Perhaps that was why the ground inside the dry cavern seemed so damp.

My head exploded in pain as I grappled to reach the hole and then climb out of it. I could not leave this subterranean hell fast enough, though I could only move by inches. When I finally extricated myself, I sat up to examine my broken leg. The slaves and the horse were nowhere in sight.

A noise behind me made me spin around. The elder stood over me with a club in his hand.

"You`re the first to ever escape the gods," he said, taking his cord from his neck and binding my hands with it. He smiled sadly. "Tomorrow, they`ll have another chance."

Professor Mendes` eyes misted up as he handed the parchment back to João Cabrilho. "Now we know," he said, putting the fingertips of both hands together to form the symbolic tent of certainty.

Cabrilho shook his head. "No," he said softly, and then again, louder. "No. We can only wonder now whose hunger was darker, the Pimuvit man, the creature in the cavern, or my ancestor, a conqueror motivated only by swordplay and riches. . ."

6

Saving the Day

JASON GRINNED AND WITH A deft slice of a letter opener, he attacked the subscription envelopes that had started filling our mailbox again. "See, didn`t I tell you? A manly adventure minus romance always saves the day."

Evie pulled a face at him and fluffed her strawberry blond mane. "Sex and glamour would do that just as well," she said, pulling a fake rose from a tired bouquet on Millie`s old desk. She placed the stem between her teeth swayed toward Jason with a little cha-cha triple step. "What we need is another story with a Green Goddess character, simpleton."

"Touché," Jason replied, glancing at her swaying hips with more than a trace of admiration. Shirley gave him a mock slap as I looked away and pretended to scan the account book.

"The Conquistadors` Surprise" had garnered mostly positive responses, one thanking the writer for turning the story on its head and giving the conquistadors what they deserved. Three more praised the unique alternate history, but one was aghast that anyone would mock European superiority.

The account receivables spoke for the many readers who hadn`t bothered to respond. My Classic Art Exposé savings was still growing steadily even though I had to make a hefty payment to our lawyer O`Neill, who was still lobbing long, convoluted letters back and forth with my father in an attempt to stave off his foreclosure madness. He was an unabashed penny pincher and I held no animosity toward him because of his thriftiness, what my mother called his "dogged stinginess." Father hated to part with his money, but I knew this stemmed from being dirt poor when he grew up.

But Mother had moved into my old bedroom and said she was gathering her nerve to file for divorce as soon as Father calmed down from his quest to undo me. I wasn`t quite sure how to feel about Mother`s revelation and still felt responsible for her marriage troubles. But I seethed with rage at my father`s treatment of me, and my head soon ached with the tension my body mirrored.

Despite my dark mood, I put my feet up on my desk and pretended to park a cigar in my mouth. "So gang, what outstanding work of art should we feature in the next issue?"

Shirley picked up the great international painters book. "Our dibs, gentlemen," she said, pretending to pull the imaginary cigar from my mouth and tossing it in the wastebasket. "How about whatever page it opens to?" She held the book out to Evie, who slid a finger between the pages and opened it with a flourish.

"Bingo!" Evie smiled triumphantly, pleased at the choice: James Jacques Joseph Tissot`s rendering of two women and a man aboard "The Gallery of the HMS Calcutta, Portsmouth." She read from the text around the photo. "'Tissot`s first characteristic period made him renowned for capturing the charms of women.` The charms of women, gentlemen. . ."

Shirley giggled. "Now all we need is a female author to win."

Jason and I looked at each other and shrugged. "Hope this one works out," he said, winking at Shirley, whom he was still sweet on, though too proud to show it since her steadfast rejection of him. I wondered if she might appreciate him more than she let on.

I laughed aloud as Evie stuck her tongue out at Jason. She definitely had a little crush on him too.

*At the heart of Tissot`s work . . . lies the idea of the modern, that which
makes the present time distinct in appearance and character from the past.*
—Curator Malcolm Warner, Yale Center for British Art

LOST MEMORIES

I ATTEMPTED, AS ALWAYS, TO stay in my stateroom to avoid mingling with the other passengers, but I couldn`t bear the close atmosphere, even with the luxurious appointments. To escape this gloom of my own making, I cast about and paced the ship`s deck.

I couldn`t help but notice two well-dressed ladies waving their farewells at the railing as HMS Calcutta broke anchor and sailed from Portsmouth Harbour, bound for the West Indies. One young woman gazed intently at the shore, her face hidden behind her fan as her companion turned boldly toward me, her face lighting with recognition.

"Excuse me, aren`t you the famous alienist that the medical world is raving about?"

"Famous? Unlikely. Dr. Gerald Kreizler at your service," I said, doffing my cap. "I don`t believe I`ve had the pleasure of meeting you."

"Please excuse my bad manners—it`s not every day I meet a celebrity, Lady Anne Whitmore."

"Pleased to make your acquaintance," I said, blushing at her assertion. I knew people talked about my miraculous mental cures, but I didn`t consider myself either famous or a celebrity. An American by birth and ignorant of protocol for greeting nobility, I took a chance by bowing, taking her gloved hand in mine and holding it to my lips. The woman with the fan, who appeared she might be Lady Whitmore`s younger sister, continued to look at the receding shoreline, but when she fluttered the fan, I could see the barest trace of a smile curving her lovely cheek.

I straightened up and gazed again at Lady Whitmore`s smooth, alabaster face. "Would you ladies care to accompany me to the lecture scheduled tomorrow?"

"Which one?" Lady Whitmore asked.

"I`m interested in the missionary speaking about her work in China."

"Why, that`s me. I`m scheduled to give a series of lectures about my work during the crossing and in several Caribbean ports."

While we conversed, a gentleman who had been setting up an easel and preparing his palette nearby stared at us intently.

Lady Whitmore leaned toward me. "Is he painting us?" she asked.

"It appears that he is." I offered Lady Whitmore my arm and we walked behind him and his easel to see his painting. All three of our images were already recognizable on the canvas. We exchanged a surprised glance, impressed by the precision of his work.

The gentleman noticed our presence and turned. "I`m Monsieur Tissot," he said. "I hope you don`t mind that I`ve included you in my work. May I impose upon you a bit more and request that you pose as you were at the railing, just another few minutes?"

Lady Whitmore nodded her assent and I readily agreed as it gave me more time to become acquainted with her. Msr. Tissot thanked us and turned to his work.

"Lady Whitmore, may I inquire about your companion. . . ?"

She smiled. "My sister, Edith. Quite shy." She lowered her voice and turned her head away from Tissot as if to share something private. "Edith always places the fan in front of her face to hide a small scar beside her mouth. I knocked her down as a child and split her lip."

"It must be a small blemish on such a radiant beauty. Why does she make such effort to hide it?"

"In her mind, an insignificant scar is a horrible disfigurement. She believes it cries out for attention."

"How sad." I wasn`t sure what else I should say, but I felt quite pleased that Lady Whitmore shared this personal information with me, so I reciprocated and shared a little with her. "I`m going to the Caribbean to visit a bokor who gave me a wonderful gift. I want to reward him for being so helpful to me." But I thought privately how I might give the man what was coming to him.

"Heavens. Could you please enlighten me—what is a bokor, precisely?"

"Of course. A bokor is a Voodoo priest," I said.

"Oh," she said. "I`m unfamiliar with that term." Her countenance clearly conveyed that she didn`t believe in any kind of priest other than the Christian type.

I enjoyed her discomfort. "Forgive me, Lady Whitmore. I believe that bokor is a term for sorcerer."

Lady Whitmore turned to glance at the nautical clock secured in its box in an alcove behind us. "You`ll have to tell me more about your amazing adventures, Doctor Kreizler. Perhaps tomorrow, after my lecture. Excuse us, please—Edith and I have a meeting with our donor committee soon."

Though I did not feel like leaving my room once I`d returned, I attended Lady Whitmore`s first lecture and sat beside her sister. Edith spoke little and continued to hide one side of her face with the fan, ducking and bobbing her head like a wounded bird.

Dressed in a more somber outfit than she had worn on the ship`s launch that morning, Lady Whitmore told the modest gathering about how she had become involved with her mission group. "Even as a young woman, I was drawn to religion. I became concerned about so many in this world who haven`t heard about Jesus and are doomed to an eternity of suffering. This alone compelled me to bring the Word to the world`s heathens. No matter how devout these practitioners of other faiths are, I knew they would never rise to heaven because they didn`t believe in Jesus."

As most attendees nodded their silent approval, Lady Whitmore continued to "preach to the choir," describing how she and her husband had converted the heathen Chinese. "I didn`t have the opportunity to get deeply involved until I convinced my husband, Lord Whitmore, of the importance of missionary work," she lamented.

Lady Whitmore continued speaking for another interminable hour. An interesting lecture, overall, if you like that sort of thing. I wondered if she thought I was going to hell along with the world`s peasants because I didn`t accept Jesus as my only savior. I would enjoy remembering vindictively her warnings about heathens many times over.

My mind went a step further. Perhaps I should thank the fates rather than cursing them for allowing me to meet the bokor, my "benefactor". . .

Lady Whitmore then excused herself from socializing due to her unusual exhaustion. We agreed to meet on the deck the following day.

During the course of our conversation that windswept morning, I politely mentioned "enjoying" her lecture.

Lady Whitmore blushed with embarrassment. "I`m afraid. . ." she began to say, ". . .Can you believe. . . I`ve forgotten every word I said!"

Through using the gifts provided by my benefactor, every word she said became stored in my memory and gone from hers. I wondered if maybe it wasn`t a good thing she couldn`t remember her opinionated views, but sensing her embarrassment, I assured her that I remembered much of the lecture and repeated some of it word for word.

"What a magnificent memory you have, Doctor Kreizler! How does one acquire a mind like yours?"

"It`s a very long story, and one day when we have time, I`ll tell it to you."

Later that evening, I attended her second lecture, in which she described how she and her husband went to China as missionaries after their marriage. Lady Whitmore`s adventure as a newlywed was rich with romantic memories of her recently departed husband.

"We were able to convert many Chinese to Christianity by making food available to any who would convert. Many Chinese were dying of starvation—can you imagine the stupidity of those people, allowing that to happen? It proved that England`s superiority allows us to better their lives. We`d never allow mass starvation or other catastrophes to happen."

Puzzled by the contradiction, I felt I must voice it. "But England rules Ireland—consider the recent famine there."

"Well, they`re Irish."

"And India, the `Jewel in the Crown`—they have famines there as well."

"Regardless, the simple-minded natives of the world must be converted and looked after. We know what`s good for them."

Her ideology annoyed me, but I absorbed all her words. I promised to attend her third lecture, and the day after, we met on deck again.

Lady Whitmore seemed agitated and perplexed. "I`ve forgotten much that I spoke about yesterday. I can barely recall what I said about my late husband. This is most distressing. How can I have feelings for someone I can`t even remember?"

I repeated some of her third lecture word for word. This seemed to ease her troubled mind.

"How are you able to remember what I say so well? Is your memory always so keen, Dr. Kreizler?"

I laughed. "Not at all. I don`t use my memory, I use yours."

"Please do explain! I have all afternoon. What is your technique?" she asked.

"It`s a long story, really, so if you`ll join me for a cup of tea, I`ll tell it to you from the beginning." She agreed and we walked together to the salon, where we sat across from one another, sipping from the ship`s heavy china cups.

"I`m dying of curiosity to understand what you mean about using my memory," Lady Whitmore said.

"Three years ago, I was diagnosed with an early case of dementia after some trouble with my memory," I confided. "I decided to travel while I still was able. I embarked for Europe, and before winter set in, sailed for the Caribbean where the winters are tolerable. I rationalized that if my memory failed completely, I could return home more easily from the West Indies. While watching the sunset and drinking some tasty rum at a public house in Haiti, I struck up a conversation with one of the locals. Everyone called him Man. . ."

❦

"I`ll buy you a drink if you tell me how you got a name like Man."

"My uncle is a village bokor. He named me Man the first time he lay eyes on me, and what my uncle say is pretty much the law `round here."

"I`m sorry, but I have no idea what a bokor is."

"Bokor is what you people call a sorcerer. Maybe he can help you."

"What do you mean, help me?"

"Anyone can see your memories be stolen."

"What do you mean, stolen? My memories are dissolving because my brain is aging."

"I`m trying not to laugh. You don`t know `bout stolen memories? Maybe my uncle can help you," Man reiterated.

"I don`t think so. I`ve been to the best doctors in America and Europe, and there`s nothing to be done."

"As long as the price is right, my uncle can help with just about anything. Buy me another drink and I`ll take you to him."

What did I have to lose? I ordered two more drinks and we were soon on our way to see the bokor. We hiked along the moonlight-drenched road from Port-au-Prince to a nearby seaside village. When we arrived at a shack in a clearing, Man yelled first in French Creole and then in his broken English, "It`s me. I`ve brought you somebody who needs your help."

The thatched door opened, and the bokor stepped outside. A big person, twice as big as Man, who was

❦
81

of considerable size himself. They conversed in whispers. Then Man introduced us and bid me farewell, a Haitian ten-gourde note tucked in his shirt pocket, a gift from me.

"So you want to learn about stolen memories?" the bokor said. "We have many different memories for sale. What kind you looking for?"

"I`m afraid Man misunderstood me. I`m not looking to buy any memories; I`m trying to find a way to stop losing mine."

He looked at me intently. "I can help, but it be 'spensive, because you need the magical amulets."

"What are you talking about, what amulets?"

"These will help you keep memories told to you."

"I don`t quite understand what you mean."

"Do you want memories or not? If the answer be no, stop wasting my time."

The way he used these phrases brought me both skepticism and curiosity. How ludicrous, a Voodoo witch doctor selling amulets that capture memories! Yet I wanted badly to believe I could avoid the nothingness of dementia. Not being a fool, I wasn`t about to give him any money, but before I had a chance to begin the negotiations he suggested a princely sum. "The price is a thousand gourdes. Don`t worry none `bout being cheated—you may try the amulets for twenty-four hours before you pay. You not satisfied, just return them."

I wondered how he could be so sure I`d return one way or the other. But I wanted to restore my memory again no matter what. "In twenty-four hours I`ll probably return the amulets, but I`m willing to give them a try."

He reached into a leather bag attached to his belt, and pulled out a gold chain with two ivory pendants that had looking glass set into one side and intricate carvings of tiny animals on the other. He dangled them in front of me and showed me how to arrange them so the words they captured could pass between the reflections. If I set them like this, he promised I would recall each memory that passed through them. He told me the amulet would function only while in the presence of the person possessing the memory I wanted.

"Do I understand correctly? You`re telling me I need to be in the room with someone who is speaking from their memory for this to work?"

"`Xactly," he said.

"How long will I retain the memory?"

"As long as you live."

"What if I want to give a memory back?"

"Put the amulets on the person you want to take back the memory while you tell it to them."

I agreed, took the amulets, and strolled down the road, heading back to Port-au-Prince.

One sweaty hour later, near the pub where I'd met Man, I came across a small theatre with a marquee hanging over the door. It advertised "Shakespeare's Hamlet * One Week Only." As it was just a few minutes past showtime, I decided to cool off and spend the evening there.

Just then, I remembered to put the chain around my neck and position the amulets as the bokor had shown me. This would be a good test of the amulets' supposed power. I settled into the back row of the little open-air theatre on a rough bench. The lead actor performed better than I expected and knew his lines perfectly. He went through the complete performance without a misspoken word. I followed his eyes and they stayed focused upon the audience. I could see he wasn't reading any cue cards or listening to a cue reader. The twenty-seven people in attendance gave him a standing ovation for his superb performance.

After a refreshing night's sleep, I remembered every word of the previous night's performance, to my amazement. Years before, even with youth's sharp memory, I could never remember some of those archaic English words and phrases. But now I could recall and recite the opening and closing sentences of each act at will, and recite any portion of the play I chose. This was absolute proof that the amulets functioned as the bokor promised. I thought of boarding a ship to save myself the thousand gourdes, but the bokor's stern countenance the evening before haunted me and I knew I'd best pay up. I hurried to dress and counted out the gourdes notes for the bokor. On the way to the village, I passed the little theatre where a man on a ladder was changing the marquee sign. I asked what happened, as the play scheduled performances for a week.

"Poor chap has lost his memory. He woke up this morning and couldn't remember one single line. There's no understudy to take his place, so we need to change performances."

My stomach turned a little at this news, but it demonstrated to me that once I acquired a memory, the person it came from lost his recall. I paid my debt to the bokor, who seemed very pleased with himself, and returned forthwith to New York, reciting Shakespeare's lines all the way. How could I put my newfound talent to good use in the city?

With the amulets, I could absorb all the memories I wanted. Since I had spent all my savings traveling and buying the amulets, I could now replenish my earnings and even make enough money to retire permanently. As a doctor of mental pathology, I knew full well there were many people willing to pay large sums to rid themselves of thoughts that, in many cases, crippled them.

Before I had retired due to my dementia, my middling practice consisted mainly of patients afflicted with a garden variety of neuroses and anxieties. I needed clients with more dramatic afflictions, so I visited a more prominent alienist in New York City, known for his work with chronically ill patients. I advanced my proposal to remove any memory, no matter how horrible or debilitating, for ten thousand dollars. If the memory didn`t return in six months, I would receive payment. Fascinated, the alienist suggested that I present my proposal to the American Alienist Association. As it turns out, our organization knew of several persons willing to pay that much and more to rid themselves of horrific memories. I informed the AAA that I would take only ten cases. I could live well on one hundred thousand dollars, even in the throes of dementia or the problems posed by other people`s memories. With the amulets, I`d always have a way to create more income if I so desired.

The AAA insisted I have a stenographer record my sessions. I steadfastly refused. I wanted to protect my clients` confidentiality, assuring them that whatever they revealed would go no further than my ears. At first, the AAA stood firm, but in the interest of science and probably great curiosity, they finally conceded. My first patient was the scion of one of New York`s wealthiest families, treated without result by the nation`s most illustrious alienists. Mr. X had done something he perceived of as so horrible that he needed to be restrained in a straitjacket or he would do anything possible to commit suicide. Two attendants in shirtsleeves dragged him into the room, flailing and screaming oaths. After considerable effort, I was able to convince him that if he told me what he had done, he would never, ever think of it again. A dim glimmer of hope lit his eyes. Mr. X tried several times to tell me, and finally, the truth came pouring out. Though shocked by his lurid memory—actually a series of dreadful memories in which he tormented family pets and then his neighbors` pets in increasingly bloody and sick exploits—his memories became completely erased from his mind and embedded in mine, thanks to the amulets. Mr. X began to smile, though wanly, and to talk in a normal voice, asking me why in the world was he bound in a straitjacket.

The AAA considered this cure little short of a miracle. "There`s no need to hold the money for six months. The cure is obvious," the AAA Director told me the following day. He gave me an envelope with my fee and motioned to the window, where I gazed down at the horses and a carriage thrown in by the young man`s family as a bonus. The director offered me an additional ten cases at twice my normal fee. The thought of this wealth was tempting, but I feared that if the other nine patients` memories were as dreadful as the first, the accumulation of twenty such memories might be detrimental to my own mental health.

During the first night after my first cure, I woke up in a cold sweat from dreams in which I had slain innocent dogs and cats and alternately dreamed of being a helpless animal in the hands of this perverse young man. I could only hope that by taking his memories, I had truly cured him. Or had I unleashed this monster back into the world? Perhaps I would never discover the truth. During the day, I grappled with obsessive thoughts, shoving them from my mind, but my nights became a trial of either experiencing these terrors or embracing sleeplessness. Over the next month, I listened to the memories of the other nine clients, and then, retired. "And here I am," I told Lady Whitmore, holding my palms up.

She remained silent during my entire narrative, but now leaned forward, anxious to learn more. "But what about your night terrors, Doctor? If the first memory gave you bad dreams, what about the rest?"

I sighed deeply. "I must admit that each new memory brought another challenge—some in the form of dreams, others in the form of obsessive thoughts. I tried many things to relieve myself of them: herbs and sleeping draughts to quiet my mind, writing notes about the memories, a process I hoped would channel the negative energies to paper, and though I`m not a religious man—no offense intended, Lady Whitmore— I also prayed to have these thoughts and dreams taken from me."

"And did none of this work?" she asked, incredulous. "Surely God would answer your prayers, as your sole motive was not profit or your own comfort, but to help others."

"I don`t believe that God has forsaken me, dear Lady, but He certainly made clear that `God helps those who help themselves,` as many wise men have proclaimed," I admitted demurely. "I`ve done my best to own up to this revelation."

"But what else did you do? You seem in fine mettle now," she said, looking me over.

"I must confess that I did some animal experimentation, though not as cruelly as the young man. . ."

There was a quiet pause and then I continued. "After one truly distressing night in which I`d experienced uncountable dreams, I decided to try giving the memories to a dog. But not just any canine, of course. I sought out a poor, stray mongrel just a day or two shy of death, put the amulets on him, and repeated all the memories given to me."

Astonished, Lady Whitmore said, "Please tell me that this worked."

"No, actually it did not. I soldiered on for a bit, then after another particularly trying day and night—the worst seemed to occur around full moons—I decided that perhaps the superior mental capacity of an ape, being closer to our own, might allow me to transfer memories to one."

"And this was not successful?"

"No, but this time I made more than one attempt. An organ grinder with a dancing monkey, a flea-bitten old creature, often performed in the park near my home. I paid the man dearly and returned the poor monkey as he was, but my scheme didn`t work. Then I approached a zookeeper at the Central Park menagerie and compensated him for some moments alone with the chimpanzees. The scoundrels took my amulets and played tag with them, keeping them out of my reach for a while, and then one finally gave them back. She also allowed me to put them on her and repeat the memories. But sadly, I walked away with all the memories intact."

"How dreadful for you. How did you ever cope?"

"I`ve exercised my will like a muscle. Each day I contemplate these memories actively, which seems to tone down the stray thoughts and nightmares." I smiled sadly. "I`m just grateful that I was able to assist these miserable people while simultaneously helping myself."

Lady Whitmore clucked over me like a mother hen. "You certainly seem to have done a fine job. Excuse my prying—did anyone`s memory ever return?"

"One young woman, the second client and victim of a terrible crime, begged me to return her memory because she was so used to it, she claimed, that she couldn`t bear to live without it."

"Oh, what happened to her? How were you able to return her memory?"

"Oh, dear Lady, Miss X was the victim of an unspeakable rape, multiple hooligans who tortured her for hours. It left her diseased and unable to bear children. I returned her memory the same way I tried to give the collected memories to the dog and the ape, just as the bokor directed. I didn`t want to, but I couldn`t ignore her pleas. I put the amulets around her neck and repeated what she had told me."

I explained the story in fuller detail as Lady Whitmore listened in fascinated horror.

"And it worked! You`re telling me that if I wear the amulets while you repeat what you recall of my lectures, that my memory will be restored?"

I nodded and removed the amulets from their place around my neck and inside my shirt.

"Please show me how to position the amulets," Lady Whitmore said.

I placed them around her neck and showed her how to position them.

"Please," she begged, "please recite my second lecture first. I miss that one dearly. I used to think of it all the time."

"Of course," I said. "I`ll tell you not only that one, but all that I`ve heard." I repeated everything I had absorbed from her, and she was so grateful to me for "restoring" her memories that she didn`t know how to thank me. "No thanks are necessary, Lady Whitmore. . ." I gestured to the table. "If it makes you feel better, would you mind pouring me another cup of tea?"

As soon as she`d emptied the pot of hot water into my cup, stirred in cream and sugar, then pushed it closer to me, she asked, "What made the other memories worth ten thousand dollars?"

I raised my hands in horror. "They`re miserable. I couldn`t possibly tell you all of them."

"They couldn`t be any worse than the tales confessed to my husband and me by some of the natives we converted," Lady Whitmore said. "Please share them, and I`ll tell you some of the dreadful things I learned. I`m sure this exchange will ease our minds."

"If you`re certain. I hate to sully the mind of a gentlewoman like yourself."

"Oh, posh, do continue."

With a heavy heart, I described the other eight memories I had collected from the victims of the criminally insane or the criminals themselves, each more distressing than the one before: madness, mayhem, murder. . . .

Lady Whitmore furrowed her brow and wrung her hands, clearly revulsed by each and every tale. "Oh, my. How could you stand to listen to those poor souls?"

"Shocking, my dear Lady, truly, but the afflicted parties` healings were well worth my own suffering," I assured her.

Lady Whitmore took my amulets from around her neck and returned them. "You are a kind, kind, generous soul. Perhaps you might talk to my sister soon. How blessed Edith would be if she could share the memory of her injury with you. It would ease our minds greatly to be rid of her compulsion to hide her tiny scar."

I promised to make an appointment at Edith`s earliest convenience and bid Lady Whitmore good day. She seemed to forget she had promised to tell me her stories and continued to sit in the salon. She began to stare into the distance and rock herself, her face twisting in horror. Tears began to flow down her alabaster cheeks and a plaintive sob burst forth from the depths of her heart, shaking her delicate frame.

As the ship pulled into port, the dear Lady continued to tremble and keen as she recalled my clients` horrendous tales, a fitting predicament for a pretentious hypocrite. I hurried to disembark before she realized she was stuck with their memories forever.

7

✣

Doomed to Disaster

ONE STORMY AFTERNOON, I STARTED to browse through the big art book for our next contest painting. "Listen to this, everyone," I said. "`Jean-Louis Forain, a French impressionist painter, is another great artist who attempted to start his own publication. In 1898, he founded the short-lived *Psst.*` What chance do I have if these famous guys couldn`t publish anything successfully?"

"Ah, come on, Pete," Jason chided, "cheer up. We`re making great strides."

Shirley looked up from her desk and joined her thumb and finger to give me an okay sign. Evie pushed the ends of her mouth up comically with her fingers and bugged her eyes out, trying to get me to crack a smile.

"Anyway," Jason said, "the guy was a violent Jew-baiter and the paper he helped found was an anti-Semitic rag. It`s a good thing he got out of the publishing biz and stuck with art."

A sudden bolt of lightning etched the sky outside the office window, and the resulting thunderclap rattled the glass. "From your lips to God`s ears," I said, laughing. I took this as a sign to go ahead and use the melancholy painting. The race theme also appealed to me as a metaphor for our struggle to make Classic Art Exposé profitable.

But my good mood was short-lived. Everything felt as if we were going two steps forward and one step back. It rained every day for a week during the time we published the new artwork, "At the Races," and the contest winner, "Lost Memories." Even though we—and especially the girls—were energized by the winning story, which was written by a woman, my spirits plummeted underground with the sun. The eerie note cast by the story didn`t help, even though the magazine gained both subscribers and contest fees. We even garnered a nod in a literary magazine for our writing contest, but it looked less and less possible that I'd meet the deadline for the promissory note. The contest brought the magazine back to life, but the note had to be settled in just twelve more months, or we'd risk losing it.

O'Neill had managed to get my father to back down on his claim, but at the cost of adding interest to the debt. And he'd managed to sweet-talk my mother into moving back into their bedroom, a development doomed to disaster, in my opinion. When I was too young to put two and two together, I was aware of a certain tension between my parents. When I got older, I noticed that Father's second passion (after money) was my mother, or at least controlling my mother, for how could you make someone you love so miserable? If he saw another man so much as glance at her, he turned red with anger. She didn't try to cultivate glances from other men, but Father's predilection sometimes caused him to imagine things.

But I kept my doubts to myself, especially since Shirley and Evie had worked so hard sorting through our record-breaking batch of stories. All I could do, really, was soldier on with the contest. I'd give it one more issue and then maybe we'd all have to put our heads together and come up with a bright idea for another fundraiser.

THE HORSE-RACE
Jean-Louis Forain, 1890

Benevolence? I do not know what it is.

THE SNOW GLOBE

OUR FRIEND SAMMY PICKED UP James and me at Clancy`s Tavern. Sammy had just turned twenty-one, and his father had given him a brand-new Ford Model T for his birthday. Mr. Jones was just a hard-luck miner, so I knew he must have saved up most of Sammy`s life to give him a gift like that. He`d never owned an automobile himself.

"Good thing he got a new T," said James. "He`s so ugly, that`s the only thing that`ll get him a date."

Sammy had never gotten over his adolescent acne and his face was still covered in pimples. Most girls didn`t take a second look at him. That, and his reputation for being a bully. "Maybe his being so ugly is why he`s so mean," I said.

When we got in the car, I rode shotgun. I made sure I got in front because if I got stuck in back I`d smell James all the way to the track. He always looked neat and clean and he spent a small fortune on his wardrobe, but he had this strange aversion to bathing, which became obvious when you were in smelling distance of him.

On the way to the track, a route we`d all walked many times, no one saw the old woman until we heard the loud thump as she flew into the air, and landed on the hood.

"Shit!" exclaimed Sammy, "my new Lizzie is messed up because that stupid old hag walked in front of me."

The poor woman`s glazed eyes pointed directly at him, as though to ask *don`t I mean anything at all to you?*

"Bitch," Sammy said, as if to answer her questioning eyes.

James looked around and grabbed Sammy by the arm. "Let`s get out of here, fool, before someone sees what you`ve done."

"Wait," I said, opening my door. "We have to help her."

"Like heck we do," Sammy said as he stepped on the gas, and then braked suddenly to throw the old woman sideways onto the ground. I almost sailed outside with her.

"I may as well finish her off," Sammy said, as he accelerated again, and jammed the gearstick into reverse.

I grabbed the wheel and yanked it toward me as hard as I could, causing Sammy to miss the old woman. I considered fleeing at this point, but these two had been my buddies since we wore short pants.

"Damn you," Sammy shouted. "Get out of my goddamn car."

"Calm down, Sammy. Dan did the right thing. You`ve got no reason to kill the old bag," James said.

Sammy sneered. "Can she identify me? She looked right into my face while she was on the hood."

I nervously picked at my lip, a habit I had as long as I`d known Sammy and James. "Let me see how bad she is. Maybe we can just give her a few bucks to forget what happened." I got out, and walked back to where the old woman was now sitting on the ground rubbing her arms.

"Thank you," she said. "I saw you turn the wheel, and I know you saved my life."

"No thanks needed," I said, squatting down beside her. "Is anything broken?"

"I don`t think so."

"Good. How about I give you twenty bucks and we forget this ever happened?"

She gave me the strangest look I`ve ever seen in my entire life.

"Money is meaningless to me," she said. "If you want to give me something give—"

Sammy walked up and kicked the old lady before she could finish. I didn`t notice him coming up behind me while I talked to her.

"The old bitch thinks she`s going to hold us up. If twenty ain`t good enough, the hell with her."

The woman bent over in pain and I could almost feel it for her. The injustice of it all just got to me. I stood up and punched Sammy right in the face with all I had. I never thought I could ever do that to anyone, but I knocked Sammy cold with that one punch. I picked the old lady up, carried her to the car, and put her in the back seat.

"Oh, brother. What`n the hell are you doing?" James said.

I got in the driver`s seat and prayed I could drive the Model T. "I`m taking her to the hospital."

"Probably a good idea," James conceded. "What about Sammy?"

"Leave him be."

"Are you crazy? If you take his car and leave him, he`ll kill us both."

"Do what you want. I`m taking her to the hospital, and I don`t give a damn what Sammy thinks."

James got out of the car. "I dunno. Maybe one of us had better stay with Sammy. That way you can take care of the old lady and I can deal with him. I don`t want him out looking for me."

"Okay, see you later," I said and started grinding gears as I tried to roll away in the Model T.

The old woman leaned toward me and spoke softly. "Thank you for helping me. I don`t need to go to any hospital. Just let me out near the old church."

"Are you sure?"

"Yes." She reached into the pocket of her sweater and pulled out a small, transparent glass ball. Like the ones you shake to see the snow falling. "And here`s a gift. Your friend will be seeking revenge on you and this may be of some help."

I took the ball and put it on the seat between my legs, concentrating so hard on driving that I forgot to thank her. I managed to get through town, past Clancy`s, the old livery, the school and finally to the old church without hitting anything or anyone else. As she opened the door to get out, I asked her to wait. I dug through my pocket but all I had was three five-dollar bills I was going to wager at the track. I held one out. "Please, I know this isn`t much, but get yourself something. I`m sorry for what my friend did to you."

She took the money, got out, and slowly walked away without looking back.

I didn`t know what to do now, go back to get Sammy or head out of town. Everybody knew how crazy Sammy was, and anybody that crossed him always got the short end.

If I hadn`t knocked him out, I probably would have gone back. His damaged pride would make him roaring mad. He weighed a good two-twenty, and for me at one-fifty to knock him cold, well, that was something he wouldn`t take lightly.

I was sadder about the old lady than the Model T, but it was also too bad about the car getting dented up. It was a nice car an hour ago, and look at it now. I gazed at my reflection in the rearview mirror. I knew if Sammy caught me I`d be saying the same about my face.

At least the drive had aired out James`s stink. I decided to drive on to the track to see if maybe I could win enough to leave town.

I paid the two bits to park, as much as I hated it. As I got out of the car I picked up the little snowball thing and shook it. I expected to see snow falling, but when I looked at it, what I saw made my heart stop. The thing was like a crystal ball with an image inside it, the tote board with the winners of the first race posted. It couldn`t be because the first race hadn`t been run yet. But I memorized the numbers 4-1-6, put the globe in my pocket, and forgot about it.

The excitement going on all around me was good for my mind, because I forgot all about Sammy and what he might do to me. I bought a racing form, and bet fifty cents on the seven horse to win.

There were twenty minutes left before the start of the first race, so I got a beer and looked through the form. I overheard a couple of guys next to me talking about this race having a trifecta. Trifectas were great—if you could pick three horses and the order they`d finish in. It was practically impossible, and a real sucker`s bet. Then it dawned on me. I recalled the 4-1-6 in the globe, and for the hell of it, I put a dollar on those exact numbers. I looked at the tote board and I saw that the number one was fifty to one. With odds like that, there wasn`t a chance in hell for my numbers to come in. But if they did, well, I`d be able to get out of here.

The race went off. My seven horse broke dead last. I started to tear up my tickets when the announcer screamed that the one horse had taken the lead by three lengths. I couldn`t believe a fifty to one shot was leading. I knew that horse would never last. I craned my neck, waiting for the nag to die. Instead of dying, the horse increased its lead with every step and didn`t die until almost at the finish line, where the four horse nosed out the one horse to win the race. I couldn`t believe my eyes.

Then they put up the winning trifecta numbers, 4-1-6. Amazing. I put my hand in my pocket and wrapped it around the globe. Then I heard the wining amount of the trifecta, $350 per ticket.

I rushed to cash out my winning tickets. As I strutted away from the window counting my cash, somebody grabbed me from behind. I got dragged kicking and yelling into some sort of janitor`s closet, all full of brooms and mops. Sammy had caught up to me fast. James was trying to hold me still, while Sammy balled his fists, ready to beat me.

"Wait! Wait, I cried, look what I`ve got for you, Sammy." I showed him the wad of bills.

He glared at me but let go of my collar and put the wad in his pocket. Then he balled up a fist and pulled his arm way back in order to sucker punch me. Again I yelled, "Wait! Wait."

Sammy sneered at me with slitty eyes. "Wait for what?"

"I got something from the old lady that`s going to make us all rich."

He dropped his hand. "Yeah, right. Show me."

I fumbled for the globe. I pulled it out, shook it, and we all looked as the tote board appeared in the globe with the second race results posted. But Sammy pulled his arm back to punch me anyway.

"A snow globe with a tote board isn`t going to make you rich, asshole. It`s going to make you dead."

"Wait! Don`t you see?"

"See what?"

The punch I hit Sammy with must have knocked something loose, as he`s usually not that slow on the uptake. "See the winners of the second race."

"Yeah?"

"The race hasn`t been run yet. You just saw the winners, and you`ve got ten minutes to make your bet."

"You`re kidding, right?"

"No, that`s how I won the wad." Sammy looked at the money, looked at me, and handed all the cash to James.

"Go bet it all on the second race, number six to win." That was the number in the globe for the second race.

James returned with the tickets, and Sammy dragged me to the grandstand to watch the race. I didn`t know if the first race was just a fluke or if I really won because of the globe. The old lady did say it would help me.

I wanted to run before this race was over, because I just didn`t believe it would happen twice in a row and I knew I could count on Sammy to pick a fight. He was holding me tight like he knew what I was thinking. The bugle sounded, the race was on. The six horse broke slow and easy, still in last place at the first turn. The race was a long one, so the horse might have time to pass all the other horses if he pulled up. The horses dashed to the halfway mark and six was still last. Now the jockey was making his move, leaning forward and thumping the horse. My heart was in my throat. It still wasn`t looking good for the six horse. Sammy tightened his grip. Like me, he was thinking the horse didn`t have a chance, and he wanted to make sure he could take out his disappointment on me.

The jockey whipped the six horse a second time and he really took off. He galloped past the horses in front of him like they were running in place. He only won by a half-length, but he paid out five bucks for a one-dollar ticket. Since there were over two hundred bets, Sammy would be rolling in dough. He relaxed his grip when he realized how much money he`d won.

"Now I can fix the T, and my dad will never know," he said.

"Hey! Don`t I get half?" James whined.

"What about me?" I chimed in.

"Let me think," Sammy said. After a minute, he said, "Give me that goddamn thing," and held out his hand.

"What?" I pretended I didn`t know what he wanted.

"The magic thing, you know, the glass ball that picks the numbers."

"You mean this?" I held up the globe.

"Yeah that, asshole." He grabbed it out of my hand and shook it. We all looked to see what numbers came up. None! Not a single number or anything else was visible in the globe.

"Here, you shake it." Sammy handed the globe to me.

I shook it like crazy, not knowing what was going to happen. I shook it and shook it, trying to stall for time while I figured out what I could do to extricate myself from this predicament.

"Alright, already, quit shaking it and let`s see."

I held it out and we all looked closely. There it was, the tote board with the third race posted. Number eleven was the winner. Sammy handed his entire wad to James and told him to put it all on eleven to win. There were only a few minutes to post time, so James hurried to the ticket window.

Sammy and I watched the tote board, looking at the odds. Eleven was going off at ten to one. Suddenly it dropped to even money, and we knew James had bet on it.

"I didn`t even think of how the odds would drop by betting so much on that stupid horse," said Sammy.

"Yeah, big difference in the pay-off. Next time we make a big bet like that we should do it through a bookie so it doesn`t affect the odds," I said.

James returned with the tickets. We were pretty subdued because the payoff was even now. I guess we were convinced of the accuracy of the glass globe, though, because the race hadn`t even begun yet and we were already complaining about not winning enough money.

The race started and we all remained seated until we saw the eleven horse boxed in on the rail as it ran past us. It looked like the fix was in. They weren`t going to let the eleven horse win no matter what. We all stood up shouting at the jockeys to make room, as if they could hear us. I don`t know why they do what they do in horse racing. I just assumed the owner knew the eleven horse, "Deliverance," was ready to win, but didn`t want him to win at these odds.

There were only eleven horses total in the race, and believe in luck or coincidence or whatever, but the lead horse tripped and there was a pile up at the three-quarter pole. The leader coming out of that six-horse collision was Deliverance, who went on to win the race.

All three of us sat down, breathless from screaming, and stunned by such an unlikely turn of events. It was unbelievable. But the tension wasn`t over yet. An inquiry was called. I`d had this happen in the past. I`d be holding a winning ticket, and an inquiry would be called; my horse would be disqualified for some infraction, and I`d end up a loser instead of a winner. Now with a pile of cash riding on this decision, we were silent and sweating it for a few moments. When they announced the winners were as posted, we all jumped up and danced a jig.

"I`m going to the best dermatologist in town now that I`ve got plenty of money," Sammy said.

"I`m getting a house with a big swimming pool, myself," said James, his eyes glazing over.

"Before we spend all the money, let`s think about making a lot more," I said. "We should think about saving and investments and stuff like that. Make this last our entire life."

"I dunno," Sammy said, "might be a good idea. Might have been just dumb luck before."

"Yeah, probably was," James said.

"Look." I started shaking the glass dome again. When I stopped shaking it, all we saw was Sammy`s face clear as a baby`s ass. The image changed, and we saw that clear face lying with its eyes closed in a coffin.

"What the hell`s that supposed to mean?" Sammy said.

"I don`t know," I lied. I knew darn well it meant he was about to die, and I`d bet my share of the money on it.

"Shake it again," James said, and I did. I held it out so we could all see at once what was in the globe. There was a picture of James, floating in a swimming pool, face down.

James`s face drained of blood. He grabbed the globe and smashed it under his boot. "This piece of garbage needs to be destroyed before anything it shows comes true."

I scraped up all the pieces and put them in my pocket. I just couldn`t leave it lying there, I don`t know why.

Well, there went my moneymaking scheme. At least Sammy gave me half my share of the winnings. "Be happy I`m letting you live after the shit you did today," he told me.

Believe me, I was just happy to be alive. Could have been even happier if I got my fair share, though.

I quit going to Clancy`s after that and didn`t see Sammy or James for a long time. I heard all about how handsome Sammy looked after his face cleared of the monstrous pimples and I heard it was no longer a problem to sit next to James after he started taking daily showers and swims at his new house.

How could I help but be jealous? Those assholes got what they wanted and I got only half of what I deserved for my trouble. In fact, that globe was supposed to be mine.

Then again, guess I shouldn`t get mad about it. Had enough money to leave town if I wanted, but I didn`t have to anymore. And I`d gotten my own Model T, which helped me get a job and woo my girlfriend Nancy. Even so, I started to wonder what would happen if I took those smashed pieces of the globe and tried to glue them back together. I pulled the shards out of the bedroom bureau where I`d wrapped them in a handkerchief and then I meticulously fitted them back together. The glue didn`t hold them very well, but maybe it could still predict the future. I put the lumpy globe on top of a coffee cup to let it dry and went about my business.

I forgot about it until the next morning. Though covered with cracks, it shone seductively in the early morning sun. I picked it up, closed my eyes, and gently shook it. Then I partially opened one eye and looked at the globe. Sure enough, there was Sammy, clear face and all. He was in a coffin again. I shook the globe again, and there was James, face down in his pool. If I had any money, I would have bet someone they`d be dead soon. Sure enough, the big news that weekend was Sammy and James dying on the very same day, different incidents.

Of course, I went to James`s wake and Sammy`s funeral. I was shocked to see the old woman that Sammy had hit with his Model T standing on the other side of Sammy`s open grave. I stared at her, and she smiled back.

After the burial, I couldn`t help but walk up to her. "How are you feeling?"

"Much better, now that you wished that monster dead."

"What do you mean, wished him dead? Sammy could be a jerk and what he did to you was wrong, but he was my friend."

"Didn`t you foresee his death in the globe I gave you?"

"Yeah, but that tells the future. I never wished him dead."

She gazed at me with a sad look. "I thought you were smarter than that. The globe is a wish grantor."

"A what?"

"You remember Aladdin and the magic lamp?"

"Sure. Aladdin rubbed the lamp and the genie appeared to grant him three wishes."

"I gave you the modern version. All you had to do was shake it to make your wishes come true."

"I wish I would have known that."

The old woman reached out and the glued-up globe appeared perfect and unblemished, gleaming in her hand. "Sorry! You`re out of wishes. . ."

8

Black Magazine Monday

THE MORNING AFTER "THE SNOW GLOBE" came out in the new edition, someone vandalized seven of the ten newsstands that sell Classic Art Exposé. The newspapers called the incident "Black Magazine Monday." A picture of one very angry newsstand vendor with an armful of magazines and newspapers dripping with black paint appeared on the front page of the NY Daily News. In seven cases, the only blackened periodicals were copies of Classic Art Exposé. Clearly, the crime was masterminded to target yours truly, but of course, it hurt the news vendors more. The perpetrator apparently didn`t know that the bulk of our readers bought their copies via subscription, or that the magazines were bought and paid for by the stands—or maybe simply didn`t care.

How juvenile these attacks were! The magazine vendors were the ones losing money and I hated knowing it was because of me. I knew I shouldn`t, but I couldn`t help but pick up the phone and call my father. How I might negotiate with him despite my anger escaped me.

"Hello, Father," I said when I finally reached him at his bank. Though I now thought of him mostly as someone annoying named Peter, I called him father in the hopes it would foster his best paternal instincts. I could almost hear his anger in the pointed silence on the other end of the line. "I just want you to know what it feels like to have someone impeding your business. When you have losses at the bank, yours are insured. Small businesses can`t always cover small expenses with insurance. . . Anyway, those magazine vendors are working their butts off. I`m working my butt off over here too, the same way I worked for you. Only I`m working for myself. I`m a businessman now." I paused, remembering how he used to talk about businessmen with obvious respect when I was a kid. "If we can avoid this petty vandalism of my property in the future, I won`t talk to the cops about you, okay? The vendors are the ones who made the police report this morning."

I didn`t know for certain if Peter was the one behind the vandalism, but I listened as he inhaled and exhaled at an accelerating rate as he tried to control his anger. At least I hoped he was trying to control his anger. For all I knew my call would make matters worse.

Finally, he spat his words out like excess saliva. "Businessman. You`ll be begging me for a job soon. Just wait. You`ll see."

I could imagine how he slammed the phone down by the way I suddenly heard the dial tone.

It hurt like hell that Father didn`t deny having anything to do with Black Magazine Monday. I was already in a state of shock and talking to him just made me feel worse.

When Jason returned from talking to the pressmen, I showed him the story. "Tell the newsstands to be on the lookout for more trouble. My father. . . went off the deep end. I thought he`d calmed down, but I guess he`s determined to see me fail."

Jason`s forehead wrinkled up in puzzlement. "You think he did it? Or paid someone to do it? Seriously? Since the police are involved, they`ll probably patrol the newsstands, so it`s not likely to happen again. . ."

I had a sudden rush of memories from my childhood about the conflict between Father and Uncle John and I shared some of these with Jason. He listened silently, shaking his head in disbelief at my father`s unreasonable behavior.

"It`s true, Jace."

"It`s a shame he didn`t support your dreams. But at least your mom did. One out of two isn`t so bad."

"I guess, but I expected him to be over it by now. That he would stoop so low . . ." My voice trailed off. It was hard for me to believe the depth of his anger, let alone explain to anyone. Still, I felt compelled to keep talking about the issue. ". . .Father discouraged me from expressing any artistic inclinations after Uncle John left town. But my bent to create became strong, and as hard as I tried to please him, I couldn`t shake the desire to express myself in pictures and in words. . ."

"So what happened when you did?"

I sighed. "Every time Father noticed me drawing or writing a story, his lost money and Uncle John came to mind, or so it seemed. It still hurts to think about it. If I left a sketchbook, a story for English class, or the student school paper on the kitchen table, he flew into a rage. He only approved of me when I studied math, science, history, or anything related to business. I wasn`t interested in sports and I suspected he might have been happier had I taken up baseball, as he played baseball in his youth. When the time to attend college arrived, he was opposed to my plans, of course, but he also seemed to breathe a sigh of relief, as though I'd reached the point where I wouldn't trouble him any longer."

"That's rough, man." Jason looked embarrassed and searched for something new to say. "Oh, you were complaining about the bums sleeping in the vestibule when you came in earlier—I've got a plan."

I wanted to vent about how my father had treated me when I applied to attend my university journalism program, but I forced my mind back to the present. Two or three guys were sleeping in the unlocked vestibule at night to soak up the heat. The stink they left behind was getting to be a problem.

"What plan? I thought we'd have to install locks on the outer doors or call the police to clear them out."

"Simple," Jason said. "Let them sleep in the truck dock in return for distributing some copies of the magazine. Community service. Gives these guys something to do, and you might sell a few extra copies."

"I don't know. The biggest part of the problem is their smell. Let me think about it."

"Oh, I almost forgot. We have another problem. Maybe three problems are a charm. Don't forget that the pressroom still wants you to hire a third person."

"That again." I sputtered for a moment. "They're barely working two full days a week!" I envisioned the business savings account taking another blow.

"The way they were joking about it last week made me wonder. But they were serious," Jason said. "Today they showed me where the union contract specifies that they now need a third worker for the current print run. It's a situation that usually isn't enforced. They know you don't want to hear about grievances, but Peter must be pulling some strings with a union steward."

I shut my eyes and imagined a two-man picket line, trucks unable to make deliveries, and subscribers looking in vain inside their empty mailboxes. "Guess I have something else to think about," I said, disheartened by dark thoughts of dipping into our savings to pay yet another union-scale salary.

"Gotta spend some money to earn some money," Jason said, making the motion of a bank teller shuffling bank notes.

I knew full well I couldn't dodge having a three-man printing crew. I gave the okay for Jason to start giving the bums all the magazine returns and unsold issues to sell to drivers at jammed intersections during rush hour. Whatever they made from these was all gravy, so I let them keep half of whatever they sold. Jason said he wouldn't be strict about counting what they turned in, either. He figured it was better to just trust them, and not worry about what little they might steal.

The trust began to pay off. I know because I kept track of how many magazines they took out and how many they paid for. Jason was right; a little trust goes a long way. I never would've thought of this ploy if it weren't for him. Another surprise—the truck dock transformed from a greasy, dingy area to a clean, welcoming site. I congratulated myself that these guys were trying to rehabilitate themselves until I looked in the trashcans behind the building and saw all the empty wine bottles. But whatever—we were all happy.

Choosing the next painting for the next contest prompt was the least of my worries. We were so busy I had little time to give a hoot about responses to the contest. Most people must have liked "The Snow Globe" because we received fewer responses than usual. A few people wrote or called with the usual subjective banter about interactions between art and literature.

Though we still needed money and lots of it, the writing contest was truly exceeding our expectations. For that, I was grateful. We were so busy that I hardly remembered the frantic afternoon when we`d edited the art features, solved some layout issues, negotiated the printers` complaints about a shipment of ink, and made a quick decision—on the enthusiastic recommendation of Evie and Shirley—to feature *The Knight of the Flowers* by Georges Antoine Rochegrosse for the upcoming contest.

A manly knight, a bevy of nubile maidens, and a sunny meadow full of flowers—what`s not to like about it?

Georges-Antoine Rochegrosse, 1894

Arthur Conan Doyle much admired the work of Rochegrosse,
and Sherlock Holmes was made to express the same sentiments.
—Geraldine Norman, *Nineteenth-Century Painters and Paintings: A Dictionary*

A LIFE IN FLOWERS

ONE MORNING IN 1894, NOT long after I commenced my internship at the city hospital before I graduated from medical school, a wealthy patient died and left several vases of fresh-cut flowers behind. As was the hospital`s custom, the nursing students distributed the abandoned bouquets on the ward for charity patients.

When I arrived on the charity ward for the last round of the day, I observed that Monsieur Mathieu, an old man almost completely incapacitated by paralysis, was teary-eyed, beset with gloom. I discovered early on my first round with the hospital`s supervising doctors that the old man could do little but talk, completely dependent upon the care provided by the charity ward. He sometimes rambled on about how his family had thought him a lunatic and disowned him years ago. Sensing his loneliness, I began to chat with him whenever my hectic schedule permitted. I made further polite inquiries about his family, but he tended to evade any question on the matter by pretending not to hear me.

On this spring afternoon, thinking Mathieu in pain or uncomfortable, I asked him what ailed him.

"Nothing hurts now that they`re in my room," he said, his voice wheezy with phlegm.

"I see." Mathieu`s statement startled me for a moment. Might he be entertaining himself by fooling me? Or perhaps his mind was deteriorating.

He spat into a handkerchief I held for him, then his eyes roamed to the vase of flowers by his bedside.

"Do you mean the flowers?" I asked.

"Yes, the flowers. They remind me of my life before I became a vegetable."

"Don`t speak that way," I admonished him. "You`re no vegetable. Why, here you are, carrying on a conversation with me—something no vegetable can do."

"I disagree with you, Doctor. Vegetables can and do converse," he replied. "They are well-rooted in knowledge of the Earth."

I began to see why Monsieur Mathieu`s family might think of him as insane rather than eccentric. "I see you enjoy having flowers at your bedside," I said, trying to steer our conversation in another direction.

"Oh yes, please leave them for me."

Our conversation wandered in another direction entirely. Soon, Mathieu`s eyelids fluttered closed as he drifted off to sleep. When I took my leave, I gave the ward nurse orders not to remove his flowers, for they usually circulated these rare gifts among all the charity patients, per the hospital`s rule.

As usual for interns in teaching hospitals, I became extremely busy and didn`t get an opportunity to visit the old man for several days. When I finally arrived at Msr. Mathieu`s bedside to chat, I was surprised to see fresh flowers again. I assumed the nurse misinterpreted my order when I told her not to remove the flowers, perhaps thinking I meant for her to keep fresh flowers by his bedside. Where she obtained them was a mystery—perhaps she cut fresh flowers from her own garden as spring blossomed into summer.

The bouquets appeared to make a marked difference in his attitude. Mathieu had always been noted as smiling beatifically in his sleep despite his melancholy demeanor during the day. But the nurse`s notes and my current observation revealed that he now smiled more often while awake. He began to bubble happily about his life before his paralysis, revealing that he used to grow flowers.

"It`s no wonder that you love these flowers, then," I said, motioning to the vase.

Mathieu nodded and warmed the room with a smile that seemed to speak of hidden knowledge. But a commotion broke out at the far end of the ward that required my assistance, and then it was time for me to return to my *pension* to study.

Another week passed before I visited the old gentleman. To my surprise, a vase of fresh flowers sat at his bedside. He seemed even happier and less careworn than before. I made a mental note to inquire of the ward nurse who was supplying Matheiu`s bouquets, when we crossed paths again. Once more, I had to hurry away to attend to other business before I could learn more about him.

During my next visit, I arrived earlier with more time to converse. I told him a little about my grandfather, of whom he reminded me a little, a revered research physician who had retired to the country to paint and garden.

"I used to be a farmer, you know," Mathieu said. "I grew the same crops as my neighbors—wheat, beans, and kitchen garden vegetables, all the usual things. Until I had a dream."

"You had a dream?" I wondered how a dream could possibly change what crops farmers tended.

"In my dreams, all the plants in the fields and our vegetable garden were alive with feelings and thoughts. Just like people." Mathieu described how the first dream didn`t affect him very much, but he had subsequent dreams in which the plants revealed their feelings and reasons for existing. "This convinced me these were more than dreams. Visions, I think," he said, waving his weak arms in expansive motions, "yes, visions of truth."

Mathieu said he decided to do what he could to make the world a better place for plants. "From then on, I dreamed of flowers. They showed me not only their obvious beauty, but the beauty of their thoughts. I began to plant my fields with nothing but flowers. My family would sell bouquets, both fresh and dried, to the villagers and the many tourists who passed through our village, but we also needed wheat for our bread and vegetables for our soup.

"Of course, my family questioned my sanity altogether when I began to refuse to harvest the blooming flowers. As our skill at growing flowers grew, they were far too beautiful to cut and harvest. Soon, I earned no money at all from my crops. My wife could not understand my passion for the flowers. `You care more about these plants than your children`s hungry bellies,` she would shout at me. As I began to spend all my days engrossed in their beauty, she drifted away with our children, and no one in our village wanted to associate with me."

Mathieu closed his eyes as though looking into the past. "I missed my family, naturally, but I had my flowers, my beauties, my life. I started to sleep in the fields, my cheek pillowed on the earth. I adored their pure minds and happy thoughts and how they turned their faces to the sun every morning. Their short lives reflected an eternal beauty."

"The flowers became your ideal," I said, empathetic to his sentiments.

"Yes, you could say that. One morning, I woke up feeling such clarity, such a sense of sweetness. My wish had come true—I was transformed, as simple and pure as *mes cherès*. All my thoughts were as clear as sunlight, fragrant as rose petals. I could no longer move a muscle below my chest, but I felt free. I became a flower in the field!"

Mathieu gazed at my face and I gazed back. For a moment, I felt as if I had looked deep into the face of a sunflower. What a happy insanity, I thought.

"What a wonderful feeling, Monsieur," I said, "what a wonderful day. . ."

"Indeed, indeed," he said, his eyelids drooping with the effort of sharing his story.

The ward nurse approached us while making her rounds. "Hello, Doctor. Monsieur. Mathieu loves the flowers you leave for him. He lives for them, I think."

"But, I thought you. . . I wanted to ask you if I could share the expense. . ."

She looked at me as if she didn`t understand.

"You aren`t bringing him flowers?"

"*Non*, Doctor. You told me not to touch his flowers and I`ve done exactly as you said."

"How can that be? Who is bringing him fresh flowers? Perhaps someone in his family. . ."

The nurse shook her head. "He has no visitors but you. Occasionally the custodian brings him a bite to eat."

"The custodian then?"

"*Non*." The nurse shook her head again.

"I guess this is one of life`s little mysteries. No matter."

Perhaps people from the countryside around Toulouse like to toy with Parisians, I thought unkindly. Impatient, I rose from the chair to leave and looked at the young woman as sternly as I could, though I was not much older than she. "Mademoiselle, do you not bring these lovely flowers? They are fresh from a garden. . ."

"*Non*, Doctor, I do not. But every day, the flowers are here—lovely, the identical arrangement. The bouquets make him so much happier."

"That they do." As I walked away, I gazed at the old man`s face, luminous now and almost angelic in his sleep. I could imagine him as a handsome young buck, frolicking in a spring meadow filled with wildflowers. Truly, I could almost see his dreams as he slept.

I had a dinner engagement that night with my artist friend Georges and mentioned the matter of the flowers to him.

"Fascinating," Georges said. "I`d love to paint what the old gentleman sees that makes him so happy."

"Maybe I can ask Mathieu if he would describe what he sees so you can paint his happiness. A good project for you and it might do him some good to socialize more."

Georges readily agreed and I made note to talk to Mathieu as soon as possible.

When I finally went to Mathieu a week later, I was not surprised that his bouquet was as fresh as ever.

"I have a friend, a painter of fine art. I told him a little about your life among flowers and he said he would love to talk to you and paint what you see."

Mathieu looked at me with that smile that spoke of hidden knowledge and he readily agreed. "It is time, I think, to share my visions with the world."

The next morning, Georges arrived at Mathieu`s bedside with his tubes of oil paints, his palette, and his knives and brushes. He set a fresh canvas on an easel, blended his paints, and made love to the canvas with his hues as the old gentleman described a day in his many fields of flowers.

"The colors, the scents, the delicate interplay of petal, stem, and leaf touched by sun and wind brought Heaven to Earth," Mathieu concluded. "The hours I whiled away in this daily meditation brought me ever closer to the Divine."

Georges returned day after day, spending much more time with the old man than I`d ever given him. The painting took over three weeks to finish. Until then, Georges tended to be secretive about it, always covering it when the nurses, assistants, or I roamed about the ward. "I`m showing it to Mathieu first," he always said, "it is his vision."

The morning that Georges finished, he had a ward assistant fetch me from another floor to see the painting unveiled. As he pulled a paint-daubed rag from the canvas, the painting seemed to explode into life. Clearly the young knight surrounded by floral spirits was Mathieu, and his fields, so drenched with flowers, so dreamlike and glowing with the sun`s radiance, was the life he had so lovingly described.

The scene made me long to step into the painting. No wonder the flowers made Mathieu smile always. The world of his flower maidens would put a smile on my face every day too.

I turned to Mathieu to watch his reaction. His smile grew broader and more beatific as he gazed on Georges` masterpiece. "Bravo," he said. "That`s it. Exactly what I see even now as I recall my flowers, *mes beaux enfants chéris.*"

I scurried away and brought back a bottle of wine from my locker, one I`d purchased from the farmer`s market on my way to the hospital one day and forgotten to take home. We each had a glass, Mathieu, Georges, and I, toasting one another and the lovely vision brought to life in Mathieu`s memories and

Georges` work. Under the influence of the fine red wine, Monsieur Mathieu beamed with more joy than ever.

Too soon, I had to continue my rounds and Georges to retreat to his studio. As the late autumn day expired into dusk and the weariness of it wrapped around my shoulders, I began to wonder how Mathieu coped with the winters when his flowers no longer bloomed. As I thought this while exiting the hospital, his ward nurse dashed through the door to stop me.

"Doctor, come quickly," she urged, tucking a stray lock of ebony hair behind her ear and into her cap. "It`s Monsieur Mathieu."

We turned and rushed back to the charity ward. At Mathieu`s bedside, the seemingly eternal flowers began to wilt, their heads drooping and dropping petals onto the floor. These petals quickly began to wither and dry before our eyes. Georges had left the painting on the easel where the old man could see it. The nurse took his hand in hers. As he shuddered, taking his final breath, I expected to see the slack, grey face of a corpse, but Monsieur Mathieu`s face and the painting seemed to fill with ever more light.

The nurse and I watched wordlessly as the knight in the painting looked up, seemingly oblivious to his beloved flowers and flower nymphs. He cast a firm gaze past all things earthly into God`s great beyond.

"The flowers and I are one," the knight simply said as he rose and vanished into the cerulean sky.

9

⁂

Two Steps Back

NEARLY SIX MONTHS HAD PASSED since I`d taken over the helm of Classic Art Exposé, but it felt like six years due to my bone-deep weariness. For every step forward, for every success we celebrated, we still took two unpredictable steps back. Despite the fact that I`d hired a third printer, fulfilling what I considered my entire obligation to the printer`s union, I suddenly received a shortlist of union grievances in the mail.

We were getting on well with our printers, so obviously there was some outside influence shaking things up at union headquarters. It didn`t take a genius to figure out whom that someone might be. The brokerage firm Peter managed under the sponsorship of Maryland First Fiduciary Savings handled the union`s pension fund. This gave him undue influence with union leaders, because he knew which closets held the skeletons. I knew a threatened strike would manifest if I didn`t rectify every grievance within thirty days. No truck driver would cross the picket line and circulation of the magazine would come to a dead halt.

I resisted the urge to call my mother or father, afraid of setting off some commotion between them that might cause further problems for them or the magazine. Instead, I called O`Neill.

"Pete, you can`t win a battle with the union," he said, his voice oozing doom. "They`ll effectively put you out of business. You`ll have to rectify every point, or believe me, they`ll strike. Even if your printers are on your side, they`ll strike because the union tells `em to."

I pounded my fist on the letter with each point of my rebuttal. "But these are bullshit issues. We have three printers working only two full days a week. They sit around and play cards the rest of the time.

They don`t have any grievances about any of this stuff. Not their hours, not the working conditions, not anything. There`s nothing I can improve. The facilities are what they are and the magazine is too small to deal with this."

"Nonetheless, the union will make good on their threat."

"Cripes. I`ll get back to you when I figure this out."

Only Jason had any experience with the printers union. When he came in, I handed him a copy of the union contract and the letter. "One more obstacle. Guess who has clout with labor unions in New York?"

"Lemme guess, Big Daddy." He skimmed through the contract. "There`s a loophole, Pete, right here," he said, running his finger along a line of fine print: "`. . .Any current managerial staff employed by the magazine are allowed to replace striking workers.`" He looked up with a smug grin.

"How does that help us? You and I are the only managerial staff. It`s a stretch, but we could probably count Shirley and Evie. We`re too damn busy to print the magazine on top of everything else."

Jason raised his eyebrows and stared me in the face. "I showed you how to think for yourself. Can`t you see the simple answer staring you in the face?"

I threw my hands in the air.

"Listen. We hire the bums who do the distribution. Give them both assistant manager titles. When the strike comes down, they can take over any job the printers refuse. Sure, we`ll have to watch over their shoulders to help them through the print run, but we can manage. By now, Shirley and Evie can handle some of our duties. Simple," Jason concluded.

I had to admit that his plan appeared to be in line with the contract language. I called O`Neill back, and he seemed a little flustered that Jason, and not he, had figured a way out of the mess. He suggested the content for the contracts, and by that afternoon and yet another legal fee plus two fifty-dollar bonuses later, I had two more assistant managers working for the magazine. I only hoped that the pending strike would fizzle out as swiftly as it had manifested out of the blue.

Evie and Shirley loved the fluffy, old-fashioned story of the old man and his flowers, and they continued to moon over it after declaring it the hands-down best story of the current crop. Though some of the subscribers thought the story conflicted with the artist`s original intent in depicting the chaste knight Parsifal from the Arthurian tradition, I found the story`s premise to be a charming but plausible interpretation of the painting. Though I`d hoped new entrants wouldn`t feel they had to insert both artist and painting into their stories, I had to concede that this author had done it with panache.

That night, my stomach ached with the heartburn that haunted my sleep and gave me restless dreams. In one of these dreams, a painting appeared on the office wall next to our print of van Gogh`s *The*

Night Café, a portrayal of a sunny, non-descript garden with unappealing, twisted trees. Such a vivid and real dream, that when I woke up, I forgot for a moment that this painting was never on our wall. Or was it? I felt confused until I dressed and left my little sleeping cubicle to assure myself that the painting truly wasn't in the office.

During a quick meeting that morning, the day after we'd signed up our still imbibing distribution team as assistant managers, we settled on the piece for the next contest. Evie randomly passed her index fingers into the pages of our art book. I gasped when she opened it to a section about van Gogh and revealed the plate of the very same painting I'd dreamed of, one I'd never known that he'd painted, a scene in the garden of St. Paul's Hospital where he'd lived as a mental patient.

I recoiled, not knowing why. "That's an ugly painting. Try again for something more inspiring."

Evie giggled and Shirley joined in. "Maybe chance or fate makes it the best choice. You always thought so before," Shirley ventured. "And you dreamed about it. Has to be the one."

Jason shrugged and nodded.

The weird choice just seemed to add insult to injury on an already crappy day. I frowned, wondering if I was projecting my revulsion. After all, a good writer *could* craft an imaginative story from even the plainest scene. But something still repulsed me. "My dream was unsettling. We've already had a van Gogh painting—"

"Let's roll with chance," Jason chimed in. "It's a challenge. It'll be interesting to see what writers come up with."

I sighed. I didn't want to expend precious energy on this issue or discuss my dream further. "Three to one it is. Indeed, let's see what the writers come up with."

It was anybody's guess what the next contest might achieve. We'd have to see what sort of stories *Jardin des Peupliers (Trees in the Garden of St. Paul's Hospital IV)* would inspire.

⁜

In the evening after our discussion of the best stories Shirley and Evie had shortlisted from the monthly entries—several dozen this time—my dreams took me again to van Gogh's painting of twisted trees and a half-hidden house. I watched with horror as the paintings, each one with an additional tree, multiplied on my wall like living things until there was no space at all. Every time I tried to pull a painting away from the wall, another took its place.

I awoke with a start, my heart racing and my armpits drenched with sweat. Worse, I felt sick with a blooming cold stuffing up my sinuses. No doubt these paintings had become a metaphor in my mind for

⚘

all the niggling problems at Classic Art Exposé caused by my so-called father. I wondered if van Gogh`s paintings of his hospital garden were simply studies he`d painted to pass the time, or if painting these was an obsession caused by his mental illness, or worse, if he had tried to reveal something sinister the only way he knew how.

By the time I grabbed a coffee and a Danish at the bakery around the corner, my headcold was in full swing. I felt as dismal as the chill gray day and sneezed my way miserably back to the office.

"Hey, Pete," Evie said when I finally poured myself into my chair and puddled up to my desk. Uncharacteristically, she waved only one manuscript around rather than the usual stack of a half-dozen or more of her and Shirley`s favorites. "There`s one clear winner here. You`re gonna love it."

"'S`not too bad," Jason punned, watching me blow my red, irritated trumpet of a nose.

"Yeah," Shirley agreed. "We were right. All it took was a writer`s imagination to turn a plain painting into an inventive story."

"So, convince me. Read some of it."

Evie turned a few pages and started in the middle somewhere. She read atmospherically about the protagonist staring at a painting on his bedroom wall, where it took on a life all its own. Then later he viewed similar paintings—many of them, lining the walls of a strange cottage. . .

I shifted uncomfortably in my chair.

"What`s the matter, Pete, don`t you like it?"

I exhaled. "It`s on the mark. Maybe too much. I had two dreams about this painting. One was almost identical to the scenes you just read, Evie. Why do you suppose I dreamed of this painting before you found it in the art book? And why would I dream of almost exactly the same scene this writer created in his or her story? I woke up in a cold sweat this morning."

"That`s crazy, man," Jason said.

Shirley patted me on the arm. "Maybe you need to rest. Look at you, a bad cold and you`ve been knocking yourself out lately, and worried sick by your father."

"I`ll say." Jason opened his mouth to say something else, but the phone`s insistent ring interrupted him.

How could I rest when I lived in the building? All I could ever think about was work. And almost every night I dreamed about work.

JARDIN DES PEUPLIERS
TREES IN THE GARDEN OF ST. PAUL'S HOSPITAL IV
Vincent van Gogh, 1889

I put my heart and soul into my work, and I have lost my mind in the process.

A TWISTED GARDEN

MY FATHER, JEAN-LUC MAURICE ANDRÉ AUDET, moved to the Netherlands from France soon after I was born. Thank God he christened me with the simple name of André Audet. An influential poet, he stopped writing after he took refuge in Amsterdam. I always wondered at the loneliness in our lives caused by the disappearance of my mother. As the years passed, we lived on his savings, and as he aged, the money dwindled and he fell ill. As he lay on his deathbed, my burning questions about our lives finally broke his silence.

"I felt compelled to leave Saint Rémy de Provence so the curse wouldn`t affect you."

"Curse, what curse? Why did you not bring my mother with you when we left?"

He sighed deeply, resigned to his lonely life and an inevitable death. "It`s not in your best interest to know. You were born under a dark star. Just stay away from your birthplace."

I found it hard to believe a learned man would utter such a silly warning. Then he coughed just once, a deep hacking gag that caused blood to flow from his nose, and he fell silent.

As I washed the blood from his face, I knew Death would soon take him. Irritated at his reluctance to share the circumstances of my mother`s disappearance, I tried several more times, each time more urgently than the last, to coax him to reveal the nature of this supposed curse and what had happened to my mother. I continued pressing him with questions even as he went out of his head, questions he seemed clearly unable to answer.

But in his final hour, he fell in and out of a delirium and mentioned the Monastery Saint-Paul de Mausole in Saint Rémy de Provence. He spoke of it just once, perhaps by mistake. He wouldn`t discuss it further and as life leaked from him, he took his secrets to the grave.

One day, soon after my father`s death, I came across an old woman dressed in the manner of a gypsy, a fortuneteller who wandered along the banks of the River Rhine. For a guilder, she told me that my birth under a dark star meant that a generational curse was upon me because of some sin perpetuated by an ancestor.

"How could I be cursed?" I asked. "Up to this point, except for the absence of my mother and the loneliness of my father, my life has been exemplary."

"A curse is a curse, and one can never know when it will befall them. The good news is that I can lift the curse for only ten guilders."

What hogwash. This hag was using old-fashioned superstitions to extort ten guilders from me. When I was born in 1853, most superstitions were long abandoned, spoken of only by country folk. Only the ones so common they had become universal were repeated, such as seven years bad luck for breaking a looking glass, or that a black cat brought gossip and bad news. I knew these were nonsense because my boyhood kitten Minnie was midnight black and sweet as could be. A curious child, I`d broken more than one looking glass to see if my luck would change. Nothing ever changed, despite these folk superstitions.

After my father`s funeral and a proper period of mourning, a burning desire overcame me to see the village where I was born to the mother I had no memory of. I returned to Saint Rémy, traveling along the River Rhine from Amsterdam. Immediately, I fell in love with the village, feeling as if I had truly come home. At my first opportunity, I hired a carriage and told the driver to take me to the neighborhood of the Monastery Saint-Paul de Mausole.

The driver slowed the horses as we approached the lane where the monastery rose like a great fortress over fields and cottages nearby. He informed me that the old refuge now held a hospital, an asylum for the mentally afflicted. At a distance, I saw a garden nestled against the monastery, dotted with twisted, deformed-looking trees composed of many colors. These hues grew throughout not only the dagger-shaped leaves, elongated much like willow or eucalyptus leaves, but the shades of red, yellow, green, brown and a peculiar blue-gray were also present in the bark. I might call these trees beautiful because of their subtle and variegated colors, but they also appeared tormented because of their deformities.

Beyond this bizarre garden and just down the lane from it, stood an ordinary cottage with a small garden of its own. Rather plain, but this garden radiated such an eerie feeling that I understood why my father spoke with dismay about the neighborhood. The modest cottage was barely visible from the lane, but a stone path wound through the garden toward it.

I immediately forgot my quest to see my birthplace, which possibly lay nearby. As the carriage passed the monastery, we came upon an artist standing on a knoll, and as we drew beside him, I saw he was dressed in a drab but paint-stained suit. One would inquire, of course, about this artist who recorded this bizarre garden—was he also strange? But no, he was not twisted or colorful like the garden. Despite his ginger-colored hair, he appeared straight-laced and drab because of his passive demeanor and his somber, threadbare suit.

The artist painted upon a canvas held by a rickety wooden easel. I told the carriage driver to stop and watched as the artist worked in an unusual fashion. He picked up a bit of vermillion on his brush, dabbed it here and there on the canvas, and with quick movements of his hand, spread the small bits into many small lines with a palette knife. Then he repeated the process with the other colors on his palette. To my surprise, this technique gave his painting a layered, impressionistic texture that dazzled the eye with movement.

I gazed at the painting and then at the garden again. Even before I learned more about the cottage and its garden, I began to consider the colors of this twisted foliage as the shades of insanity and the trees' twisted branches as the result of some revulsion.

"Excuse me, sir," I called to the artist. "Why did you choose this particular garden to paint?"

"Can`t you see? Are you blind?" he shouted.

Intimidated by this outburst, I braced myself and calmly asked, "See what?"

"See what sort of twisted individual must live near these gardens!"

"I can`t understand how you can tell who lives there by looking at a garden. Look, the cottage has the same trees in its garden as the Monastery Saint-Paul de Mausole." I pointed at the large garden and then at the smaller one.

The artist stared at me. "Yes. You. You could live here."

"Me! Why me, Monsieur?"

"You with your colorful attire and tidy coiffure—just like those gardens, you`re perfect and twisted at the same time."

No one had ever spoken to me in this manner before, and I wanted to slap the artist`s face for his impudence until I realized he must have seen a special beauty in the gardens or he wouldn`t be painting them. Though I felt uneasy about the gardens and especially the cottage, I could extrapolate that because he perceived a similar quality in me meant that his remark was complimentary.

"How much do you want for this painting? Tell me what you want, your price is immaterial to me."

His face registered surprise. "I`ve only sold one painting before," he said, signing it "Vincent van Gogh" with a flourish of his brush. "A few guilders are enough."

I didn`t recognize the name when he signed the painting, but I easily produced the petty cash he requested. As soon as I returned to my newly leased home, I poured a glass of wine and hung the painting in my bedroom where I gazed at it by candlelight, appreciating the colors and the artist`s unusual brush strokes. My attention was drawn for the first time beyond the twisted garden and to the barely visible cottage. When I saw movement in the painting, it caused me to question first my eyesight and then my sanity. My skin tingled with the excited sensation of a voyeur, as if I were peeking at things not meant for my eyes.

As I looked closer, the front door of the cottage opened, and a gentleman and a lady walked along the stone pathway to the gate. They stood talking at the gate, and I watched in horror as the man performed an act upon the woman so dreadful, so horrible that I can hardly bear to describe it—he drew something from his pocket, a thin wire, and wrapped it around her throat and strangled her, nearly severing her head. I watched her eyes grow wide in surprise and then glaze over with fear as he twisted the wire around her neck. Finally, the light dimmed in her eyes and she slumped to the ground.

Chilled with horror, I wished I`d never encountered the painting or the artist. Why did this twisted garden even exist? I blew out the candle and lay in the dark wondering how I might fall asleep.

But fall asleep I did, and at dawn`s first light I believed either I dreamed all that I had seen in the painting or that my wine was tainted. My day progressed normally, and after a day of sorting my belongings out, I endeavored to fall asleep without gazing upon the painting. But after quaffing my evening glass of wine, the painting had a nearly magnetic effect upon me. When I gazed upon it again and it came alive once more, I knew it wasn`t a dream or the wine. How that plain Mr. van Gogh could put such life into this macabre painting was unfathomable.

I held my breath as the gentleman from the cottage came outside again to shovel dirt into a hole where he planted a sapling. But I soon exhaled because there was nothing sinister at all about his labor until the tree slowly twisted into a misshapen form that mimicked the other twisted and deformed trees. Confused and intrigued, I could only conclude that he must have buried the girl there after his heinous act, and that the tree must have tried to twist itself from her grave in disgust. I recoiled in horror, my heart thumping in dismay. Did this mean someone was buried under every tree in the garden?

If so, why? For what reason did this gentleman kill so many? Night after night, I felt inexorably drawn to scrutinize the painting, to look for some clue that would answer my questions. I resolved to do a bit of detective work, but how could I discuss what I saw with anyone? I thought if I went to the library and researched supernatural phenomena that I might find a clue as to what transpired at the yellow cottage.

I dressed and proceeded to the village square. My inquiries led me to the library of the hotel I`d stayed in for a few nights upon reaching St. Rémy. Not knowing where to begin looking in the modest room dimly lit by gas lamps, I approached a young woman reading at a desk.

"What can I do for you?" she said in a soft voice, looking up from her book.

The light from a nearby lamp flickered across her lovely face. Charmed by the Provence mademoiselle, I introduced myself. "André Audet at your service," I said, "or rather, I`m badly in need of yours. I don`t quite know what I`m looking for. I observed a very strange happening. . . a waking nightmare, perhaps. I`m wondering if you have any books on the supernatural?"

The way she smiled told me that either my admiration was returned or that she had no belief in the supernatural.

"Monsieur Audet, as you can see, this library is quite limited. There are one or two such books located along that wall." She pointed a slim finger at a shelf across the room. "If you`re looking for something about a recent event, you won`t find anything but old classics in this library. You`ll have better luck at the newspaper office. They have a morgue, a room where they file newspaper clippings about about such things."

"Thank you, Mademoiselle. . ."

"DuBois," she said, blushing, "Danielle DuBois."

"May I visit with you again tomorrow, Mlle. DuBois?"

"Ah, I`m afraid not—"

Embarrassed, I took her words as a rejection. "Forgive me, I`m sorry for assuming—"

Danielle blushed again. "I`m afraid I only work here on·Mondays. On Wednesdays and Thursdays, I assist my father at the newspaper."

"Oh? And that`s why you know so much about it, then."

"Yes, my father is a news editor. I write a column critiquing new art and literature in Provence."

"I shall look forward to reading it then. May I call on you there sometime? Perhaps we could dine after your work." I was encouraged when her cheeks bloomed with color again and her eyes sparkled with her consent.

I walked from the hotel to the weekly newspaper office across the square, and requested permission to peruse their files. After an intensive search, I came across an article from two years prior that described a cottage in St. Rémy where wicked and hateful things had happened for over two centuries. It was located in the very same neighborhood as the Monastery Saint-Paul de Mausole that my father had mentioned in his delirium. Shocked, I never considered that a cottage might be wicked or hateful. After watching my painting come alive night after night, I realized there might be some truth to this story. I scanned through the article for details.

Back in 1680, the authorities discovered six bodies buried under the garden of what I now know for certain was the yellow cottage. The owner, a sculptor by the name of Yves Gagnon, claimed he was forced by an unknown entity to perform murderous acts. He testified he had to kill anyone who couldn`t appreciate the beauty of his work. What the madman did exactly to his victims was not detailed, but he was hung for his efforts.

I left the newspaper mentally exhausted by my search, but endeavored to walk to the courthouse located on the far side of the city square. Perhaps I could find out more about the Gagnon case in records of the murder trial.

I looked up the incident in court records. These revealed that the stone path of the yellow cottage was the length of many "last walks"—a metaphor for the walk of a condemned prisoner to the gallows, and later, the guillotine. As in my painting, Gagnon felt compelled to walk his guests along his stone path to the gate and choke them to death. He methodically buried his victims in the garden, planting a sapling over each one. Naturally, his sanity was questioned by the court, and physicians and clergymen were consulted. One suggested a diagnosis of melancholia leading to insanity and two declared Gagnon to be possessed by demons.

I asked the clerk if there were any more criminal cases concerning the cottage near the monastery. He paused for a moment and left his desk for a cabinet, where he located and extracted three more documents. Exactly one hundred years later, in 1780, nine bodies were found buried in the garden of the yellow cottage. Eugenie Beaulieu, by all descriptions a beautiful creature, was a writer of epic poems and tragedies. She also gained infamy as the first female serial murderer in French history. That a poetess so dainty and cultured could commit such ghastly crimes was unbelievable to many until the garden was dug up. She said she was forced by an unseen entity to poison her victims because they couldn`t appreciate her poetry. The next court document went on to describe how the new owner of the cottage had hired painters to change its color to a drab brown that blended into the woodsy surroundings. Within a few months, the hue had supposedly faded back to a soft butter yellow, but I suspected this was an old wives` tale.

The final incident happened exactly twenty-seven years later. The body of a young woman had been buried without her head and hands. The authorities dug up the entire garden at the yellow cottage after her husband reported her missing, but they had never found her severed parts. Both the legal record and the trail grew vague. The decomposed body couldn`t be adequately identified and it appeared that both the owner of the cottage, who was issued a summons to appear before authorities, and the young woman`s grieving husband had both left the country. Or were they one and the same man? The case had closed in confusion.

This happened the year I was born. Could it have been my mother`s body, I wondered? Impossible. If she had been a victim of the owner of the cottage, how had she come to be there? Why would my father not relate this terrible tale to me so that I might resolve the issue? My mind reeled with exhaustion and macabre thoughts. If the garden were dug up today, how many bodies would be found?

I resolved to do more direct detective work. On the next moonless night, I walked through the village and to the lane past the monastery. I crept through those twisted trees and hid in the cottage garden. I had a clear view into a window, fortuitously left open. A dim light shone through this open window and the voices of those inside floated into the garden. The gentleman living there had a lady guest and they conversed about art.

"My friend is an artist," he said, "would you care to see his latest painting?"

"Yes, please show me his work," the lady replied.

The room went silent for a moment, and I crept into the lowest branch of one of the twisted trees to get a look. The gentleman carried a painting covered with a sheet into the room. He set the painting on a table and uncovered it with a flourish. She gasped, I gasped. It was exactly like the painting I had purchased, save for an additional tree.

"How hideous! Whoever painted this monstrosity belongs in an asylum," she said hastily, then covered her mouth with a dainty hand, remembering that the artist was the gentleman`s friend.

The gentleman calmly drew the sheet over the painting and took it from the room.

The woman stammered when the gentleman returned. "I apologize for my outburst. . . it is getting late—

"Have no fear," he said cordially. "May I walk you to the gate?"

She stood and offered the gentleman her arm. They strolled down the yellow brick path, arm in arm, chatting softly. When they arrived near the gate he did to her what I had witnessed him do to the other girl in the painting.

I remained in my hiding place. How I shivered as he fetched a shovel and measured an exact five paces from the latest tree he had planted, a mere sapling. He dug a new hole, placed her body into it, and placed another sapling on top of her. Once he shoveled the pile of turned earth onto the roots, he watched as the tree twisted and turned as if in horror at being placed atop a newly murdered woman.

The next day I couldn't resist returning to the scene of the crime. I strolled past the cottage and the artist stood exactly where he had before, daubing at an exact replica of the painting I had purchased. This painting, upon observation, had a small difference: there were two more trees in it. Absorbed in his work, the artist said nothing to me as I walked past him.

Why a man would kill someone because they didn't like a painting intrigued me, to say the least. Should I go to the police? I felt disinclined to engage the authorities and simultaneously felt disgusted with myself for not doing the right thing. I decided to contemplate the murderer's behavior and my own motivation. The most direct way to solve both mysteries would be to engage the killer in an interview and try to discern his motivation.

Upon the pretext of being interested in purchasing the property, I strode confidently to the front door of the yellow cottage. The name plaque above the bell said Tristan Duhamel, whom I recalled as an art dealer who worked from the business districts of both Paris and Amsterdam. I was curious that the plain Mr. van Gogh was a friend of such a prominent man, and I wondered how much he knew about the businessman's nefarious activities.

The distinguished-looking gentleman answered the door. "May I help you?" he said briskly.

"Please pardon my intrusion, Monsieur Duhamel." I quickly mentioned a feigned interest in buying the property, and he promptly attempted to close the door in my face.

"You had better listen to my proposition, because I know what you did last night."

At these words, an incredulous look spread across his face. "I don't know what you're talking about."

"I know why your new trees are twisted and growing so quickly," I said, secretly quivering in my heart of hearts.

At this, he knew that I knew his secrets and he invited me inside.

I stepped through the doorway with my hand on the grip of the snub-nosed pistol I'd concealed in my coat. My jaw dropped in amazement at the interior of the cottage. From the outside, it appeared to be an ordinary two-story house, but inside I discovered it had only one floor and very high ceilings.

The walls were painted a creamy white that seemed to both absorb and reflect light, and the floors fashioned of polished, multi-colored marble. The hand-carved ebony interior doors were nearly ten feet high and the frames reached nearly two feet higher—massive proportions much greater than a simple cottage called for. What amazed me even more were the paintings, all hung in perfect sequence. There were landscapes of the cottage with no trees, with one tree standing beside it, two trees, and so forth. Each painting added one more tree to the twisted garden. The gentleman stood silently watching as I rushed from painting to painting, counting the trees. The final painting looked and smelled damp. This one held over a dozen trees, reflecting the number of bodies that must be buried in the garden.

An empty space on the wall marked the spot where my painting would have hung if I hadn`t purchased it from his friend. I felt the pull of that space exerting itself. The spot beckoned for my painting. I was nearly overcome by the same irresistible force that coursed through me whenever I felt compelled to view the painting at my home. I felt I needed to rush home and bring the painting to hang in the reserved space, but I managed to resist the impulse. Alarmed, I judged myself foolish for not alerting the authorities because surely I had discovered a serial murderer in our midst.

Truly this cottage *was* evil and beyond reproach. Did the thing that possessed this cottage need the paintings to survive? Was I drawn here so it could recover the one painting it didn`t have? Or had it drawn me because my mother had perished here?

Feeling faint, I pulled my pistol from my breast pocket and leveled it at Duhamel.

He met the barrel of my pistol with a brazen smile. "Ever since van Gogh told me you purchased one of his paintings, I`ve been expecting you, Monsieur Audet. He told me your demeanor matched my garden, so it was easy to recognize you. After he sold the painting, I was prepared to offer you a generous sum, so I recently hired a detective to find you. I learned that once you graduated from your university studies, you became a writer, but your work was harshly criticized. Once I read your literary stories, I knew you were a kindred spirit and would understand."

I raised my pistol higher. "Understand?"

"I know you`re trying to understand me, or you would have taken this matter to the authorities. You know that I`m intent upon making the world a better place."

I tightened my hand on the pistol grip. "How can you possibly imagine that killing anyone makes the world a better place?"

"Do you know how many are buried out there and who they are?" He pointed in the direction of the twisted trees.

"I know there are fifteen, but I don`t know who they are." All I had to do was look at the trees, even in the paintings, and know every tree meant a body buried beneath it.

Duhamel tossed his head back in an eerie laugh. "Art critics, each and every one of them a critic! I gave them all a chance, just for once, to appreciate true genius by showing them these paintings. Not one grasped their beauty or their significance. That`s why I waited for you. I know your soul believes in artistic beauty, be it in painting, sculpture, music, or letters."

Because he told me all he killed were art critics, I put my pistol away.

"A job well done," I heard myself say as though someone else spoke through me.

Duhamel, looking relieved, retrieved a bottle of fine whiskey from his kitchen.

He poured two fingers of the amber liquid in each glass, handed me one, and held his aloft in a toast. "To your new home," he said.

I raised my glass as well, thinking of Duhamel`s drab friend, Vincent, and his fancy that I could be the owner of this cottage. How strange this was happening so quickly!

As we warmed ourselves with the whiskey, we agreed on a purchase price for the cottage. A satisfying price, exceedingly low, because I solemnly promised I`d take very good care of his garden—and continue with the planting!

After we shook hands on our deal and discussed the particulars of the banking issues that would allow Msr. Duhamel to slip out of St. Rémy, I glanced up at the paintings again.

My paintings, all my lovely paintings.

Then a movement in the first caught my eye—the one with no trees at all. A young woman, dressed in the fashion of well-bred ladies three decades before, walked toward the gate with a dark-haired gentleman dressed in an old-fashioned greatcoat. For a moment, they stopped and looked over their shoulders at me and smiled. My mother. My father. Together and home at last!

I could hardly wait to invite Mademoiselle DuBois to dinner to share my good fortune. . .

10

✿

Trouble in Spades

MY COLD DRAGGED ON FOR more than a week and I continued to think only about work. Or anything related to Peter's regular attacks. Sometimes I couldn't stop thinking about how he always needed to distance himself from John or put him down when I was a kid. Mother always seemed to like Uncle and praised his gentle ways and his writing, and when she did, Father's face turned fiery red. I was only nine the first time I recall my father twisting and turning in his chair while my mother gabbed on about my uncle's achievements. I imagined him every time I'd confronted him over the phone, twisting and turning in his chair at the bank with that same bright red face.

After the business debacle that lost Peter money, John moved from Baltimore to New York City to try his hand in the publishing industry. He worked in a publishing house mailroom for a while, then moved to an editorial assistant job upstairs, and later on, started Classic Art Exposé. The magazine was no cash cow, as I'd painfully discovered, and though Uncle John eventually repaid Father nearly every cent he lost on their venture in dribs and drabs (as I'd confirmed from his books), Father had never truly forgiven him.

Just a young boy, I'd missed Uncle John terribly when he left town. Only he and Mother ever encouraged my budding talent as a writer. His last birthday gift to me was a glossy anthology of the best science fiction stories published the year I turned twelve. Uncle John never forgot my birthdays and at Christmastime, there were always art supplies or books under the tree from him. I think my father tolerated this because he hated any confrontation on holidays and also because it saved him time and money on Christmas shopping—he was a bit of a Scrooge.

Finally, on one uncharacteristically sunny morning when I`d rather have taken a long walk in the park nearby just after another anxiety-inducing chat with O`Neill about the upcoming payment deadline on the note, I pulled our big art book from its place on one of the old library tables we used for layout. "I`m choosing the artwork this time," I announced, flipping the book open to *New York Harbor with the Brooklyn Bridge Under Construction* by A.T. Bricher. "There you go, a strong composition, well-rendered, and yet basically neutral in character."

Jason, Evie, and Shirley looked at me with concern because of my brisk, detached manner, but they nodded their agreement. Bricher`s painting had a serene atmosphere even with the brewing storm in the background, unlike the van Gogh painting with its frenetic, unpredictable energy bubbling underneath the sunshine. The sailboat scene had the potential to be interpreted in dozens of different ways that probably didn`t include a crazy artist or the painting itself. I felt more shaken than I wanted to admit about the van Gogh story and the recurring nightmares. I didn`t want to feel unsettled during the next round of stories or have any more dreams about them.

"Well," Jason said, breaking the silence. "The bad news is, we`ve reached a plateau in the number of contest entries and subscriptions, but the good news is we`re still holding steady."

"Yeah, and the *best* news is that we`re going to make that deadline with Peter Rizzo`s bank," I said, creating some distance from my father with my words while grabbing for a tissue to mop at my runny nose. "Barely, but we`re making it."

Bricher`s obituary in Art News (November 21, 1908) stated, `[Bricher] did not receive the notice in the press that the artist`s ability and reputation deserved`—a sentiment shared by today`s finest scholars of American nineteenth-century painting.

—Hollis Taggart Galleries

THE ISLAND

ISABEL MORRELL NOT ONLY BELIEVED that spirits exist; she had seen them with her own two eyes. On the summer morning of her tenth birthday, her parents had hired a sailboat for a jaunt to a little island near Manhattan, just across New York Harbor. Wide-eyed and receptive to searching for the pirate treasure rumored to have been buried there almost two centuries before, Isabel insisted she would find the chest that would spill open with pearls and pieces of eight sparkling on the wet sand. She wished she could have a pirate party on the island with all her friends, but her mother and father said they couldn`t afford to rent a bigger sloop.

Isabel adored the hum of the sails in the wind and the cries of seabirds over the harbor, and she didn`t want the day to ever end. Once they reached the island`s shore, her mother unpacked a picnic lunch and they enjoyed a leisurely meal of her favorite egg salad sandwiches with watercress. Afterward her mother and father sang Happy Birthday over a little chocolate cake. Then they became too serious, poring over some old map, walking off measured paces and poking around in the ground. They seemed to forget this was *her* day, *her* birthday adventure.

Isabel decided to entertain herself by building a sand castle while her parents dug holes all around the shore like eager dogs searching for bones. She decided to dig deep too, to accumulate enough wet sand for a giant castle that would be her masterpiece. When her parents finally found the treasure, she thought, they would be happy again and she could pretend to be the fine lady of the castle. She found a flat stone and started to dig fast and deep. Before long, she had a hole she could sit in, more than a foot deep.

Startled, Isabel looked up when a voice broke through the endless play of wind and surf. "Let me help you," said the boy. Dressed in strange, raggedy clothing, he appeared to be just a little older than she, tanned and freckled with long, sun-streaked and windblown hair, as if he always spent his days at the shore.

Isabel nodded. When the boy scraped sand from the hole, he pulled his cupped hands out and the sand passed through them. A look of determination crossed his face and he tried again. This time he picked up a handful of sand that didn`t pass through his fingers. He threw the handful aside and started digging like a machine. They continued to dig the hole, content to work without speaking. Isabel had no idea where the boy had come from, but was happy for the company. In the distance, her parents continued to move from place to place, digging small holes and then changing their minds and starting in another place again, oblivious to her.

Finally, when the hole was over two feet deep and more than two feet across, Isabel and the boy stopped digging to cool off.

"You have a funny accent. Are you English?"

"Almost," he said. "Me mam was born in Cardiff, Wales, but me grandmam packed her off to London when she had me in her belly."

"Did you sail over for the day too?" Isabel asked, dangling her legs into the cool hole.

He shook his head. "No, I was kidnapped by pirates, and forced to work for them before I died!"

Isabel frowned. The boy spoke as if he wasn`t joking, but maybe she didn`t hear him correctly. "What do you mean, you died?"

"I`m to keep guard over the treasure until someone removes it from the island. But no one`s likely to do that while the crew is protecting it," he said, picking up a handful of wet sand and kneading it between his palms.

Isabel laughed. "But you`re flesh and blood. You`re teasing me."

"I can prove what I say is true." The boy picked up his stone and started digging again.

"How are you going to prove something like that?"

He stood and plucked at her hand for an instant, then walked a few hundred yards to the nearest tree, a scrappy, wind-twisted oak. "Put your arms around it to be sure the tree is solid."

While Isabel hugged the tree, the boy walked toward her and then right through her and the tree, both. She looked at him with her mouth open.

"Is that convincing enough?" He turned around and walked through her and the tree from the other side.

Isabel felt more curious than frightened. After all, although the boy just walked through solid things like a ghost, he still looked solid. "So what`s it like to be a spirit?"

"To answer your question, I best tell you how I landed on this island. I`d worked as a cabin boy for just two months when pirates waylaid our vessel. These mutineers attacked and sank HMS Loyalty in a furious row on the high seas near the West Indies. They killed almost all hands aboard. Then they forced the rest of us, all raw recruits, into conscription on their schooner. Just a few weeks later, the pirate schooner was thrashed far off course during a two-day storm, the likes of which I`d never seen before. Afraid of being found and captured near the colonies, the cap`n decided to bury much of our booty and return for it later. He figured the coin and jewelry was better safely buried right here, not sunk on the bottom of the sea or recaptured by the British Navy. Cap`n Morgan brought four of his men and me with `im, supposedly to bury the treasure and map its location."

Isabel listened to his tale, spellbound, and couldn`t help but blurt out more questions. "What do you mean, the colonies? But you`re so young. How come you went to sea? Did you try to get away from the pirates?"

The boy smiled at her flurry of questions. "In those days, your States were all forts and colonies, of course, British and French and Dutch and Spanish. Many poor boys in Britain were bound out for apprenticeships, as they probably were in the colonies, and in Europe as well. I was a year too young but said was older, grateful to eat and for the adventure as well. The slums of London made life dull, and mean. It meant little to me whether I got ordered about by the Navy or ordered about by pirates. . .

"Anyway, the cap`n and mates found a secure spot for the booty here. In fact, it`s right under that oak tree. Cap`n had us dig deep, over six feet deep, before we put a chest in the hole just in front of that big boulder. Two of the men were in the hole setting the chest in place when Cap`n told the other two,

`Alright, then, do it now.`

"They drew two pistols apiece, and shot those in the hole. Cap`n ordered the two alive to fill the hole. He was in a right jaunty mood as he strolled back to the schooner. When we least expected it, he drew two pistols and shot the other mates. He ordered me to push the bodies further into the waves so they would float out to sea.

"Then Cap`n looked at me with an evil grin. `I`m sorry, boy, but I can`t leave anyone alive who knows where the treasure is buried.` He ran his sword through my midsection and I died on the beach." He pointed to a spot where the biggest waves crashed ashore and lifted his shirt.

Isabel couldn`t see any scar, but she shivered with the gloom that suddenly engulfed the island. She hardly knew what to say. "Why did you become a ghost?"

"I dunno," the boy said, shrugging his shoulders. "Maybe it`s the luck of the draw. After everything went dark, I seemed to be conscious the whole time, though I couldn`t feel my body. I was scared of the dark, but after a while, I woke to sunshine. I wondered if I was dead or alive until a wild boar ran directly at me. I froze with fear, knowing if I wasn`t already dead, I would be as soon as those tusks ripped me apart. To my amazement, the boar passed right through me and I didn`t feel a thing. Then I knew for sure I was in the life after death. I`d always heard preachers speaking of heaven and hell, but it didn`t appear I`d arrived at either place."

Isabel found the courage to ask lots of questions. "What do you eat? Or does a spirit have to eat? Do you have to bathe or wash your clothes? Can you stay awake all night without sleeping? Do you ever go to bathroom? How many people come to the island hunting for the treasure? Did the captain ever return for it?"

The boy laughed. "Whoa, whoa, whoa, lass. Let me begin by telling you my name is Rhys Morris. I was thirteen when I died, and I would now be two hundred and seventy-three years old. Today, in fact, is my birthday."

"I`m Isabel Morrell and it`s my birthday too!" She quickly figured in her head. This meant Rhys and the treasure had been on the island for two hundred and sixty years. "You`ve been here a long time. It must be boring. Why don`t you leave and go somewhere else?"

Rhys sighed, and the wind seemed to capture his sigh and carry it audibly out to sea. "I tried to leave several times on ships and even little sailboats that anchored at the island. I would board one, and when it sailed a mile or so away I would find myself back on the island. Some mysterious force holds me to this spot."

A puzzled look spread over Isabel`s face and she was silent for a moment. "How do you like living here?"

"I wouldn`t exactly call it living, more like existing. The existence is pleasant enough, aye. I have friends here." He gazed in the direction of a tree, where a group of men and women gathered. He waved to them, and they waved in return.

Isabel looked at the motley crowd, dressed in the clothing of many different eras. "How did all those people end up here?"

"Most of them were treasure hunters. A few of them drowned and washed up here, and of course, four are my crewmates. Being a ghost or spirit, whatever you call it, is somewhat a comfort. When I was alive, I often suffered from hunger and pain. I don`t experience either now. Nor do I worry about money or other worldly things. The best part of being dead is that there`s no longer the fear of death."

"When I die, can my spirit return here?"

"I can`t give you a definite answer. Some of the people who died here stayed dead, or else went to another place. I could never figure out why some stayed and others didn`t."

She started to think, maybe, just maybe, that this boring little island might be a nice place to spend eternity.

She blushed as Rhys Morris took a long look at her. "Aye, I`d be happy if you did stay, Isabel Morrell," he said, as if he could read her thoughts.

But the day turned darker then. While she and Rhys talked, her parents had managed to find the right spot near the boulder and the oak tree. She and Rhys watched, amused at first, at his crewmates and the other treasure hunters` attempts to scare the couple away. But something about their energy caused her parents to quarrel.

Isabel looked at the ghosts swirling about her parents and shivered. "They won`t hurt my mom and dad, will they?"

"Spirits aren`t able to do more than make a racket. Or cause eerie feelings in the living, sometimes," Rhys assured her. He seemed amused by his friends` efforts, especially because her mother and father were oblivious to the spirits wailing like banshees and passing back and forth through their bodies and the oak tree. "It`s the treasure itself that makes people behave badly."

Isabel relaxed then, not quite understanding Rhys`s second remark. She began to enjoy the spectacle, still attached to her girlish fantasy about how much fun her family would have after they found the treasure. But her mother and father seemed to grow dour and tense as they dug deeper, disappearing into the hole, their pick and shovel clanging in contact with something.

Curious, she walked over to look inside the hole. She thought her mother would call her, happy for the find, but could see her parents` faces harden as they extracted the bones of Rhys`s old crewmates and dug around the chest, making room to pry it away from the soil and rocks embracing it. The crewmates` skulls and leg bones looked scary as they flew up from the hole and scattered on the ground.

The ghosts brandished cudgels and one even waved an old cutlass about, howling and raging around the hole. Isabel eyed them with increasing dismay.

As her mother and father muscled the chest from the hole, sweating profusely, they seemed to not see her at all, as if slowly fading into the background. She backed away and went back to her sand pile, where Rhys stood watching. She watched from a distance as her parents climbed from the hole and began to argue again. She could hear them disagree, first trading angry words, and then pushing and shoving one another. Her mother almost fell into the hole and her father almost looked glad of it. She had never seen her parents argue so vehemently or abuse one another before.

Isabel`s memories always grew sketchy at this point. She recalled only a deep, empty, miserable sadness and Rhys Morris trying to console her as her parents took their place among the group of ghosts. Somehow, Rhys`s crewmembers reburied the treasure despite their formlessness. Her parents tried to console her later as she nearly died herself of hunger and thirst while she remained stranded on the island until yet another group of adventurous young people discovered her there. With Rhys`s patient prodding, they had finally stumbled upon her on the far side of the island, although they couldn`t see him like she could. Isabel barely remembered saying good-bye to her parents and Rhys as she was hauled away to wake up alone in the orphanage under the watchful eye of Father Donahue.

Isabel gradually recovered from her ordeal, and no one believed that she had murdered her parents. Yet there was no clear evidence that they had killed one another, either, the most likely explanation. The only conclusion the authorities could offer was that the Morrells had scuffled around a tree on the island while searching for some legendary treasure, a family argument gone bad. There was no blood on their shovels or pickaxe and none around their bodies (probably due to the rainy weather that had started that evening) and there was nothing else near the bodies but a dozen muddy and abandoned shallow holes to show for their labor. But their wounds were obviously grievous and the deaths very real. There were no leads to speak of and the police closed the double murder investigation quickly. For a long time Isabel had longed to be dead, to join Rhys Morris and her parents, but she had no opportunity to get back to the island from the orphanage.

On her eighteenth birthday, Isabel stood aboard a small sloop that left New York Harbor on a cloudy morning, heading for the island that lay only twenty miles distant. Father Donahue looked unusually grim as he scanned the horizon in the direction of the island, as a man calling himself Captain O`Reilly steered his sailboat toward it. In a strange twist of fate that always seemed present in Isabel`s life, the craft bore the name "Spirit."

When Isabel had finally confessed her story for the first time just weeks before, Father Donahue seemed taken with it. He said she would only find peace by confronting her fears and revisiting the island. He claimed only to support her quest when he offered to take her there, but Isabel knew enough about human nature by now to wonder if his real motive involved the treasure. Or was he more interested in the spirits that inhabited the island? She also figured that O`Reilly must also have his own motive for agreeing to transport them.

Thirty minutes later, their tension grew as the sloop neared the island`s shoreline. No one spoke about what awaited them once they stepped ashore. Perhaps nothing. Perhaps something. Isabel had discovered she wasn`t the only person who`d had strange experiences there. In the eight years since her rescue, she`d learned that many recreational boaters instinctively stayed away from the rocky shore. Even before her parents had taken her to the island, she was vaguely aware of some dreadful stories about it, ranging from warnings about dangerous currents to tales of cursed treasure. Some stories were colorful and paranormal and others leaned more toward cautionary tales of vague, random accidents that befell visitors to the island. Her parents had downplayed all these, presenting the trip as a birthday adventure.

Father Donahue was probably right. She needed to face her trauma and that`s what she would do. She took off her shoes, lifted her skirt, and waded through the surf, headed straight for the oak tree while the priest and the captain tugged the sailboat onto the shore. Father Donahue soon followed her while Captain O`Reilly secured the craft.

Isabel wondered if her parents` spirits were still on the island, since authorities had removed their bodies and buried them in a city graveyard for the indigent. Her memories of Rhys Morris enticed her even though she still felt tormented by the nightmare of her parents` violent deaths. As if in response to this thought, she suddenly saw her mom and dad in the distance, walking hand-in-hand. She ran toward them, but they faded and disappeared when she reached the spot where they stood.

As if answering her second thought, Rhys Morris appeared beside her and spoke to her as though the eight years` absence meant nothing in his world. "They`re embarrassed by what you saw them do to one another. They think you will never forgive their stupidity."

Isabel leaned forward and cupped her hands around her mouth. She shouted as loud as she could over the brisk wind. "Mom, Dad, I love you!"

Three times Isabel shouted into the wind. Slowly the pair materialized an arms` length away, their heads down. She tried to embrace the misty spirits, but of course, her arms passed right through them. For some reason, they weren`t solid-looking like Rhys. She stepped back, embarrassed by trying to hug ghosts. But she could still communicate with them, even so. "Why?" she simply asked.

Her parents gazed at her with deep hurt in their eyes. "As happens to many who lust after material things, once we discovered the treasure, we couldn`t control ourselves," her mother said.

Her father nodded. "Greed is a sickness that, once indulged in, cannot be controlled. We each wanted the treasure for ourselves and couldn`t bear the thought of sharing it."

To Father Donahue, who stopped nearby to watch her, it must have appeared as if she were gesturing and talking aloud to herself. He must think she`d snapped under the strain of returning to the island. As the priest strode over to comfort her, Captain O`Reilly arrived with a revolver in one hand and a pair of shovels in another.

"Show me where the treasure is buried," he demanded. "Now."

Father Donahue stood and stared at O`Reilly.

"I said now!" O`Reilly shouted. "I knew there had to be some truth to the stories about the treasure." He spat on the ground and threw a shovel at Donohue. "Start digging!"

Father Donahue let the shovel lay at his feet. "I`m ready to meet my God, if that`s His will. Go ahead and shoot."

O`Reilly raised the pistol and cocked it. "I knew the girl had to know something when I read about her parents` death in the papers. You opened up the door to my dreams when you called me to charter the sailboat for *poor* little Isabel."

Isabel cringed and pointed at the boulder by the oak tree as Rhys put his arm around her. Her parents shouted and rushed toward O`Reilly, but this had no effect on him.

O`Reilly lowered the pistol and then re-aimed at Isabel. "Are you ready for her to die, God-man? Because that`s what`s going to happen if you don`t start digging."

The priest slowly, carefully picked up the shovel and started to dig next to the boulder, chanting a prayer in Latin under his breath.

"What`s that you`re saying?" O`Reilly asked, spading into the damp ground near Donahue.

"An old ceremonial verse said to send spirits to their final resting place."

O`Reilly rolled his eyes. Isabel looked at her parents and then Rhys, wondering what this meant for her. At least now she could see her friend and her family, even if she couldn`t be with them fully. What if they had left her entirely? She would have to wait a lifetime to see them again in heaven.

It took some time to dig to the depth of the chest. Both men stood inside the deep hole, exhausted and panting, after Donahue`s shovel finally struck the chest. Donahue abandoned the prayer as O`Reilly finally stooped to clear away the rest of the dirt with his hands. O`Reilly motioned with the pistol for Donahue to pull the chest up and out of the hole. When the two clambered out, O`Reilly lifted the lid with the toe of his boot, and both men stood transfixed, immobilized by the sight of the gold coins and roughly cut gemstones.

Isabel's parents edged closer to her, fragile as rainbows. They urged her to run. But she didn't want to leave them, or Rhys. Rhys leaned toward her and whispered, "Just watch their eyes."

The two men's eyes sparkled with delight, then desire, and finally, greed. Donahue seized a shovel from the ground and knocked the gun from O'Reilly's hand. O'Reilly leaped on the priest, punching and kicking him, but the man of God seemed to give as much as he was getting. Soon, the two men stumbled and rolled on the ground as if doing their best to kill one another. After a minute of intense wrestling, they rolled right into the hole.

Suddenly, Rhys's companions and some of the dead treasure hunters appeared. They pushed and kicked the high piles of dirt on top of the two men, who tried to scramble up from the hole, screaming oaths. Somehow, much to Isabel's horror, the ghosts managed to keep them inside the hole, and she shut her eyes tight as an eerie silence soon replaced the screams.

When Isabel opened her eyes again, she wanted to dig them out. "It's too late. Buried alive," Rhys said. "A fitting end for greedy bastards."

"I'm not so sure about Father Donahue. . . He seemed nice enough to me. . ." Isabel felt her chest tighten to the point of not being able to breathe as tears welled up in her eyes. She had seen four people die over this wretched treasure. She didn't know what to do but cut and run.

Not even the calls of her parents or Rhys could draw her back. She didn't know how to sail, but as she shoved and tugged and swore at the sailboat, she knew somehow that the high tide would take her back to the mainland.

As the wind began to hum in the sloop's sails, and she heard the cries of the seabirds circling overhead, Isabel wondered why she wanted to go back to the city. She had no one there any more, not even Father Donahue. She would have to leave the orphanage and her friends there soon. Was life with all its contradictions really worth living?

She turned to gaze at the island, so innocuous looking in the misty light. Her family was there, and her friend Rhys would be happy if she stayed. He had said so long ago. He was eternally thirteen, of course, but taller than she was and wise for his years, even so. And she and Rhys were so much alike, even had the same birthday. Maybe he was right about Father Donahue. . .

Isabel's parents stood silent, watching her. Isabel imagined they were still shamed by their condition. She missed them and hungered to wake up in the sunshine with them and without her worldly concerns. To awaken to a life without end on the quiet island, even with her parents' regrets, seemed idyllic.

Isabel could hear Rhys calling her back, his Welsh accent flaring in the wind. Mesmerized, she slid over the side of the sloop. She had never learned to swim against the sea. The gray-blue waters tumbled around her. It wouldn`t be long. . .

As Isabel`s head went under the last time and her lungs burned with saltwater, she prayed she`d be one of the lucky people who lived forever on the island.

11

Treasure Map

THIS TIME AROUND, I WAS surprised that the winning writer had created a paranormal suspense inspired by the Bricher painting, because it was a reasonably neutral composition in my mind—perhaps somewhat melancholy and mysterious, but not paranormal genre gloomy.

"I love the female protagonist," Evie confessed.

"Yes," Shirley concurred. "And the love interest with a ghost. . . "The Island" shows a surprising abundance of spirit in more ways than one!"

"Hear, hear," Jason muttered. "Better romance with a spirit than a troublesome human," he added, apparently still raw from Shirley`s rejection.

Privately, I felt uneasy that the van Gogh-inspired murder mystery was followed by another creepy tale. A few vocal readers complained too, some that the story was for teenagers, not adults, others that the story was too gritty to have teenaged protagonists and that the sad ending encouraged teenage suicide. I worried about liability at first, then accepted once more Jason`s opinion that art is controversial and that we`d encouraged the submission of dark fiction through our previous awards. I began to see the story as a non-prescriptive cautionary tale that teenagers would enjoy. Still, I hoped "The Island" wouldn`t spur any more bad dreams because I was still having more than enough negativity to contend with in real life.

"Hey," Jason said at the conclusion of our meeting, "How `bout we print a treasure map with the story? Maybe we could build a refreshment and magazine stand near the harbor. After all that sailing around in circles, people will need a drink!"

I never knew whether to take Jason seriously or not. Shirley rolled her eyes and Evie giggled uproariously at

Jason`s ideas and his hoarse, stuffy-nosed speech We`d all passed my cold around the past month and he was the final victim.

"The Island" caused a boating boom when many people really did sail across New York Harbor trying to find the fictional setting after the story`s publication. Some street vendors who heard about the story had thoughts similar to Jason`s—they printed and sold a few fake treasure maps and helped the island myth gain more momentum. It was amazing how some people would take literally anything in print as gospel truth. It made me pause and think again about journalistic responsibility. If we`d done a radio play of "The Island" in a "War of the Worlds" vein, I could imagine the unforeseen results.

The best part of this success was that our subscriptions and entries for the next contest put Classic Art Exposé on the map again. We were approaching a circulation of thirty-six thousand and a few more than five hundred contest entries, a cool $2500. I had no qualms about holding back $2000 and giving the contest winner $500. We had a lot of financial catching up to do after our most recent run-in with Peter.

The printers went on strike, but our new manager assistants printed the magazine with some help from us editors and our contest interns—and a little paid overtime helped to sweeten the deal. The strike grievances turned out to be so vague that even the union didn`t try to back our printers up when they got tired of marching back and forth in front of the building with their placards. They finally asked to go back to work after three days. So, all was going mostly right in our world again, although the deadline for financial solvency was rushing toward us like a bat out of hell.

"So people," I said when it was time to pick another contest painting. "Since we`ve garnered many positive responses to work by American artists and to our recent Classic Art Exposé feature articles about them, how about this landscape by T.C. Steele for our next contest?"

"Simple," Jason said with a grin.

"Poignant," Evie said, grabbing the opportunity to use one of her favorite words.

Shirley picked up the book and studied the picture closely. "*Morning by the Stream* should challenge our writing enthusiasts to capture the sweet desire it exudes."

"Isn`t it about time we attracted another sweet story?" I said to no one in particular.

MORNING BY THE STREAM
T.C. Steele, 1893

*It is light that gives mystery to shadow, vibration to atmosphere,
and makes all the color notes sing together in harmony.*

NICOR

ONCE THE ALEXANDER COUNTY DEPUTY said, "I don`t believe anything you say," and the cell door locked with the sharp finality of a steel trap, Molly started to pray silently. *Please, God.* Then she remembered she`d uttered the exact same words when Nicor had first appeared.

She`d been at work in the drugstore uptown just months earlier when her new friend Angela burst through the door. "Wait 'til you meet my cousin, he`s as handsome as any movie star," she said in her snooty Chicago accent.

*Her cousin`s probably a dog like the rest of the guys who come in here,* Molly thought. But she put on a happy face, not wanting to appear rude. "I can`t wait to meet him," she lied, turning her face to look at the cash register so Angela wouldn`t see her eyes blink as they always did when she fibbed.

"Maybe we can all go to a movie or something?"

Molly hesitated. "Well, maybe. I`m pretty busy." Angela seemed overly friendly and accommodating for someone she`d only known a few days. Maybe the new girl just had that social type of personality. Still, she had no intention of going anywhere with Angela and her cousin if she could help it. Not yet.

But Angela returned the next day with a picture of her cousin at a swimming meet. He had a swimmer`s physique, the broad shoulders, small tight waist, and long, muscular arms under a face that really was movie star handsome. Molly wasn`t sure of the color of his hair, since it was short and still wet in the picture.

"Maybe we *could* take in a movie one night," she said impulsively. She regretted it afterward, knowing she`d never get permission from her mother to go back to town after work on a weekend, let alone a weeknight. Her mother tended to be overprotective even though she`d just turned eighteen, something Molly didn`t mind most of the time because she was slow to warm up to people anyway.

Molly was at the register again when Angela came into the drugstore the next day. Angela waved at her and sailed past to the cosmetic counter to try on a sample lipstick. When her boss told her to assist Angela, probably worried that she`d swipe something, she looked over Angela`s shoulder into the mirror. As Angela turned her head this way and that, pouting like Marilyn Monroe with her short bouffant hairdo and her painted lips, Molly noticed for the first time the small lines around Angela`s eyes and mouth. She wondered if the girl might be older than she said. She dressed and acted eighteen, but none of Molly`s friends that age had lines on their still-plump faces. Maybe Angela just had a hard life.

When a stranger walked into the drugstore, the sight sent chills up Molly`s spine. She suddenly felt childish in her homemade pink and white gingham dress. But he looked like, well. . . like a man. His thick, wavy chestnut hair hugged his perfect, chiseled forehead. Dressed in blue jeans, a plaid snap-button shirt, and cowboy boots, he sauntered over to the counter and looked her right in the eye.

"Can you help me, ma`am?" he said in a Texas drawl, his lips curving into a winning, suggestive smile. Molly thrilled to the timbre of his deep voice and wanted to hear more of it. He somehow looked familiar to her even though she knew she`d never seen him before.

His boldness emboldened her. "I`d be happy to help you in any way I can," Molly said. She opened and closed the register drawer while she talked to him. He smiled again, revealing the whitest, most perfect teeth she had ever seen. He looked to be around twenty-two. Old, she thought, but not too old for her. She looked down at her hands, then lifted her face and smiled coyly at him, keeping her lips pressed together for fear her teeth weren`t nearly as perfect as his.

The young man put one hand on his hip. "You don`t even know what I need help with, and you`re willing to help me in any way you can?"

"Um, if it`s something pertaining to the store," she stammered. He smiled, exposing those perfect white teeth again. Angela walked over from the cosmetic counter right up to the stranger and threw her arms around him.

"Tom, I see you`ve already met Molly. Molly, this is my cousin, the one I`ve been telling you about."

Now Molly knew where she had seen him before, Angela`s picture. How could she not recognize him? The Texas drawl must be fake because she knew he was really from Chicago, like Angela.

"Angela and I are having a picnic this afternoon," Tom said. "Why don`t you join us?"

An afternoon picnic sounded less threatening than going out at night for a movie, but her mom probably wouldn`t let her go on a picnic, either. Not until she was properly introduced and felt as if she knew their family. "Sorry. I have to work until three. That`s too late for a picnic, but thanks for asking."

"We`re just going to the woods outside of town for a couple of hours, so we can leave at three. Come on, we can get you home before dinner."

Tom looked directly into Molly`s eyes. "Pretty please?"

Molly suddenly felt hot and sweaty, made almost dizzy by Tom`s hypnotic brown eyes. "Um, yeah, okay, why not?" She figured she could tell her mom that Mel wanted her to work two extra hours.

"We`ll see you at three, then. I`ll run home and add a few snacks to our picnic lunch, and get my camera and tripod so we can snap some pictures," Angela said. While Tom wandered away and browsed through a sports magazine, she whispered, "Isn`t he as handsome as I said he was?"

Molly didn`t answer, but knew if she didn`t go now she might never get another chance to hang around with Tom.

Three o`clock came, and Molly stood in front of the drugstore to wait for Angela and Tom. She imagined him riding up on a big white stallion like the Lone Ranger because of his presenting himself like a movie-star cowboy. When he pulled up in a white Thunderbird convertible with the top down and Angela in the back seat, she knew it was the next best thing. He smiled; she melted when he said in that now-sexy, slow drawl, "Jump on in."

She almost pinched herself as she slid across the soft leather seat. The car smelled of fresh, new upholstery and paint. "Is this beauty new?"

"Yes ma`am, I just picked it up before I came to Cairo," he said, revving the engine and peeling away from the curb.

Molly loved the way the wind blew through her hair as they sped along the highway. It made her feel as glamorous as Angela. Tom soon pulled off on a dirt road leading to a stream in the woods where many local people had picnics in the summertime. This spring weekend, most people would still be over at the high school or at the park for the local baseball games.

"You seem to know where you`re going," Molly said. "Have you been here before?"

"I checked it out just yesterday," Tom said.

Angela nodded. "A lot of kids say this is where people go for picnics."

Molly wondered what Tom meant by "checked it out" but Angela pointed to a large oak tree and declared it the perfect spot, and this distracted her.

Tom parked and wrangled the big basket from the Thunderbird`s small trunk while Angela spread an army blanket in the shade of the big oak. Angela set out the tin plates and sandwiches wrapped in waxed paper, a melmac bowl of potato salad covered in tin foil, and some cookies and crackers folded into small brown paper bags.

Enthralled to be near Tom, Molly wasn`t much interested in eating. To avoid staring at him, she gazed around at their surroundings. The warm sun drifted down through the tree branches at the edge of the woods, just budding out with the first spring leaves. Over a fence in the distance, she could see a farmer`s orchard crowned in pink blossoms.

Tom pulled a bottle of wine and three glasses from the basket and handed her a glass.

"Do you have any Pepsi or Coke?"

Angela giggled. "Come on, Molly, have a glass of wine. That`s what grownups drink at picnics, not soda pop."

Embarrassed, Molly let Tom fill her glass with red wine. She took a sip, hoping she didn`t look goofy. The wine tasted rich and fruity, not unpleasant, and before she knew it, she`d emptied the glass. She reached for a sandwich, thinking she`d better eat something with the alcohol.

"Have another glass, Molly." Tom reached out and refilled her glass with the last bit in the bottle.

She nibbled at her sandwich while Angela and Tom jabbered about their family. She really didn`t know what to say, so she just listened. Suddenly, she felt relaxed and found it difficult to sit up.

Angela smiled at her. "Oops, feeling a little tipsy, are we?" She giggled and let Molly lean against her.

Molly gazed into the woods. All the bright green buds, brown tree trunks and pretty spring flowers whirled around and blended together until she felt like she was in some surreal painting. Every movement she made felt difficult, like she was stuck in the mud.

Angela moved away and Molly found herself lying on the blanket, staring up at the sky. Tom began to unbutton the top of her dress. Normally she`d be appalled, but she could have cared less until she put two and two together and realized the possible consequences. Then she tried to lift her hand to stop him, but it felt too heavy to bother. She formed the word No! with her lips but it came out soundlessly, a poof of air. With great effort, she turned her head to see Angela snapping pictures of everything Tom did. When he finished undressing her, she waited for him to rape her. *Oh, my God, I'll probably get pregnant. Or maybe he has the clap and I'll have to visit Dr. Martin's office. . . then everyone will know.*

Angela went to the car and brought back another camera and a tripod. *What did this mean?* Molly struggled to find logic in her thoughts. But she could hear Angela and Tom talking as if they were all under water.

"What'd you give her?"

Tom laughed. "Just a sleeping pill in her wine. Doesn't take much for a hick like her."

Angela smirked. "Good, she'll be able to feel the pain."

Pain? Molly wasn't so out of it that she didn't feel scared. *Why didn't I follow my intuition and not come? Too late now!*

She struggled to get up, to scream at the top of her lungs, but all she could do was make some flailing motions and groan.

"You need to do it different this time," Angela told Tom. "The buyers are getting bored with the same old stuff. We need something more exotic."

Tom nodded at Angela with a peculiar gleam in his eye.

Molly's body racked with the sobs that almost choked her. Would they murder her too?

"Listen, this is the best idea ever. These woods are known to have a few bears. We'll chain her to that tree, and coat her with honey. We can prop the camera over there on that other tree, and set it to start up to fifteen minutes from now." He showed Angela how to delay the timer.

Tom retrieved some chains from the Thunderbird trunk and a small jar of honey from the picnic basket. They stood Molly up and secured her to the tree. While Angela focused the movie camera and propped it up in the crotch of another tree, Tom stuck two fingers in the honey jar and smeared it over her face, breasts, stomach, and thighs. She flinched at his touch.

"You like that, don't you, little girl?"

The drug must have been wearing off because she managed to say, "Please don't."

Tom mocked her, imitating her high voice and Southern accent. Without another look, the kissing cousins piled into the Thunderbird and peeled away in a cloud of dust, leaving her naked and alone, chained to the tree.

Molly knew there were fewer bears in these woods than Angela and Tom thought, that they were rarely sighted, but it was true that hunters encountered them from time to time.

Molly shivered and tried to wriggle free of the chains. Despite her discomfort, she'd gotten sleepy and dozed as the sun went down. Now it was dark and the woods seemed to close in around her. Her legs felt like they were on fire, as if mosquitoes and flies had bitten her hundreds of times. She wondered if anyone would find her alive. At least Tom hadn't raped her, a small consolation considering she'd be found naked. *What must Mom be thinking?*

She held her breath when she heard something shuffling in the undergrowth nearby, getting ever closer. She hoped it was a skunk or a badger, or maybe some stray cow that had escaped its pasture. But no; a low, growling snuffle rose just behind her and she caught the rank odor of a meat-eating animal.

"Dear God, help me," Molly said aloud. She wasn't religious and she didn't know how to pray, but what else could she do now but turn to God?

The dark form rounded the tree and sniffed at her feet. Smelling the honey, it stood on its hind legs and braced its forepaws on the tree beside her head. The eyes gleamed green for just a moment as a moonbeam penetrated the darkness.

Molly trembled with fear, wishing she could merge into the tree trunk. Though she could barely see the outline of the bear's muzzle just inches from her face, she could imagine the rows of large, pointed teeth within. She closed her eyes and clamped her jaw shut, fearing that if she made any more noise it would arouse the bear.

The hot stink of its breath oozed onto her face as it opened its maw. *God, how can you let this happen?* Suddenly, a strange crackling sound like the bristle of electricity, accompanied by an eerie glow, surrounded her. In that split-second, Molly watched the bear's thick tongue lap out and touch her face to lick the honey from it. She closed her eyes tight and held her breath again, waiting to die. At least the movie camera couldn't possibly still be running this many hours after Angela had set the timer, or even work at all in the dark without a bank of floodlights.

Just as suddenly as the light appeared, it seemed to surround her with a silky, soothing sensation. Curious, Molly opened her eyes. The light still enveloped the tree and the bear seemed to be undergoing a metamorphosis. Its thick fur was thinning, smoothing, and becoming more flesh-like, and the snout seemed to be pulling into the face, flattening into lips, the eyes centering into human eyes. Within seconds, she found herself face to face with Tom.

Molly prayed harder. "Oh, my God. Let this be a nightmare." Was she going crazy? She remembered her science teacher saying crazy people don't know they're crazy.

"Your prayers can be answered if you're willing to make a sacrifice," Tom said.

Molly turned her face away and struggled to free herself from the chains.

The thing in front of her laughed. "You have to make a decision. I can`t stay in this body for long. It tasted the honey and wants more. Will you make a sacrifice for me or not?

Molly stared as Tom`s eyes began to shift sideways and his lips bulge forward.

"Who are you?"

"I am called Nicor. God gave me permission to make people prove their faith."

"Are you an angel then?" She couldn`t imagine God sending anything else but an angel for this travail, but why would it take the form of a bear and an evil person?

"Let`s say I was an angel once. You better decide. . . I feel the overwhelming hunger for honey." His tongue licked the half-formed snout that began to sprout fur, and he passed a hand condensing into a paw over the wavy dark hair matting down into a pelt.

Molly could hardly believe her eyes, but she believed in her fear. "Alright! I`ll do anything, just don`t let the bear get me." Anything was better than being eaten alive.

Immediately the snout shrank again and the fur disappeared. Tom unfastened the chains that held Molly and picked up her dress and underwear from the ground. He led her to the stream deeper in the woods, and she gratefully washed the honey off. Shivering in the cool night air, she dressed. When she turned away from the steam, a bear was once again rooting around the oak tree, searching out any remnants of honey.

She stumbled away from the tree and down the dirt road to the highway, trying to make sense of everything. When she reached the payphone near the edge of town, she found a dime in the coin return and called her mother. She threatened to ground Molly for life. "I`m so sorry, Mom, I`m so sorry. I`ll never, ever do this again." Shaking, she made up a story about going over to her friend Pam`s house after work to finish a school assignment and forgetting to call. Her mother didn`t buy it, but at least she could walk home in peace. When she passed the town square, the clock on the tower said just half-past nine. She`d thought it might be past midnight.

After her mother grilled her about her disheveled appearance and threatened to make her quit her job, Molly showered. Afterward, she eased the medicine cabinet open to avoid making it squeak and took one of her mother`s tranquilizers, scooping water from the lavatory with one hand to swallow it. She lay in her dark room, the covers pulled up to her chin, but whenever she closed her eyes, images of Tom`s gloating face and the bear haunted her.

And Nicor. Where had she heard that name before? Maybe she could look it up at the library tomorrow. Or would it be in the encyclopedia? She crept downstairs to the small bookshelf that held the row of Encyclopedia Britannica volumes. She pulled a lamp over toward the sofa and blocked the light with a cushion so it wouldn`t shine toward her mother`s room, then seized the Volume N and paged toward the middle. *Nice, Nicor.* She closed her eyes for a moment and let her forefinger rest on the name. When she opened them again, she took a deep breath and began to read. *In Teutonic mythology, Nicor are malignant water monsters who drown people. According to Scandinavian mythology, Odin takes on the name of Nickar or Hnickar when he acts as a destroyer. Under this name, he frequents lakes and rivers, where he causes tempests, hurricanes, and hailstorms.*

How can this be? Why would God send a demon to help her, and what had she agreed to do in exchange for her life? In stories about Satan, he often tricked humans. Worse, Nicor had made itself look like Tom. Were Tom and Angela demons? What promise had Nicor extracted from her by pretending to be both Tom and a bear? Why were there no storms? What sacrifice would she make?

Safe now, Molly`s fear turned to anger. *Angela, that bitch, she set me up. She must be Tom`s shill.* Befriending unwary teenage girls and luring them into unsavory situations to film them. . . She was damn lucky she hadn`t been raped or murdered.

Dawn`s first dim light began to seep through the curtains when Molly finally slept. In her dark dreams, she found Nicor lurking in a shadow. He told her to return to the oak tree where she would find a baseball bat. "Use this to avenge yourself," he said, as though speaking of something ordinary. "You promised to make a sacrifice."

When she woke, she thought it was only a dream. If she jumped into her clothes and ran, she could still make it to the high school before the last bell. Then she saw a note on the refrigerator. Her mother had already left for her job in the five and dime uptown. Maybe she wanted Molly to run an errand after school. But her mother always wrote in cursive, not in big block letters in a similar slant to her own writing.

BE THERE BY 10 AM

NICOR

Molly stuffed the note into her English text. She`d have to check the tree later. If there was a baseball bat sitting against that tree, then she`d know it wasn`t just a dream. Or better yet, maybe she shouldn`t go at all. What if Angela and Tom planned all this to lure her back again? Maybe Tom just pretended to be Nicor and she was hallucinating when she saw the bear. She opened the back door and stood on the stoop for a moment, gazing across the hills in the direction of the woods.

Her mother sometimes walked to work and left the green `53 Chevy in the driveway to save money. She grabbed the keys from the kitchen, not even bothering to change from the pretty velveteen robe her mother had given her for Christmas. With a shaky hand, she started the car and put the gearshift in reverse. She had her license, but her mother rarely let her drive. She gnawed on her lower lip as she concentrated on making all the proper stops and turns, hoping no one she knew was out and about to see her like this. Finally, after what seemed like hours, she reached the turnoff for the woods. She parked in the same place that Tom had parked his Thunderbird and turned to look at the trees. A baseball bat leaned against the big oak like it was waiting for her.

Molly chided herself for not dressing and going to school. She turned the key in the ignition and restarted the car. But she hesitated for a moment, turned the key off, put the transmission in park, and got out. She stared at the bat, then eased toward it, her slippers making a hushed shuffling noise in the grass. The bat looked so, well, innocent, as if it belonged to a local kid, the kind who called himself Slugger, collected baseball cards, and knew all the famous players` statistics. She picked up the bat and felt a sudden surge of strength course through her body. If she had a ball to hit, she would have slugged a homerun.

She remembered a fallen tree in the stream, where the water had backed up and allowed her to bathe. It looked like picnickers had even thrown some rocks there to dam the stream and make the pool deep enough for swimming. She sensed there was something she needed to do there. But the sound of a car coming startled her and she slunk behind a tree much like the one she`d been chained too, just a few yards away.

Tom and Angela were joking and laughing as they got out of the Thunderbird, until they looked up and noticed her mom`s car. Their faces sobered up as they gazed around the woods. The chains that had bound her still lay on the ground, looped around the oak. Angela looked panicky as Tom unfastened the camera from the tree, but he simply laughed and said he couldn`t wait to see the film.

He looked more evil than handsome now. The jerk assumed she was dead, mauled and carried away by the bear.

Her anger became uncontrollable. Tom handed Angela the camera and while she placed it in the trunk of the Thunderbird, he inspected the chains.

Here was her chance. "Tom," she said softly.

He turned at the sound of her voice, and she swung the bat right on that bright smile with every ounce of strength she could muster. When Angela turned toward the dull thud that echoed into the woods, Molly ran to her and smashed the bat onto the top of her head.

Molly could hear Nicor`s voice in her head, telling her to pull the film from the camera. She struggled with it for a few minutes, finally prying the back open with her fingernails. She ripped the film out in a frenzy, held the wadded and tangled celluloid in the sunlight to expose it, then threw it and the camera into the back seat of the Thunderbird. Satisfied with that handiwork, the voice said to put Tom and Angela into the car too and to push it into the water.

It took some time and effort to drag the heavy, unconscious, but still-breathing bodies and to stuff them inside the little sports car. Finally, sweaty and exhausted, the hem of her robe rimmed in dirt, Molly put the gearshift in neutral and released the brake so it could roll downhill into the stream. It caught on some brush and teetered on the edge for a moment, and she had to thrust the bat into the bumper a few times until it rolled forward again. She watched the cousins` bloody faces as the car bobbled on the surface for a moment and then tilted underwater. She sobbed with relief as she threw the bat into the water, still broiling with bubbles made by the sinking car.

She fled to her mother`s Chevy and drove home, weeping all the way. What had she done? That stream wouldn`t hide the evidence. It emptied into the Mississippi or the Ohio somewhere, but it wasn`t big enough to swallow the crime forever.

Nightmares began to disrupt her sleep and bad memories haunted her days. During the final two months of her senior classes and at work, she felt transparent, like a ghost. Her mother suspected the worst as she withdrew, accusing her of being pregnant because of that one night away. Rather than growing plump, though, Molly grew stick-thin and hollow. While her classmates celebrated at the prom and senior banquet, attended commencement parties, and planned for summer weddings or for college that fall, she wandered around like a wraith, void of direction. She clung to her familiar job at the drugstore and didn`t care about moving beyond the routines she`d already established.

But the bad dreams and memories eventually became thin too, light as air. As spring turned to summer and the long, hot, lazy days made everything feel better, the darkness seemed to lift. That is, until summer disappeared into autumn and hunting season came around. One rainy Saturday morning, two hunters found a white Thunderbird partially submerged in the stream with the remains of a man and a woman inside.

Molly panicked when she read the news. *But no one would ever suspect me of having anything to do with it,* she reasoned. *The film and the camera are ruined. Wouldn`t the water remove fingerprints from everything?* A few days later, a deputy sheriff stood on the front porch with a warrant in his hand when she came home from work. *How could they possibly know?*

As the deputy put Molly in handcuffs, she heard her mother scream from far away, as if everything was happening in a dream. Then, in the sheriff`s office, she saw Angela`s camera on a desk, and a waterlogged baseball bat, both tagged as evidence.

Had Nicor tricked her into killing Tom and Angela? After all, they really had chained her to a tree naked, she was certain of that. And she`d survived a bear—was it really a demon? She hadn`t seen Nicor since that awful evening at the river.

Am I Nicor?
Molly didn`t know what else to do now, so she prayed again.
Please, God.

12

Clout vs. Integrity

AGENT BARNES SHOOK MY HAND with one strong downward tug after walking into the office uninvited and introducing himself and Agent Grabowski. "We suspect you were involved with dumping paint at magazine newsstands to discredit Peter Rizzo. In case you didn`t know, it`s a federal offense to damage property that`s deliverable by U.S. mail."

Barnes and another FBI agent were friends of my father (I almost choked on the word, but gave Peter the respect of having raised me). Their unexpected late morning visit had to be just another ploy to ruin me.

Even knowing this, my jaw must have hit the floor, judging by the smug looks on their faces. "What a stretch," I said, my voice too loud. "For one thing, I had nothing to do with this. Why would we dump paint on our own magazines? We need every sale we can get. What happened only hurt the vendors because we sell at a reduced price to them and they pick up only a small profit at the cover price. For another, we post magazines by U.S. mail only to subscribers. We deliver the remainder of the print run to the magazine stands ourselves. And I never pressed charges—that was up to the stand owners. I heard that NYPD handled the case and found evidence tying Peter to the crime—"

Grabowski leered at me. "We`re looking at NYPD records at this time. A prosecutor will likely subpoena you for a deposition."

I couldn`t help but roll my eyes and make a tooth-sucking sound. "I don`t believe this. Peter`s done everything he can to obstruct my success," I said. "Just like he drove my fath. . . my uncle out of his newspaper business and tried to destroy this magazine years ago." The instant I`d said it aloud I wished I hadn`t.

Barnes cast Grabowski a look that said I was a moron. "We`re more inclined to believe Mr. Rizzo`s side of the story."

"Peter Rizzo may have clout but Peter John Rizzo has integrity. I had nothing to do with the incident, and I`m pretty certain you two assholes know it."

Grabowski stuck his fat mug in my face and spittle flew with his words. "Listen buddy, I strongly suggest you tone it down before you find yourself locked up. Good day."

I could feel my face flaming in anger as the suits turned on their expensive heels and walked out. Was this a bluff or for real? I didn`t see any way they could frame me for the crime, but maybe I could make things better with Peter anyway. I picked up the phone receiver and then put it down three or four times. I`d woken up in a cold sweat having a nightmare about some dark creature pursuing me after a weird evening while visiting my mom the night before.

Finally, I grabbed the phone again and dialed Peter`s number at the bank.

When he picked up his line, he snarled at me. "Ready to roll over?"

"Dad," I said, almost choking on the word. "I overheard you arguing with Mother last night. I stayed over after I took her out to dinner."

I`d wanted to do something nice for her birthday while Peter went out to a business meeting. Mother and I returned home from dinner so late that I`d decided not to commute back to Brooklyn until morning.

The silence on his end spread like ink on water.

"I know how painful it must be. I never, ever suspected it. I`m shocked, really. I can see how much you love Mom. She must love you very much or she wouldn`t have tried to smooth things over. Maybe you and I didn`t always agree about things, but you were always a good father."

Relatively good, I thought to myself as the uncomfortable silence on the other end of the line deepened. Despite his stubborn aversion to my artistic endeavors, I still thought of Peter as a decent person. He spent more time with me than many of my friends` fathers, who were so enmeshed in their businesses that their families became an afterthought. They served the almighty dollar rather than the dollar serving them.

The long silence ended with a deep grunt from Peter. "You`re damn right. It was a deep disappointment. If you`re so grateful, then you`d follow my advice."

It was my turn to simmer in silence. Obviously, he didn`t understand my shock.

Apparently he`d accidentally awakened Mother before the row broke out. She mentioned later that she`d intended to tell him I was staying over. But I`d awakened to his loud baritone voice yelling, "Quit your goddamn sniveling."

"John`s your brother and you act like you`re happy he`s dead," Mother yelled back.

"I am happy! That son of a bitch came sniffing around whenever I went out of town on business." Father`s voice went up the scale as he ranted. "Don`t give me that bullshit about him looking out for you while I was gone. Do you think I`m so stupid that I don`t know that bastard kid of yours is his, not mine?"

The statement took a moment to penetrate. That bastard kid was *me*.

My mother`s sweet voice dripped with venom. "Do you think I`m so stupid I didn`t know you knew?"

What the hell? Mother seemed almost to agree with Father. I could hardly breathe through the cloud of my disbelief. Surely they must have said these hurtful things in anger.

"I saw to it that he moved out of town and away from you and this kid of his," he said.

"Do you think I don`t know you threatened all the merchants in town? I heard you tell one that if he advertised in John`s paper you`d foreclose on his outstanding loan. Or reconsider his credit requests. You drove John away, all right. I`ve always hated you for sending Petey`s father away."

I felt as if someone had knocked the wind out of me. Uncle John was my biological father and my stepfather is Peter! I considered for a moment how Uncle John must have struggled to pay for my schooling while my stepfather, the man I called father, refused to pay for my degree in journalism and hoarded his money. That was another long, hurtful story. I wanted to jump up from bed and intervene in the quarrel, but I settled for rolling over and covering my head with a pillow. I rose extra early, started coffee for my mother, and headed back to New York City on the first train.

I stewed as the train clacked along, my emotions joggling this way and that. On the negative side, Father was never cruel, at least not physically, but his strong opinions caused him to browbeat people for whatever he wanted. If he`d had more than one son, perhaps he could have allowed me my interests in art and literature. A highly successful banker, my father carried his title, President of Maryland First Fiduciary Savings, the biggest bank in the state of Maryland, with pride. Being his only son, he insisted I had to follow in his footsteps. Most of our arguments stemmed from this fact.

Finally, I decided that by taking over the helm of the magazine, I`d not only honored my deep interest in the arts, I`d also honored my biological father by rejecting the lucrative banking career nurtured by my legal father. It was no wonder that Peter was so angry and bitter. It took only a few moments to realize that deep in my heart, I owed both my fathers a lot. Uncle John had not only scraped by to give me a university education through his secret scholarship, he`d probably protected Aunt Millie from his misdeeds with my mother, and helped my mother and me as well. And the fact that Father admitted he`d driven his brother out of business made it all the more difficult for me to ever go back to work for him. He was using the same dirty tactics on me. Running the magazine now held more than a particle of intrigue for me, a task synchronous with the writing life I`d worked so hard to launch. If Uncle John hadn`t died, I might have been mired in the banking life with Peter for ages. For this, I double owed him.

I cleared my throat and forced myself to speak. "You taught me to be hardworking and resourceful. But I have my own interests and talents. I`m sorry these remind you of . . . Uncle John."

Peter`s bitter laugh rattled my nerves. "It`s not so much that you remind me of him, Petey. It`s that you need to learn there are more important things in the world than to scribble pretty pictures and entertaining stories. I also raised you as my own to keep your mother from embarrassing herself and to deprive my brother from beating me."

Peter always kept his eyes on the prize, I had to hand that to him. "What are you talking about, beating you?"

"I`m talking about winning and losing. If he`d taken you and your mother, it would mean that he beat me, and believe me, nobody but nobody beats me."

"Hold on, you`re saying that Mom wanted to go to Uncle John, but you used me to keep her for yourself?"

"She couldn`t go to John; John had Millie. Even so, your mother belonged to me, and I wasn`t about to let her get out of line because she loved the half-wit`s stupid poetry. I always told her "try eating poetry and see how it fills you up."

I sighed. Every insult Peter directed at John and my mother basically galled me too. Did this man ever give up?

"Look, apparently it hurts you because I love art and literature as much as you love banking and business. But this doesn`t mean I don`t ignore your accomplishments or respect you. . . love you. . . any less. You`re making it really hard to love you now, but when I was a child—"

The line clicked abruptly and buzzed with a dial tone. I gently put my receiver on the cradle and sighed again.

Jason returned from the pressroom, took one look at me and said, "Syndicate, man."

"What?" I snapped back.

Used to me going up and down with breaking events, Jason diplomatically ignored my rudeness. "Write a regular Art Exposé column. It would indirectly advertise the contest nationwide. Hell, maybe even worldwide. Syndication`s where the money`s at."

I never considered syndication before. Jason just might have something there. Maybe I could use Classic Art Exposé`s old contacts and put out some feelers to newspapers. We`d be under significant pressure to write a weekly, biweekly, or even a monthly column, but it might be the substantial financial boost we needed.

"Hey," I said. "You forgot to say simple. . ." I gave Jason a fond punch on the shoulder. "Thanks, my friend. You`ve done more to help this operation than I have."

Shirley and Evie walked in during the last bit of conversation. "Operation? Dr. Jason? I think I`ll stick with an apple a day," Shirley quipped. Jason stuck his tongue out at her.

"We may as well have a staff meeting," I said. "Jason has the great idea of trying to syndicate a regular AE column to help meet our financial deadline."

Evie waved her hand and hopped up and down like a schoolgirl. "Print a separate magazine or even a book with all the stories and pictures from the contest. Get a national distributor to place them in bookstores or sell them mail order through CAE and other magazines," she said. "For one thing, all the writers and their families and friends would like a copy. Some people might even buy them for the artwork."

Yeah," Shirley said. "Sell them for a buck or two."

"All those color plates in one publication would cost more than a buck or two, but we might be able to work something out here with the printers` union to keep the expense down," I said. "We`re already set up with the plates from the magazine, so we may as well do a special edition."

Jason nodded. "And we could do some advertising for the special edition to make up for the expense. It`s a shame John limited advertising. He never liked the cluttered look. It helped when we raised the rates, but a special edition would give us a chance to use advertising to our advantage. Maybe we should aim for one special edition every year."

Jason never let my brain rest. "I`ll have to sleep on this. So, what`s the word on the latest contest, ladies?"

"I guess we`re definitely known as the art mag with the weird stories," Shirley said. "For the last edition, the sweet 'Morning by the Stream` painting only inspired a flood of horror, suspense, and paranormal stories like 'Nicor,` except for one straight-up romance and one well-written but not very interesting story about married couples divorcing."

"If weird sells more magazines, always go with the weird," Jason said. We all laughed for a moment, until Evie stuck her finger into the art book and opened it. "Whaddya think?" She held up a plate of *The Knife Grinder* (*Principle of Scintillation*) by Ukrainian artist Kasimir Malevich.

The bright cubist painting dazzled Jason. "Cool, man," he said.

I nodded. "Let`s do it."

I had my doubts about always picking dark or odd stories—the contest was supposed to be open to all genres. It would be interesting to see what sort of stories the Malevich painting would inspire.

I ripped through the blue shade of the constraints of color.

MASTERPIECE

THE HAUNCH-SLAPPING AROMA OF beef stew emanated from the tavern`s kitchen. Usually all I could enjoy was the scent. But this day was different and my stomach did somersaults as I stepped through the door.

Boris, the tavern keeper, wiped his hands on a rag and waved his arms at me. "Out, I`ve told you a hundred times we don`t feed starving artists here."

I swaggered a bit on my way to the bar and lay a gold piece down hard, making it clank against the polished wood. "Give me a bowl of stew and a mug of beer."

"Kasimir, will miracles never cease? Where`d you get the gold?" Boris pocketed the money and before I could answer his question he said, "All right, this pays your previous debt—a bowl of stew and a mug of Boris`s fine brew coming up." He returned with a steaming bowl and a sweaty mug.

I pulled my mother`s old silver spoon from my pocket and dug in. Boris watched me with his chin propped on his hands. "Kasimir," he said, "you have a reputation as one of the best artists in the land. I`ve seen you perfectly reproduce almost any image, so why is it you never have any money?"

"Unfortunately, my reputation doesn`t yet assure me any income," I mumbled with my mouth full, "but it did get me a commission to paint a portrait of the mayor`s daughter." I held up a hand and swallowed. "He wants it finished in time for his wife`s birthday so he can present it to her in front of the entire town."

Boris blinked and stared through me as he always does when he`s trying to find an answer. "That`s wonderful. If the mayor is satisfied, everyone of means will ask you to paint their children`s portraits." He picked the stoneware bowl and turned away to refill it.

When he returned with my stew, I said, "The problem is, it sometimes costs more for the paints and canvases than my payment for the finished work. Then if I want to paint, I have to rely on taking what I can get for other work to replenish my supplies."

"So why don`t you just charge more? Make sure your commission is enough to cover your materials."

"Often people offer me only room and board with a reduced fee. When I`m lucky, a patron offers me a commission for a portrait or a mural. Only then am I assured of getting enough money to buy my materials."

I shoveled down the rest of the stew like there was no tomorrow. I held the bowl out for another refill. Boris gave me his famous "you`d best go now" look. Then he sighed and went to fill it.

I sometimes considered other ways to earn a living, but I couldn`t imagine not painting every day. Ever since I started scribbling with bits of charcoal in my childhood, I felt alive and fulfilled. I`d always been a creator. What else could give me that feeling?

Boris had been trying to marry off his daughter for years. When he returned with the second bowl of stew, he played matchmaker. "Once you start painting the mayor`s daughter, you`ll need a wife to take care of you."

If her mustache wasn`t thicker than mine, I might have considered it, if only to keep my bowl full of stew.

I wracked my brain for another excuse to avoid his offer and held up my mug for a refill. "I often sleep in someone`s barn when I can`t pay rent, and no woman would put up with that."

"Maybe after this job you`ll be able to pay rent steadily."

"Yes, but the mayor has to like my painting before I can even hope to get another job. What if he doesn`t like it and I become the laughingstock of the town?"

"With your talent? Boris scoffed. "No chance. All you have to do is sell more paintings at a higher price. Soon you`ll be painting royalty."

❦

When I began to paint the portrait of the mayor`s daughter, he told me I could sleep in his barn. This was good news because the well-kept barn wasn`t as drafty and cold as most. I knew he might send me some table scraps occasionally as well.

Because his wife`s birthday celebration was scheduled in only two weeks, I purchased an already primed canvas. I couldn`t gesso it myself as usual, because I didn`t have time to wait for it to dry. I stretched the canvas, readying it to receive my skillful brushstrokes, gathered my paints and brushes, and marched with pride from the barn to the mayor`s fine house. I knocked on the door, confident of painting the best portrait of his daughter ever.

A sour-faced housekeeper opened the door. "Servants use the rear door," she huffed. This was not the first time my appearance had inspired door slamming. But this time the back door hung open for me, revealing a large, airy kitchen where two cooks and a young maid were preparing food that smelled so good I lingered to beg for a taste. The housekeeper grabbed me by the arm, steered me from the kitchen and through a dining room; and stopped before a tall wooden door. "She`s in there."

When I opened the door, I was again impressed by room`s size and the French provincial furnishings scattered throughout. With her back turned to me, the mayor`s daughter gazed at the sky through one of four tall windows. She wore a blue dress decorated with red ribbon, the proper gown for a portrait.

Although the girl must have heard me come in, she didn`t turn to greet me. I set up my easel, opened my paint box, mixed some oils on my palette, and asked if she was ready for me to begin. As she slowly turned to face me, I was mesmerized by her beauty. An artist always appreciates beauty, but her radiance was all-encompassing. Her face overwhelmed me, made me want to surrender to those fogbound eyes, those cherub cheeks, those pouty lips. I had painted dozens of pretty women but I`d never felt my heart soar like this before. Then she spoke in the voice of an angel, and her beauty intensified.

"Hello, I`m Julia. What`s your name?"

"Kasimir Malevich," I stuttered, because her beauty made me almost speechless. I could only point to the chair where I wanted her to sit.

My ardor made my fingers fly as I sketched her outline in pencil. I stirred a bit of extra oil into my paints to keep them pliable for blending. I knew the portrait wouldn`t be dry in time for the celebration, but it would be finished and could dry wherever displayed.

Now that I could see Julia`s face, I adjusted the hues for her gown, primary colors that were simple enough, but to match her exquisite gray eyes I spent a considerable amount of time, and also for the glossy blue-black hair and nearly snow-white complexion. With my palette in order, I took a deep breath and started to paint her portrait. I could feel the heat of her eyes staring at me as I worked, and I wondered if she could feel the heat that threatened to burst from my loins. I couldn`t help my randy thoughts; blushing a deep red, I kept my face turned to the canvas.

I nearly fainted of fright—more than a fear of failure, I think I feared success. If my painting was as brilliant as Julia, how could I ever create another portrait as fine? If my daydreams of Julia were made manifest, how could I ever love another of my own station? My circumstances as a starving artist didn`t boost my ego in any way. I peered at her face again. She appeared to be about seventeen years old—at the ripe old age of twenty-two, I felt almost too old for her, and at the very least, outclassed. To be on the safe side, I attempted to do my job, praying to ignore this beauty from heaven and to simply finish her portrait.

"Kasimir, I`m surprised that an artist like you is so bashful. Artists go around painting naked girls all the time, don`t they?" When I looked up at the sound of her voice, Julia looked directly into my eyes, placed her index finger in her mouth, and sucked on it. She batted her eyelashes at me as she removed her finger and inspected it. This lovely creature was definitely no angel.

And Julia wasn`t content to sit peacefully or in boredom, as was the case with most of my subjects. She was a sprite, a mischievous vixen who wanted to play, and she continued to sexually provoke me by displaying her ankles, or smiling sweetly at me and then suddenly flicking a long, sensuous tongue across her full lips. When she sucked on her finger again, I almost lost control. Where was this girl`s mother? Why didn`t the family provide a chaperone? But I was too embarrassed to ask, afraid I might get Julia or myself into even more trouble.

As the days went by, Julia became bolder with her advances. I resisted them only by constantly reminding myself of my place as a poor artist. I knew if I surrendered to Julia`s charms, the mayor would probably have me killed, if she didn`t reject me and laugh at me first.

Finally, the last day of painting arrived. I needed only to do some blending and the portrait would be finished. Just in the nick of time, for Julia`s mother`s birthday celebration was the following day.
I entered the room where the painting stood and started my blending. Perhaps I`d used a little too much linseed oil in the paints, for they were softer than I expected.

Julia entered the room wearing only a dressing gown and wanted to know if she could see the portrait.

I wondered at her boldness, but I lay the portrait on the floor in front of the window where the sunlight would fall on it, illuminating her image.

She stood beside me and we both gazed at the perfect likeness. "Brilliant," she said, untying the cord of her dressing gown to let it fall onto the painting. I knew it would smear the wet colors, but at the sight of her perfect body, I could only say one word. "B-beautiful."

We embraced and sank to the floor atop the dressing gown and painting. We had studied each other day after day, and desiring one another more each day than the last, we fell upon each other hungrily. If I could paint the picture of our union it would have to include the solar system, the stars, perhaps even the entire universe. . . at last, we both moved beyond descriptive words and images into pure ecstasy.

Afterward, we lay in each other`s arms for a few sweet moments, until Julia broke the spell when she stood and picked up the dressing gown to wrap herself in. I stood up too, grappling with my trousers, afraid that someone would burst into the room. We both looked down at the portrait at the same time. Fortunately, the canvas had held up to our passion but our movements had smeared all the colors together. My happiness soared away like a raven into the dark woods. Julia felt my dismay and left me too, apparently not wanting to share the responsibility for wrecking weeks of work.

Dumbfounded by this turn of events, I cursed my poor judgment. Why had I given in to Julia at the last moment? The mayor expected a painting of his daughter the next day to present to his wife before the entire town at her party.

I didn`t know what to do. I wanted to run away, but I had no place to go, and little money. I tried to think of a way out of this dilemma, but no ideas came. The mayor came to the barn the next morning in a jolly mood, wanting to preview the painting. I insisted he wait to see it unveiled with everyone else, for good luck, I explained. He seemed charmed by my eccentricity, but I sweat like a pig all day, wondering what to do next. I had visions of the mayor having me beaten or perhaps arrested for fraud. I`d taken his advance and had nothing but a smeared canvas to give in exchange.

I tried to see Julia, but a maidservant told me she wasn`t to be disturbed. I ached to the bone with misery that she could walk away from what we had shared yesterday. And yet I understood. Why should she risk everything she had for a talented but unknown artist?

I crept near the house to assess the situation as the celebration for the mayor`s wife began. As I watched through a tall, many-paned window, all the townspeople began to arrive at the grand house. The mayor`s groundskeeper set up a makeshift stage of sorts in the great room and an orchestra tuned up and then began to play a waltz. A few early, enthusiastic revelers began to whirl about. I crept away again, sick to my stomach. What in the world would I do when it was time to unveil the painting? Could I somehow delay the presentation? What if I said the painting needed to dry, or even that it needed to age another week? But it wouldn`t matter because I couldn`t produce another painting so quickly in either case. I was stuck like a fly in ointment. In despair, I rushed at the painting and slashed through the paint with the handle of a paintbrush, wishing I could scratch it into oblivion.

When a large number of people had assembled and I could hear that the orchestra retired for refreshment by the quiet that flooded the estate, the mayor sent his manservant to the barn to retrieve me. Resigned to my fate, I covered the portrait with a sheet and carried it with an easel to the makeshift stage where the musicians` instruments leaned upon their chairs. Numb, I stood the easel at the front center of the stage and placed the draped portrait on it. I had no idea what I could possibly say to make a difference.

With many happy pleasantries, the mayor introduced me as the soon-to-be famous artist who painted his daughter`s portrait as a gift to his lovely wife on her fortieth birthday. I stood with my heart pounding, avoiding everyone`s eyes. The orchestra percussionist returned to his seat and played a drum roll that stretched out until I thought my head might explode. To applause and the lofting of glasses in a toast, the mayor took hold of the fabric and whisked it off the smeared painting.

A dead silence more potent than any sound filled the room. I looked up and saw Boris and his daughter across the room, looking at me with pity. The guests stared at one another with guarded looks, and then at me with outright astonishment. No one knew what to think of the jumble of colors that covered the canvas.

The mayor frowned. His gracious wife, almost a twin to gorgeous Julia, stood with one hand over her mouth, her eyebrows raised higher than a spitting cat`s back. The guests began to chatter. Suddenly I heard Julia`s angelic voice cut through the air like a bell.

"Brilliant, absolutely beautiful," she cooed to the crowd. "Just like I told Kasimir to paint me—as he saw me, not how I look." Dressed in the same blue and scarlet gown I had painted her in, she drifted to me like an angel, took my arm, and nudged me to turn so we could also admire her portrait.

Someone in the crowd shouted, "Yes, brilliant!" Another said, "True art!" And another trilled, "Bravo, a masterpiece!"

Before long, loud applause pattered through the room like a refreshing summer rain. The mayor`s wife took my hand and bid me to take a bow after thanking me for the unique and revolutionary portrait. I never dreamed, never even dared to consider such a happy ending for this misadventure. As we waltzed the night away, Julia confessed that she had only withdrawn to plot with the sour-faced housekeeper (who had also served as her nanny) to find a way to elope with me. My heart went boom and would never beat for anyone else ever again.

After that night, my work earned acclaim throughout Europe and I became known as a great modernist painter. Soon, I easily won the hand of the mayor`s daughter. I`m often asked about my painting technique, but it remains our greatest secret. Once I have my colors blended on the canvas, Julia and I lay it on the floor, cover it with her old dressing gown, and make love atop the painting. And now I paint as many canvases as I can because of all the joy they bring us.

13

✿

On A Roll

THE DAY OUR PRINTERS BUNDLED up the new issue for delivery, the City of Brooklyn Department of Streets and Sanitation began digging up the street in front of our truck dock entrance.

"Hey, who`s the man responsible?" I shouted at a guy shimmying on a jackhammer.

He pointed to a short dignified-looking man wearing a suit, standing near a work truck with a clipboard in hand.

A suit on a road digging crew meant Peter Rizzo was behind it. I couldn`t believe he`d start another conflict so soon. I made a note to stop calling him because the only result that would ever satisfy him is if I quit the magazine and rolled over.

I eased over to the truck. "Excuse me sir, I need to get our delivery truck in and out of this driveway. Are you going to provide a ramp?" I pointed to one of the holes, already almost four feet deep.

"Ramps? We never provide ramps. You got adequate notice about when this work would start. You should have figured out what to do by now." He turned to one of the foremen and barked an order.

I held my hands out in bewilderment. "Sir, I never received notice."

"Tough titty, son," he said, barely paying me any mind.

I had one day to figure out where to get some sheet steel or some sort of ramp. Could I reach over this guy`s head at the city government? At the very worst, I figured we could hand carry the boxes to the truck. After all, there weren`t that many boxes, but it was important to our reputation to get the magazine distributed on time.

A call to City Hall sent me in circles that yielded nothing. Apparently, the guy in the suit was the person who had the last say about road construction issues, and he clearly wasn`t going to yield. Peter must have paid him a pretty penny to do his dirt.

I asked Jason if he had any ideas. We walked around the building once. We stood in front of a window-lined wall designed to let light in, a common architectural feature in these old factory buildings. Finally, Jason lit up a reefer and said, "Simple man. See those windows?" He pointed to the wall. "They had to put a lintel beam above them to support the roof and wall weight, so all you need to do is knock out those windows and the lower wall. You`ll have a brand-new doorway for your truck."

"Thanks. I`d never thought of that in a million years."

Jason laughed. "But that`s the hard way, man. The easy way is that I simply cart them out by hand. Our delivery truck only picks up about thirty-six boxes of a hundred magazines each."

I slapped myself on the forehead. I was always so busy with editing work and formatting details that I`d forgotten that our shipments weren`t very large.

So when our driver arrived for the boxes, Jason stacked them four high on a dolly and carried them to the truck by hand six times. "I could use the exercise anyway, man," he told me. The remainder of our subscriptions were always handled by Shirley and Evie, taken in two boxes and dropped to a newsstand vendor nearby who saw to it that the others were distributed around the borough. Any new subscriptions that were ordered late were posted by Shirley or Evie at a branch post office just down the street. What had seemed like a huge predicament was really just a little bump in the road, not the huge obstacle my stepfather must have imagined, or that I conjured up with my anxiety about it.

But Peter managed to catch up with me another way. Just before our driver pulled away with his load, a police cruiser arrived to ticket my truck for blocking the sidewalk.

I fumed when Jason came inside to show me the citation, but he told me to relax. "The judge will throw this citation out if you appear in court. Even the cop said this citation is BS."

I called O`Neill and left a message with his secretary. He called me back later that afternoon. "Hey, Pete. Looks like the cop was directed by his sergeant, who was called by someone in City Hall, to cite your driver. They`re trying to do something illegal. City code 277:14, Section 11, fourth paragraph from the top states, `Where an entrance or exit exists for a vehicle, said vehicle shall have access to the roadway and cannot be blocked.` Then the code goes on to list sidewalks as something that cannot block an entrance, so don`t worry about the citation. Have the driver go to the court date shown on the citation and the judge will throw it out."

The following morning, the street crew patched up the holes without any further work and minus the guy in the suit, confirming my suspicions about Peter being involved. Maybe O`Neill`s call to City Hall had shaken things up a bit.

Anyway, for our nearly delayed issue, we had selected a charming light romance as our winning story. The tale featured the artist and the painting, a quirky diversion redeeming us from the dark ambiance of the preceding stories, and one appealing to both male and female readers. The author had cleverly inserted a little alternate history about modernist painting as well. Though we`d struggled with distractions and hit a plateau during the last few issues, we started gaining subscriptions and contest entries again.

On this round, we engaged in more deliberation than usual when choosing the next contest painting. Jason pulled the art book open to another maritime picture. I figured we`d had enough sailing and seagoing themes for now. He tried again, and opened the page with a flourish to a rather haunting painting, *Avenue de Clichy: Five O`Clock in the Evening* by Louis Anquetin, a French painter. Shirley and Evie oohed and aahed their approval.

"It`s intriguing, and the painting will probably spawn the dark stories that Classic Art Exposé is becoming known for," I said. "That`s a yes. Let`s call it a day."

Vincent [van Gogh] met Louis Anquetin, Henri de Toulouse-Lautrec, Camille Pissaro, Émile Bernard, Paul Gaugin, Paul Signac, and Georges Seurat. The colour and light of the Impressionist and Post-Impressionist painting and the carnivalesque action captured made him giddy.

—Modris Eksteins, *Solar Dance*

LOOKING OUT FOR HARRY

VIDOCQ'S EYES ASSESSED ME COOLLY as he made his inquiry in a soothing voice. "I must talk with your brother about a woman he may have had contact with in Calais. Can you help me?"

I nervously toyed with my door handle, avoiding the detective`s gaze. "Of course, I`ll be glad to help."

"Relax, Henri. Please don`t consider this an interrogation; think of it as a conversation between friends."

"Friends, eh. Maybe we used to be friends. The day you became a snitch for the police, our friendship died."

Vidocq looked away. "If you tell me what happened, I`ll do everything in my power to make certain things go easy for you and your brother."

"I had to do it."

"Do what?"

"Stop Harry before he did what he told me he would do. I promised our mother on her deathbed twenty years ago that I`d take care of him. We were only fifteen at the time."

"I recall you telling me about your mother`s death when we first met."

"Yes, I`ve looked after Harry ever since. I always kept my promise and looked out for him."

Vidocq looked at me the way detectives and informants always do when they try to get into your head. Only he was worse than others, because we had shared a flat for a time when we were students at the university and I could see he felt that he knows me well.

"So, Harry has killed before?"

"Of course not. I`ve always seen to it that he doesn`t act on his impulses, just as I promised."

"Then you have nothing to share?"

"Only that I`ve made certain Harry hasn`t hurt anyone."

"I should like to talk to your brother." Vidocq`s eyes drilled into mine as he reached into his breast pocket and produced a business card. "Have him call the lieutenant at his convenience, and they`ll send me here again."

I nodded. Vidocq brushed a finger on the brim of his hat to bid me good-bye and turned on his heel like a soldier.

I closed the door carefully, making certain it made no noise. I paced the room like a panther. Why was the Sûreté Nationale questioning me? Who was this woman that Vidocq alluded to? She could be a lady of the night, or some secretary or nanny, or even a socialite who rubbed shoulders with the world`s elite celebrities and politicians. Harry could charm the panties off any woman, just as Vidocq used to do before he recanted. The only way to find her would be to retrace Harry`s footsteps.

My brother Harry had arrived in Paris from Calais just the day before yesterday and already he`d wanted to harm someone. I thought to trace his trail and find those he had talked to would be no problem. But Harry had visited with dozens of girls since his arrival. Good old gregarious Harry, always engaging the nearest attractive mademoiselle in repartee.

He had called me along his way and said, "I`m upset. I feel like killing her." Harry has made this threat before—haven`t we all done so casually? In the background, I heard the tinkle of female laughter as he shared his intention. Because I protect my brother from evil, I knew when he said he wanted to kill someone, a feminine someone, that she must be thoroughly evil. Otherwise, Harry would never breathe those words.

He explained his system to me long ago. "I work on the law of averages. If I wait until I see the perfect one,

I may only talk to a single woman all day," he`d told me. "And then if she rejects me, the day is over. If I talk to every desirable woman I encounter, the odds are with me. Out of the many whom I ask for a date, I`m sure to receive acceptance from one or two. I usually keep my appointment with the choicest one."

Obviously, Harry played the numbers game by dating many women in a short timeframe.

I had to find out quickly who he wanted to kill and why. Vidocq hadn`t said whether someone had died, so perhaps someone had felt threatened. I traced his footsteps backward, and took the next train to Calais. I began my investigation at the docks where Harry had debarked from the Dover ferry yesterday. I showed his picture to the ferry service ticket taker, as hostlers and tourists surged around us with freight and luggage in the stinky, fishy air.

"Do you remember this man?" I asked him, and discovered Harry had befriended a hostess, a friend of this man, on the evening ferry. She had spoken to her friend about allowing Harry to spend the night with her.

Once I found lovely Mademoiselle Fontaine at her flat by the river and inquired about Harry, she said, "Oh, Harry, I just love Harry, I have nothing but good things to say about him."

But I could trace Harry`s footsteps from Mademoiselle Fontaine`s doorstep. I could sense which way he strolled from her apartment because I understood him so well. Sure enough, right around the corner from Mlle. F.`s flat stood a beauty college. I stopped in. The perky blonde receptionist was young and giggly, as were the girls poised around the room with their scissors and combs, playing with one another`s hair. "Did any of you see this man two nights ago?" I showed her a photo of Harry and she circled the room to show it to all the girls.

A petite, flat-chested brunette with her hair pinned up in a bun came forward, not Harry`s type at all. "I remember him. My friends, Shirley and Giselle, and I made a date with him, but he never showed up. Is something wrong?"

"He`s my brother and I`m trying to help him," I said. "Did he say where he wanted to go next? Was he angry when he left?" I needed some idea of his state of mind. I hoped I wasn`t too late. If so, this would be the first time in twenty years. It was nearly twenty years ago today that I made the promise to my mother on her deathbed to look after Harry. It seemed like yesterday and I can picture every detail of her passing, and of my assurances to her.

I left the beauty college and headed intuitively in the direction I surmised Harry had traveled. He must have headed for the train station to catch the early train to Paris. He had insisted upon finding his way to my flat, wanting to enjoy the adventure, he said. I knew him quite well, as we`d been born five minutes apart, me first, then Harry. Mother used to call me the evil twin and the two of us double trouble because of the mischief I masterminded as a small boy. But once I showed her that Harry was truly the evil twin, she asked me to look out for him. Harry had this monstrous habit of threatening to kill people at the smallest provocation, but I made certain he didn`t hurt anyone. If Mother were still alive, she`d praise me for stopping Harry from killing so many people.

I clearly recalled the promise I made on her dying day.

"Promise me you`ll make sure He—Ha—Harry won`t hurt anyone," she`d begged in a weak, reedy voice, lifting her head from the pillow for emphasis. At first, I thought she was trying to say Henri, my name, though I knew she meant Harry.

"I look after myself quite well, thank you very much," Harry said, looking at our mother disdainfully from the doorway.

I never could understand our mother giving us such similar names, but she did, and as she slipped away, she couldn`t keep them straight. But she remembered that I was tough and that Harry needed someone to look out for him.

"A promise like this means I`ll have to devote my life to looking out for him." I said. "But you know I will."

Harry cast me another withering look.

Our mother knew what her request entailed. "Please just promise me. . ." she said, her voice even raspier and weaker this time.

She passed away shortly after my promise. Almost immediately after the funeral, keeping an eye on Harry became a full-time job. Sometimes I wanted to give up and let him get what he deserved, but a promise is a promise.

Mother first became concerned when the authorities had accused twelve-year-old Harry of killing a little girl a few years younger than us. She`d borrowed his bicycle without asking. Harry let his temper get the best of him and said he felt mad enough to kill her in front of four witnesses.

When the little girl`s mutilated body turned up the next day, everyone assumed Harry had committed the crime because of his angry statement. I knew for a fact that it wasn`t Harry. Other than his threat, there wasn`t any evidence, so Harry wasn`t charged. Harry had threatened to kill a lot of people these last twenty years, and a lot of people had died. But not by Harry`s hand. I`ll guarantee he didn`t kill a single one. After all, I should know because I`m looking out for him.

I took the next train back to Paris—the same one that Harry had reservations on. There was no chance I`d find any of the women Harry had encountered as he travelled, so I settled down for a nap and afterward, lazily pulled out my sketchbook to draw caricatures of my fellow passengers until we reached the city. At the station, I followed my nose. On the next corner stood a betting parlor, and I figured Harry wouldn`t pass by without stopping to bet on something. I went inside. "Have any of you gentlemen seen my brother?" I showed his picture around the room.

"Yeah, yesterday," said a man wearing a pink shirt. "He won big, and left with a hooker named Polly."

My next step, find Polly. Simple. Because when the whores weren`t working they shopped, sometimes for clothes, but usually for drugs.

I went to the red-light district where the whores and addicts hung out. I approached a man loitering on a corner who dressed the part of a pimp with a fancy, tailor-made suit and a wide-brim hat. I handed him a fistful of francs. "I`m looking for Polly. Do you know where she is?"

"What do you want with a tart like her? I`ve got some nice girls right around the corner."

He didn`t expect what I offered him next. My knuckles crushed his nose and blood spurted onto his fancy clothes. "My brother doesn`t hang around with tarts," I informed him, "now tell me where Polly is." I made a fist again and drew my arm back.

"As you wish. Polly came here a couple of hours ago, and she copped enough dope to kill a horse," he said, wiping blood from his nose using the sleeve of his fine coat. He gave me her address. I gave him a few more francs. "For the cleaning," I said.

Polly lived atop a tavern called Sourire—better known as Smiley`s, after the English gent who owned it. I knocked hard on her door. No answer. Worried she might be the one, I went back downstairs to the bar. "Are you acquainted with Polly, who lives upstairs?" I asked the bartender.

"Who`s asking?"

I reached into my pocket and set the notes on the bar.

"Over there," he pointed. There Polly sat, tipping back a pint with an uncouth-looking character in dreadlocks and rags. Harry`s type all right—long, endless legs clad in fishnet stockings. A skirt so flouncy and short, she`d wasted her time when she put it on. Pierced ears with giant gold hoops, as if she were a gypsy queen. Her hair wasn`t blonde at all, but a deep blue-black that caused her milky white skin to stand out like a lighted movie screen in a darkened cinema. All the better to show off the purplish lipstick and lavender eye shadow that highlighted her deep cornflower eyes.

I came right out and said, "What did you do to piss Harry off?"

Polly glared at me as if I were insane. "Harry pissed off? You`ve got to be kidding. I can`t imagine Harry upset about anything. He`s such a nice guy."

"So where did he go? I`m his twin brother," I said in answer to her questioning look. She pointed in the direction Harry had gone, and I hurried in that direction. Did Harry ever fool Polly, I thought. If she only knew how often Harry lost his temper, she wouldn`t be calling Harry a nice guy.

The clock behind the bar showed five o`clock, and the avenue became crowded with people rushing home or to their favorite café or bar. I pushed my way through the crowd, searching for a clue—any clue—to help me find the woman Harry had become angry enough with to kill.

A few blocks down the avenue, I came across a sign that read "Girls, Girls and More Girls." I knew Harry couldn't pass up a sign like this. I paid my entry fee and entered a dark, smelly, smoke-filled club. The "girls" turned out to be transvestites. I must be getting close to whoever Harry wanted dead. If he ended up with one of these lady-men and he stuck his hand down her crotch that might have been enough to piss him off. *Oui*, I figured, I'm real close.

I flashed Harry's photo around the pub, and as usual, they recognized him immediately. A group of lady men told me how Harry had come in the day before with a blonde on his arm and had bought champagne for every one of them, a treat they usually had to hustle to get someone to buy.

I thought my search over, but now I had another blonde to find. I continued my trek down the avenue until I came across an outdoor café. I knew Harry just loved to sit outside and drink coffee while the girls paraded by.

I sat at an empty table, and when the waitress came over, I showed her Harry's picture. She recognized him right away. "He came in yesterday with Sheila."

Now I was getting somewhere. "Sheila who?"

The waitress shrugged. "Sheila the model, that's all I know."

Not much help.

After she poured me a cup of coffee, she thought of something and turned back. "Sheila's modeling at the museum," she said.

I chuckled. "Which museum? Paris has more than one."

The waitress glared at me. "Musée du Louvre," she said in a tone that indicated I must be a moron. I tipped her though there was no need, thanked her, and rushed to the Louvre. I found Sheila modeling all right. She stood beside an ancient sarcophagus holding a bejeweled perfume bottle with an Egyptian name, surrounded by lights and cameras on tripods. At the sight of her, my feet became glued to the floor. She was the spitting image of the neighbor girl who got herself murdered twenty years ago. This had to be the woman Harry was pissed at. She must have returned to haunt me, I mean Harry. I could see why Harry wanted her dead, just like he wanted the girl dead twenty years ago.

I found a men's room and made my preparations, drawing from a vial the snake venom that would paralyze and then kill her. This would make great headlines, if only I had a snake handy to blame it on. But being a museum, everything here had died long ago.

I waited until Sheila finished her job, and as she walked toward the exit, I bumped into her. I pricked her arm with the needle. She jumped from the pain, but she could only glare at me as paralysis overtook her. A curator and some visitors surrounded her, rendering aid and making phone calls to Emergency Services.

But she died on the way to the hospital.

I had to give Harry the good news. When I finally reached him by telephone, we arranged to meet at a new bar he had made his hangout.

I thought of Mother smiling from heaven, proud that I killed Sheila so Harry wouldn`t do it. I know she`s watched me look after Harry all these years. Mother knew I never killed anyone for the fun of it. If I did, I`d be the evil twin, as she used to tease me. But Harry is the one who really wants to kill, and that makes *him* the evil twin. Helping my brother stay out of trouble is a good thing. I`ve done many good things in the last twenty years, and I`m sure I`ll do many more in the next twenty. The gates of heaven are going to open wide when I come knocking.

As soon as I walked into the crowded, frenetic bar to meet Harry, I observed him surrounded by people, as always. He rushed to my side.

"Henri, I was just sharing the good news. I`m marrying my soulmate, Sheila, the famous model. You have heard of her, no?"

Stunned, I could only smile at his announcement. Marriage! Harry had never mentioned this word before. I ordered a drink and when the topic changed and I could get a word in edgewise, I asked Harry what woman had made him angry. I didn`t mention the word "kill."

"Oh, I bet everything on a filly in the last race, and she came in second. I could have killed her right then, I was so upset, but an inquiry disqualified the winner, and my filly was declared first place," he said, nonchalantly waving his cigarette in the smoke-laden air.

Oh, Mother. I`ve made my first mistake. But hey, we all make mistakes, don`t we, Vidocq?

14

Stumbling Blocks or Stepping Stones?

WHEN WE HEARD A COMMOTION—laughter and catcalls—at the back of the building late one afternoon, Jason and I rushed to the pressroom. A few women of the night were parading their wares outside the pressroom windows.

"What`s going on? I demanded, exasperated with the noise.

"When we made inquiries, the girls offered us uh, suggestive poses and free bottles of wine," one of the printers said.

I didn`t know whether to laugh or cry. "Obviously Peter sent them to do this," I said to Jason. I motioned the printers to move away from the windows. "Back to work, you guys."

My order didn`t mean much since it wasn`t one of our print days and all anyone interrupted was another card game. The printers and my reformed transients ignored me and continued to hang out along the windows, laughing and making eyes at the girls.

Jason excused himself and returned to the office. When I didn`t think the situation could get any weirder, an unruly handful of men turned up, turning the spectacle into a party. The ladies, their wine, and their new johns soon wandered away. I noticed then that Jason had returned, a big smile lighting up his face.

"How did you cause that?"

"Simple, man. I called the local *Talk of the Town* radio show and told them about the free party in back of our building, courtesy of your father`s bank."

I didn`t know whether to laugh or cry again. "I`m not sure that was a good idea, Jace. On the other hand, there isn`t anything that Peter won`t take offense to, so no harm done."

After all, I`d always encouraged Jason to help run the business. If it weren`t for his help, I`d probably have crashed and burned long ago.

The printers returned to their card game and Jason and I returned to the office, where Shirley and Evie were still reading and arguing the merits of the latest contest shortlist.

"We picked only five favorites from almost five hundred stories this time," Shirley said. "Out of those, I think this one is the most interesting hands-down." She held out a dog-eared manuscript typewritten on onionskin paper. "Not necessarily the best writing, but the riveting whodunit plot makes up for any lack of literary pizzazz."

"Unique in your book sounds like another dark horse. Am I right?"

"Hmm-hmm," Shirley said with a wry smile. "I`m not one to challenge tradition."

Evie pulled a pretend pout. "That story`s pretty neat, but there`s a heartrending romance I liked better."

I asked Shirley to read a page from her favored manuscript. Her smooth reading voice paradoxically filled the office with simultaneous solace and mystery. I loved the protagonist`s point of view and the sudden plot twist of the climax. And as always, I enjoyed how the author had turned the artist`s ordinary daily scene inside out into an eerie tale.

"Let`s go for it," I said. "Any objections?"

"I`m in," Jason said.

Evie stuck her lip out further. "Oh, okay. I don`t wanna get left out of an almost unanimous vote. Hey, by the way—don`t you think the contest is making enough money now for a runner-up award?"

Jason and I looked at each other. "That might be a good idea, Pete. It`ll cost a little more, but it just might pay off as well."

"We may as well give it a shot," I said. "The second place award could be a flat fee, that way we wouldn`t risk much if our hopes for more entrants don`t pan out. In fact, I have some good news for you. Yesterday I got a call from The Village Spoke. The editor there subscribes to CAE, and they`d like to run the old contest stories in their weekly Arts Beat supplement, since so many have turned out to be local writers. They`re even willing to run some of the shortlisted stories. There`s nothing in it for us directly, but the publicity is good for both us and the writers. Jason, I leave this project up to you and the girls to figure out."

Jason circled his fingers into an okay sign. "Simple," we all said simultaneously, sharing a much-needed laugh.

"Hey, I`ve got a question for you all," I said. "I`m both a writer and an artist. In your opinion, do you have to be crazy to be an artist, or does being an artist drive you crazy?"

"Well, sure," Jason said, "there seem to be plenty of literary greats who have or who have had mental disorders, and many artists too. Mental instability and creativity plus intelligence seem to go hand in hand."

"Most writers and artists I know are pretty kinky." Evie giggled, blushing, and then turned her eyes downward.

"I think you mean eccentric," Shirley corrected her sister.

Evie giggled. "Great artists go crazy because they`re different!"

"Sure, different is one way of defining crazy. After all, if everyone acted weird then weird would be normal," Shirley said. "Weird would be ordinary."

"Exactly," Jason said.

"I believe that artists of all sorts are more socially awkward rather than outright insane," I added.

"I`m an artist and a musician. As far as I`m concerned, if most people are normal, I`m grateful to be considered `insane,`" Jason declared. He pretended to light and deeply inhale from an imaginary reefer cigarette to highlight his position.

"But who is qualified to fairly define sanity?" I asked. "Are doctors and psychologists any less afflicted than the rest of us? The sci-fi writer Phillip K. Dick writes a lot about `sanity` and the perception of reality, and his best novels have deep insights. The artistic life is an outlet for many creative people who can`t stand the artificiality and monotony of daily life."

Shirley and Evie nodded, and Jason added an afterthought. "Who can say they`ve never done anything crazy, or haven`t sometimes thought they might be insane themselves? I don`t see much difference between the `sane` and the `insane` except that the insane are interesting and unpredictable and the sane tend to be ordinary and predictable. To achieve a masterpiece in any craft, you have to go the extra mile and search beyond normal boundaries. To go the extra mile is to be obsessed, to be obsessed is to be insane."

"Good observation," I said. "I guess if we examine the lives of famous artists and writers, we find that most were obsessed with their craft. . . Well, I guess we better leave that tangent for now. What`s the verdict on artwork for the next contest?

Jason looked pleased, like the cat who`d just swallowed the canary. "How about the painting I wanted to use the last time? Napoleon oughta inspire some interesting stories."

I pulled the art book open and thumbed through pages until I found the plate of *Napoleon on Board the Bellerophon* by Sir William Quiller Orchardson. The quiet but commanding piece certainly had charisma. "Indeed. Indeed he will."

NAPOLEON ON BOARD THE BELLEROPHON
Sir William Quiller Orchardson, 1880

The truth is that [Orchardson`s] spaces—and, I confess, they are often ample enough— are seldom empty. They are filled with subtle colour modulations, with the infinite echoes of a harmony which never dies completely into silence.

—Walter Armstrong

THE IMPOSTER

A MAN WITH A SHOCK of gray hair and dabs of orange paint still damp on his white shirt and trousers sat down next to me. He dropped a faded, discolored envelope on the bar, one large enough to place unfolded letter-sized pages inside. Then the painter motioned for the bartender.

"I thought I`d found a goddamn treasure. I discovered a niche under the wallpaper but this was the only thing in it," he grumbled, pointing at the envelope, which seemed to be handmade from a large folded sheet of parchment.

"I wish you would`ve found a treasure so you could pay your tab," the bartender said, folding his arms across his ample belly.

I wondered why a tradesman would drink at this pricey tavern at the corner of Chartres and St. Louis Streets in the French Quarter. The painter pulled pages from the envelope and handed one to the bartender, who squinted and pulled his reading glasses down from his forehead.

"Jesus, Jasper, what kind of trash you bringing me? This is written in French." He threw the page on the bar.

Curious, I glanced at the upturned page. "I speak French. May I?"

The painter nodded and the bartender continued his lively verbal smackdown.

> *J`ai parlé à personne; juste regardé fixement au-dessus de la balustrade gauche jour après jour. Enfin j`ai été transféréau HMS Northumberland qui avait été indiqué pour me prendre.*
>
> Louis-Napoléon Bonaparte

Handwriting covered almost the entire page. I had to reread the first paragraph twice to be certain my translation was accurate.

> *I talked to no one, staring over the port railing day after day. Finally, I was transferred to the HMS Northumberland, a ship designated to take me into exile on St. Helena. On 7 August, I left the Bellerophon, where I spent over three weeks without ever landing in England. I then boarded the Northumberland, which sailed for St Helena to spend my remaining days on an island in the Atlantic Ocean, under British supervision.*
>
> Louis-Napoléon Bonaparte

If this document was authentic, it had historical importance and could be valuable. I figured I could coax the painter to give it to me for a few bucks and a few beers. I picked the page up off the bar, so it wouldn`t get wet. "Hey buddy, where`d you find this?"

The painter took the page from my fingers, placed it with the other pages, and put the envelope under his arm.

"I`m working at the Cabildo, repairing the fire damage. Can you believe it burned in 1948? It`s taken four years just to begin to clean up the mess. We have another year of work before we`re finished." He chugged the final bit of beer from his glass and stood to leave.

"Let me buy you another beer, Jasper," I said, reading his name in red embroidery over the left pocket of his shirt. Mention of the Cabildo and the letter itself piqued my curiosity. The Cabildo served as the headquarters of colonial government in New Orleans, and the final transfer of Louisiana Territory from France to the United States was held there in 1803. Before the Cabildo underwent another metamorphosis as a state museum in 1908, it served as a city hall, a courthouse, and a prison. Anything found in that building could be old and valuable.

"Just one more. I`ve got to get back to work." Jasper`s eyes told me he`d sit there and drink beer all afternoon if I was buying.

"You mentioned a niche that had been wallpapered over?"

"Yeah, I was stripping at least six layers of wallpaper, and once I got down to the plaster wall, there was a copper panel that I lifted out of the hole. I got excited, daydreaming of a hundred different treasures I might find in there. All I found was this crummy letter. Why the hell would anyone hide something like that?"

I could think of a thousand reasons even if poor Jasper couldn`t think of one. "Well, what will you do with it now?"

"Probably end up wiping my ass with it." He brushed the back of his hand across his mouth and stood to leave.

I offered him ten bucks. I could almost see the wheels turning in his head when I mentioned money. I hoped I hadn`t made a big mistake by showing my eagerness to acquire the document.

Jasper looked at me closely for the first time and dollar signs appeared in his eyes when he realized my clothing cost a month of his paychecks. "I can`t wipe my ass with ten bucks. How about I give you one page for twenty bucks?"

Afraid he might actually use the letter for toilet paper, I gave him a twenty-dollar bill, and he pulled the first page from the stuffed envelope and handed it to me.

"How much for all the pages?" I watched his mental wheels turning again.

"Ask me tomorrow." He turned on his heel and marched through the door.

I motioned to the barkeep. "Does Jasper the painter come here for lunch every day?"

"Yeah, lunch and dinner, he drinks them both here." The barkeep thought I wanted to start a conversation, because he began to relate the history of the building that housed the bar. "This is called the Napoleon House because the mayor, Girod, offered it to the Emperor in 1815."

New Orleans must have loved Napoleon. The Hotel St. Hélène, located next door, is "dedicated to the memory of Napoleon Bonaparte" according to a plaque I read there. For the first time in years, I congratulated myself for my ability to speak and read French. But I`d made my visit home to "Nawlins" on a whim, not thinking about French heritage. Nor all this Napoleonic history. . . I`m not generally skeptical, but I began to question the situation. Show up in a tourist bar named "Napoleon House" disguised as a workingman and claim to have found one of Napoleon`s letters. Good scam.

I called the bartender over and asked for a match. He took a cigarette lighter from his pocket, lit it, and held it out for me. I obstinately held out the page I`d just paid twenty bucks for to demonstrate I wasn`t taken in by this little charade.

When the corner caught fire, the bartender immediately pinched the flame out with a thumb and forefinger. "Jesus Christ, are ya trying to set off the sprinklers?"

I never gave the sprinklers a thought, but he was probably right. If the flame became large enough, perhaps it would have set off the low-hanging sprinklers above the bar. "My apologies. I meant to show you that I`m not falling for your scam."

"You can think whatever you like, but since Jasper got that job, he brings me old stuff for sale every day. Look at these." He reached into a drawer below the till and showed me a handful of Civil War medals. "Fifty bucks for all these."

I thought these were also part of the painter`s scam until he said, "I thought Jasper was bullshitting too. But the Louisiana State Museum is in the Cabildo, and they were throwing out all kinds of stuff damaged in the fire. Jasper must have picked these out of the garbage."

He returned the medals to the drawer. When I attempted to bend the page to put it in my pocket, I found the paper thick and heavy. The page was as thick as three sheets of typing paper. I knew there was more to this piece of paper than met the eye. Professional investigators could use a number of analytical tools ranging from standard optical magnification to sophisticated molecular spectroscopy to determine its age.

I took a cab to Tulane University, and looked up Professor Boudreaux, an ethnohistorian and an old family friend. One of his many hobbies was papermaking. I was certain he could tell if this document is a fake or not.

I was lucky to catch the professor between classes. It took him only a moment to examine the page.

"The feel of this tells me this paper is not manufactured today. In the 1800s, Europeans used rags to make their paper. See the texture? This page is quite different from today`s smooth papers made from wood."

Despite his French heritage, the professor couldn`t read the language fluently, so I translated the page for him after he scrutinized the handwriting. Once I finished reading, he said, "The letter looks old, but before I can positively give you a time frame in which it may have been written, I`ll ask our lab to analyze the paper and ink. It`s possible this page is an old forgery, but there`s an equal chance it`s authentic. If it is, you have quite a find. Museums will be clamoring to buy it from you. We should also have a linguist from the

Anthropology department check it for the proper translation."

I knew then that I`d return to the Napoleon House for lunch the next day.

❦

"Hey, Jasper, how ya doing?" I strolled toward his table with two beers in hand, acting as if we were buddies from way back, aiming to buy his remaining pages.

He looked up from his heaping plate of red jambalaya, the same lunch he`d had the day before. "Hey. You never did tell me your name."

"Rick. Rick Taylor."

"Rick, I sure could use a shot of whiskey to go with that beer chaser you just bought me." Jasper looked me squarely in the eye, to see if I`d flinch at the price of a shot.

I ordered his whiskey and after a little small talk, I asked him if he was ready to sell me the rest of the pages. Jasper pulled three pages from inside his jacket and laid them on the bar. "What`re you offering for these?"

"These are worthless. The ink is so faded you can`t read anything." But I knew Professor Boudreaux`s lab had methods to decipher the writing.

"If they`re worthless, I`ll use them to wipe my ass."

"How many more pages are there? Are they faded too?"

"They`re all pretty much the same as these. I have five more besides these three. But what do you care if they`re so worthless?"

I ignored Jasper`s remark. "I`ll give you twenty bucks for all the pages," I started low, thinking he might let them go cheap, and then hoped I hadn`t made another mistake.

Jasper turned his back and pretended I wasn`t there.

"Bartender, bring another shot and a beer on me."

That nabbed Jasper`s attention and he turned back to me. "I`ll give you these three pages for a hundred bucks, take it or leave it." He tossed back his shot and then almost emptied the twelve-ounce bottle of beer in one long draw. He stood up and headed for the door.

A C-note wasn`t a lot of money to me, but I still wasn`t sure if Jasper was taking me for a ride. I`d know later that day when Professor B received his lab`s analytical results on the first page.

"Hold on, Jasper," I said. "If I give you a hundred for these three pages, what will you charge me for the other five?"

He shrugged. "Depends. I`ll let you know tomorrow."

I handed him the hundred in exchange for the pages and rushed over to Tulane.

When I found the professor in his office, he waved the page at me, wearing white cotton gloves this time.

"Richard, when you showed me this page, I thought perhaps it was aged by soaking it in coffee or tea. But the test results reveal that the paper was made in the early 1800s."

Professor Boudreaux was the only one who ever called me Richard in deference to my famous father, the novelist, and occasionally, a visiting professor of English at Tulane. Wary of being called Richard Taylor, Jr., my moniker became Rick and Icky Sticky Ricky for my love of cherry Tootsie Roll pops during my teenage years, or alternately, Richie, or even Dick by some members of the fairer sex, but never Richard.

I pulled the three pages I had just bought from a modern manila mailing envelope. "I`ve got more work for you, Professor. These have to be restored somehow."

He took them from my hand and studied them in the sunlight streaming through the single window behind his desk.

"The words are faded beyond recognition, but ink on an old and faded document can be restored. The lab will give it a chemical treatment that will turn the iron salt still remaining on the pages into ferrous sulphate. In fact, let me show you how it`s done," he said, standing up and motioning me to follow him to the lab down the hall.

"Does it take very long?"

"Not at all." The professor put a long white lab coat on over his plaid button-down shirt and khaki trousers. First, he pulled a small wooden box from a cabinet, four inches deep and a few inches longer and wider than the page. He grunted softly to himself as he spread a net of fine white cotton threads inside at about one-half the depth of the box, and then placed two saucers containing yellow ammonium hydrosulphide in the bottom of the box. Then he used a clean sponge to moisten the paper with distilled water from a dispenser and placed the page on the net with the writing side down. Finally, he placed a plate of glass on top of the box. The vapor from the ammonium hydrosulphide caused the obliterated writing to slowly turn brown, then black.

"Interesting," I said, "like the invisible writing we used to do with lemon juice and heat when we were kids."

"Mm-hmm," the Professor said, distracted as he scanned the text and started another page. "I`ll make a hand-traced copy with tracing paper now, because it won`t be long before the writing disappears again."

After he painstakingly traced the writing on the pages, he placed these and the already fading originals in an inbox with a note to the department secretary. I translated the pages for Professor Boudreaux:

We met in 1802 when Napoleon arrived on holiday at his birthplace
in Corsica. A lowly peasant, I had just appeared at the outdoor market to

sell my vegetables when several members of the Imperial Guard queued up in front of my stand. They stood at attention, staring at me for the longest time. The superior officer dispatched one of the soldiers, who soon returned with Napoleon himself. He too stood and stared at me. Uncomfortable, I knew not what I had done to attract their attention. I tried to ignore them, and to carry on with my business, but the great one himself walked up to me and asked my name. He inquired in French, and I answered in French.

He questioned me about my family and connections. I told him my entire family had died of the plague the previous year, and I was alone in the world. This answer appeared to please him. He offered me a job with his Imperial Guards. I thought this an odd request because all of his guards were at least six feet tall and I stood no taller than the emperor. I wondered what Napoleon`s plans were for me.

I accompanied his guards to Paris, where I was measured by a military tailor for clothing in the style worn by the emperor himself. Then a military attaché schooled me upon use of the many eating utensils placed on the imperial table, as well as my manner of speech and etiquette. Napoloeon`s barber coiffed my hair in the style of Napoleon`s. When I thought there was no more to learn, the attaché instructed me how to walk in the proper manner, and even how to properly listen during conversations

The attaché instructed me to memorize many sayings that Napoleon favored, such as `A resolute determination is the truest wisdom,` and `A leader is a dealer in hope.` When I could easily recall these, I was given more to learn: `Imagination rules the world,` was one, and `Courage is like love; it must have hope for nourishment` was another. As I memorized these aphorisms, I began to see the truth in them and asked for more.`

You become strong by defying defeat and by turning loss into gain and failure to success,` became one of my favorites, as well as `The human race is governed by its imagination,` which struck me as absolutely true.

Living in the manner of the wealthy was a pleasure I had never experienced. Life as a farmer`s son hadn`t provided many opportunities. So being treated like royalty without a clue as to why made me dread even more the thought of returning to my miserable existence as a poor farmer.

One evening I was summoned by an Imperial Guard to dine with Napoleon himself. My servants dressed me in a suit of powder-blue silk, the likes of which I had never worn before. The barber came to trim my hair and apply powder to my face. I looked in the mirror, pleased with my appearance.

A servant led me to a huge dining room filled with a massive table long enough to sit twenty to a side. A butler, dressed in crisp black and white, the only other person in the room, seated me at the far end of the table. In walked Napoleon. I stood and bowed out of respect for the man. When I stood straight, I found he had walked to me and stood right in front of me. I gasped; it was as though I gazed in the mirror again. I was looking at an identical reflection of myself, right down to the trousers and coat of blue silk. A look of pleasure lit his face as he told me to sit. He then took a chair next to mine.

Napoleon shared with me the heavy responsibilities of his office. It seemed he always needed to be two places at once. When his guards had seen my uncanny likeness to him in the market that fateful day, they sent word to Napoleon, and he had to see for himself. Once he was satisfied that what they said was true, he ordered them to hire me.

He asked me if my "hosts" were treating me well. Naturally, I couldn`t thank him enough for the care I received. He told me that if I would always do as he said, I would enjoy a high-quality lifestyle normally unattainable by someone like me. I vowed to do whatever he wanted, and meant every word.

My place was to allow him to rest when he needed it by appearing for early morning reviews of his troops while he slept late. I would also appear at routine state functions in his stead. This routine evolved into a rich, full life for me, until he decided to invade Russia.

When I finished translating the pages, the professor shook his head in amazement. "Is that the entire letter?"

"No, the painter has five more pages and the envelope he found them in."

"Richard, whatever you do, try to get those remaining pages in case they turn out to be authentic. I may be able to help with university funds because this narrative may contain proof that the rumors about Napoleon circulating among historians for years are true."

❧

The following day I sat at the bar, waiting for Jasper to come in for his lunch. I didn`t expect to pay much for the remaining pages. With three thousand dollars in my pocket, half mine and half from a university fund, I was sure to have more than enough to meet Jasper`s demands.

"If you`re waiting for Jasper, you`re wasting your time. He spent that hundred you gave him in here last night, and you can bet he`s hung over." The bartender wiped the counter in front of me and pocketed the five-dollar tip I`d left on the edge of the bar.

How would I find him if he didn`t show up for work again tomorrow or got fired?

"Hey barkeep," I called, as he turned to wait on someone at the far end of the bar, "Where can I find Jasper with his hangover?"

After he served a drink, he gave me directions to a bar at 438 Bourbon Street, otherwise known as Fat Catz, where Jasper sometimes nursed his hangovers after a binge. Along the way, I passed a statue of Napoleon in a square. It seemed the little emperor haunted this city, because there were mementos of him all over the place. I had done a little research the previous day and found that many of Napoleon`s officers had settled in New Orleans after the wars.

When I walked through the door at Fat Catz, I saw why Jasper chose this place to recuperate from his hangovers. If you could stomach the repulsive smell of stale beer, it was cool, dark, and silent, perfect for nursing a headache. I spotted him right away, sitting at the end of the bar holding an empty beer glass. I sat next to him, and he turned to look at me.

"What`re you doing? Following me?" He stared at his empty glass and I ordered another for him.

"I have to leave town soon, Jasper, and I`d like to buy your envelope and the remaining pages."

"Tough shit. I got fired for showing up drunk this morning. You can forget about getting the rest." He rambled on about how he had hidden the envelope back in the niche where he`d found it, and how he`d hung a sheet of vinyl wall covering over the hole so no one would know it was there.

"Is there any way you can get inside the Cabildo and get the envelope for me? I`ll make it worth your while."

"Only if we bribe the night watchman, because my boss said he`d have me arrested if I showed my face on the job site again."

We negotiated for over an hour and I had to give him the entire three grand before he agreed to accompany me to the Cabildo. We`d retrieve the papers that night. I took thirty hundred-dollar bills from my wallet, showed them to Jasper, then tore each one in half. I handed him one-half of the torn bills and put the others back in my wallet. "You get the other half when I get the papers."

I had to get more cash from the professor because by that time, the banks had closed and I needed to bribe the night watchman at the Cabildo. This guy didn`t like being called a watchman, Jasper told me. He said his correct job title was security guard and he liked to be addressed as Officer LeMay.

We showed up at nine dressed as painters. Jasper banged on the entrance door that the tradesmen used to enter and leave the Cabildo.

"What are you guys doing here this time of night?" LeMay demanded through a security speaker.

I let Jasper do the talking. He pulled a pint of whiskey from his overalls and displayed it to the security camera.

The door buzzed and then the lock released with a loud click. Jasper led the way inside. "Have a swig, Officer," he said, offering the stout watchman a pint of whiskey from his overalls. He reached for it and took a long pull.

"Officer LeMay, I left my keys in my work bucket. Without them, I`m screwed. I can`t get into my car or house. Not only that, I didn`t finish hanging the wall covering I was supposed to install today. If you`ll just give me an hour or so, I can finish what I was supposed to do. Then I won`t get fired, and I can get my keys at the same time." Jasper pulled another pint from a different pocket, and handed that along with a folded twenty to the watchman.

"Okay, I`ll give you an hour. Not one minute over. And your friend waits here."

"Officer LeMay, it`ll take both of us to finish in an hour." Jasper handed him another twenty.

"Let`s get going, then." He waved us up the stairs.

Jasper led the way to the hallway where carpenters, painters, and other craftsmen were restoring a section of rooms. The watchman sat in a chair and watched as we started rolling out wall covering. Half of the large room, marked with a plaque in the hallway as the Sala Capitular (meeting room), was covered with a deep red velvety wall covering. The other half had bare plaster walls. The odor of burned wood and wiring still lingered there after four years.

Jasper pasted a few eight-foot-long sheets of vinyl, and had me carry them to the wall, where he directed me to carry one sheet up a ladder and unfold it. I held it away from the wall to block the watchman`s view while he peeled back the edge of the sheet of vinyl that covered the hiding place. It revealed a small door of copper with a greenish patina. He lifted that off from a deep hole, reached inside, pulled out the old envelope, and tucked it inside his overalls. We proceeded to hang the sheet of vinyl next to the one Jasper had pulled back. He squeezed some excess paste from the sheet we hung first to re-stick the one he had peeled back to get to the door. We didn`t want the watchman to start asking any questions, so we hung two more strips before we left.

Outside, I breathed a sigh of relief and handed Jasper the other half of the torn bills. He took the pages from the envelope and handed them to me.

"What about the envelope?" I held my hand out, expecting him to give it to me.

"The deal was for the pages only."

I sputtered in protest because we`d specifically negotiated for the envelope, but he put it in his overalls and walked into the night.

Even so, I couldn`t wait until the next morning to translate the pages. I called Professor Boudreaux at home. He was anxious as well and agreed to meet me at the university.

The professor again performed the process to make the writing on each page legible, hand-traced them, then placed the pages in an inbox with a note for the department secretary to make mimeographed copies of the tracings. As soon as he handed them to me, I started to read aloud:

> *Then my status changed. I was to accompany the infantry advance, to actually lead the columns, and in doing so, mislead the Russians. Naturally, everyone thought I was Napoleon, and the emperor traveled in disguise to study the Russian troops and discern their next move. Everything went well with my leadership under Napoleon`s orders.*
>
> *We met often, and with my efforts to imitate even his most subtle physical movements, we became so much alike that any physical difference became unnoticeable. However, when it came to intellect, Napoleon`s thoughts were always miles ahead of mine. Sadly, even his focused mind wasn`t great enough to defeat the Russian winter. We retreated to Germany. He led the army to a series of victories, but there were just too many troops arrayed against him. Surrender was the only option.*
>
> *Napoleon signed the treaty of Fontainebleau, and the Sixth Coalition drove him into exile on the island of Elba. He soon escaped and returned to France. The French army still adored Napoleon, so when he*

appeared to Marshal Ney and the regiment who had served under him in Russia, Ney proclaimed "vive L`Empereur!" and they marched on to Paris together.

One of the first things Napoleon had done upon his return was to send an envoy to my farm in Corsica to implore me to return to his service. To live as royalty again thrilled me. My life as a farmer seemed especially hard and dirty after all the comforts I`d experienced. I vowed to do anything to live the good life again. Unfortunately, Napoleon`s luster had waned and he was soon defeated in battle.

He called me before him. "You can go back to your life as a farmer or you can replace me as a prisoner," Napoleon told me. "The choice is yours."

I certainly didn`t want to be a prisoner.

"The British will only exile me, not lock me up in some dungeon. Even in exile, your life will be a thousand times better than a farmer`s."

The last time Napoleon lived in exile, he still had his personal staff, and enjoyed luxurious accommodations. The more I thought about it, the better it sounded. I had no family left, so no one would miss me.

"I sold our territory in North America to the United States with a stipulation that should I ever need sanctuary, they would supply it. I will travel there incognito and no one will ever know I am there. But should someone discover my presence, the U.S. government is sworn to protect me."

"What will happen to me if you`re discovered?" I asked.

"All I can promise is that I will do my very best to remain anonymous for your sake." He held his hand over his heart as a promise.

It only took me but a few minutes to think it over. I decided it well worth the risk to live out my life in luxury. I agreed and dressed in Napoleon`s uniform and surrendered while he sailed for the United States.

Whoever reads this letter will know I died faithful to the last.

A Poor Corsican Farmer

My excitement made me speechless for a moment. "This letter suggests that Napoleon was here in the United States while his double replaced him on the island."

The professor`s face suggested caution. "The paper dates from his era, but other than that, we have no evidence to verify the identity of the writer. If we could somehow establish provenance, we`d be able to declare the narrative original and true. But how could this letter wind up in New Orleans when it`s allegedly written by a Corsican farmer exiled to St. Helena?"

I was despondent. The money was no issue, but I felt the disappointment of spending so much time and effort to acquire a letter that could very well be a hoax, the figment of someone`s imagination. I needed a drink and invited the professor to help me drown my sorrows. I knew the perfect bar, and we headed in a taxi for the Fat Catz bar.

The professor and I sat in the smoky gloom, lamenting what could have been. Several drinks later, I heard a familiar voice near dawn. "Give them two gents a drink on me."

Jasper stood at the bar arrayed in a brand-new black suit with a salmon-colored shirt. "You`ve bought me drinks, so I`m returning the favor," he said, still flush with whatever remained of the three grand I gave him. He sat beside me at the bar and we raised our glasses in a toast.

"To Dr. Antommarchi," Jasper said.

"Who the hell`s he?" I said, perplexed.

"Dr. François Carlo Antommarchi was the doctor who performed the autopsy on Napoleon," the professor said. "He also donated the death mask of Napoleon to the City of New Orleans shortly after he immigrated here in 1834. The mask was displayed in the Cabildo, along with the instruments he used at the autopsy."

"Are you a history buff, Jasper? Is that why you`re toasting Dr. Antommarchi?" I asked.

He grinned. "No, I`m toasting him for the money I made from his letter."

The letter! Then I remembered the envelope had legible writing on it. I hoped and prayed Jasper hadn`t disposed of it yet. "By the way, Jasper, I`d like to buy the envelope the letter came in."

"I knew you would, that`s why I`m here. You can have it."

I held my hand out.

"For six thousand," he said.

I looked at the professor, searching for a hint. He shrugged.

"Jasper, that letter is old, but it could have been written by anyone. I can`t give you that kind of money for an old envelope. I`d like to have it for its historical value."

The professor cleared his throat. "Just a minute. May we examine it first?"

"All right, but don`t try any funny stuff." Jasper opened his jacket and pulled the envelope from his sleeve where he had it stashed. It wasn`t hard to miss seeing the shoulder holster with the butt of a pistol sticking out of it.

I read the barely legible writing aloud. "`To Dr. Antommarchi. Do not open until my death.` There`s a handwritten note on the back that says in English, `Item # 23, donated by Dr. Antommarchi` with a date stamped 1835."

Professor Boudreaux`s eyes lit up. "*This* is the provenance we need. The doctor was there when the double died. He made a death mask and moved here. There should be a record somewhere in the Cabildo to prove this stamp and the #23 on the envelope is valid. Maybe the doctor came here to notify Napoleon of the death of his double, or perhaps he had a more Machiavellian purpose for bringing the death mask and letter here. It appears there`s an immense amount of research to be done here in New Orleans. Let`s go to the bank, wait for it to open, and get Jasper his six grand," the professor said.

We passed a statue of Napoleon on the way to the bank, and for the first time I noticed the smirk on the statue`s face. . .

15

Ⓐ

Slow Afternoon

ONE SLOW AFTERNOON, I SAT leafing through an old legal book I found at the bottom of a stack on our lobby bookshelf. "Jason, I`m wondering when it`s necessary to post a disclaimer with fiction."

Jason looked up from the layout table. "Um, what kind of disclaimer?"

"You know, like the disclaimers you sometimes see at the end of movies or the beginning of novels: `All characters appearing in this work are fictitious. Any resemblance to real persons, living or dead, is purely coincidental.`"

"Oh. Why do you ask?"

"I`m thinking of folks who have been sued for libel or defamation. But that usually happens with memoirs or biographies, right?"

"Any particular story you`re worried about?"

"Well, no. Not really."

"Writers usually disguise real events and characters in their fiction, and mix these with purely fictional characters and events," Jason said. "You *possibly* could get sued over something imaginary. There`s always the possibility that if your characters remotely resemble real people who might claim they were harmed by the story. Must be a rarity because I`ve not seen this. And I also think most authors could prove they weren`t intentionally modeling a character or events in question upon real people or events."

"Do you think anyone might sue us or any of our authors over the contest stories? I mean, we really don`t know where any of our authors got their ideas."

Jason looked at me as if resisting an eye roll. "Of course, anything can happen, but it`s a pretty remote possibility," he said. "The contest stories are mostly paranormal or fantasy. Imaginary stuff that`s not likely to cause problems. I wouldn`t worry about it. If lawsuits about characters in fiction were a real worry, these would happen frequently. I guess publishers are printing disclaimers in every novel or short story collection now to be on the safe side."

I lifted my hands in front of me and shrugged. "Just trying to think ahead."

Jason aimed a little smirk in my direction. "Pete, don`t create trouble by anticipating it and picturing it in your mind."

Just then, the phone rang. Joseph Ragmora, publisher from *The Village Spoke*, rushed into a breathless, cheerful report. "Great idea, Pete, printing your contest in my paper as well as your magazine. My circulation has increased by 9% since I started carrying the pictures with the entry form. But—and this is a big but. You`re getting many more entries to your contest at five dollars apiece. Consider that."

"Rags, the money goes toward prizes and expenses for running the contest. I`m up against the clock with some obligations. My uncle John left the helm with some debts to repay. There`s not much left to share."

"Well, think it over, Pete. Perhaps we can expand this contest together somehow in a way that benefits both of us. If not, I can always start my own contest, you know."

"Sure, Rags. I`ll give it some thought."

I put the receiver down with a deep sigh. "Well, Jace. You`re probably right. I need to stop thinking about trouble. But here`s one I never expected. The Village Spoke isn`t simply happy that their circulation increased. Now they want a cut from the contest. Since we can`t help Rags right now, he`ll probably start one of his own. One thing after another, isn`t it?"

Still concentrating on his work, Jason just looked up and shook his head. "That may or may not hurt our contest. After all, there are plenty of writers around. And you really don`t owe Rags anything. Legally, I mean. But maybe if you make the magazine lucrative enough to let him in as a partner somehow, you could go for a little palm greasing. Maybe the column project will turn everything around. You can pay the magazine debt, take Rags on and give him a cut of the entry fees or something. But only if you want to. I don`t think you owe him anything legally. He agreed to help you out and he`s benefitting already."

"That`s a thought," I said. "So gang, what`s up for the next contest? The Napoleon theme in "The Imposter" is a hard act to follow. . . Evie, what`s the verdict from the legendary art book?

Evie set aside her filing at the cabinet and picked up our dog-eared art book. She stuck a pretty finger inside a page and opened it. "How about this? *Snow at Louveciennes.*" She turned the page around so Jason, Shirley and I could take a gander, then she turned it around to read again. "`Alfred Sisley was born in Paris of English parents. He was one of the creators of French Impressionism`. . . wow, get this. . . `Sisley, with a family to support, was reduced to a state of penury, and lived in poverty until the end of his life`. . . poor starving artist. Then blah, blah about his paintings becoming more popular after his death. `He retained a passionate interest in the sky, which nearly always dominates his paintings, and also in the effects of snow, the two interests often combined to create a strangely dramatic effect.`"

"That painting looks a little dull to me, for an artist who liked dramatic effects. But it`s sort of neutral and moody at the same time, like the Bricher painting. It`s a scene that would challenge writers," Shirley said.

Jason and Evie looked at one another and nodded.

"Good, we`re all on the same page," I said. "Let`s do it."

The mailman strode in and left the usual rubber-banded stack of mail on Shirley`s desk. She spent a minute sorting it out into piles and handed me a small stack of envelopes.

I sighed again. More bills. But when I opened the first envelope, a jaw-dropping check dropped out. From my uncle`s estate, said an attached stub. But there had been very little money involved in Uncle John`s estate. . . what was up with this? I picked up the phone to call O`Neill.

"Hey, Pete here. I just received a check for a substantial amount from John`s estate," I blurted out when he answered the phone. I waited for his answer with my eyes closed and my fists clenched.

"Must be fake, Pete. Your uncle didn`t have any funds or you would have had the money from the get-go. That`s why he placed conditions on the magazine inheritance."

I turned the check over and examined it. Would Peter send me a bad check and hope I`d cash it and pay bills? He understood better than anyone the difficulties I`d find myself in if I deposited a bogus check and paid all my creditors. All my checks would bounce sky high. My credit would be ruined. I might even get charged with criminal offenses by an overzealous prosecutor.

I sighed once more. I never dreamed of all the odd troubles I`d face when I went into this business against Peter`s wishes. Now I`d have to decide whether to ignore this challenge or take the check to the authorities. I put it in my top drawer of my desk and locked the drawer for the first time ever.

Every picture shows a spot with which the artist has fallen in love. . .

ALONE

AT SOME POINT EVERY WINTER, a major snowstorm isolates my father`s village from the world. And now, with twenty miles of unplowed mountainous backroads between the village and the city, Jacob and I are waiting for our past-due baby to make an appearance. I warned my husband that this sudden snowstorm might happen. But Jacob, ever-positive athlete that he is, cast my worries aside. "Don`t fret about anything. The hospital is only twenty miles away, and if need be, I can carry you there."

Transporting an injured person or a woman in labor were two different things entirely, but I let the statement go as male bravado. Jake might have seemed callous to anyone overhearing our conversation, but after all, when my due date approached, I had made the last-minute decision to birth in the quiet village with a midwife rather than in the hospital with my obstetrician, a brooding man who sometimes annoyed me.

"I`d feel better if you didn`t go out, honey. My mother died giving birth to me here twenty-three years ago. You know that."

Jake wrapped his arms around me and kissed me on top of my head in a way that felt simultaneously comforting and dismissing.

"I really need some fresh air, Missy. Your father is here to take care of you, and the midwife will be here in minutes once you call her," he said, pulling his down jacket from the clothes tree. "I won`t be long. You haven`t even had a labor pain yet."

I crossed my arms over my sagging belly and gazed at him.

"Have you?" Jake pulled me to him again, holding me longer this time before he pulled his skis from a corner and strode off into the gathering storm.

I didn`t like talking to Jacob about the other reasons I felt uncomfortable without him. Whenever I visited my father in the old house, he seemed every bit as distant as he had been during my childhood. Even the people in the village kept a polite distance, as though both they and my father blamed me for my mother`s death.

I shut the cottage door against the chill wind and still-falling snow after watching Jacob put on his cross-country skis and shuffle into the hills like a giant hare. After pouring another cup of raspberry leaf tea, said to make birthing babies easier, I went to find my father in his study. He was nestled down in a worn leather armchair, poring over his morning newspaper with my mother`s old mohair shawl around his shoulders. I cleared my throat to get his attention.

He looked up at me, startled, his eyes large and owlish behind his reading glasses "With your full figure, you look so much like your mother, Marissa. . . He shut his eyes and inhaled deeply, as if seeing her, a shadow of a smile crossing his face. "Bless her soul, while she lived, people in this village practically worshiped her. Even as a small child, she had this healing power. It started when she found a wounded bird and nursed it to health. Then she began healing small animals. Before long, she treated animals of all sizes, horses, cattle. If any farmer`s livestock suffered injury or illness, they would call for your mother. She had the knack to restore any animal`s health. Then, when Farmer Beran`s wife fell ill with cancer, your mother visited her daily for a month, feeding her a soup of herbs and vegetables, tending her fire and reading to her. I think Leah thought to show Madame Beran kindness before she passed away, but miraculously, the cancer disappeared, never to return."

Leah—how my mother`s name rolled musically from his tongue. Whenever Father uttered it, I imagined his mind springing to life. The lilt of two simple syllables charmed flowers open, caused rain to splish-splash through pine branches, and enticed the soft babble of water over smooth stone. She was the sun, the moon, and the stars to him, yet I had never known her. He had related the same facts about my mother many times over the lonely years of my youth. How I had wished she hadn`t died. Sometimes I even wished I`d never been conceived, so that she would not have perished.

"The doctor who practiced in this village moved elsewhere, because whenever anybody became seriously ill, they`d seek out your mother instead." Father stood and padded to the window in his slippers and drew the lacy curtain aside, gazing at the snowflakes dancing against the windowpanes. "With each healing, her abilities seemed to grow stronger, until she could heal anyone. She always cared for people without charge or any discrimination, so it`s understandable why the villagers were shocked when this healer, of all people, should die while giving birth."

Father`s face became mottled as if he might cry. My stomach churned, then the baby churned its head against my bladder, and I excused myself to run to the toilet. Now I wondered again if I faced the same fate as my mother. I feared this birth would be tough when nine months passed and I hadn`t started labor. Ten days past due now, I felt as swollen and as round as a full moon.

I felt tempted to run a hot bath and relieve the load on my aching hips and swollen ankles. Just as suddenly, I felt sleepy. I opened the squeaking door of the guest room to lay down in the canopy bed, my mother`s and father`s old room. He`d removed his things from the room and taken to sleeping on a day bed in his study after my mother`s death. I`d never asked my father if it were the same bed she had labored and died in after delivering me, but I knew it had to be. Thrifty to a fault, my father would never get rid of a perfectly good piece of furniture.

I napped fitfully for less than an hour and awoke with a start. The soft, intermittent contractions of late pregnancy had gone sharp. I rose from the crisp white sheets, wiping away sweat from my brow with the back of my hand. I startled when I opened the door and found my father just outside, leaning against the wall.

"It`s time," I told him, at once excited and filled with dread.

Without waiting for an answer, he stepped back as if to make room for my bulky body, his face alarmed. "Missy. I`m sorry. I can`t watch you, this situation, this room, this bed—your face. All reminders of the morning you were born." He looked away, as if checking the hallway for imperfections. "Where`s Jacob?" he mumbled.

A contraction gripped my abdomen like a clenched fist and I couldn`t answer. I bent forward, rested my forehead against the cool plaster of the wall and suppressed a groan. Where *was* Jake? He`d been gone for over an hour. He probably would carry me all the way to the city, if only he`d come back.

I steeled myself against another searing bolt of pain. "*Oh.* That hurt. . . Jake went out for some fresh air, just a short time, he said. . ."

Looking away again, my father said he would call the midwife. "I still say you shouldn`t have come with the baby past due, away from your doctor," he muttered as he headed downstairs.

Under normal circumstances, I`d feel hurt by my father`s distance, but I understood that this situation would be unsettling to anyone. I went back inside the guest room and sat on the edge of the bed to await the next contraction. I`d heard my doctor and older women talk about dilation and I wondered if this would be a long labor or a short one.

As the next contraction gripped me, I gazed at the portrait of my mother hanging on the wall. She was my age in the photograph, and for some unknown reason her lips turned down in a sulky frown, her eyes dark with passion. I`d often gazed at this portrait when growing up, either yearning for her or hating myself for causing her death. The contraction peaked and ebbed, but within seconds another long contraction clawed at my belly, holding me immobile and almost breathless in its interminable grasp. I forced myself to breathe deeply and then panted a bit to ease the pain.

When my mother`s face turned in the frame to face me, I assumed the birth pains caused me to hallucinate. Then her expression softened and her lips moved. *Don`t worry. I`ll take care of you, Marissa.*

I shook my head, confused if I had heard her or if I`d imagined her voice. Oh, how I wished it were true, that she`d take care of me. I`d always wanted to know my mother, but grew to resent her by the time I was a teenager. All I ever heard was how saintly she was and how sorely she was missed. I knew I could never measure up to the love of a dead saint.

As the pain passed, I turned to the window. The falling snowflakes swirled into the grooves left by Jake`s skis, filling them up and adding depth and sparkle to the already fallen snow. Soon there would be no tracks at all to testify to the fact that Jacob had left the house. I began to worry that he was unable to find his way back. I prayed this birth would not be like my own. Even the village`s highly experienced midwife might not be able to handle an emergency. If the snow became much deeper, the roads would not be clear for days.

Another contraction ripped through my belly. There was no time at all between contractions and my father had not yet come back upstairs. I feared being alone while I delivered this baby. When the contraction peaked, panic overwhelmed me until I looked at my mother`s picture again. Her eyes softened. "I told you not to worry," she said in a low, sweet voice. "Peace, be still."

The contraction trailed off. Relieved, I let out a deep sigh and lay back against the pillows.

I rested that way for a moment, almost falling asleep in the few seconds between another wave of excruciating pain. Suddenly, I felt the baby pushing with its legs, helping to position its head into my birth canal. Somehow, I knew then the baby would be a girl and that she would soon arrive. Another contraction like white-hot lightning consumed not only my belly, but my entire body and soul. I screamed with agony, a shrill scream like bone scraping bone that echoed from the walls.

I took a sobbing breath and screamed again until I felt a cool, soothing hand resting on my brow. "Breathe deeply You`ll be fine. Trust me."

I opened my eyes and looked up. My mother stood between my legs with her hands outstretched, softly urging me on as I gave one last long, nearly involuntary push, grunting from the effort to bring my baby into the world. As the baby slid free, I felt lighter, and the room grew brighter as if I passed away to a heavenly place free of gut-wrenching pain.

When I came to just moments later, my baby was squalling face down on my chest, a cotton baby blanket spread over her. She rooted for my breast and I loosened the buttons of my gown and helped her find a nipple. My hand brushed something aside that lay next to the baby.

Frowning, I held the old-fashioned perfumed stationery up to the light. "Marissa—Please name my granddaughter Leah after me."

I stared in surprise at my mother`s photograph. She stared back at me, her face frozen in time now, her frown dissolved into a serene smile. A great surge of relief coursed through me. My mother had come to me when I needed her most. . .

❧

Six-year-old Leah ran into the room, a small brown wren perched on her little forefinger, her generous mane of my mother`s cinnamon curls bouncing against her shoulders.

"Look, Mama, Papa, I fixed his wing. He can fly again." She held the small bird near the open kitchen window of the old village house, our home since Father took ill and Jake retired from his sport.

The small bird raised its wings and flew away without a sign that only yesterday it had dragged one broken wing behind it.

"Bravo!" We smiled and applauded Leah`s victory, I with flour-covered hands, and Jacob while nestling our infant son.

"I fixed Alley Cat`s sore tail, and the goldfish Grand-père thought dead is now swimming in circles. And Grand-père feels so much better too. Can I go outside to play now? Perhaps someone else needs me. . ."

193

16

Competition

I SLAMMED THE PHONE RECEIVER down hard on the cradle after O`Neill said good-bye. Evie startled, eyes wide over the stack of contest manuscripts she had just started to browse through. Jason looked up from his cutting and pasting on the storyboards at the "long table."

"What`s up, Pete?"

"O`Neill heard that my fath . . . I mean, Peter, has made an offer to purchase L`Artiste." Our biggest rival in the art mag business was an old, well-established periodical embraced by America`s artistic elite.

Jason tried and failed to suppress a grin. "Guess Big Pete lost his distaste for the publishing biz, eh?"

I paced from one end of the office to the other. "Maybe I`m over-reacting. Classic Art Exposé is also well established and we`re growing. But what if L`Artiste manages to surpass what we do? They already have a much larger *and* a more sophisticated readership."

Jason tipped his head and stared at me for a moment. "Competition`s good, man, don`t worry. They`ve got their readership and we`ve got ours. In a way, Peter is inadvertently helping you. He may not see it that way, and you may not see it that way, but watch what happens." He checked the clock and stepped out, probably to smoke some of his exotic tobacco. Evie and Shirley stepped out on errands, the press guys probably mulled over their millionth card game, and soon I heard the clock click-clack every time the minute hand moved.

I cleared my throat with a fake cough when Jason resumed his cutting and pasting. "So, Jace, do you know which American writer became a millionaire first?"

He glanced up from his work with an expression that said he wondered if I knew the answer and was quizzing him, or if I didn`t know and wanted him to tell me.

"Okay, sorry. It`s too damn quiet around here. I just need to talk. You must know a little about Jack London . . . he`s one of the first American authors to achieve financial success."

Jason nodded and stepped back to assess his handiwork. "I read he served time too. For vagrancy, I guess."

"I didn`t know that. But I do know he was in the right place at the right time. Wri-ite time . . ." I chuckled at my lame pun, but Jason didn`t respond. "Anyway, London started publishing just as new printing technologies enabled lower-cost production of magazines. This started a boom in popular magazines and a strong market for short fiction. In 1900, he made $2500 for his writing, the equivalent of about $75,000 today."

Jason looked up from his work. "Why are you talking about London?"

I shrugged. "Remember, we chose a Remington painting for the next contest. Evie says the best story for our next issue might read like something he could have written."

"Oh, cool."

"Yeah, I guess we`ll take a look when the girls get back. By the way, the story inspired by the Sisley painting was a big hit with our female readers. I pointed to a stack of letters on Shirley`s desk. "I think it`s time to add some space to our Letters to the Editor column."

Jason didn`t seem to hear me. I sighed and went back to sifting through my perennially anxious and antagonistic thoughts about Peter.

THE COWBOY
Frederick Remington, 1902

*I knew the wild riders and the vacant land were about to vanish forever. . .
and the more I considered the subject, the bigger the forever loomed.*

CHEATER

I HELD MY PEPPERBOX PISTOL beneath the card table and aimed at the head of the cheating cowboy. `Twasn`t hard to see his hand held too many cards. "You know eight cards in five-card stud is called a `dead man`s hand` don`t you?"

He made a move. I pulled the trigger. The bullet hit him under the chin and exited the top of his head, followed by what brains he had. The saloon filled with silence as I stood up and walked to where he fell. All eyes were on me as he lay at my feet, blood pouring from his wound. Then the same pairs of eyes all looked the other way. None wanted to be a witness to a shooting.

I gathered my winnings off the table and hit the trail to the next town before some do-gooder tried to get me locked up for killing someone`s son, husband, or father. Emotional relatives often overlooked the fact that their loved ones got caught cheating.

I had won enough to get myself a little business. Tired of gambling and killing, I headed for Denver, the biggest burg in Colorado, looking for an opportune investment. I`d been traveling and gambling since the war ended in `65. My aim in life now was to settle down, hang up my guns, and never look at a deck of cards again.

The mountains were just turning green, but snow still topped most peaks in the Rockies. I knew I`d best keep an eye out for hungry grizzlies this time of year. When I reached town, I rode down the main street and saw people beginning to gather around a man who talked in a voice loud enough to echo up and down the dusty lane. With promises of easy money, he soon drew a crowd. He set up his "tripe and keister," a display case atop a tripod, on the wooden sidewalk.

"All right, folks, step right up. My name`s Soapy Smith and I`m gonna make you an incredible offer you can`t refuse." He held up a cake of soap.

Hell, I knew cowboys only needed that once a year or so. How he`d make money selling soap piqued my curiosity, though, so I clambered off my horse to hang around and watch. He placed ordinary, rectangular, homemade cakes of soap onto the keister top, and he began to expound on their wonders. As he spoke to the curious onlookers, he pulled out a roll of bills and began to wrap paper money around a few cakes of soap. He used notes ranging from one dollar up to one hundred dollars. Then he finished his handiwork by wrapping plain brown paper around each cake of soap and mixed the money-wrapped bars in with the plain ones.

"Cleanliness is next to Godliness, but the feel of a good crisp greenback in the pocket is paradise itself. Step up, my friends, and buy some heaven-scented soap to please your ladies for one measly dollar. You just might make a ninety-nine-dollar profit when you peel the wrapping off," he shouted.

I watched a man, who I figured to be a shill planted in the crowd, buy a cake. He tore it open and loudly proclaimed that he`d won some money, waving it around for all to see. The shill looked enough like Soapy to be his brother.

This performance had the desired effect. The crowd clamored to buy the soap for one dollar a cake. I laughed as some of the victims rushed to buy several cakes before the performance was complete. Another shill hollered in excitement when he tore the wrappings off the soap he had bought and showed the crowd the note wrapped around the soap.

Soapy Smith announced that the hundred-dollar note yet remained in the pile. He started to auction off the remaining soap and the highest bidder could choose which one he wanted. My carefully trained eye had seen his manipulation and sleight-of-hand. I stepped forward. "If I win the auction, I can choose any cake of soap I want, is that correct?"

"You can choose any soap I have if you win."

Soapy Smith started the auction. I got my choice for seven dollars and fifty cents, a royal sum. The crowd watched in suspense as I approached and pointed to his right-side jacket pocket where I saw him stash the cake he'd wrapped with the hundred-dollar note. He attempted to do the old switcheroo once more, but I grabbed his soap-filled hand, reached into his pocket and withdrew the soap. I unwrapped it in front of the crowd to show them the money. Once they saw I had won the big one, they quit bidding and walked away. Not a one demanded their money back. I figured they must be scared of this hombre for some reason.

"I'll get you for this," Soapy Smith mumbled in my direction.

I looked him dead in the eye, ready to draw both my hidden pistols. "No time like the present," I snarled.

He could tell I wasn't bluffing. He packed his keister, folded his tripe, and strode away muttering threats under his breath. I tied up my mount and sauntered into the Elite Saloon and Hotel where I rented a room and a tub full of hot water. I paid with the crisp hundred-dollar note, and I put the cake of soap to good use. Had a meal in the dining room, and then I slept until sunbeams shining through the grime-covered window woke me.

Feeling refreshed after the meal, the bath, and the long sleep, I headed downstairs where I knew a poker game would be in progress. Sure enough, before I hit the bottom step I spotted a table occupied by five men playing seven-card stud. I grabbed an empty chair, pulled it to the table, and sat.

Out of the five, four were cowboys, but the fifth I recognized from the day before. He was the first shill in the crowd to buy soap from Soapy Smith. Today he was dressed as a cardsharp in his costume of black jacket, trousers, and hat decorated with silver studs. His bolo tie, tipped in gold with a gold nugget for a slide, showed off his prosperity. When I caught his eye, I tipped my hat.

He tipped his in return. "Bascomb Smith here," he said.

Definitely Soapy's brother. Cooking up a card scheme, no doubt.

An older, distinguished-looking gentleman who held the deck ready to deal nodded at me. "Ante's five dollars, high card bets, twenty-dollar limit on raises."

"Percival Morse," I said, and threw my five dollars into the pot.

The dealer started tossing cards. "I'm Bradley Broome, the barber and undertaker in this here town."

The other four didn't say a word, just watched Brad's hands as he dealt the cards. Time passed and the game progressed. Slowly, I began to acquire a substantial amount of their money. The players were making snide remarks to each other about me being a dude with my clean white shirt, something they didn`t see very often. They figured me as a dude, and any dude had to be stupid. Most cowboys wouldn`t think I`d be brave enough or smart enough to cheat them. I was both and cheated them out of their gold every chance I got.

One of the players, Billy, had been smashed in the head with an Indian tomahawk some years ago. The tomahawk must`ve scrambled his brains—he played and talked like a half-wit, but his money was good.

Smith`s hand showed aces and eights. He bet all the coins and paper money piled in front of him. To match his bet I had to use my entire take and the lucky twenty-dollar gold piece I`d carried all through the war. I rubbed it hard before I threw it on the table. Smith held three hole cards, and the aces and eights in his hand would have turned into four aces when he added the two I saw him pull from his sleeve. These young whippersnappers thought because they could handle a deck of cards smoothly, no one could catch their shenanigans. Darn stupid cowboys, they all think I can`t spot a card cheat. But they better learn to cheat good, or don`t cheat at all.

This pot turned out to be the biggest my eyes had beheld in a long time. I had two kings showing and two in the hole. I wasn`t going to let someone beat my kickers with palmed aces.

I shot Smith smack in the middle of his forehead. His eyes opened wide in surprise, and as the light drained from them, he tried to stand but fell to the floor. I wasn`t about to let anybody cheat me out of my lucky coin.

I held my four-shot pepperbox pistol aimed at the other players while I gathered my winnings from the table. I had three shots left in the pepperbox and under my left sleeve, another seven shots in my .22 Rimfire revolver. Billy the half-wit grabbed my lucky twenty-dollar gold piece from the table and put it in his mouth.

"Spit it out, Billy, or you`ll lay beside Smith." I looked at Smith`s body laid out on the floor and Billy`s eyes followed mine. "I`m going to count to three, and if that gold piece isn`t on the table, you`re going to have a hole in your head to match his." I put the pepperbox against his forehead. I couldn`t believe he`d give up his life for twenty bucks. His eyes dared me to shoot. I squeezed the trigger and a small bloodless hole appeared in his forehead. He slumped back in his chair. I didn`t want to do it, but I couldn`t let him call my bluff. If I did, I`d be dead meat in minutes.

I gazed around the table to warn those still alive they wouldn`t be for long if they did anything stupid like Billy. I tried to open his mouth to retrieve the twenty-dollar gold coin, but I couldn`t get it to open.

"Locks up like a safe when they die biting down on something," Brad said.

"What are you talking about?"

"I`m telling you when someone dies biting down on something their jaws lock. The only way you`ll get that gold piece is to break his jaw loose. I know what I`m talking about. I`ve had to break many a jaw to make their faces look normal for viewing and picture taking."

I swung the butt of my gun against Billy`s jaw and heard the bone crack. He toppled from the chair to the ground. I stooped down and tried forcing his jaw opened with my free hand. "Don`t make a move," I warned them and put the barrel of my pepperbox between Billy`s lips and fired. That`s one way to force a mouth open. I laughed and shot a look at the undertaker.

"Didn`t do much good, did it?" the undertaker said.

I looked at Billy and there was a hole blown through his lips and teeth, but his jaws were still locked. I put my gun to the undertaker`s head. "You know how. Open his jaws and get my gold out of his mouth."

I watched as he put one hand on the cadaver`s head and one on the jaw. He twisted hard in opposite directions. Then he repeated the procedure by twisting them back and forth. I heard a loud snap, but he still couldn`t get the mouth open to retrieve my lucky piece.

A figure plowed through the swinging doors, guns in hand, ready to shoot someone. "Bascomb," Soapy cried out when he saw Billy lying on the floor with a spreading puddle of blood around his head. His eyes burned with hatred as he spotted me. "You! First you rob me, now you`ve kilt my brother. You`re going to pay and pay big." His guttural voice turned to tears as he holstered his guns and bent over his brother.

Pitiful, a grown man crying. I should have shot him then, but I didn`t have it in me to shoot a crying man. I hated to leave my lucky piece in the mouth of a dead half-wit, but I knew I better skedaddle before help for Soapy arrived. I gathered my winnings and rode hard.

My horse headed toward Colorado Springs, but that town was said to be awfully refined and devoid of liquor, so I stopped for supplies in Colorado City. I spotted a wanted poster with my image on the front of the town Marshall`s office declaring a reward of five hundred dollars, dead or alive. I ripped the poster from the wall. Five hundred dollars would get a lot of people hunting for me. I knew I`d better change my appearance. I slunk away, wandering until I found a general store and traded in my matching pants and jacket for cowboy duds. My shoes were replaced by a fine pair of sculptured boots. I decided not to shave for a long time. With any luck, no one would recognize me as the same man on the wanted poster.

Over twenty years had passed since the gold strike at Pikes Peak, but there was still plenty of loose gold floating around in the saloons. I figured I`d have time to play some poker before I moved on. I went to the best hotel in Colorado City, the Hoffman Hotel, a hole in the wall by the grand standards of

Colorado Springs, and rented a room for a week. Right upstairs, the Hoffman Saloon bustled twenty-four hours a day. There I found four cowboys playing a game of five-card draw poker. They eyeballed my starchy new clothes, but cowboys usually buy a new outfit when the old one wears out, so they welcomed me as one of their own.

As usual, I began to accumulate the money bet back and forth, small change for me. These were working cowboys, and only earned thirty dollars a month, so it didn`t take long before all four were out of cash.

"One more hand," one of the cowboys said.

"Sure. Put up your ante if you want to play."

"I`ll put up my brand-new gun," he said. "It`s a new-fangled .44 Colt. Packs enough power to kill a grizzly, if you hit it between the eyes."

I threw up twenty silver dollars against his gun. "Five card stud. Just turn them all face up, no bets or raises."

He smiled when his first card was an ace and mine, a deuce. He got a jack and another deuce landed in front of me. His next card gave him a pair of aces and he smiled again as I got a three of clubs. We watched each other warily as he was dealt another jack. I got a four of diamonds. He wore a big smile now, anticipating how he would spend the twenty. When the last round fell, he got a ten of spades and I another deuce.

As soon as he saw the third deuce, he grabbed the gun from the table and trained it on me. "Get his gun," he told his buddy.

The buddy came up behind me and relieved me of both my weapons, then struggled to remove the wad of cash from my rear pocket.

But a shot rang out. Soapy stood by the door with his pistol smoking. "Stand back, he`s mine. I`m taking him back to Denver where he`s going to hang for killing my brother."

He strode to the cowboy who pointed the .44 at me and removed it from his hand. Scooping up the twenty silver dollars with one hand, he gave them to the cowboy. "For your .44, now git."

We headed toward Denver with me tied to my saddle like a sack of potatoes. I started saying my prayers. I knew if Soapy got me that far, it was all over. But Providence intervened and sent a powerful rainstorm with thunder and lightning that crashed through the mountains and spooked the horses. We found a cave, but the horses wouldn`t enter. After dismounting, Soapy untied me from the saddle but left my hands tied together. He tethered both horses to a tree, and we ran for the cave.

A bear smell told us a bear lived there—that probably spooked the horses as much as the storm.

"Nothing pisses a grizzly bear off more than someone entering its den. I`m putting you between the opening and me while I get some sleep. If the bear comes back while I`m sleeping, it`ll eat you, not me." Soapy laughed and slapped his thigh.

Soapy tied me with the lariat he pulled from his saddlebag. I looked at his holster and saw the new .44 in it. He left me lying on the cold damp cave floor between him and the opening. He stretched out by the fire and fell asleep with the .44 on his chest.

Bear bait for Soapy and not much I could do about it. When he began to snore, I began to pick at the knots he`d tied me up with, the bear in mind all the while. If he shot at the bear and missed, it would only piss it off. But not many could shoot as straight as me. These thoughts encouraged me to work harder on untying those knots. Once the first knot unraveled, the rest of the knots came undone easier.

I stared at Soapy with that .44 lying on his chest. My legs shook and my belly froze up as I crawled over the cold damp ground to his sleeping form. Sweat dripped from every pore, even in the chilly air. Finally, I scooted up beside him and slowly reached for the gun. My hand was on it when we both heard a grumbling roar.

The grizzly had gotten a whiff of us. I quickly grabbed the gun and aimed it at Soapy.

Soapy sat up and uttered a not so funny laugh. "I figured you might try something like that, so I emptied it." He opened his big right hand. Six .44 cartridges rested in his calloused palm. I shook violently now. That bear crept forward. I had to deal both with it *and* Soapy, and no way I could do either with an empty gun.

Soapy stood and stretched above me with his considerable height. "Percival Morse, give me my gun back and I`ll take it easy on you when I beat the crap out of you for taking it."

The bear growled and then roared, lunging forward in a way that made me jump back.

"Give me that damn gun and I`ll tell the law not to hang you," Soapy said, raw fear quivering in his voice.

I refused. The bear was close now. It couldn`t yet see us because of the fire`s glare, but we both knew what would happen once it could.

Soapy began to plead in his best shyster, soap-selling voice. "Please. Before the bear goes past the fire." His shaking hands betrayed his quiet words.

I again refused. "Give me the bullets so I can shoot the bear."

"And once you shoot the bear, you`ll turn around and shoot me."

"I`m not giving you the gun," I said, as another roar poured from the beast.

Soapy and I stared at each other.

"All right, I`ll give you one bullet to shoot the bear with." Soapy tossed one to me, which I hurriedly loaded into the gun and aimed it at him

"What`re you doing?" he yelled. "Shoot the bear, you fool."

"I think I`ll shoot you to get the rest of the bullets for the bear."

Soapy`s hand went to his mouth. I pulled the trigger, and a round hole appeared between his eyes just as he locked his jaws around the bullets.

That`s cheating, I thought.

I closed my eyes as the bear`s steamy, berry-scented breath grazed my face. . .

17

Who, What, When, Where, Why & How?

ONE DREARY MORNING WHILE WE wrote and edited our features for the next edition of Classic Art Exposé, Shirley, Evie and I discussed what cultures started written language and when. To settle our questions, Evie went out to the waiting room to pull a dog-eared book about writing from the old bookshelf. She thumbed through the opening pages until she found a passage that satisfied her. "It seems the early writing systems of the late 4th millennium BCE were not a sudden invention," she read. "Rather, they were based on the more ancient traditions of symbol systems. These systems conveyed information but were devoid of linguistic information. The symbols gradually increased in complexity over the years. The hieroglyphic scripts of the Ancient Egyptians seamlessly emerged from such symbol systems."

"So we know when writing systems developed, but these may have been based on even earlier systems," I said.

"Looks like it," Evie mumbled as she turned more pages, absorbed in the pictures and the text.

"Hey, what about novels?" Shirley said. "When did they get started?"

"About the seventeenth century, if I remember correctly," I said. "Evie, does the book cover novels?"

Evie turned the pages back to the index, ran her finger down a column, turned toward the last chapter of the book, and began to read again. "The novel is usually considered a modern genre of literature. Its history began in the seventeenth century. However, there are several ancient and medieval texts that fully qualify as novels in the sense of being extended `fictional narrative in prose.` Following the medieval romance, it is time and space consuming to list all the genres that finally culminated in the novel as we know it today. . . . " Evie paused to turn a page. "The earliest dated printed book known is the `Diamond Sutra,` printed in China in 868 AD. However, it is suspected that book printing may have occurred long before this date."

"Wow," Shirley said. "I had no idea printing happened that early."

Jason looked up from his work, apparently with his mind on other things. "How `bout a new contest plan? We award two prizes a month from now on, a first and second prize. It risks splitting the money on the first round because we might not get extra entries. But it might increase the entries exponentially. We have to try it to find out. The second story won`t take up a lot of space if we`re careful to keep an eye out for the best and shortest stories, if necessary." He looked at Evie`s disbelieving look as she mimed hitting him over the head with the book, but he shrugged and launched back into his monologue. "Or heck, maybe we can cram the second story in without adding pages. Our readers will appreciate getting twice as many cutting-edge stories to read. Speaking of reading, if you`re going to split the entry fee with other publications, make them read and judge part of the entries. Maybe we can run separate contests in the future with dueling stories. Maybe let the readers pick their favorite stories from a longlist and offer a best of the winners` prize."

"Um, I think not. We`re already doing a runner-up, though we don`t print that story. I`d rather not change anything just yet." I knew Jason could solve any logistical problem that came up for either the contest or the magazine`s business affairs. But I couldn`t very well change the rules midstream for this contest.

Shirley waved the arts page of the New York Times from her desk. "Listen to this, Pete. `Peter Rizzo, Baltimore banking magnate, recently finalized the purchase of L`Artiste magazine.`" She read on silently for a moment. "Get this. `Rizzo indicates that his premiere issue of the prominent magazine will announce a $5,000 prize for the best short story inspired by a famous piece of artwork.`"

My mouth dropped open. L`Artiste was our biggest competitor in the world of art magazines. And as much as Peter loved money, I couldn`t believe he`d throw that much around on only one contest just to annoy me.

However, with all the talk generated about dueling contests in art mags in the NYT, we received twenty-five hundred entries for our contest that month—a whopping total of $12,500. Normally, I`d sock a larger percentage into paying the magazine debt down, but Jason suggested we fight fire with fire and offer a 5k prize for a "best of" or "reader`s choice" prizewinner to cap off the contest, just to get Peter`s goat. In the end, we finally decided that since the earliest winners` prize had been so much smaller, that we should instead run one last painting as a grand finale contest and allow both non-winning writers and the earliest monthly winners to compete with new stories for our $5 entry fee. We already had the prize money earmarked, but it would be far less risk to generate more income than to stage a free "best of" or "readers` choice" contest. Then we`d have some funds earmarked for the launch of a new contest cycle with a more consistent prize payout.

Evie and Shirley breezed back into the office and overheard us talking about contest biz. "Hey, there`s a really sweet Renoir painting in our art book. How about we do something for the ladies since we just did that Western piece?"

"Eh, romance, shromance," Jason teased.

Shirley looked up from the filing cabinet where she`d started to match shipping receipts to invoices. She raised her crossed fingers. "May our success be a lot less dark and a lot more romantic!"

I scratched my head. "What do you mean?"

Shirley wrinkled her brow. "Um, I don`t know why I said that, Pete. Maybe my intuition is telling me something about the next winning story."

I laughed. "Madame Fortuneteller, let the good times roll!"

DANCE AT BOUGIVAL
Pierre-Auguste Renoir, 1882

When young Henri Matisse asked the suffering old man why he kept painting,
Renoir is said to have replied, "The pain passes, but the beauty remains."

SUCCESS

AFTER I SOLD MY FIRST book, I clandestinely took dancing lessons, and now the lessons were paying off. Suzanne had finally agreed to dance with me. I shared my new skills, twirling her around the dance floor with the expertise of one of those fancy ballroom instructors whose salons line the streets of Paris. Gazing coolly at Suzanne`s face as we danced, I drank in her radiant look of contentment, the lashes of her closed eyes fluttering like butterflies.

Some dancing couples nearby stopped to watch us, and soon the entire room gathered `round to watch us dance. When the music paused, many young women giggled, their cheeks filled with roses as they lined up before me, holding their dance cards out with downcast eyes in a plea for my signature.

It wasn't long ago that if I'd asked Suzanne to dance, she would have looked at me with disdain. She came from a well-to-do family and traveled in social circles where a workingman like me wasn't welcome. And I never, ever placed myself where I wasn't wanted. Until I met Suzanne. The fact was, when I arrived at her family home in Bougival to repair her bathtub plumbing, she was unusually friendly, letting me enter the house through the front door rather than the kitchen door used by the family's servants and the occasional workingman. I immediately got the idea that class didn't matter to Suzanne. But my first impression must have been mistaken, because she treated me like a servant when her mother walked into the room.

Still, I never let my position in life stop me, because I knew I would be a successful author one day. Despite our difference in social class, I found every excuse to visit Suzanne, using our interest in the arts as an excuse. I would bring her books loaned to me by a neighbor, or take her news of the weekly gallery shows by the finest artists in Paris.

Every time I popped in to see 'Zanne, as she began to call herself, I was entranced by both her beauty and intellect. If she was bored, she'd spend time with me, talking about my scribbles. But her two-faced treatment of me continued. Whenever one of her friends or her siblings or mother appeared, she'd dismiss me as one dismisses a servant.

After one particularly painful dismissal by 'Zanne, I took a job as a sailor so I could travel to faraway, exotic places, and acquire knowledge of different cultures for my writing. I learned so many amazing things in a short period of time. After a year, I returned to Paris, and secured a job working as a plumber. I used every spare moment to write about my experiences in South America, the South Pacific, and other ports of call. In fact, I had so much to write, I eventually quit my job to devote all my time to my writing.

Alas, as is the case with many writers, money soon became a difficulty. I was unable to pay my rent and could barely afford to feed myself. Yet I continued to write enthusiastically, eight or more hours a day, every day. I incessantly sent my stories to magazines and any publishing house who might be interested. All my stories and essays were rejected repeatedly.

I tried to see 'Zanne, but she knew of my penniless condition and seemed embarrassed to be seen with me. Whenever I tried to read any of my work to her, she would belittle it. "You must get real job, Pierre," she lamented. "At least work as a plumber again. You are much too thin."

I often heard the whispers of other people around me—*why doesn't that crazy young man work?* But I had work. My job was to write the stories bottled up inside me. The problem was that no one paid me to do my job.

At least my landlord tolerated my predicament. Even though my rent was several months in arrears, he would invite me to dinner weekly. He liked my stories and said he didn`t want to see me starve to death. I always related to him my most current story as we dined, and he let me fix his plumbing when he had trouble.

Finally, at last, one fine day I received a letter of acceptance from a magazine. One of my stories would be published, and I received a check for the princely sum of one hundred francs. It wasn`t much, considering all my debt, but enough to inspire me to renew my efforts. I continued to write and mail out manuscripts every day. Oh, the glorious beginning of my success! One after another, my stories were accepted and published. Slowly I began to receive larger and larger sums for each piece.

As my fame grew, so did `Zanne`s affection for me. I could now bring her flowers and books and trinkets, and for Christmas, even a fine golden bracelet set with emeralds that matched her eyes, a sparkling trifle that she had admired in a Parisian shop. Her family began to invite me to her home for dinner, and afterward, `Zanne would ask me to read one of my stories. She now adored everything I wrote, even if I repeated stories she had rejected before my luck turned.

But the more I was welcomed in the homes of the gentry, the less I liked it. When I needed support, there was none. Now that I`m successful, I get more attention than I want. Human nature is flawed, marred by its hunger for celebrity and lack of compassion for those in need.

Now `Zanne whispers in my ear as we dance. "We should get married soon, darling." Her counterfeit emotion turns me cold. Here is a woman who held me in disdain while I earnestly struggled to please her, no good to her as a plumber or an emerging writer, yet now she wants to marry me. Only a fool would marry a woman like this.

How cruel life is! I have everything I ever dreamed about: `Zanne, fame, fortune, and social status. But how meaningless it all is! I`ve wasted my life in pursuit of these worthless things I now possess.

A feeling of darkness overtakes me on the dance floor. I no longer want to participate in this facetious society. After I kiss `Zanne on the steps of her family`s home, pretending to love her, I return to my flat. I pull out my writing paper, dip my pen into a nearly empty ink bottle, and scrawl one last piece: my last will and testament. I leave everything I own to my landlord, the only person who tried to help me when I needed support.

Afterward, I mount the steps to the platform at the train station downtown. There are freight and passenger trains, and only passenger trains stop at this station. I, unlike the crowd around me, wait for freight train, as these speed through the station without stopping. As it rumbles up the tracks, tooting its whistle, charging ever closer, I take one last look at the faces in the crowd. That last look assures me I am doing the right thing. I step to the edge of the platform. As the engine comes so close that I feel its heat and taste its iron, I leap, soaring through the air with joyous relief. . .

18

Breaking Even

I KNEW MY FATHER WOULD go ballistic rather than be happy for me if he realized that the magazine was breaking even, and that I`d paid my monthly invoices on time though I could barely pay for printing supplies just a few months ago. I wondered what devious scheme he`d come up with next to try to thwart me.

"Syndicate, man," Jason quipped suddenly.

"What are you talking about? We already have the column syndicated. Do you mean to expand that?"

"Sell our contest to other publications nationwide; hell, worldwide. That`s where the money`s at," he said.

Except for working with some other local papers, I`d never thought of trying to go nationwide with the contest before—our subscribers were mostly regional—but Jason was right. If we got a host of other magazines and newspapers to pick up our contest, we might get thousands of entrants. At five bucks an entry, an even larger pot looked feasible. Of course, taxes would eat up some profit and there would be shared profits with the syndication group, as well as bigger awards. We`d have to either hire more staff or find pre-reader and judge volunteers.

To test possibilities, we strategically contacted a sampling of publications around the country. They liked my revenue-sharing plan and Jason and I started to draw up written agreements to syndicate the contest, including a cut for every participating venue.

"It`s a little mindboggling," I confessed to Jason. "It`s going to take O`Neill and an accountant to handle all this."

Jason shrugged like he always does. "Simple, man. Every rag that syndicates will print a serial number on their entry forms so we know where each one comes from. If we need to do the reading and judging, we deduct a fee for each entry. That way it`s advantageous for them to run local contests, but if they don`t, the money we hold back covers the reading costs. Either way, it`s good publicity for us."

We skipped our usual contest meeting and I again picked a painting from the art book myself for the next contest. Joaquin Pallares y Allustante, whose birth and death dates are unknown, was a genre and landscape painter from the Spanish school. We`d had some nice stories with settings in France, so why not another, I thought. Allustante`s painting, *Y Une Place Animee a Paris,* looked like a winner.

❦

Peter had heard about my column and contest syndication and no doubt tried to prevent the deal, but his influence dwindled away from New York, Baltimore, and Washington D.C., and this gig involved too many different media outlets around the country. It suddenly but belatedly occurred to me how he kept "finding out" about so many issues regarding my magazine business, but I pushed the thought of an inside leak away. No one could stop me now. I was on a roll and had more than enough cash on hand to pay off John`s debts in full.

"Are you sure you want to use your entire cash reserve like this?" O`Neill asked when I called to tell him the good news.

"I agree it`s a risk, but things are moving along and I`d like to see how it goes with no outstanding debt hanging over my head." My mind drifted to positive future possibilities.

"It`s your call, Pete. By the way, your father`s bank has been involved in some bond fiasco. I don`t know the full details yet, but the breaking news is that the Feds are considering bringing fraud charges against him."

My mind began to spin with worries about how this would affect my mother. With the current run of good luck at the magazine, I could care for her, and surely if she did file for divorce, she would be eligible for a handsome monthly alimony even if Peter were prosecuted. . . so I shoved my concerns aside as I stifled a cynical chuckle. "How can that be? My father`s dead."

O`Neill went silent for the first time since I`d known him. I realized what I`d said and that he had no clue about my father-uncle debacle. I didn`t want to elaborate, so I said, "I`m sorry, I was daydreaming. Now what`s this about my father?"

🌱

Y Une Place Animee a Paris
Joaquin Pallares y Allustante, 1898

The success of Joaquin Pallares y Allustante`s `costume painting,`
an offshoot of romanticism, depended on the expressiveness of
the characters, a quality directly derived from history painting.

THE JONAH

THE WARNING SIRENS HAD JUST faded and the post-explosion silence grew more deafening by the moment. "You did it again, Michel. Get your stuff and get the hell off the property." Georges growled and waved his hand at the cave-in caused by God knows what—inappropriately placed explosives or too many explosives.

As Michel picked his cap and lunch pail up from the lacerated ground, he watched LeMonde, the mine owner, dog his foreman`s heels. They made no attempt to lower their loud voices. "Is that a good move? You know how difficult it is to find a competent dynamiter."

"Michel may be an explosives expert, but he`s a Jonah," Georges growled again, gesturing again toward the site.

"You know as well as I do that these peculiar accidents always happen on his watch."

Michel wasted no time hitching a ride to his favorite tavern to tip a few back and whine to his favorite tavern keeper. "I`ve worked the mines all my life. I did my best, but this last explosion somehow injured two men. I set all the explosives just right, spent days calculating the field and the results. I doubt I`ll find another job anywhere." He drained his first pint of lager and started on the second, already beaded with sweat in the dank heat. He ran his fingers around the circular watermarks on the scarred wood of the bar.

The drinker sitting next to Michel pulled a frown and waved his half-empty glass for emphasis. "I hear they`re building a subway underneath Paris. Seems there`s a shortage of dynamiters down there. Goddamn city canards are blowing themselves up. They don`t know how to use that shit." He turned and cast Michel a cold look. "You can go up there and help them, you fucking Jonah," he spat in an ugly voice, as if his thick words could take form. "My father died when I was a boy because of an expert like you." The workingman turned back to nurse his beer, facing the mirror with a self-satisfied expression.

"Accidents happen, you know," Michel said, trying to force an even tone into his shaky voice. "Over time, dynamite sweats nitroglycerine, which then pools in the bottom of the storage area. Crystals form on the outside of the sticks. This creates a dangerous situation because that shit can explode at any time."

The workingman slammed his empty glass down and barged through the double doors of the tavern, letting them dangle open. A whoosh of warm air rushed inside and some flyers tacked on the wall behind the bar fluttered in a limp way that made Michel feel sad. He fingered his glass, considering the move to Paris. He left the tavern after only one pint, gathered his few possessions, packed a small trunk, and paid his landlady for an extra week to keep her mouth shut. Paris was only a half-day`s train ride away.

On the train, Michel kept his cap pulled low on his forehead and his face behind a newspaper. Perhaps his bad luck had run out now. He really did know the ropes with explosives. . . this time, he wouldn`t let greedy mine owners and their greedy foremen push him into risky decisions. They were more complicit in these accidents than he was. Michel knew he certainly was no Jonah—he`d been unlucky in his jobs, to be sure, but was cooperative, knowledgeable, and hardworking. Mistakes happen in the mining business no matter the good intentions. His father had been a sailor in his youth, and then a ship`s captain in later years, and he had sometimes used the expression after coming home from a particularly trying voyage fraught with disobedient sailors and bad experiences. No doubt Georges and the workingman at the tavern had a sailor in their families as well and how they had learned that simple but pejorative term.

Once in Paris, Michel found a cheap *pension* for the night and headed straight for the excavation site in the heart of the city. He clipped his curly mane of dark hair short and with a fresh shave, he hoped he looked different from the photos that circulated in newspapers all over the country. He approached a man in overalls and a soft derby hat with a hard leather brim shouting orders over the din of jackhammers and dump trucks, and asked if the company were hiring. "The only hiring we're doing is for experienced dynamiters," the man said brusquely, turning away to his work again.

"I worked mining operations in Wales for several years," Michel said truthfully, as he truly had worked in Britain before working in the American mines and then on the last disastrous job in Noeux. "I came home to help my mother when my father died recently, and I consider myself an expert."

The foreman looked him over so carefully that Michel's forehead began to bead with sweat. He asked several questions about explosives that Michel answered quickly. With a satisfied grunt, the foreman introduced himself as Emile and gave him a paper to sign. "This job pays well, of course. We've had some accidents, though, so make certain you don't have any. All you have to do is keep extending the tunnels. Once the dynamite does its job, you wait until workers clear the debris from the last explosion. Then repeat the process over again. You'll find the work is quite routine." He directed Michel to a metal shed filled with explosives, held tight with a thick door lined with padlocks.

To Michel's relief, the new job was truly less complicated than mining work. Those who had fallen short on this job must truly be canards. All day long that first day, he walked underground into the already excavated tunnel segment and drilled several small holes into the back wall to fit the dynamite sticks into, and then set the long fuses to give him time to walk away. He had only to limit the number of sticks and keep the explosions small enough to shatter the rock without collapsing the tunnel, no more. Even a canard could do it.

Whenever the dynamite exploded, it made the street above shudder softly, the muffled boom sounding no more frightening than the heartbeat deep in his chest. Even so, his was one of the most dangerous jobs on the project, though certainly not at the danger level of his mining jobs. There, the life expectancy for dynamiters depended upon their skill and experience—there was always a shortage of dynamiters because the middling ones kept blowing themselves up.

The crew came in after each explosion with picks and shovels to load the loose rock into gondola cars that ground slowly to the surface. Other workers emptied these into the trucks. The operations were similar to mining operations but on a much smaller scale. Sometimes it took two or three hours to clear the tunnel after an explosion, so Michel had plenty of free time between rounds of setting dynamite. Emile didn't care what he did as long as the explosives shed was secure, so he often spent his time reading a book or gazing at the sky. Sometimes the white-collar people who worked downtown would stroll nearby at lunchtime to goggle at the project. Then Michel would watch the lovely ankles of the young women in their heavily starched skirts, hoping for a breeze that might expose a shapely calf.

Michel had just put his book down and was striding into the newly cleaned tunnel to continue blasting a solid rock face when Emile tapped him on the shoulder.

"Will you plant adequate explosives to crumble enough rock so that the diggers are busy for the rest of the day?"

Michel didn`t answer the question as he thought it stupid. If anything, he always used a touch more explosive than he needed. Never not enough. But he reconsidered, and turned to say yes, of course, there was enough work for weeks. Emile was the only other guy working in the tunnels who spoke the same regional French dialect, and probably why the foreman had hired him so quickly. Even though he didn`t particularly like Emile, it felt good to converse in the familiar way.

Both men quickly began to sweat in the stuffy air of the tunnel. Emile removed his cap and shoved into his trousers pocket. His bald head took on a glowing sheen and Michel could feel rivulets of sweat trickling down the back of his neck and past his shoulders. There was no possibility of cooling off in the humid heat. It should be cooler underground, Michel thought. "Emile, why is it so hot down here?"

"Because we`re so close to hell," the foreman said, laughing and mopping his head with a dirty white handkerchief.

For a moment, Michel imagined he could hear the faint cries of the damned. He resisted rolling his eyes and ignored this stupid answer. The humidity had to come from the moisture that seeped through the rock they were blasting. The season was warm. There was no hell. Science answered everything.

They watched the dozen or so men who trailed inside the tunnel to dig in the glare of the new electric light bulbs. Michel felt transfixed as he gazed at the electric lights. The mines he had worked in Wales and the American West had no electrical lighting.

"Emile, you should see the miners` equipment in America. They carry a two-compartment lunch bucket, a carbide lamp, and a pick. Old-fashioned."

Emile grunted. "I suppose those mines aren`t located in the middle of the city like this project."

The next day Emile approached Michel with a plan. "There are old tunnels said to exist under Paris. Excavations that are hundreds of years old. If we find these, it`ll knock weeks off our schedule. I`ll get a bonus and I`ll share it with you. All you have to do is spend your free time digging in places on this map." Emile handed Michel a short-handled shovel. Then he reached into his sweat-soaked shirt and extracted a rolled-up parchment of dried animal skin. When he unrolled it, Michel saw some old symbols and a map drawn with some sort of ink that looked much fresher than the skin. In fact, the map looked as though it were recently drawn. But the skin showed its age. The map had tunnels drawn on it, but Michel couldn`t understand the symbols or the language on the map. Emile pointed out the placements in the map related to existing city streets, and what landmarks Michel should look for.

"Who built tunnels here centuries ago?"

Emile shrugged. "Who cares? A friend who likes history told me about them. What`s important is to find them."

The symbols gave Michel the creeps and he wondered what supernatural phenomena might lurk underground but he pushed this out of his mind. He had several hours of daylight left to start searching for the old tunnels when he finished his day shift. At least one old tunnel was already accessible from underground, but he would have to look for signs of others above ground, like archeologists looking for old cultural sites without monuments. He located all the areas Emile had shown him on the map. At first, he`d shuffled around in the dirt like a dog and hadn`t found anything interesting. Blinded by his own salty sweat in the late afternoon sun on the first day, he cursed at his failure, swearing that Emile`s map was a fake that had sent him on a wild goose chase. Some sections of tunnels on the map were inaccessible, with too many cobblestone lanes, buildings, or other obstructions over them.

Finally, on a long fruitless Sunday, just as the thought of quitting this foolishness weighed heavily on his mind, Michel`s walking stick broke through a slightly depressed area at the east end of a public park. He got on his knees to tap and dig with a small spade. It was easier on his tired back to dig on his hands and knees, and it drew less attention. After that first success, he quickly developed the knack to locate many other tunnels. He walked farther and farther from the city`s teeming center, puttering along the grassy shoulders along roadways, and sometimes even upon the hard-packed dirt of the roadways themselves, avoiding the curious eyes of motorists and pedestrians wherever the map indicated he would find a tunnel. Once he even found a tunnel entrance that lay deep in the weeds and brambles of an unkempt, derelict cemetery. Michel felt a chill go up his spine as he imagined the phantoms that might be loosed by digging there. He laughed aloud at himself, thinking again of science.

Giuseppe di Anti of Venice, Italy had studied carefully the Rosicrucian manifestos and Freemason documents he had accumulated over the years. He found everything had a price, and with the support of the prosperous backers of this quest, he could afford to pay whatever it took. His backers were fortunately not only interested in treasure, but also in the knowledge they had acquired along the way. Di Anti had learned that the Rosicrucians had descended from The Knights Templar, the original owners of the treasure. The legend presented in their *Fama Fraternitatis*, an anonymous Rosicrucian manifesto published in 1614, was interpreted through the intervening centuries as a narrative ripe with metaphor and symbolism:

> *We speak unto you by parables, but would willingly bring you to the right, simple, easy and ingenuous exposition, understanding, declaration, and knowledge of all secrets.*

Historians weren`t lying when they said that the Rosicrucians spoke in parables, di Anti conceded the first time he`d read the manuscript. He`d found nothing clear or simple in it. He felt tempted to abandon his quest many times because of the complexity of the manuscripts, charts, and graphs now scattered throughout his library. He practically had to learn a new language just to understand the various symbols, signs, codes, and languages in these old documents. But through his painfully slow and labored study, success now appeared to be in reach. The greatest treasure ever hidden was about to be discovered.

He called his trusted assistant to relate the conclusion of his search. "See, Marco, by using astrological charts, I have determined the location of the buried treasure, a park situated in the center of Paris, France. Right here." He tapped on the dot representing Paris on an atlas map.

After sorting through the old documents, di Anti had found that the Rosicrucians, and later, the Masonic brotherhood, had kept meticulous records of the Knights Templar and that it wasn`t hard to acquire the needed documentation. He made a list of the leaders, and from this list, determined who was in control of their treasury.

"Look, Marco, right here it says that vast treasures were hidden from the king who persecuted them." His finger rapidly scanned back and forth across a tattered document, a palimpsest he had painstakingly restored in two years of daily work. "And right here," he pointed to a paragraph, "it tells of the progression of secrets handed from one generation to the next until finally one of them put the secret in writing lest it would be lost if he died before passing it on. Here`s the secret, but it`s in code. Fortunately, I deciphered the code and I know where to look for the treasure. The written directions tell me there`s only one day every hundred and five years that the planet Venus is positioned to enable anyone to find the treasure. Listen:

> `On June 8 1793, Venus passed directly between the Earth and the Sun, appearing as a large black dot travelling across the Sun`s disk. This event is known as a transit of Venus and is very rare: the next one is this year, 1898, and after that, in 2004, and then again in 2012 during a*

*retrograde when Venus appears to travel backwards, and not until 2117
will this transit happen once more.*`

"I need the exact measurements of these three landmarks in the Place des Vosges–Square Louis XIII." Di Anti showed Marco how the public park was dotted with fountains and structures. "The objects must date prior to 1793, so this narrows it down to these three statues. These are mentioned in the secret code for the treasure`s location." He pointed out three dots on the map, in close proximity at the park`s eastern perimeter, and then traced his finger along a line of his written notes. " `On 28 June this year, Venus will pass in front of the sun, and the sun`s rays will point to the location of the treasure by passing across these three landmarks.` My calculations show this location will be revealed at exactly five-fifty a.m."

Marco frowned. "How can you be so sure of the exact time?"

"By the varying positions of the sun above the Earth. Sun time is also expressed in hours, minutes, and seconds, but the length of solar days varies by seconds. So, by interpreting the triangulation methods used in the documents, I`ve come to this conclusion. Of course, with Venus passing directly in front of the sun, it will change the angle of the rays slightly and reveal the location of the treasure. That`s the reason I need you to measure the structures exactly for me, so I can be certain the calculations are a hundred percent accurate. If we make a mistake, the treasure can`t be discovered for over another century."

Marco left by train for Paris within the week accompanied by a trusted six-man crew carrying the latest surveying equipment to measure the landmarks. When he arrived, Marco and his men headed straight to the park in central Paris. The measurements matched di Anti`s exactly, and he sent a dispatch immediately to Venice to confirm this.

Di Anti sent a return telegram, instructing Marco to secure a permit to dig in the park by bribing someone who worked on the new subway system. The reason for this was twofold. First, they could help dig up the treasure when located, and second, they needed to be certain there wasn`t the slightest vibration coming from the tunnel excavation on the day they pinpointed the treasure`s location.

Marco learned what tavern the superintendent of the subway excavation drank at after work every day. He`d already positioned himself at the bar when the superintendent came in the next afternoon.

The workingman downed his drinks the instant the barkeep set them on the bar.

"You have quite a thirst," Marco said. "Let me tell you about a drink that dates from the Crusades that`s guaranteed to quench it."

"Hell, I`m not thirsty. I just love to drink," the superintendent said.

"Then let me buy a fellow tippler a drink." Marco waved the barkeep back and ordered two drinks made of liqueur and fruit juices specially measured and stirred. Soon both men became friends of a sort.

Marco showed up at the tavern for lunch or late afternoon drinks for a week. The superintendent`s name turned out to be Jacques. On Friday afternoon, Marco asked Jacques if there would be an underground station at the park they were digging near.

Jacques became animated. "That`s exactly what I wanted, but the commissioner overruled me on the matter."

Marco paid the commissioner a visit as the business day concluded, and a large sum of cash changed hands. When he returned to the tavern on Friday evening, he gave Jacques the commissioner`s change orders to build the subway station at the east end of the park. On Monday, the excavation company declared 28 June a day when all miners must be above ground until seven a.m. to do various tasks, but they didn`t tell anyone it was because of the transit of Venus across the sun. This assured Marco there would be no vibrations from underground to interfere with the statues` alignment with the sun.

Marco negotiated with Jacques to allow him and his six men on the vanguard of the dig. Another sum of cash changed hands. Not as much this time, just enough to persuade Jacques to allow space to observe, and to secure any artifacts uncovered rather than reporting these to the metropolitan museum or to the city fathers. To assure Jacques` silence, Marco assured him that if Emile`s crew found anything truly valuable during the park excavation, that he would also benefit.

In Venice, di Anti built a scale model of the three landmarks to see if by shining a light on them in the exact angle of the sun on 28 June, he could determine the treasure`s location in advance. But he couldn`t quite get the beam of light to touch the statues, which were not situated in a straight line, no matter how hard he tried. When he placed the light where the sun would rise over the horizon, it never struck all three statues. There must be a hidden prism in the statues or some inexplicable anomaly that could not be determined by using a model. He sent word to Marco to have a camera set at each statue to record the path of the sunlight at five-fifty a.m. on 28 June.

27 June 1898. Michel emerged from the tunnel to signal to the diggers. His carefully calculated first blast of the day shattered the back wall of the new tunnel under the park.

"Good work." Emile patted Michel on the back. He left and returned with a string of electric lights and a large battery. The lights wobbled to life, dimmer with the battery than when the workers used the direct current downtown. "Let`s get moving," Emile said, "before the batteries weaken." He handed a small kerosene lantern to Michel. "Be mindful and watch the flame in case there are gases underground."

They entered the newly excavated length of tunnel together. Six or seven yards into the tunnel stood a cement pillar about six feet in diameter. "Blast a hole big enough for us to get through. It may be a support, so we don`t want to take it out entirely, but we need to make more room around it to see what`s behind. Can you do that?" Emile, though cautious, beamed with excitement now that they`d found all the old tunnels but one and might complete the digging weeks ahead of schedule.

Michel nodded. When the blast was finished, they discovered that it exposed more of the old tunnel, confirming the marks on the map. It wasn`t much of a start, just enough to reveal that it connected at right angles to the tunnel they were constructing, one scheduled to stretch quite far in another direction, right along the park boundary.

"We`ll explore more later. For now, help me hang these signs," Emile ordered. He handed Michel a stack of hand-printed signs that they posted on wires over the tunnels and at the entrances, giving strict orders that no one was to enter the tunnels before seven a.m. the next morning. Emile gathered groups of workers to make certain everyone understood, as there were employees who spoke various languages.

28 June 1898. The day had finally arrived. Marco entered the park with his crew long before the sun rose to set up cameras, surveying tripods, and theodolites at each of the three statues of interest in the eastern end of the park. The park slowly filled with excavation workers, still curious as to why they had been assigned various tasks aboveground—"make work" tasks, many grumbled. But they went about their business anyway, inspecting tools and equipment and taking inventory.

The sun began to rise in almost slow motion as Marco`s crew gathered near the statues.

Michel had arrived a few minutes before dawn, wanting to be certain that more debris would be quickly available by the time the workers were due to start work again. Despite the orders to stay out of the tunnel, Michel felt it would be no problem if he simply drilled the dynamite holes to ready these for blasting. He carefully drilled three holes into the remaining concrete and rock, and inserted a stick of dynamite into each one. Then he hooked a long fuse to each stick. Then he absentmindedly lit the fuses and ran.

Only when he reached the mouth of the tunnel did Michel realize with a heart-dropping start what he`d just done. He turned as if he could run back and extinguish the fuses. For an instant, he felt his body poised in mid-air, torn between two opposing forces. He glanced at his watch, illuminated by glowing numbers. Five forty-nine a.m. He wrenched his body around from the mouth of the tunnel to scramble up the ramp to the surface.

Michel shook his head and tried to focus on the activity around the park. In the distance, he saw the group of foreign surveyors near the statues. A ray of sunlight broke through the early morning mist and shone on the easternmost statue. When the sunlight touched the tip of an upheld sword in the hand of the historic horseman, the sunbeam flared to the second statue, a female draped in Roman garb and holding the scales of justice. Michel gasped when the third statue, a dashing musketeer with a wide-brimmed hat topped with a feather, seemed to shudder for a split-second as the sunbeam zigzagged from it and then to the ground, almost like a bolt of lightning. The surveyors cast each other knowing looks, then all stumbled backwards with the shock wave and the muffled sound of the underground explosion. In another split-second, the musketeer suddenly disappeared into the ground.

Emile, standing midway between Michel and the surveyors, went pale and slack-jawed, as if he envisioned his bonus sinking along with the statue. He tossed his clipboard to his feet.

Marco fell to his knees, deflating like a balloon losing air. He pounded his fists on the ground.

Michel stepped back and trembled behind the wide trunk of an oak tree sheltering the explosives shed near the ramp, looking behind him for a way to disappear in front of so many people. *Fucking Jonah*, he thought. What trouble had he unleashed now?

Emile, Marco and his crew, and the excavation workers scrambled away as a sinkhole began to widen from the remains of the caved-in tunnel.

No one else seemed to notice the churning demonic forms raising their dark, claw-like hands over the park, their mouths circled in silent howls. As Michel stumbled forward, pulled by a mysterious force, they rose like mist from the gaping sinkhole, the blast`s dust and debris scattering around him on the morning wind rather like the weeping, deadly sirens noted by Michel`s father in his fogbound days at sea. . .

19

New & Improved

JUST AS I HAD PREDICTED, the winning contest story had entered the realm of the fantastic, a paranormal story set in Paris. And the circulation of Art and Literature Exposé, our new and improved magazine, increased again because of the contest. On the first morning after the new issue reached subscribers, I deliberately chose a dark and suggestive painting for the final contest myself—*Dante and Virgil in Hell* by William Bouguereau. Jason, Shirley, and Evie all agreed that this painting should inspire many compelling tales.

In the afternoon, I made the final payments on John`s notes per the bequest agreement, just in the nick of time. Full of good cheer about the magazine`s future prospects, we all went out to celebrate that night after work. First, we went to see *Citizen Kane* playing at a local art theatre that specialized in old flicks. Afterward, we walked to a club nearby, one with live rock and roll on the weekends, but nearly empty on this off-night Tuesday. The barmaid fed some dimes into the jukebox in the corner to liven the place up as we walked in. "Geez guys, I`m real sorry to hear about it," she said as she opened four bottles of Bud.

"Hear about what?"

"On the radio. The fire. What a blow."

I looked at her like she must be out of her mind. Then she looked back at me like I must be out of my mind. Then it hit me. "What fire? Tell me it`s not the magazine," I said, knowing that was why we heard so many sirens at a distance from inside the theatre. No doubt the city was trying to get in touch with me and maybe even thought we`d perished inside, if the fire had been bad enough. By the look on the barmaid`s face, it must have been a doozy.

I stood up to leave and then, hit by despair, sat down again, holding my head in my hands like it might fly apart.

I rubbed my eyes against the searing vision of the building grasped by flames, with water streams from the firehoses futilely arcing into the fire, and steam and smoke rising from broken windows as if issued from the pits of hell. Decay, despondency, and despair punched me in the gut and it was all I could do to keep from weeping.

Shirley and Evie fluttered and clucked around me like mother hens. Jason cast a concerned look at me, but shrugged. "Relax, Pete. The place is insured and needed remodeling anyway. We`ll just have to take this a step at a time."

At least Jason hadn`t said `simple.` I stood up and sat down again. "Holy crap. What the hell. We just got out from under all that debt. We`re only an issue away from picking the final winner of the short story contest. There`s no way I`m not finishing the contest at this point. . . C`mon, Jason; use that brain of yours to figure out what we can do now. I don`t even know how good our insurance policy is."

Shirley patted me on the shoulder. "If it`s the same one your Uncle John had, it`s probably okay, don`t you think?"

Evie`s eyes teared up, but she nodded vigorously.

"I`ll have to check with O`Neill." I looked at my watch. Ten thirty. "I`ll have to call him tomorrow. No sense trying now."

Jason smugly took a long swig of Budweiser. "Simple man, just use one of the local distribution centers to print the magazine."

Why couldn`t I ever think of simple solutions like that? My mind raced with multiple scenarios of the disaster and our uncertain future. "Peter, he`s probably the one who torched the place," I said, slamming my bottle down on the table. He hated to lose any challenge, and my star was rising while his was sinking. He just had to drag me down with him somehow. But why would Peter risk even more prison time over a personal vendetta that seemed trivial by comparison to his legal woes? It would make more sense for him to gruffly concede I`d done fairly well for myself and move on. . .

"Let`s talk about the Impressionist movement," Jason suddenly said, his enunciation thick and slurred.

Shirley glared at Jason. "Impressionism was a nineteenth-century art movement, what about it?"

"Did you know the name of the movement is derived from the title of Monet`s painting, *Impression Sunrise?*

What the hell. What was Jason up to? This diverting behavior was strange, even for him.

❀

223

"How would I know something like that?" I didn`t know if I knew or not. My brain roiled with conflicting thoughts of filial loyalty and revenge. Peter hated me so much he`d torch the magazine? But why the hell did I even care?

Jason`s hand motions increased to arm waving. "Impressionistic literature can basically be defined as when an author centers his attention on the character`s mental life, the character`s impressions, sensations, and emotions, rather than trying to interpret them."

I stared at Jason. That`s exactly what I was doing, centering my attention on my impressions, sensations, and emotions. What would I do if I found out for certain that Peter had burned my building?

Tipsy now, Jason continued his bizarre monologue. "The Impressionists broke the rules of academic painting. They used short brush strokes of pure and unmixed color, not smoothly blended, as was the custom at the time. Instead of physically mixing yellow and blue paint, they placed unmixed yellow paint on the canvas next to unmixed blue paint, so that the colors would mingle in the eye of the viewer to create the impression of green—"

"I`m about ready to give you the impression of a black eye, Jason. Come on, Evie." Shirley headed for the ladies` room with Evie in tow.

I suddenly had an "impression," a daydream of Peter in handcuffs, hauled off to the penitentiary. This inspired more mixed emotions.

Jason was silent for a moment. I turned my eyes away and stared at the wall to discourage him.

"Let`s talk about time," Jason suddenly said.

I glanced at him. "Shit. Okay, what time is it?"

"I mean *what* is it?" Jason reiterated. "There are many questions about it. Whether time exists when nothing is changing; what kinds of time travels are possible; whether the future and past are real; whether there was time before the Big Bang; what are the neural mechanisms that account for our experience of time? Does time exist for beings that have no minds?"

"I don`t know how to answer all those questions. What the hell, Jason."

"I`ve got more questions. If we have the intuition that time flows, but science implies otherwise, then which view is correct? If the future is real, then is it fixed now, and would we have the freedom to affect that future?"

"Why are you asking me these unanswerable questions? You know they`re all theoretical and can`t be answered. Hell, we`ve got a crisis on our hands, guy." I nearly started banging my head on the table but held it in my hands instead.

"Wait, listen to my theory; humans are time travelers. The human mind moves through time in any direction or speed. We are a race of time travelers. We can create any past or future we want—"

"Jesus. Jason. Knock. It. Off." I stood up and put my jacket on. "You make sure the girls get home okay. I`m outta here."

I slammed through the club door and took off at a slow jog toward the office.

❧

I stood for over an hour shivering in the cold night air, fuming and staring with dismay at the smoking ruins of Classic Art Exposé. The building's burned-out shell still glowed with searing heat, too dangerous to get near. After speaking with a Brooklyn Fire Department captain as the fire brigade packed their equipment and readied to return to their station, I found a cab around the corner a few minutes past midnight and spent the night in a cheap hotel. First thing in the morning, I called BFD to see about an arson investigation. If it turned out Peter had burned my business to the ground I'd. . . Anger mixed with myriad painful emotions almost blinded me. Honestly, I wasn't sure what I'd do.

The arson probe turned up conclusive evidence the fire had been started in a trash can in the pressroom and aided by some sort of propellant. The damage was so great that there were no recoverable fingerprints in the area. Otherwise there would have been plenty of fingerprints belonging to the printers, me, Jason, Shirley and Evie, maybe even to John and Millie, on various surfaces.

The insurance company settled quickly so I could start rebuilding. Fortunately, due to the Black Magazine Monday incident, I wasn`t an arson suspect, at least not for long, even though the running joke about fires is that the business owner always sets them to collect insurance money. Luckily, I also found the property had increased in value since I`d inherited it, something O`Neill hadn`t mentioned and probably assumed I knew. I could sell the property and make a tidy profit if I wanted out of the business.

The insurance settlement was decent, generous even, and I located some office and living space in a warehouse nearby as a temporary address while I researched old Classic Art Exposé building plans from the city Planning and Building files. I wanted the old historic brick structure copied and a modern interior designed. I'd add an extra floor with an eye to business expansion and rent it out as office space until we needed it. Our truck had burned too, but it would soon be replaced along with the building and the press. I hired a messenger service to haul our mail back and forth the extra distance to our rented quarters because Evie and Shirley were busier than ever—so busy that I budgeted a real salary for Shirley's promotion to an editorial assistant and Evie's promotion to official contest reader.

The local distribution center did a fine job of printing the magazine and the thought of letting them continue to print it crossed my mind. Well, for about five minutes. While it was tempting to cash in on

⚶

the land, I'd grown to love Brooklyn and the publishing business, and even as I sat in the club after hearing about the fire, I vowed that a new Rizzo enterprise would rise from the ashes. I'd made a name for Art and Literature Exposé, and even though I could probably run the business from anywhere, I felt completely at home in Brooklyn. Maybe we could even start a second magazine or get into publishing art books—*Rizzo Publishing, Incorporated.* I liked the sound of it. Uncle John must be smiling from heaven, if there is such a place.

I arranged to move John's and Millie's caskets from the Fairhaven Cemetery in Baltimore to a nicer cemetery in Brooklyn, where they belonged. My mother bought a plot near them, devastating me with her plans to "come home to you, Petey," when I told her about feeling at home in New York City. She was considering her options, whether to remain married but formally separated, or to divorce and secure her share of assets that the Feds couldn't seize. Peter had substantial holdings and she would live well even if he went to prison.

I was feeling so good about the future, I didn't even mind when Jason, Evie, and Shirley voted on my least favorite story in the final round. I was surprised that the girls hadn't insisted upon naming their favorite Green Goddess tale as the 1961 Art and Literature Exposé Writing Contest grand prizewinner since it had the smallest field of contenders and had won the smallest pot. There were a few other deserving tales, old and new, but I had to concede to Jason that "Heaven or Hell" definitely had some clever moments and would appeal to many contemporary readers.

DANTE & VIRGIL IN HELL
William-Adolphe Bouguereau, 1850

*Each day I go to my studio full of joy. . . if I cannot
give myself to my dear painting I am miserable.*

HEAVEN OR HELL?

MY OLD FRIEND ANDY BOUNCED into my room and flashed that sideways, shit-eating grin he always got when he started coming down from a trip. "Guess what, Joe? I`ve learned how to tell if you`re dead or not while I`m hallucinating."

I looked up from my book, wondering what kind of drug Andy had experimented with this time. "Um, how can you tell?"

"Look in a mirror. If you see yourself, you`re alive. If you don`t see a reflection, it means you`re dead." Andy leaned toward the dresser and checked his reflection in the mirror.

"If you`re hallucinating, how do you know what you`re really seeing?"

Andy reached into his shirt pocket and shook a plastic pill bottle filled with little tablets. "I don`t know how it works, but it`s a proven fact. If you see yourself, you`re alive, and if you don`t, you`re dead."

"A proven fact? How the hell do you prove something like that? Besides, if you`re looking in the mirror, you`re pretty much alive." I put my hand out and Andy dumped a half-dozen yellow pills into my palm.

"Not so, Joe," he said. "Everyone who died while hallucinating on this mixture and got resuscitated swore they didn`t see their reflection while they were high, and everyone who didn`t die saw their reflection."

I stared at the little pills and wondered what my chances of dying were if I took them. "What good`s it going to do if you know you`re dead?"

"Then you don`t have to worry about dying anymore."

I guess that made sense since the biggest human worry, especially when you get up in years like me and Andy, is death. After Andy got tired of rattling on about his trip and went to bed, I decided to eat one of the little yellow pills. I`d make sure I looked in a mirror if I could find one during my trip.

Almost immediately after swallowing the pill, I saw colors so bright and sharp they felt like they cut through my skin. I felt, tasted, and heard every single color as they entered my body. The world became bright and crowded with colored lights and textures—it seemed as though my favorite artist, van Gogh, had painted the world.

Suddenly, nausea overtook me. All the colors turned into a revolting, swirling dark purple and black vortex that spun ever faster, whirling me along the hallway to the bathroom door. I leaned over the toilet, opened my mouth, and tried to heave a ball of liquid fire from my stomach.

I tried my best to expel this broiling ball, but nothing emerged other than a dry heave. With the next forceful heave, I could feel the muscles of my legs and my back straining. I heaved again and again until finally, I`d filled the toilet with regrets. I puked up regret after regret until I had to flush the toilet to make room for them all.

Any sickness is worth the pain once your regrets are gone, I thought. For a moment, I figured part of my brain must have emptied into the toilet too. But when I looked again, there were only regrets, each one neatly marked with a bright yellow label with black print stating what I did, and the date and time I did it. It seemed that thousands and thousands of these swirled around the toilet bowl. How had there been any room in me for things I didn`t regret?

This wasn`t the experience Andy had shared with me. But I could live with it. Now that I had no regrets, I went back to my room and took another little yellow pill. After a minute or two, the colors of everything around me became textured again and I felt another ball growing in my stomach. I ran to the toilet and puked up my beliefs. It wasn`t as painful because I had few beliefs. These had pretty blue labels with a flowing, handwritten script in dark navy. I knew the last little yellow pill had gone down the toilet with my beliefs, so I went back to my room and took another.

Just as the colors and textures began to form again, I had to vomit once more. I rushed to the bathroom. This time my sins came pouring out. I needed to flush three times before they were all gone. The sins were marked with white print on a red label that named the sin and the date and time. I hadn`t realized I`d been such a sinner. I would have guessed these were no more prevalent than my beliefs. But stuff I`d considered natural was labeled as error. I wanted to weigh myself, because after ridding myself of all these regrets, beliefs, and sins, I felt twenty pounds lighter. I searched for the bathroom scale, but I couldn`t find it.

I felt more and more tired with each episode of vomiting. My abdomen, back, and leg muscles ached from the continuous heaving. Maybe my time to die had come after all. The idea didn`t upset me. I had no regrets as I`d flushed them all down the toilet along with all my sins and all my beliefs. So I had nothing to worry about if there was such a thing as an afterlife. One thought crashed into another, and then I wondered what it would be like to pass from this life to the next. A voice in the back of my mind asked, "Isn`t there one thing you want before you die?"

"Yes, I`d like to fall in love, to remember that experience for eternity," I said aloud.

Somehow, thinking of love gave me the strength to reach the phone and call 911. The ambulance arrived in minutes. By the time they arrived, the attendants had to inject me with a stimulant and administer mouth-to-mouth resuscitation. At the hospital, an ER doctor took blood and hooked me to a heart monitor, and after disappearing for an hour, returned to say I`d had a heart attack. When he was finished with me in the ER, an orderly wheeled my gurney to a room on a cardiac unit, where I`d stay under observation for a day or two. I felt undecided about feeling happy or sad, because even if I`d died for a little bit, it seemed pleasant enough.

As soon as Kate, my daytime RN, walked through the door, my question was answered. I felt happy to be alive. In fact, it was love at first sight. I`d read dozens of love stories, but never believed true love was possible for me. With her angelic smile, halo of soft blonde hair, and the bluest eyes I had ever seen, Kate stole my heart and soul the instant I laid eyes on her. *Stunning, stunning,* I said to myself.

"How are you feeling, Mr. DiBuduo?" If angels could speak, they would all have Kate`s voice. "Is there anything I can do for you?"

"You`ve already done what no one else could in all these years." I asked her if she`d be my nurse as long as I was in the hospital.

"Along with other patients on this ward, I`m your assigned nurse."

She held my wrist to take my pulse. It raced at her touch.

"I`m still a little nauseous and—"

I clapped my hand over my mouth and gagged. Kate grabbed the stainless steel emesis basin from my bedside table and handed it to me. I vomited a few spoonfuls of what looked like multicolored confetti.

"What in the devil is that? Before my heart attack, I vomited my regrets, beliefs, and sins, but I never puked up anything like this."

"Oh," Kate said, "I wouldn`t worry—it`s just a bit of stray creativity. You can afford to blow some off once in a while."

"Oh," I said. That sounded reasonable. I drank some water and as soon as she left, I called the hospital personnel office to see if I could hire Kate as a private nurse. I received a disappointing answer and racked my brain for a solution. How could a sixty-five-year-old man attract a beautiful, angelic twenty-year-old? Impossible, I knew. Depression overcame me.

A few days passed and upon my release, I asked Kate for her phone number.

"Whatever for?" She gave me a strange look.

Whatever for, whatever for rang repeatedly in my thoughts that day. What should I have said? Could I have told her I loved her without her laughing at me? My wish had come true—I`m hopelessly in love and there`s nothing I can do about it. If I thought life was uncomfortable before I fell in love, it felt ten times worse now. I couldn`t stop thinking of Kate. I found out where she lived and followed her everywhere until she finally called the police and told them I was stalking her. I was warned. "Keep harassing her and we`ll be harassing you," a policeman said. "We`ve recommended the victim file a restraining order."

At least I found out what it`s like to be in love. I felt fortunate this had never happened before. By now I was prepared to die, so love didn`t hurt me as much as it could have in my youth. The loss of Kate and threat of jail prompted a new decision. I swallowed an entire bottle of sleeping pills, never expecting to wake again. But after what seemed like a long period of darkness, I heard faint questions bubbling in the back of my mind. Once I passed the threshold where one reality unites with another, a question became clear. "Are you finished, or do you have another wish?"

I couldn`t believe what I heard. Was this my imagination? Or God?

"Answer, you don`t have much time."

"Please, God, please—"

"No one said God is here."

I felt presumptuous to assume that God would care about me or my wishes. "Okay. I do have another wish.

I wish I could wake up in the hospital and Kate would love me."

I woke up in the same hospital room. I remembered my delusion, and got a kick out of the thought that somehow, someone had granted my wish. Then my joy turned to embarrassment as I recalled my suicide attempt. Everyone would know how weak I really am.

The biggest surprise was Kate`s behavior. Even though I`d troubled her, she seemed delighted to see me. When I saw her radiant face, I knew my wish had come true. After she took my vitals, she lingered to read to me, massaging my shoulders afterward. She never once mentioned my suicide attempt.

As Kate turned to leave the room, I felt emboldened. "May I have your phone number?"

"Of course! I thought you`d never ask!" She reached into her pocket and scribbled her name and number on the back of a matchbook.

With Kate`s loving care, my doctor signed an early release. I`d already set up a date with her. I took her to a fine Italian restaurant where singing waiters trilled around a waterfall cascading down a long, polished crystal wall and into a channel dotted with floating rose petals. The water flowed musically around the perimeter of the room. I was thrilled by Kate`s gaiety and innocent enthusiasm for everything life had to offer. Watching her made my heart race and when I fantasized how we might connect when I took her home, I almost passed out from my excitement.

Our meal progressed with fine wine and flirtatious conversation. Kate leaned her head on my shoulder in the cab as we rode to her apartment. I paid the driver and after I`d walked her to her door, I held her in my arms and leaned over to kiss her.

She wiggled free, giggling like a schoolgirl. "What on earth are you trying to do?"

A half smile remained on her face until I said, "Why, kiss you, of course."

"Kiss me!?" Her smile disappeared, replaced with a grimace.

I hesitated for a moment. "Yes, kiss you. I love you, and I know you love me, Kate."

A look of astonishment swept over her face. "You`re forty-five years older than me. The love I have for you is for the grandfather I never had."

I felt humiliated. She loved me all right, like a grandfather. My wish had come true again, but not in the context I wanted. Who granted these distorted wishes anyway? I couldn`t take the embarrassment and disappointment so I went home and swallowed another bottle of Valium.

As I crossed the threshold into another place, I heard the question again. "Are you finished. . . ?

I quickly answered, "No, no, I`m not finished. I want Kate to really need me."

I felt my direction reversing. I hoped I`d made the correct wish this time.

I woke up in the same room, where Kate began to treat me with loving care that went beyond granddaughterly love. I wondered what I had done to deserve so many chances. Whatever the reason, I felt overjoyed and within hours, I proposed to Kate. We decided to get married before my release from the hospital.

After our decision, I noticed one of the doctors, a youthful, handsome man of Indian descent, angrily pulling Kate aside in the hallway. I strained to listen and overheard her telling him that "I really, really need to be with Joe, and I don`t know why." He stalked away, his footsteps echoing from the walls.

The wedding went off without a hitch in the hospital chapel and without a honeymoon, doctor`s orders.

Soon after the wedding, a voice shouted from the PA system, announcing a multiple Code Blue, urgently directing any available staff to report to the ER immediately.

More than an hour passed, but Kate didn`t return. Finally, after I`d waited another hour, the Indian doctor opened my door and smirked at me. "Kate`s going to need `round the clock care. She really, really needs you now."

As it turns out, Kate was the first to reach the ER. She`d pushed through the swinging doors, but rather than offer her services, she was met by a fiery explosion. An inexperienced respiratory therapy student had foolishly stacked oxygen containers near a heater. Kate wasn`t killed, but it`s debatable if she might have been better off dead, as she was left paralyzed and sustained burns over seventy percent of her body.

I began to wonder if I`d actually died the first time I`d taken those little yellow pills. Perhaps after emptying myself of all my regrets, beliefs, and sins, my new wishes had more power to torment me. At this thought, I rushed to the bathroom mirror to see if I was alive or if I was dead. I flipped the light switch on and I looked into it. All I saw reflected was the wall behind me.

Goddamn it. The one question I forgot to ask Andy was how would I know if I`m in heaven or hell?

20

Story of a Lifetime

AS HAD HAPPENED WITH MANY other winning stories, we received our share of postcards and phone calls praising and denigrating "Heaven or Hell." One poetic soul pointed out that the contest stories had traveled full circle from absinthe to psychedelics, a fact with which Jason became enamored. At least this story—and all the rest of the contest stories—had made vivid life`s deepest paradoxes even if some hadn`t struck me as notable. But I felt workplace democracy was more important than my being right. I also couldn`t help but see how my life had twisted and turned right along with the contest and the winning stories, full of gobsmacking surprises.

To acknowledge his hard work and invaluable assistance, I rewarded Jason with a trip to the Caribbean, using some of the extra money that Evie`s special edition story magazine had earned. He`d joked about wanting to study stolen memories in Haiti ever since we published "Lost Memories," one of our earliest contest winners. Jason sailed around the West Indies for two weeks, and when he returned, I asked him what he`d learned while Evie and Shirley went out to meet some college friends for lunch.

"I don`t know, man, somebody stole my memories." He tilted his head and gave me his signature crooked grin, just shy of a smirk.

Smoking too much reefer on his vacation was probably what stole his memories, but I didn`t want to press the point because I wanted him to think about next year`s contest. Clearly, we`d have to keep running one to get situated in our new building.

He looked at me sheepishly when he didn`t get a rise out of me. By now I knew this look meant something was bothering him. "All right, spit it out, what`s going on?"

"You've treated me decent, Pete. Never thought I had a conscience, but I couldn't get it out of my mind while I was on vacation."

He sucked hard at the last bit of reefer cigarette gripped between his thumbnail and the nail of his forefinger, inhaling some loose pieces of leaf and ash that made him hack and cough.

I slapped his back. "You can tell me, Jason. When have I ever gone off on you?"

"I think it's the dope down there that caused my conscience to kick in. God, what great stuff they have."

"Jason! Let's stick to the point." I drummed my fingers on my rented desk. "What in the hell are you trying to say about your conscience?"

"You know? Your father. . . uncle. . . " He relit that last nub of reefer and tried to inhale the smoke until he scorched the tip of his forefinger. "Damn," he said, tossing the brown fleck of rolling paper into the wastebasket.

Bringing Peter into the equation made my blood boil. "Goddamn it, what are you talking about?"

"All right. I'll tell you, but first you've got to promise not to get mad at me."

"How can I do that when I don't know what you're talking about?"

"At least promise you won't fire me or beat the heck out of me."

I knew if I didn't agree, we'd go back and forth all day. So I said, "Okay. I promise. Now tell me what you're talking about."

Jason sat up straight, bowed his head and folded his hands in front of him as though he were in prayer or a confessional booth. I soon found out the confessional was appropriate when he said, "Your father bribed me."

Jason's face drooped with such a forlorn look I almost felt sorry for him. He had my attention now. I asked him a question I already knew the answer to. "Which father are you talking about? Uncle John or Peter?"

"Peter." He avoided looking into my eyes.

"Come on, Jason. There's no way you'd let Peter bribe you."

"But I swear I did."

"Wait, wait a minute. Even if he bribed you, it was your ideas that made this magazine a success." I put my hand on his shoulder in a gesture of friendship. "What did you get bribed to do?"

"The contest."

The contest had stimulated subscriptions and had helped pay off John's old debts. "What about the contest? What in the world did Peter have to do with that?"

"He promised me reefer from México every month if I did whatever he wanted. I didn't have a problem in the beginning. I figured your magazine would go bankrupt anyway, so why not get some free dope by agreeing to his madness?"

Jason looked at me coolly with calculating eyes.

"And what else did you do for him?" Anger caused my voice to rise to a taut, hard level. I`d never heard myself sound like this before.

"Some of the ideas I gave you came from him."

"But all your ideas worked out fine. How were any of them supposed to sabotage me?"

"Yeah, they did work out in your favor. Believe me, I`m happy they did. But Peter suggested many of them with the intention of torpedoing your efforts. First off, when I told him about your idea for the contest, he misjudged our ability to pull it off. He thought by starting the contest, you`d stretch your resources and end up closing up shop. It was his idea to syndicate, not mine. He thought everyone you approached would copy you and start their own contest, effectively minimizing your effort."

Jason`s hands began to tremble—his confession seemed as traumatic for him to verbalize as it was for me to hear.

"I can see being duplicitous bothers you. Though I`m pretty sure you could have scored your own dope. Why did you let Peter bribe you?"

"The thrill, man. The thrill."

Coming from Jason, I believed it.

"You got your thrill, but—"

The phone rang. I picked it up and O`Neill launched into an immediate monologue the way he always does.

"Pete, I don`t know what`s going on between you and your father, but right now you`re the only one who can help him. Everyone else has turned their backs on him."

A myriad of emotions swirled through me again. "Slow down. What are you talking about?"

The person I`d looked upon as a friend had just admitted he betrayed me at Peter`s bidding, and now my attorney wanted me to help the man who did everything in his power to see me fail.

"The government has frozen all his assets, or at least all they could find. He`s been arrested and just got whacked with a $100,000 cash bond. No one in the banking business will touch him with a ten-foot pole. You`re his last hope."

Why was Uncle`s John`s attorney, the man who had also briefed me about legal matters for the last eighteen months, concerned about Peter? The question was on the tip of my tongue, but I bit it back. I`d become, after all, a far less bitter, more compassionate and resilient man than Peter could ever hope to be. I`d truly taken after my mother and my biological father, and for that I was even more grateful than for my modest success in the publishing business. . . How far Peter had fallen while I`d struggled to survive!

It wasn`t too long ago I`d asked for a truce and he`d told me that he never compromised. I could see his humbled face in my mind`s eye and knew how much he must detest himself to ask me for help, typical of his passive-aggressive behavior.

Would I reach out to the man I`d known as my father or reject him as my antagonist for the past year? Maybe I`d help him and maybe I wouldn`t. I wanted to finish with Jason before I decided.

"Let me think about this. I`ll call you back," I told O`Neill.

Clearly, I didn`t have a hundred grand in cash to bond Peter out, and no way would I raise money against the mortgage on my property and new building. . . that would be a little too compassionate. I thought of my mother, who was still married to the fool and probably completely embarrassed by his actions. . . Maybe she had access to some cash the government didn`t know about. Or maybe she could convince one of Peter`s banking associates to help if she thought it was the right thing to do. I hung up the phone and strode to the table where Jason sat at the storyboards.

"So, what about the fire, Jason? Did Peter have you set that?"

"Hey man, I was with you that night."

"Sure you were. Simple, man." I made a fist and drew my arm back, packing all my weight into the punch.

Jason fell backward off his stool, and in an attempt to right himself, planted his face on the edge of the table. Then he fell backwards, landing with a thud on the floor, groaning and clutching his nose. Now he`d think twice about selling me out for the thrill of it. Maybe he`d find this scene thrilling, the story of a lifetime.

I sure hoped so, because I wanted Jason to direct the new contest.

Suggested Reading

Alfred Sisley. The Complete Works.
www.alfredsisley.org/

Alfred Thompson Bricher (1837–1908).
www.questroyalfineart.com/artist/alfred-thompson-bricher/

Art Renewal Center.
www.artrenewal.org

The Art Story. Kasimir Malevich.
www.theartstory.org/artist-malevich-kasimir.htm

The Athenaeum. Georges Antoine Rochegrosse - Artworks.
www.the-athenaeum.org/art/list.php?m=a&s=du&aid=2327

The Athenaeum. Jean-Louis Forain - Artworks.
www.the-athenaeum.org/art/list.php?m=a&s=tu&aid=341

Cleveland.com. "Louis Anquetin`s `Avenue de Clichy` is more than just a street scene: Close Up."
www.cleveland.com/arts/index.ssf/2009/10/louis_anquetins_avenue_de_clic.html

E. Blair Leighton: The Prominent Outsider by Kara Ross.
www.artrenewal.org/articles/2011/Leighton_Prominent_Outsider/Leighton_Prominent_Outsider.php

Edmund Blair Leighton. White and Blue Mountains.
www.youtube.com/watch?v=NEbAUyluhfI

Eksteins, Modris. *Solar Dance: van Gogh, Forgery, and the Eclipse of Certainty.* Cambridge: Harvard University Press, 2012.

The Famous People. Louis Anquetin Biography.
www.thefamouspeople.com/profiles/louis-anquetin-365.php

Frick Art Reference Library / Frick Research Library Online.
www.frick.org/research/library

The Friends of TC Steele State Historic Site.
www.tcsteele.org/

Hoocher.com. Pagina Artis>Alfred Thompson Bricher, American Artist, Hudson River School 1837-1908. http://hoocher.com/Alfred_Thompson_Bricher/Alfred_Thompson_Bricher.htm

I Am a Child. Children in Art History: Joaquin Pallares y Allustante.
http://iamachild.wordpress.com/2012/06/09/joaquin-pallares-y-allustante-1853-1935-spanish/

Impressionism. Biography of Alfred Sisley, 1839-1899.
www.impressionniste.net/sisley_alfred.htm

Metropolitan Museum of Art. Heilbrunn Timeline of Art History: Auguste Renoir (1841–1919).
www.metmuseum.org/toah/hd/augu/hd_augu.htm

Metropolitan Museum of Art. Heilbrunn Timeline of Art History: Nicolas Poussin (1594–1665).
www.metmuseum.org/toah/hd/pous/hd_pous.htm

MoMA. Kasimir Malevich.
www.moma.org/collection/artists/3710

My Daily Art Display. James Tissot and Kathleen Newton.
http://mydailyartdisplay.wordpress.com/2012/08/16/james-tissot-and-kathleen-newton/

The National Gallery. Titian.
www.nationalgallery.org.uk/artists/titian

Nineteenth-Century Art Worldwide. Jean-Louis Forain (1852–1931), "La Comédie parisienne."
www.19thc-artworldwide.org/autumn11/review-of-jean-louis-forain-18521931-la-comedie-parisienne

Norman, Geraldine. *Nineteenth Century Painters and Paintings: A Dictionary.* University of California Press, 1978.

Open Culture. Astonishing Film of Arthritic Impressionist Painter Pierre-Auguste Renoir (1915).
www.openculture.com/2012/07/astonishing_film_of_arthritic_impressionist_painter_pierre-auguste_renoir_1915.html

Pierre-Auguste Renoir. The Complete Works.
www.pierre-auguste-renoir.org/

Sir William Quiller Orchardson, British Artist.
www.britannica.com/biography/William-Quiller-Orchardson

The State Tretyakov Gallery>Vasily Grigorievich Perov.
www.tretyakovgallery.ru/en/collection/_show/author/_id/76

Van Gogh Museum.
www.vangoghmuseum.nl/en

The Vincent van Gogh Gallery.
www.vggallery.com/

William-Adolphe Bouguereau. The Complete Works.
www.bouguereau.org/

ABOUT THE AUTHORS

JOE DIBUDUO

KATE ROBINSON

ON A DULL, COLD authors Joe DiBuduo and posteriors to chair and finish quirky short stories inspired vivid imagination and Robinson DAY IN FEBRUARY 2011, Kate Robinson decided to apply polishing and publishing some by artwork. DiBuduo sports the wields the word-whacking toolbox.

iBuduo is a retired house painter, and a budding sculptor and glass artisan who stays busy filling his front yard with giant sculptures and checking off adventures on his bucket list. He earned a certificate in Creative Writing from Yavapai College in Prescott, Arizona (2009). Bookwise, he`s the author of two mixed-genre paranormal novels, *The Mountain Will Cover You* and *Cryonic Man: A Paranormal Affair* (JD Books, 2016 and Tootie-Do Press, 2015); a connected collection of short stories, *Story Time @ The Chicagoua Cafe* (JD Books 2016); a historically relevant memoir, *Crime A Day: Death by Electric Chair & Other Boyhood Pursuits* (Jaded Ibis Press, 2015); and a popular nonfiction narrative, *A Penis Manologue: One Man`s Response to The Vagina Monologues* (JD Books, 2009). He`s also the author of *The Big Breakout*, a children`s chapter book (JD Books 2012), *Out of This World Sci-fi Poetry* (JD Books, 2010), and quirky flash fiction and "flash fiction poetry" featured in anthologies and journals.

obinson promises to dance always with paradox and absurdity. She earned an MA in Creative Writing (with Merit), from Aberystwyth University, Wales (2010) and she whacks words at Starstone Lit and Tootie-Do Press on California`s Pacific coast. Her fiction, poetry, and creative nonfiction appear in international anthologies and journals. Bookwise, she`s the author of a metaphysical sci-fi novel, *Heart of Desire: 11.11.11 Redux* (Tootie-Do Press, 2014), and two history books for middle-graders, *The National Mall* and *Lewis and Clark: Exploring the American West* (Enslow, Inc., 2005 and 2010). *Loop*, her magical realist novella created from dreams, shortlisted for the Texas Review Press Clay Reynolds Novella Prize in 2010. She attended the SLS Kenya / Kenya Between the Lines program in December 2010, and the November 2016 *Silence.Awareness.Existence* residency at Arteles Creative Center near Hämeenkyrö, Finland. Her work in progress includes a memoir, nature essays, poetry, short fiction, retold folktales, and picture book stories.

Redwood
Highway
101